Death by Association
Vol. 1 *Retaliation*
Vol. 2 *Deception*

A two-volume novel

By Anthony Ellis

Anthony Ellis has delivered a murder mystery masterpiece.

A Meredith *Etc* book

Meredith *Etc*
1052 Maria Court
Jackson, Mississippi 39204-5151
www.meredithetc.com

Keywords: murder mystery, fiction, Memphis, TN, prison contraband, prison guards

First Printing
Trade Paperback Edition printed by CreateSpace
Published by Meredith Etc
Black & White on White paper
Vol 1 & Vol 2 - 288 pages

ISBN-13: 978-0692462652 (Meredith *Etc*)
ISBN-10: 0692462651

Available on the World Wide Web as an eBook
Printed and bound in the United States of America

Printed simultaneously in Hardback by Nook Press
ISBN-13: 9781681011233 (1st printing)
ISBN-13: 9781681019536 (2nd printing)

COVER: Ellis Island, Psychopathic Ward, New York Harbor, NY
LOC Reproduction Number: HABS NY-6086-U-1

Visit Anthony Ellis' author page online.
http://meredithetc.com/death-by-association/

Blog: meredithetc.com
facebook Meredith *Etc*
Meredith*etc*

Meredith *Etc*
1052 Maria Court
Jackson, Mississippi 39204
www.meredithetc.com

ACKNOWLEDGMENTS

I thank my mother, Brenda Ellis, who has been my inspiration; and Meredith Coleman McGee, my acquisition editor/publisher, who has supported me in my efforts to create a best seller. Without their support, this book would not have been produced.

DEDICATION

This book is dedicated to my Mom, Brenda Ellis, who has loved and encouraged me my entire life.

Meredith Etc

a small press

Blog: meredithetc.com

facebook **Meredith** Etc

🐦 **Meredith***etc*

Make comments on Anthony Ellis' Author Page

http://meredithetc.com/death-by-association/

This book is a gift to:

_____

From _____

Date _____

CONTENTS

Anthony Ellis's detective character Jack Webster differs from Walter Mosley's Easy Rawlins because he sticks out like a sore thumb, and investigates his way through the underworld rather than blends into it.

Meredith Coleman McGee

FOREWORD

DEATH by ASSOCIATION, by Anthony Ellis, is an excellent detective novel in two parts: Vol. 1 *Retaliation* and Vol. 2 *Deception*.

In writing *DEATH by ASSOCIATION*, Anthony Ellis has followed the first rule for authors, which is: choose a subject of which the writer has broad background and knowledge.

Ellis has written a crime novel set in contemporary Memphis, Tennessee in a dozen gritty locales within the city, such as the famous Beale Street tourist scene, police headquarters, the city morgue, crack houses, rough nightclubs, homeless hangouts, and, memorably, a prison farm near the city. Nothing occurs at Graceland, but there is action along Elvis Presley Blvd. Ellis describes the local culture including the cuisine, the weather, the music, and the famous Peabody Hotel - with detail and love.

Homicide Detective Jack Webster of the Memphis PD is an admirable character in almost all respects. He cares deeply for his family, friends, and co-workers. He is an excellent cop: honest, ethical, respected by his peers, and motivated to find and bring vicious criminals to justice. As a former local football star, he is well known and well liked in the community. He has deep, genuine love for his daughter and he also finds new love.

Jack is an African American as are the majority of the characters in the book, however, race is not a significant issue.

This is a murder mystery, a carefully crafted "whodunit," replete with "red herrings" and "straw men." Ellis displays vast knowledge of prison subculture, notably, descriptions of how contraband flows into the cell blocks. He has equally deep knowledge of the drug culture, displayed in descriptions of several of the characters' daily lives.

The writing is taut and well-plotted. There are at least a dozen major characters and each is deftly introduced. Few words are wasted.

In my opinion, Anthony Ellis has created a believable cast of characters operating in a real and unique American city. There is potential here for a sequel. I would love to see Jack find a decaying body in Elvis's bedroom at Graceland! Maybe it's the King himself. In this case, I'm along for the ride!

By John Spicer "Spike" Wilds, Retired Attorney

Mr. Wilds worked for the federal government, having served for 35 years in a variety of law enforcement assignments within the U. S. Customs Service.

INTRODUCTION

Memphis, Tennessee

Shelby County Penal Farm is the largest correctional institution in the state of Tennessee. Nearly 140 years ago, this facility was a workhouse, and the county leased inmates to private contractors for 10¢ per day for profit.[1] Today, institutions on this land house thousands of inmates with charges ranging from DUI to murder.

This city-within-a-city stretches five country miles. Thirty feet of triple razor wire fences and stone walls surround this fortress which houses some of the toughest criminals in America. Mysteriously, the first sight of the Penal Farm from the window of the bus causes the harshest criminals to break down and cry.

Only one inmate, Sonny Albert, a 66-year-old white male, who was known for a protruding cut on his lower lip, has ever made it to the fence without being mortally wounded by a prison sniper. Rather than execute Sonny, the shooter aimed straight at his right hand, which was gripping the fence, and retired its use and flexibility forevermore.

Jail time presents two outcomes. The high road offers many positive opportunities: education, self-development, and rehabilitation. Unfortunately, too many in this city take the low road: corruption, personal abuse, and rebellion.

Criminals sentenced through the courts are transported to the Penal Farm to be processed and booked into the prison system. During the booking process, inmates are tested to see if they can read and write on a ninth-grade level. Then, they are examined by a state physician and screened by a mental health counselor; next, they are escorted to a temporary housing assignment until their classification process is complete.

After processing and classification are complete, inmates are given a permanent housing assignment and escorted to a building containing four dormitories which includes a dayroom, restrooms, showers, and an area with 20 bunk beds that has the capacity to hold 40 inmates.

Being incarcerated consists of a basic, daily routine: same things, different days. However, inmates serving light sentences get a change of scenery and are allowed to leave the compound to work off their fines. On the other hand, inmate leaders, who are emboldened by risky behavior, with more time on their hands, run all the prison rackets.

On July 1, 1993, the Tennessee Legislature passed a law banning the use of all tobacco products in Federal and State buildings. Inmate advocates complained the ban breached the constitutional rights of prisoners, but nobody important cared about infringing on the rights of inmates. A large percentage of inmates who were locked up smoked cigarettes.

Inmates with work details outside the compound could smoke with permission. The criminal element, inside the compound, deemed the sale of contraband marketable, profitable, and necessary; however, inmates who were caught trying to smuggle cigarettes and other illegal drugs back onto the compound were written up and charged with new crimes extending their stay.

But then again, as the good book so eloquently said, "The love of money is the root of all evil." Well, at the Penal Farm, evil reigns by men with iron fist, brass chest, and dark minds.

To curb the import of cigarettes and other illegal drugs, Warden Luca Grasso ordered any inmate who left the compound for any reason to be stripped searched upon entering the premises. There was no exception to the rule. This slowed the smuggling business down, but it didn't end it. Not much stops desperate men.

Contraband smugglers soon learned inmates would pay more for cigarettes, herbs, or cigars than nude photos, cell phones, electronics... So, inmates came up with another way to get tobacco products and drugs onto the complex. Some of them persuaded their love ones, or anyone for that matter, to bring cigarettes and drugs on visitation day in return for financial gain and a false exemption of being caught.

But, a series of arrests which aired on all the local news channels soon made it apparent that the risk of being arrested and charged on sight was highly likely. Therefore, new drug smuggling techniques - involving the use of small balloons - were created. Smugglers packed marijuana, crack, and powdered cocaine into balloons. They took the product out of the packs, wrapped it into plastic, flattened the packages and taped them around their stomach.

Once the guest was inside the visitation area, they went to the restroom, stood on the toilet, removed a square ceiling fixture, and placed it there for a trustee to retrieve after visitation was over. Each package was marked, so inmates could identify their packages.

Some smugglers placed the balloons inside popcorn or potato chips bags without the guards noticing. Once the inmate came and sat down, the visitor shared the snack with the inmate, who swallowed the balloons as they ate.

When the visit was over the inmates were stripped, searched and sent to their respective building. Once inside, the inmates forced the balloons to come out by regurgitating. This trafficking system existed for years.

When Warden Luca Grasso grew disgusted with drug trafficking reports, he stopped contact visitation completely. Non-contact visitation stopped the smuggling business altogether, but not for long because criminal minds are usually busy devising novel ways to break new rules.

Correctional officers worked for the prison, and with other staff to enforce the rules, but some officers engaged in criminal activity for financial gain to supplement their modest state salary.

The prison contraband smuggling business transformed correctional officers into big fish, club members, high income earners, and regrettably turned comrades into foes.

As if US political leaders in Tennessee have forgotten the outcome of prohibition, they banned cigarette use to prisoners. Liquor bans in the 1920s opened opportunities for bootleggers, gave rise to speakeasies, gang violence, and crime.

And, so it is, a quarter of a century after Prohibition, cigarette bans increase crime in this city-within-a-city where money ain't always green, but clever money transfers pile up, are counted, and make average men spineless, powerful...

Advance Praise for
Death by Association

Vol 1 *Retaliation* & Vol 2 *Deception*

"Anthony Ellis uses his observations as a previous prisoner to give authentic detail to this murder mystery he has created. While in prison, he learned the craft of writing which helped turn his life around by strengthening a talent he could use to sustain himself upon release."

- **Starry Krueger**, NY Member

PEN Prison Writing Committee

"Anthony Ellis has an incredible gift of creating and developing characters. The reader becomes intimately involved in these personalities as Ellis brilliantly weaves the 'sit on the edge of your seat' plot."

- **Judy Alsobrooks Meredith**, Ph.D. Author

The Glass Ceiling

"Anthony Ellis's Book, *Death by Association*, provides ongoing reading adventures. There are many sub-stories with well crafted, sensory details which moves the story forward to its end."

- **Dorothy Mays James**, Author, *A Story About James H. Meredith: A Civil Rights Leader.*

"Anthony Ellis composes a suspenseful novel that describes in graphic detail how gruesome and tragic crime is for the victims. This book will hold your curiosity and interest to the very end."

- **William Trest Jr.**, Author, *Reverse Guilty Plea*

Monday 5:00 a.m. – Johnson Murder Scene
November 18, 2013

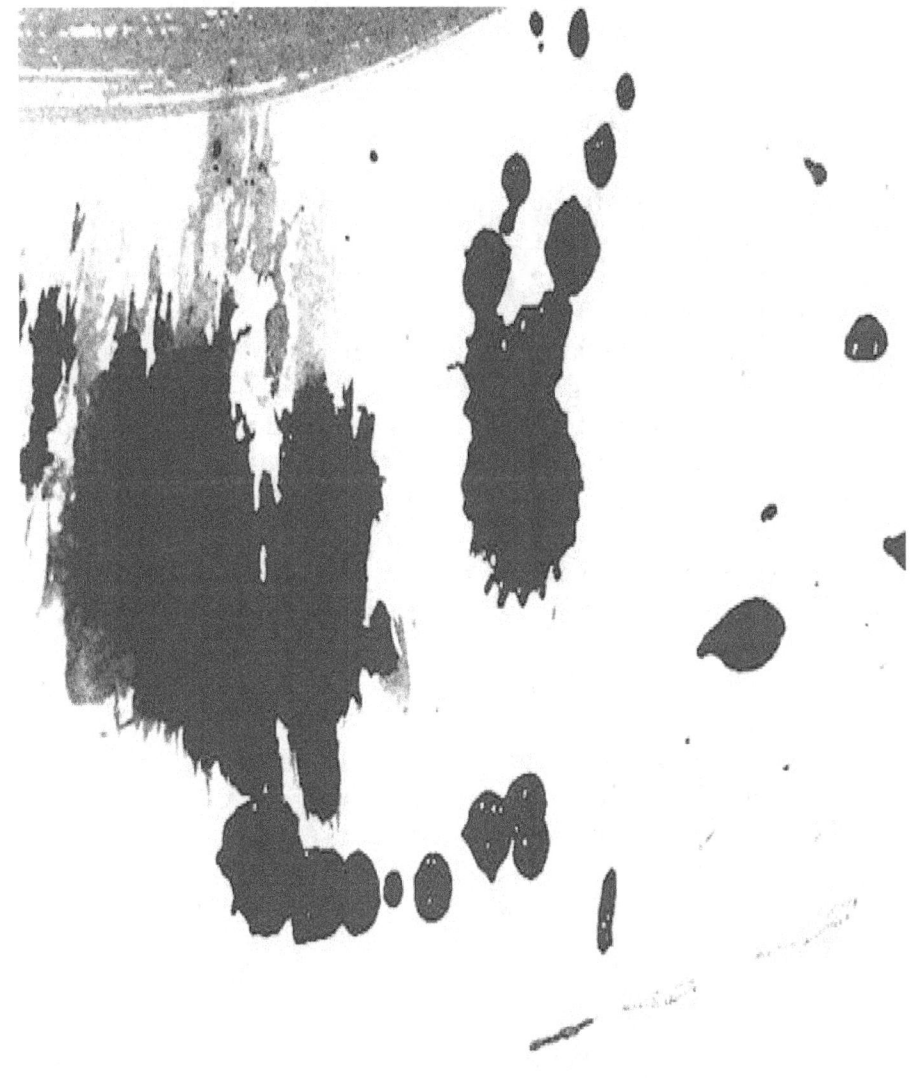

Double Murder at 1298 S. Parkway E.

Amos pulled in front of James' house in his black Nissan Titan, two door, four seat truck listening to the song *Up Down* by T-Pain; when the song ended he turned his ignition off and blew the horn twice.

Amos felt a little fatigued because he had stayed up late at a party the previous night. The beat of the music gave him a second breath, but something about the mist in the air lacked normalcy. After taking a full look at the house, he noticed it was dark, and the garage door was open. The morning got eerier by the second.

By 5:00 a.m. James would typically be on the porch sitting in the chair, legs cocked, hands free, like he owned the space he occupied. But, today unlike any other, a 7-11 plastic cup was on the porch, the house was dark, and there was no sign of family about their Monday morning business - none. The white rim of the cup was facing the garage.

The presence of the cup was unusual to say the least because at the Johnson resident, Cassandra maintained a spotless house which she cleaned herself and demanded even the youngest child put trash in the garbage and complete her chores.

The thick fog paralyzed Amos' view of the house temporarily, but he soon became aware there were no lights peering through the upstairs window of the sitting room in the corner, opposite the garage.

Minutes later, Amos became concerned he and James would be late for work unless he rushed James out of the house; so, Amos got out the truck, walked up to the old Victorian style house, and rang the doorbell. No one came to the door. Then, he turned around and went back to the truck to get his cellphone to call James.

Amos walked over to the garage and looked inside. Cassandra's car was gone and the door to the house was open. He could see the green light from the ADT Security panel blinking. He stepped inside the dark garage and walked up to the door and yelled, "Hello," but he got nothing back, not a sound. As he approached the kitchen, he heard several ice cubes fall in the tray in the freezer.

He walked back to the garage because his sense of fear kicked in and his heart beat accelerated. Wide awake, Amos slowly stepped inside the house, looked around the wall, hit the light switch in the kitchen, but the lights did not come on.

Suddenly, his heart thumped rapidly and he felt a little warmer than usual. He walked through the kitchen and bumped into the lamp sitting on the desk in the den. He could smell an odor as he stood at the bottom of the staircase; then, he became consumed with a sense of dread.

While he stood in the dark, unimaginable thoughts came to life inside his head. With the tip of his thumb, he turned on the lights, and a crime scene revealing the horrific sight of death came into full view. He stepped back, moving fast, panting. He ran back out of the house through the garage to the truck, yanked open the driver's door, reached inside, grabbed his cellphone out of his green jacket pocket, and dialed 911.

"What's your emergency?" a woman asked.

"He's dead! My brother! His little girl! They dead!" he yelled as loud as he could into the cellphone gasping desperately for air.

"Please try to calm down sir. What is your location?" the operator asked as Amos yelled, "You hear me. They're dead!"

"Sir, I need you to stay calm. I need your location," the operator pleaded.

"My brother's house!" he blurted out hysterically.

The operator asked, "What is your brother's address? Is there an address on the front of the house?"

He responded, "Yeah! 1298 South Parkway East."

"Are you in any danger sir," the operator asked.

"No, I'm, I'm okay!" he responded. "Is your brother inside

the house?"

Amos yelled "Yeah! They dead! I saw the bodies!"

"Stay calm sir. Help is on the way," she said in a consoling tone of voice.

"Are you inside or outside the house?" asked the operator.

He said, "I'm outside," and the operator said, "Good. I need you to stay outside. Officers will be there soon."

"What is your name?" the operator asked. "Am-Amos Johnson," he said in between deep breaths pacing in front of the truck."

"Amos, the officers will be there shortly," she added.

The operator inquired, "Amos are you still with me?"

Amos felt a horrible sense of loss, dropped the cellphone in the street, and sat on the curb. Within minutes, he heard sirens as patrol cars drove up from all directions. The uniformed patrol officers went into the house with drawn guns and flashlights in their hands.

After evaluating the gruesome crime scene, the officers made sure the house was clear, came out, and called in the homicide unit. Amos was still sitting on the curb in shock, looking terrified and distraught. A short female officer with a pale face and blue eyes walked up to Amos.

"Is your name Amos Johnson?" she inquired. He nodded his head back and forward signaling, yes.

"Please come with me," she gently told him.

He nodded his head indicating he agreed, and she escorted him over to one of the patrol cars and assisted him in the back seat. "Be patient, we will need to get some information from you," she stated.

Are you okay?" she asked him softly, but Amos did not respond.

He sat there in a state of shock looking straight ahead. Minutes later, a female officer answered her cellphone and conversed in Spanish with someone on the other end. Then, she approached Amos. Moments later she tapped Amos on the shoulder and asked him if he needed any medical attention.

"No, I'm okay," he said.

A male officer reached inside the patrol car and grabbed a

brown notebook off the passenger seat to record his observations and to ask Amos some questions, but before the officer could conduct an inquiry, Amos wanted a question answered himself.

"Are they dead?" Amos asked in a low voice with a worried look on his face.

"I don't know bro', but everything will be okay. The detectives are on the way," the officer said, then he asked, "What is your brother's name?"

"James." Amos replied after a very long pause. Then, the officer closed the door to the patrol car and walked off.

Amos sat in the patrol car and stared through the front glass window oblivious to the movement of people around him. Deep down inside, he knew things were not going to be okay.

He was the older of two brothers. Amos and James worked at Shelby County Penal Farm as correctional guards. His brother, James, had a truck of his own, but Amos, who lived five miles away always picked James up on Monday mornings. James' truck was inside the garage. There was no sign of James' wife Cassandra, and her BMW was not in the driveway.

By seven o'clock the sun was shining bright, and the commotion at the Johnson home drew the neighbors outside. The crime scene unit, emergency vehicles, more patrol cars, the captain of the homicide department, and television news trucks arrived on the scene. News reporters jumped out the trucks searching for answers to report the news to Memphians.

The officers blocked the street off to traffic at South Parkway and Elvis Presley Blvd. and at South Parkway and Wilson St. Spectators drove up and parked their cars next to the curb and observed the scene. People were taking pictures with their cellphones and conversing with one another.

This upscale neighborhood became crowded in a matter of seconds. All the neighbors knew each other; their children played together, attended the same private schools, churches, and shopped at the same retail malls. Now, death removed several Johnson family members from the earth leaving the community with a wide range of memories.

The chief medical examiner, Dr. Alice Avery, and the crime

scene unit along with the rest of the team were going over the murder scene. The inside of the house looked like a blood bath. Spatters of blood was on the wall, in the hallway, and on the stairs. Bloody shoe prints were all over the house and the garage. From the horrid scene, it was obvious quite a fight took place before the adult victim was killed. First responders discovered two bodies at the top of the stairs in a puddle of blood. James, a black male, was lying on his back with an infant laying on his chest. She was covered up to her neck in blood; she was in apparent distress, but alive; she was immediately transported to Le Bonheur Children's Hospital in midtown.

The body of a little black boy was lying in the first bedroom on the left side of the hall. Half of his head was blown off. Blood, flesh, and gray matter was scattered all over the bed, the wall, and the floor. The coroner estimated the victims had been dead for 11 hours. Most of the rooms in the house had been ransacked as if the murderers were looking for something.

Amos was transported to the Criminal Justice Center (C.J.C.) - police headquarters which is known for its famous address, 201 Poplar St. The detectives needed a statement from Amos as soon as they could. When the officers made it to 201 Poplar St. with Amos a mob of reporters and television news camera crews swarmed them. The officers tried to make their way down the walkway with Amos but they were overwhelmed by reporters.

"Is he the killer?" a short black female reporter asked as she quickly stuck the microphone in the officer's face. Amos pulled his green shirt over his head. The lights and flashes distracted the officers as they pushed their way through the crowd. When they made it inside with Amos an armed officer escorted them to the elevator.

****

The Johnson Family Murder Investigation

Detective Jack Webster

I made it to the office at 7:40 a.m. on the morning of November 18, 2013. Ronald Stipanik, my new partner, who prefers being called Ron, walked in the door seconds behind me. He is in his late 20s, too young to be a detective, if you ask me. He made detective two weeks ago. We've been working together since then and he is already mimicking me. I don't know if this is good or bad.

I have to give him credit; he has great potential. He wants to learn as much as he can, as fast as he can. I guess, I was like that too, when I first made detective. Man! That seems like forever, but it was only 15 years ago. I was sitting at my desk thumping through a pile of reports when the phones started ringing off the hooks which is normally a sign to a homicide detective a hectic day is in the making.

Right now, I'm not worried about the flood of case work coming in because I only have four days before my vacation starts. Two weeks of fun in the sun is almost knocking on my door. It is November in Memphis. The weather is strange this time of year. You never know what to expect these days. Ron walked over to the receptionist desk and answered the phone.

He turned to face me and said, "Jack it's for you, sounds urgent!" I didn't like the tone of his voice. I stood and limped over and grabbed the receiver from Ron. My limp is the result of an old football injury.

Captain Dunn was on the line, "Jack, we got two dead bodies and a missing wife who is possibly a suspect. I need you on this case!"

"I go on vacation in four days Captain, can't you get Cruz and Jackson to take it?" Jack inquired.

Captain yelled and said, "It's pretty bad Jack the son-of-a bitch killed a little boy!"

"But Captain! I got four days to go!" Jack said piteously.

"I need my best detective on this case Jack! I'll find a way to make it up to you," Dunn solemnly stated.

Jack rolled his eyes and said, Dammit Captain, what's the

address?"

The captain pleasantly said, "1298 South Parkway E." Jack slammed the receiver down as if the captain would feel the lick, walked back over to his desk, and grabbed his car keys.

"Bad news?" Ron mockingly asked as he walked over to Jack's desk sipping hot coffee from a brown paper cup.

"Two bodies and a missing wife. Captain wants us on the case," Jack stated with a sense of defeat in his tone of voice.

"You don't seem too thrilled about it," Ron proposed.

"Nope', I didn't want another case this week," Jack said to Ron as they walked out of the office.

I already have a lot to deal with. The night before, my daughter called and told me another teenage girl walking home from her school was abducted and raped. There are five unsolved rapes of young black girls in the city. Nobody up high wants to make these rapes a priority, and that bothers me a lot.

Unfortunately, the city doesn't have enough man power to solve all crimes, but I personally wished we did. Some of us put in overtime trying to solve cases.

I got on I-55 at Alabama St. and headed south to Parkway. Ron is very quiet because this is his first murder case. He looks a little nervous, like he is preoccupied with his own thoughts. I remember the very first case I had which was thrown at me like this one. I was nervous too.

Ron has only been a police officer for three years. He made detective pretty fast; it took me seven years to make detective. Ron is one of the best shooters on the force. He can hit a fly on an apple at 200 yards away. He is waiting for a call to go try out for SWAT any day now. When that call comes, he must be ready to go. I wish him nothing but the best. Our job is serving and protecting the citizens of this great southern city which we do with great honor.

Ron wears a different colored suit every day. Today he is sporting a brown Italian suit and a crème, silk shirt with no tie. I like his brown eel skinned shoes, but they don't look like they are made for standing all day. I guess we all wore suits when we first made detective. The prestige of making detective gives men an elevated sense of pride. It sort of comes with the territory. My suit wearing days are over. I settled for blue jeans and plaid shirts after being a detective for two years. I'm more interested in simple things now like spending quality time with my only child, finding the perfect lady, solving crime, and being a civil person.

The Johnson murder scene was crowded with spectators when we drove up. Television news vehicles were parked in the vicinity; reporters were interviewing people - the whole nine yards. The size of the crowd had reached rock star status.

Ron took out his notebook and walked over to the uniformed officers standing in the front yard. I don't really like looking at a murder case until everyone is gone, but in this case 'I have to get in where I fit in.'

This murder case involved an innocent child. Personally, I despise thugs who commit crimes against children. We grabbed masks off the front porch, covered our noses, and went inside the house. There were several people working at the scene, the place was a mess. Ron and I were careful not to step on any bloody tracks which were everywhere. I walked up to the crime-scene unit officer who was on her knees and touched her shoulder.

Glenda Burton looked up, stood on her feet, and spoke. She had been collecting blood samples from around the house.

"If it isn't Jack Webster himself," she said with a big smile on her face.

"That would be me," I said.

"Tall, light, and handsome as hell. Quite the lady's man I hear."

I managed to smile when she made that statement knowing we were from different planets. My most recent date was in a dream. Glenda's body was covered from head to toe in a blue paper uniform. She is a very fine and attractive, a shorter version of Vanessa Williams. A state-of-the-art camera hung around her neck. She proceeded to tell us the long narrative about the bodies and the toddler who was taken to Le Bonheur Children's Hospital.

The baby had crawled on top of her father and went to sleep. She was too young to know he was dead. My eyes tightened when she told us the story. I never said a word while she gave us a tour of the crime scene. I just listened intently to every detail. Ron was standing next to me writing notes, looking carefully at each scenario.

I was so engrossed in the scene I forgot Ron was in the room at first. Ron jotted down as many notes as he could, but Glenda was talking faster than he could write. It's hard for people accustomed to taking notes to switch to the use of recording devices or tablets. But, notes can be very important in any investigation.

Ron and I headed up the stairs when Glenda finished showing us the scene. A short time later, she completed her part of the investigation. A dead man was lying in the hall when we made it to the top of the stairs. I could hear people talking in one bedroom up the hall. I peeked in the room and saw the Chief, Captain Dunn, and two men in black suits engaged in a conversation. If I didn't know any better, I suspect the men in black are FBI agents.

We came to the bedroom where the little boy was killed and stood in the doorway. Dr. Alice was examining the child's body. I noticed the door in the room had been kicked in. I tapped on the door to get her attention. She turned and waved us in. I introduced Ron to Dr. Alice when we stepped inside. She greeted us. Dr. Alice was tall, blonde, had a nice body with a real nice ass, and beautiful deep, blue eyes. She is my kind of woman - classy, sexy, dutiful, smart...

She was wearing hospital scrubs. Her nose and mouth were covered with a thick mask. She sounded funny when she spoke, but we understood her perfectly. Suddenly, Ron started holding his stomach with a strange look on his face like he was about to be sick. He walked out the room in a hurry. The sight of seeing the boy's brains all over the bed got to him. I guess I should have prepared him because detectives engage in horrid, dirty, nasty work and see disturbing things. He will learn to stomach routine events but gruesome scenes can haunt you and enter your dreams at night.

"Is he okay?" Dr. Alice asked, then added, "You may need to check on him."

"He'll be okay, but I will!" I assured her. Then I asked, "What do you have for me Dr. Alice?"

She responded "Well, the little boy was shot in the top of the head at point blank range. He died instantly. The body of an adult male at the top of the stairs was shot in the back and once in the back of the head."

I thanked Dr. Alice and walked out the room. Someone really did a number on the house. I looked inside the bathroom. There was water in the tub. There was a lot of expensive things in the house, but none of it seemed to be touched. I grabbed one of the family portraits off the wall to have a recent picture of Cassandra Johnson. She was very attractive. I wondered if she could have done this as I stared at her big brown eyes.

I went back to the room where the little boy's body was, stood in the doorway, and wondered why the little boy was killed. Dr. Alice walked up to me and asked, "Are you okay?" My eyes slowly shifted from the corpse to Dr. Alice. I was lost for words but I managed to tell her, "Yes, I'm okay."

"I just don't see how... I hope you catch whoever did this!" Dr. Alice said. I nodded at her as she walked off.

The sight of the boy's brain and body matter was horrible. The scene lingered in my mind as I walked into the garage to have a look around. I noticed there were several cartons of Newport cigarettes and rolling tobacco sitting on a black work table. I followed bloody shoe tracks to a black Yukon, reached into my pants pocket, took out a handkerchief, and opened the door. I didn't touch anything with my bear finger prints in case the crime-scene unit had not dusted the truck for prints.

The registration of the car and various items were scattered on the floorboard and on the seats of the car. A gold-plated Berretta 9mm handgun was lying between the front seats; what a beauty. I laid the gun on the driver seat and saw several one hundred dollar bills rolled up in a rubber band in the middle console. That was strange. Why not take the money or the gun? I wondered what type of work the Johnsons did on the side as I stepped out of the garage and stood outside.

The uniformed patrol officers did a good job of keeping

the noisy crowd assembled across the street under control. I walked around to the back of the house and surveyed the scene while Ron was next door talking to one of the neighbors.

A news reporter walked up to Ron and asked, "Are you a detective?"

Ron replied, "Yes."

The reporter said, "Can you give me a statement about this murder investigation?"

Ron stopped briefly and said, "I don't have any comments at this time." My man! Ron is catching on fast.

The crime-scene unit would be at the house at least another day or so. I plan to come back when the house is empty so I can get a good look inside. I need to find out what happened in the house last night before the murders occurred. Dr. Alice came out of the house and told the medics to get the bodies and prepare them to be transported to the morgue. A short male reporter with straight, black hair hanging down his neck tried to force his way across the yellow police tape to get a statement from Dr. Alice. A uniformed patrol officer grabbed him by the shirt and led him back across the tape.

I walked over and asked Dr. Alice "How long have they been dead," as she got into her car.

"About 12 hours, give or take," she said before driving off.

Ron walked up to me and we headed to my black Dodge Charger. He told me a neighbor said James worked at the Penal Farm as a correctional guard and Cassandra was a bank teller. Their house and lifestyle didn't exactly fit their professions. We headed back downtown to 201 Poplar to talk to Amos. As we drove up in front of C.J.C., there was a mob of reporters camped outside the front entrance.

I decided to drive around to enter the building through the garage on Poplar Ave. to avoid the media. Reporters and television news channel crews practically lived outside C.J.C. looking for the opportunity to solicit statements and comments about crimes from detectives. The news traveled fast about the murders because James Johnson worked at the Penal Farm.

I never give a statement to the media unless I am absolutely sure about things. I don't have anything to go on in reference to the Johnson murders. I hope Amos Johnson can give me a lead. Amos was waiting in one of the interview rooms when Ron and I made it to the office. Ron sat in the surveillance room to observe the Amos inquiry.

I grabbed a bottled water out of the fridge, and headed down the hall to the interview room with my tape recorder and a notebook. Amos was resting his head on top of the brown, oak table when I walked into the room. Once he raised his head, I introduced myself, and sat down directly in front of him. He looked tired, and his eyes were blood shot red.

He was wearing a green uniform, black boots, and had a worried look on his face. All the correctional officers at the Penal Farm wore those uniforms. I offered him a bottled water, but he turned it down. The small interview room included a table with four black chairs; the walls were solid white. The clock hanging on the wall over the door had a hidden camera inside.

The interview lasted almost two hours. Then, I told Amos he was free to go. We stood at the same time and I escorted him to the door. A seductive black woman wearing a lot of jewelry, and a dark brown silk coat, in 4-inch heels was waiting for him in the office.

"Are you okay baby," she asked as she hopped out of the chair, walked to him, and gave him a hug.

"This is a nightmare," he told her in a light tone of voice. Then, he swung his hand to hers, they held hands, and left.

Amos's truck along with his brother's truck was towed to the crime-scene unit garage. They had to be processed for evidence. I walked over to my desk and sat down; it had been a long day. I was kind of tired. I hadn't been able to sleep much thinking about the rapist on the loose. Now, a double murder which included a child occupied the back of my mind. The office was quiet and most of the detectives had left for the evening. Ron came out the room and asked what I thought about the interview.

I looked at Ron and said, "I think he knows a lot more than he said, but he's not the killer."

"I think he did it," Ron said as he walked over to the desk

and sat down.

"I'm telling you Jack, he's our guy. I think he was having an affair with his brother's wife. His brother comes home, catches them in the act. They get into a fight, and he kills him."

"Get out of here!" I said to Ron with a smile on my face.

"If he killed his brother, why kill the boy? Where is Cassandra?" I asked. Ron continued pecking away on the keyboard.

He replied, "I know you don't believe it, but did you see how his expression changed when you mentioned Cassandra's name? I bet you $50 she's waiting for him at a hotel somewhere. They're going to run off together."

"If you want to give your money away. I'll take it. You got a bet!" I added extending my hand so we could 'seal the deal' with a hand shake.

I turned around in my seat and studied the Johnson case files which the receptionist left on my desk. The name and ages of the family was on the first page. Asa Johnson, 10 months old; Marcello Johnson, five years old, he was killed on his birthday. Cassandra Johnson, 27 years old; and James Johnson, 39 years old. The couple had been married for six years. Cassandra was missing. There was a state wide all-points bulletin out on her BMW.

I sat at my desk and stared at the family picture. Images of the little boy's body in the bed kept crossing my mind. I had a tough time dealing with the thoughts. Ron had finished his report and was long gone. It was 9 p.m. when I looked at the time on the computer screen. Everyone left the office, except John. He was sitting at his desk talking on the phone. I decided I was going up to the hospital, first thing in the morning to see Asa Johnson. Then, I turned my computer off and walked out the office and headed home.

Day 2 of the Johnson Investigation Tue. Nov. 19. 2013

I woke up the next morning at 9:00 which was later than normal. The sunlight beamed through the bedroom window directly into my face. I had a long day ahead. Ron called last night and told me he had been taken off the case. The Church of God in Christ Convention started today, and his name was selected for security detail.

The convention is held in Memphis every year in the month of November. It is one of the largest church conventions in the United States and people come from all over the world to attend. The event generates a lot of money for Memphis. Therefore, the city provided security to ensure the safety of visitors and attendants.

I worked better alone when it comes to paper work, but I like having Ron as my new partner. He reminds me of a younger version of the actor Mel Gibson. Ron's hair is longer and he wears a ponytail. Ron is almost as tall as me; he's 6'1. I have a feeling Ron is going to be a good detective and a good partner. In some ways, he reminds me of my last partner, who was killed in the line of duty two years ago. I had a hard time dealing with his death when it first happened, but I got through it with a lot of help from friends and coworkers. I have gotten to the point now where I don't really talk about it anymore, but I will never forget it.

By 10:00 am it was 52°. I skipped breakfast and walked out the door ready to start my day. Not too long afterward, I was standing at the nurse's station at Le Bonheur Children's Hospital. An elderly female nurse who kinda' resembled Betty White walked up to me and asked me politely, "Can I help you with something?"

I told her I was a homicide detective and showed her my badge. "I need to see Asa Johnson," I noted.

The nurse told me to wait and walked down the hall. As I walked I heard several children crying. The waiting area was full of parents and family members who had worried looks on their faces. I really hated hospitals, especially hospitals for children. Finally, the nurse returned and told me Asa had just fallen asleep.

"She has been crying a lot since they brought her in yesterday. Would you like to come back later on?" she asked with a sincere expression on her face.

I reached into my back pants pocket and pulled out a little

brown teddy bear I had brought from the gift shop for her.

"Will you give this to her when she wakes up?" I asked the nurse.

"I sure will," she said with a smile.

I turned to walk away and the nurse said, "Wait!" she opened a drawer and handed me a green pocket size notebook. "I almost forgot. One of the nurses found it in the pouch of her dress when they brought her in."

I thanked the nurse, walked away, and flipped through the blood stain pages on my way to the car. I wondered why the notebook was placed on Asa. Maybe the notebook had something to do with the murders. When I walked in C.J.C., it was crowded and noisy; there was a sticky note on my desk which said the chief wanted to see me ASAP. I wondered what he could have wanted, as I sat down and looked in the notebook again.

There were hundreds of 14 digit numbers written on the front and back of every page. I thought the numbers represented bank account or credit card accounts. I stood and walked over to the new secretary. It was only her second day at work. I asked her if she could find out what Cassandra's last job was before she worked at the bank. I didn't want her to feel pressured, but urgency comes with the territory.

The secretary told me, "Cassandra used to work here at C.J.C. as a deputy jailer. She worked all over the jail. It's been all over the morning news. She worked in the property room for a while; then, she transferred and became a court clerk. She was accused of fixing cases in the computer for inmates and accepting bribes. She quit and got a job as a bank teller at NBC Bank downtown."

"I remember her now. What ever happened to the case?" I asked.

"It was dropped" she responded, "They never could prove anything and they never caught her in the act."

"Thanks a bunch," I said and walked out of the office, and headed to the Chief's office.

I stepped off the elevator and walked into the empty waiting area. My shoes sunk into the thick brown carpet as I walked in his office. The receptionist was glued to the phone and typing away on the keyboard of a Dell desktop. She looked up and told me the chief was expecting me in the same breath. She didn't miss a beat. I was impressed she was such a skilled typist; she was petite, very attractive, and youthful looking. The chief sure did know how to pick a beauty. She was revealing a lot of skin and to think all this time I thought we had a dress code.

As I opened the door and stepped inside the office, I wondered what the chief's wife thought about his secretary. She was hotter than July. He was sitting at his huge mahogany desk watching the 12 o'clock news on a large Sony flat screen television hanging from the wall. We exchanged brief pleasantries; then, the chief offered me a seat in the chair in front of his desk. He reminds me of the actor James Earl Jones, not due to any sharp resemblance but because the chief has this air of authority about himself. He even rolls his bulging eyes around as it they are a part of his conversation.

I could see my reflection on his shiny desk when I bent over to sit down. There was nothing out of place in his nice, cozy office. His pictures with politicians, local celebrities, and awards were precisely aligned on the wall in full view of incoming visitors.

The chief opened the cigar box, took out a Cuban cigar, bit the tip of the off; then, he lit it. Cigar smoke is annoying. Maybe the chief sensed my discomfort because he laid the cigar in the ashtray rather than take more drags off it.

"This case is receiving a lot of media attention. I know you'll do what you can to solve this case Jack," he said giving me intense eye contact.

"Do you think the woman is responsible for the murders?" he asked in a really deep voice.

"I don't know yet sir, but I'm going to get to the bottom of it. You can count on it!" I'm going to solve this case if it kills me.

"Do what you got to do, but keep me informed," he added with a serious look on his face. I had never seen him this interested in a case.

I brought up the five black girls who had been raped. I asked the chief if I could check things out in the area where the rapes occurred. He gave me the okay. I stood and nodded at the chief.

"You catch this bastard Jack," he said with cigar smoke coming out of his mouth. I walked out of the office and closed the door behind me.

The chief never called a detective up to the office unless it was serious. I took the notebook out of my pants, took a quick peak inside, and walked to the car. I thought about the two FBI agents I saw at the house. I wondered why the FBI were involved. I got on the highway at Alabama St. and took I-55 to I-240 and headed east toward Nashville and got off at the Summer Ave. exit heading to the Penal Farm in search of some clues.

I wanted my first destination at the Penal Farm to be at the captain's office on the first floor, but I had to settle for Timothy Woods, who according to sources was James Johnson's supervisor, and his childhood friend. Of all the people who worked at the Penal Farm, I thought Timothy would know what was going on. About 15 minutes later, Timothy walked through the door. I stood and shook his hand and we greeted each other.

He was short and muscular with a low haircut. He looked like he was in his late 20s. He was wearing a green uniform with three yellow stripes on the sleeves. I sat down and Timothy pulled the chair from underneath the desk and sat it in front of me.

He looked at me and said, "How can I help you today Detective Webster?"

"I hear you and James were very close." I said.

Timothy said "He was my best friend. We grew up together."

"Did he have any problems with anyone? Any enemies, inmates, coworkers anything at all?" I asked.

He answered, "Not that I know of, I mean we get threats from inmates all the time. It's mostly just talk. Nothing ever happens. James was a good man. I don't know who or why anyone would kill him." He paused to cough, then he continued.

"He did have a big argument out in the parking lot Saturday which was before the party Sunday night."

"Who was he arguing with?" I asked. Timothy began to look very emotional, as if he was about to cry. His eyes looked shiny and glossy like new marbles.

He looked at me and said, "Amos... He was arguing with his brother." I was surprised at his answer. Amos didn't mention anything about an argument between him and his brother when I interviewed him yesterday.

"Do you know what they were arguing about?" I asked. I noticed a tear roll down his face. His voice was a little choky, and he held back his tears during the interview.

"I'm not sure, but I think Cassandra was having an affair with an inmate. She may have been pregnant by him," Timothy said as he wiped his face with his hand. Then, the thought of an affair as the motive crossed my mind.

"Did anybody else know about this?" I asked.

He responded, "Check with Anton Norwood. He and James worked together out on patrol. Maybe he can tell you more about it. He didn't come to work today."

"Were James and Cassandra at this party?" I asked.

He said "Yes, but they seemed distant from one another, and they came in separate cars. James didn't stay long. He left early."

"Where did y'all have the party?" I inquired.

"The B.B. King's Blues Club on Beale St." I stood and thanked Timothy Woods for his time, and he escorted me out of the office.

The sun was shining like it was July and the sky was beautiful. I thought about the argument Amos had with James, as I drove down Summer Ave. on my way to the bank where Cassandra worked. Maybe somebody at the bank could give me some leads. I needed a tip to go on, and I needed it fast. Facts are fresh in people's memories during the first 48 hours of a murder investigation. I wanted to find out what the numbers in the little notebook mean.

2

Clues & Dead Ends

On the third day of the Johnson investigation, Wednesday, November 20th, a runner working for a local law firm observed a black Mercedes sedan with dark tinted windows and a North Dakota license plate which was clean as a whistle pull up to a blue GMC van with dark tinted windows in an alley off Front St. in downtown Memphis.

A tall dark man with short wavy brown hair emerged from the driver's side wearing a green camouflage jumpsuit and dark shades. He surveyed the scene, then he walked up to the driver's side of the Mercedes.

The window opened just enough for the driver to stick a large brown envelope out. The man grabbed the packet and opened it. Inside was a white piece of paper with six names, three addresses, and $40,000. He counted a stack of bills and measured a quick count of the money.

"It's all there, you don't have to count it," a woman's voice said.

"It's business lady, nothing personal," the man said with a piercing accent.

"What happened at the house?" the woman asked.

He chuckled as he stated, "Somebody beat me to the punch. The little boy was dead when I got there. I made the woman suffer, just like you wanted."

"What about the package?" she asked.

"It wasn't there, and somebody ransacked the house," he said.

"I need you to take care of the others and bring the boy to me," she nodded and said.

He rubbed his hands together as he stated, "I'll take care of it, but it's going to cost a lot more."

She yelled, "Don't worry about money just get the job done!"

The man walked back over to the truck, hopped inside, and drove off. The Mercedes drove up to Front St. and disappeared into the thick traffic.

Detective Jack Webster

I patiently sat in the lobby of NBC Bank on Union Ave. in downtown Memphis waiting for the branch manager. A gorgeous young woman with long, blonde, curly hair and nice legs, I might add, finally walked up, and escorted me to her office which was in the center of the building, enclosed with glass doors. The inside of the bank looked like the lobby of a five-star resort. I could see my reflection in the black and white checkered marble floors as I walked through the facility.

She told me to have a seat, shut the door behind me, and I sat down and looked around the very busy bank which had six tellers and a long line of people in each line waiting for service. She walked over to the small counter, got a cup of coffee, and offered me a cup, but I declined. The name on the glass desk said Samantha Morris, Assistant Branch Manager. She is one hot and sexy executive – pleasing to the eyes – great early morning view.

She walked around the desk and sat down. "How can I help you Detective Webster?"

"Please, call me Jack!" I responded. "For starters, what can you tell me about Cassandra Johnson? Was she having any problems with anyone at the bank?" As you may know, her husband and one of her children was found dead at her house the other day.

She drunk a little more of her coffee and said, "No, not that I know of. She was just fine. She got along with everybody. There was this one time, we were all on our way to eat lunch. This car drove up to us, stopped and let the window down a little and threw out a brown teddy bear, then it drove off fast. Cassandra started acting weird, like she was afraid."

"Did you see who was driving the car?" I asked.

She responded "Nope, the windows were too dark."

"What kind of car was it?" I asked.

"It was a new model Lexus. Black, real clean looking," Samantha said.

"One more thing," I said as I took the notebook out of my pocket and handed it to her.

"Do you know what the numbers inside this notebook symbolize?"

She flipped through the pages; then, she handed the notebook back to me and said "They're not bank account or credit card numbers. I'm afraid I don't have any idea what they are."

"Thanks for your time," I said.

I stood and shook Samantha's hand and walked out of the office headed down Third St. to 201 Poplar St. I wasn't getting far with the case and that bothered me. I thought about Timothy's claim that Amos and James had an argument the night before the murder. Besides the argument between the brothers, I was still pondering over the tip about Cassandra having an affair with an inmate.

That news was shady. It's really bold of a woman to have an affair with someone who is incarcerated where her husband works. A group of lawyers stood near me as I waited on the slowest elevator in the world to arrive. When I hopped in the elevator, a group of men were debating in my presence about a case. Their language and legal jargon was a little amusing to me, but I kept my feeling to myself.

Amos ran across my mind again when I walked in the office, and I wondered if he could be involved in the murders. I walked over to my desk, sat down, and continued to think about the case. If Cassandra was having an affair, her lover could definitely have a motive to kill James.

If Amos was the killer, why did he come to the house that morning to pick James up for work? Why not leave the bodies for someone else to find? If Ron was right and Amos was having an affair with Cassandra, why didn't he leave town with her? Amos should have known he would be a suspect once he called the murders in. If Timothy was right and Cassandra was having an affair with an inmate, where was he and who was he?

Nothing about the clues were adding up, and in reality, speculations are just a guessing game. I opened the Johnson file and looked at the family portrait. There was nothing in Cassandra's record which indicated she was involved in any criminal rackets. Ron walked into the office and spoke to me on his way to his desk. I took the notebook out and looked at the numbers again. I was disappointed the bank manager couldn't reveal what the numbers meant.

I called Ron over to my desk and handed him the notebook. "The nurse at the hospital found this notebook on the baby when they brought her in," I told Ron.

"What are these?" Ron asked as he flipped through the pages.

"I have no idea. I was hoping you would know," I said. "I found out at the Penal Farm that Amos had a big argument with James in the parking lot Saturday."

A smile came on Ron's face, as he handed the notebook back to me. "See, I told you he is the killer!"

I wasn't going to tell him just yet, but I was beginning to think he might be right about Amos. But, I needed to follow-up on the tip that Cassandra might be having an affair with an inmate. Amos was being watched like a hawk but so far nothing incriminating surfaced.

"Do you think the notebook has something to do with the murders?" Ron asked.

"I don't know. I went to the bank where Cassandra worked and showed the notebook to the manager. She didn't know what the numbers represented, but she was sure they weren't bank account or credit card numbers," I said.

Ron was getting ready to head back to the church convention. "Oh yeah Jack, I almost forgot. I ran into Glenda down at the canteen this morning. She told me to let you know the crime scene is all yours. She said she would have some photographs for you by the end of the week."

Ron grabbed his car keys off the desk and walked out of the office. I sat at my desk and tried desperately to put things together but nothing was adding up. Why kill the boy, and leave the girl alive? Maybe the girl couldn't talk, or she didn't see anything that night. I wondered if Cassandra was having an affair with a man that could kill her own son. I wasn't sure what it was, but there was no doubt in my mind that Amos was holding something back.

Suddenly, I got a strong desire to visit the crime scene, and I stood and walked out of the office to my car. I took Danny Thomas Blvd. to Union Ave, and got on I-55 and headed south. As usual at 5:00 p.m. there is a lot of traffic on the highway with people racing home from work. But, I had to go to the Johnson murder scene.

I am good at going over murder scenes and reenacting what I think might have happened. In my head, I hear the great Melvin Bush saying "Think like a killer." Melvin was a FBI criminal profiler and good friend of mine.

I got off the highway at South Parkway E., headed across Elvis Presley Blvd. and pulled up at the Johnson home. The neighborhood was quiet and still. I got out of the car and walked up to the house and opened the door to inspect the lock. The door knob seemed to be intact so I ruled out forced entry. I wondered if James knew the killers and let them in.

I walked to the den and looked around. I remembered there was some white bed linen lying on the sofa the last time I was here. Maybe James fell asleep on the sofa while he was watching television, and an intruder made some noise and woke him up. Then, James tried to run upstairs to protect the children, or to get his weapon. The intruder runs up the stairs behind James and gunned him down at the top of the stairs.

Amos said the lights were off inside the house when he came in, but I wondered if the television was on. I made my way up the stairs and stood in the hall by the little boy's room. I believe the boy was in the bathroom getting ready to take a bath. He heard the gun shots, walked out of the bathroom, saw the killer, ran to his bedroom, locked the door, and hid in his bed. The killer kicked the door down, went inside, and killed the boy. The killer didn't kill the infant girl, because she's just a baby. If Amos killed James and his nephew, where was Cassandra when the killings were taking place? I continued walking around the house thinking about the case. I walked back to the little boy's bedroom and stared inside.

I thought about the boy so hard I felt head pressure on my forehead. I tried to control my grief, but it was impossible. I eventually calmed down, regained my composure, and thought about Cassandra as I walked down the hall. Maybe she wasn't at the home the night of the murders. I made it to the large master bedroom and stepped inside. I observed all the expensive furniture. That was one of the things that puzzled me the most about the case was the fact that James and Cassandra's valuable jewelry, clothes, and cash had not been touched. The killers could not have been street robbers.

The only thing missing was Cassandra and her car. I headed back downstairs and walked out of the house. I looked inside one more time, then I moaned and closed the door. The sun was fading away quickly as I drove down South Parkway and got on the highway. I took I-55 north and headed toward downtown. I turned the radio on to ease my mind. Then, I sped past traffic to 201 Poplar St.

HAH! Never get too hungry, too lonely, and too tired. I try to remind myself of that. The aroma of fresh food met me at the door when I walked inside C.J.C. The busy crowds were gone and I was hungry as hell. I decided to get a bite to eat and luckily the canteen was located on the first floor. I went over and ordered two cheeseburgers and a large fry to go. The dining area was empty, except for a couple of secretaries sitting at the table holding a conversation.

I reached into my pocket, took out my cellphone, and recognized my ex-wife's phone number scrolling across the scene of the phone. I wondered what she wanted as I said,

"Hello!" I thought about my daughter's game, and said, "Okay, okay! I won't forget!"

She said, "Okay just checking to make sure you don't forget." Then, I hung up the phone.

My ex-wife called to remind me about my daughter's big basketball game next Friday night. But, I wouldn't miss it for the world. I grabbed my food and walked off.

We have been divorced for two years now. I try to spend

time with my daughter whenever my job permits. My ex-wife fell out of love with me; my job got in the way of things. I was never home and she got tired of the lonely nights. One day she walked up to me with the divorce papers and I signed. We've managed to have a good relationship for our daughter's sake; she eventually remarried.

The office was quiet and for once the phones weren't ringing. Most of the detectives were out in the field or gone for the evening. Angie, our new secretary, was standing at her desk talking on the phone when I walked pass her desk. I nodded, and sat down to eat my food. My stomach was pounding.

I admired Angie's beautiful body as I ate my food. She was 5'10 and she looked like a super model. She was wearing a red dress and some red 3" heels. She had all the curves in all the right places. There wasn't a mark, tattoo, or scar on her smooth mocha skin. I walked over to her desk and asked her for Cassandra's parents' address to see if I could stop by their house tonight. I needed to have a talk with them about the case.

"Sure Jack," she said as she grabbed the Johnson file off her desk and looked inside.

I was hoping Cassandra's parents could tell me what the numbers in the notebook represented or give me any leads because the clock is ticking. I don't want this case to go cold on me, like so many murder cases.

About 15 minutes later, Angie walked over and handed me a piece of paper and said "They'll be expecting you tonight."

"Thanks," I said to Angie and walked out of the office.

Cassandra's parents lived in Whitehaven on Oakwood Dr. not too far from where my ex-wife and daughter live. It is also just six minutes away from C.J.C. and highway. I headed south on I-55. The lights were on inside the house when I drove up. I could see a black woman shuffling pass a small window. It was kind of cool outside and it was actually a nice night for walking. The moon was shining bright as I walked up to the house and rang the doorbell.

A short black medium build woman opened the door and said, "You must be Jack Webster?"

"Yes, I am," I replied.

I shook her hand as I stepped through the door. She told me to have a seat at the large brown dinner table and she closed the door. She walked over to the stove and looked in the oven at the food. I glanced around the kitchen; it was nice and clean inside. Her house was well kept. There was a large oil painting of Jesus hanging on the light green walls alongside a picture of Martin Luther King Jr.

The kitchen smelled like a restaurant. There was a small pot of chicken frying on top of the stove. The smoke from the grease hovered over the pot. She walked over to the sink and washed her hands. Then, she grabbed a napkin off the counter, dried her hands, walked over to the table, and sat down directly in front of me.

She wiped the sweat off her forehead with the napkin and asked, "How can I help you?"

"I'm working your daughter's case and I need to know if she mentioned anything to you about any kind of problems she may have been having with anyone, a friend or coworker, anything at all?"

She responded, "Well, she wouldn't talk to me about it, but I knew something was going on with her. I could feel it. She was acting real strange, like she was afraid and nervous."

Mrs. Ellison had a sad look on her face when she talked about Cassandra. It was hot inside the kitchen, and humid in the den; sweat rolled down my forehead. I asked her if there was somewhere else we could talk. She stood and grabbed a napkin for me, then we went to the living room.

She turned the lamp on, sat on the sofa; then, she continued. "She wasn't acting like her normal self. A mother knows her child Mr. Webster."

Mr. Ellison walked into the room holding little Asa in his arms. Mrs. Ellison became very emotional when they walked into the room. He sat Asa on the floor, and gently held her by the hand trying to comfort her. I gazed at the picture sitting on the glass coffee table. It was a picture of Cassandra and her friends in high school. She was a cheerleader.

There were several pictures of Cassandra and the family

hanging on the walls. Asa was wearing a pale pastel green, dress, and green and white laced trim black socks. She tried to stand, but she immediately fell to the floor. She tried again but was unsuccessful. She looked very happy and healthy. She crawled around the room trying to talk. I asked Mrs. Ellison if she knew who Cassandra's closest friends were and if she knew where Cassandra or James hung out.

"Well, her best friend's name is Yolanda Jenkins. They grew up together and did everything together. They were like sisters," she said.

Mrs. Ellison excused herself and went to the kitchen to check on the food. She walked back into the room, picked Asa up and continued. "Yolanda and Cassandra use to hang out at that club on Beale Street. What's the name...Alfred's? That's it, Alfred's."

I reached into my pocket and took the notebook out and handed it to her and said, "Do you know what this is? The nurses at the hospital found it on Asa."

She slowly flipped through the pages studying the numbers, then she gave the notebook to her husband. Asa was moving around and making sounds. She was struggling to get out of her grandma's arms. She was ready to crawl around on the floor again. Mr. Ellison handed the notebook back to me. They told me they didn't know what the numbers in notebook represented.

"How did James treat Cassandra? Did they have any problems with the marriage or with money?" I asked

She immediately said, "No! They were as happy as any married couple. They were even talking about having another child. They had money. Cassandra told me James had this big promotion at work. They paid our mortgage off last year. James was a wonderful man. He was good to Cassandra and the children. He really loved his family. Cassandra bought a brand-new car, and James gave my husband a new truck."

Mr. Ellison never said a word the whole time I was at the house, but he smiled when his wife spoke about James. He finally lost the fight with Asa and sat her back down on the floor. Mrs. Ellison asked me if I wanted to join them for dinner.

I told her I had already eaten. I thanked them both for their time and stood to leave. Mr. Ellison couldn't hold back the tears any longer.

"I'm going to do my best to solve your daughter's case Mr. Ellison," I said looking at him; then, I secured the lock on the door and walked out of the house.

3

Memphis, AR Double Murder

About three o'clock the morning of Thursday, November 21st, a man driving a blue van headed over the Arkansas Bridge to West Memphis. Even though it was raining lightly, he drove his truck slowly moving down the street with the head lights off.

He came to a complete stop in front of a house and looked at the address on the mailbox: 1301. He pulled up next to the curb, hopped out of the truck, and examined the scene. Not a soul was in sight. The street was dead, and the house was dark inside.

"Perfect," he said under his breath as he walked up to the side of the house wearing a green camouflage jumpsuit and black combat boots. He moved down the side of the house beneath a dim street light shadow, reached into his pocket, took out a pair of wire cutters, cut the phone line, walked up to the back door, and picked the lock; within seconds he was inside the quiet house.

He glanced around the room, took out a 45-caliber pistol with a silencer attached to it, tiptoed down the hallway, and went inside the first bedroom on the left. There was a black boy lying in the bed, sound asleep. He walked up to the bed and shot him twice in the head. He came out the room, looked around, then he moved to another bedroom, but no one was inside. He backed out the room and proceeded down the hall. He could see the light from the television shining into the hall as he got closer to the door. The sound of music was coming out of the room.

He stepped up to the door and looked inside. There was a black woman lying in the bed asleep. He walked up to her like a thief in the darkness of night, pointed the gun to her forehead and pulled the trigger twice without blinking an eye.

He felt nothing for either of them. No love, no hate, no remorse whatsoever. He searched through the house with a small flashlight looking for a package but came up empty handed. He walked out of the house, got in the truck, and vanished into the morning fog.

Detective Jack Webster

I made it to the office a little after seven in the morning. The first 72 hours of the investigation had passed. The fourth day of the investigation was underway. I walked in the office in good spirits, wearing my LA Lakers jersey and some Levi's blue jeans. At the top of the hour, there was no sign of Cassandra Johnson. I believe there was a good chance she was already dead. Even though she was reported missing, I started investigating her whereabouts as if she was dead.

The office was like Grand Central Station in the morning. People are constantly coming and going, and moving around and about like there is no tomorrow. Cell phones and land lines were ringing simultaneously. Around 29 male and female homicide detectives are employed here, and that didn't include maintenance, administrative, and other personnel. It seemed like all of us were in the office this morning. The department had its share of work because the homicide rate was up this year, 397 murders so far.

We have worked our butts off on several cases this year, but half of them had gone cold. We still hadn't caught the person who was responsible for the murder of my last partner. His unsolved murder bothered me most of all. He was working on a big case, but I didn't know anything about it. He told me he was working on a secret project, but it wasn't a murder case. He promised to fill me in on it when the time was right, and I didn't push any buttons. That day never came.

He was killed right outside C.J.C. about 1:00 a.m. I was gone out-of-town on vacation when it happened. There were no witnesses, at least no one came forward. It was hard for me to imagine a cop getting killed right outside Police Headquarters and no leads – not one. This was the one case I needed to solve, the one case that nearly drove me to the edge, and almost ended my career as a police officer. My obsession with the case lead to the downfall of my marriage. Things got so bad for me that Captain Dunn ordered me to take a leave of absence so I could go to therapy. No one in my family ever obtained professional help before me, but it actually works. Those days are behind me now.

I was sitting at my desk typing on the computer when Angie walked in the office wearing blue jeans, a black Nike shirt, and white-gray Airmax shoes. She glided across the floor like she was a beauty pageant contestant and went to her desk. I was giving her a few minutes to get settled in before I went to her desk and started making requests.

After she settled in at her desk, I walked over and asked her if she knew Yolanda Jenkins.

"No Jack, who is she?" Angie asked.

I responded, "She's Cassandra's best friend. She works in the building. Find out where she works for me."

"Sure thing Jack," she said. I walked back over to my desk and sat down to finish my report.

Monica, one of the homicide detectives, was arguing with three detectives across the room. I went out with her a few times about a year ago. She was sexy as hell, and a good detective but she talks too much, and always complains about life or money. She isn't getting anywhere in life fast enough. Her grumpiness renders her completely repulsive as a date. Besides, we weren't meant to be, and thank God it ended before it got started which kept us both from breaking the fraternizing personnel policy.

A few minutes later, Angie walked over to my desk and said, "Yolanda works down in the property room, but she didn't show up for work today."

That's a restricted area. No one comes or goes down there. "Call the personnel office and get an address on her for me," I said.

Angie walked back over to her desk and picked up the phone. The property room is off limits. You have to get special clearance to get on the elevator which goes down to the property room. It is top secret. It was a don't ask, don't tell kind of thing. The sheriff of Shelby County kept it that way. It was hard for me to finish my report with all of the loud chit chat going on across the room with the detectives.

I gave up on the report, opened the top drawer of my desk, took the notebook out, and glanced at the pages hoping the meaning of the numbers would reveal themselves to me. The numbers were still a mystery to me. Angie walked back over to my desk and handed me a piece of paper containing Yolanda's address.

"What would I do without you? I said as I stood.

She smiled at me with her pearly white teeth and walked back to her desk. I grabbed my car keys off the desk and walked out the office. Yolanda lives in West Memphis, Arkansas. It wasn't too far from C.J.C. just over the Arkansas Bridge. There were two cars, a gray Lexus and a red Dodge Charger with expensive wheels parked in the driveway when I arrived.

The house was large in an exclusive neighborhood. This whole street reminds me of the show MTV cribs. I thought I was working in the wrong department as I walked up to the house. I don't know many people working in the same building I work in who can live this large.

There were two large golden statues of pit bull dogs standing guard on each side of the double doors at the end of the walkway. The doors were trimmed in gold and the yard was well kept. As I walked up to the front door to ring the doorbell an elderly white woman with a white house coat on came outside and asked me, "Are you looking for Yolanda?"

"Yes, I'm a homicide detective from Memphis," I replied.

She said, "I haven't seen them all morning. My grandson goes to kindergarten with her son. He didn't get on the bus this morning."

"Is that normal for Yolanda to take off like this?" I asked.

She responded, "No, it's not like her at all. I called the police, but they told me it hasn't been 72 hours and they weren't going to take a report?"

I stood there a few seconds and looked at the house. It was imperative I speak to Yolanda. I asked the woman if she would give me a call if Yolanda came home.

"I sure will," she said softly.

I handed her one of my business cards and walked back to the car and drove off. It was 11:22 am when I looked at the time on my watch.

It was warm outside and the skies were relatively clear. I headed back over the Arkansas Bridge to Memphis on my way to Beale St. and Third St. I decided to poke around to see what I could come up with. Maybe someone at Club Alfred's could tell me something or answer some of my questions about Cassandra and her associates. There was a short, single line of people standing outside when I drove up to the club.

I parked on the corner and got out the car. An oversized flashing red Alfred's lighted sign was in the front of the black building. There were a lot of people walking on the street. The sound of Blues music played out of the large black speakers on the walkway. I walked up to the front of the line, flashed my badge, and stepped inside the club.

There was some soft music playing in the background and the club was packed. There were a lot of men wearing suits and most of the women seemed to be in cocktail style dresses. As far as my best estimation was concerned, the crowd consisted primarily of white collar working people. The club is nice inside. It definitely was not what I expected to see. I always thought Alfred's was just another hole in the wall; however, I was wrong. The aroma of food was appetizing and the club smelled like fresh scotch.

"Can I help you?" a blonde headed waitress with a pretty smile asked as she walked up to me.

She was dressed in a black uniform with a black apron around her waist. I told the waitress I wanted a table out on the patio. She escorted me to one of the small white tables outside. The back of her shirt said Alfred's in big white letters across the top. She studied my face and asked me if I had ever been to Alfred's before.

"Man, do I stand out that bad?" I asked smiling.

"No, it's nothing like that. I mean, I haven't seen you in here before," she said.

"Would you like something to drink," she asked.

"I'll have a coke please," I answered.

The waitress walked off and disappeared through the black swinging double doors. I glanced around the patio. Everyone seemed to be enjoying themselves. The scent of cigarette smoke polluted the air. She returned, placed a large glass of coke and a menu on the table. I asked her how long she had been working at the club.

"Bout' five years now. My uncle owns the place," she said.

"I was wondering if you know Cassandra Johnson." I said.

"Are you a police officer or something?" she asked with a disappointing look on her face.

"I'm afraid so," I said as I took out my badge and showed it to her.

"Dammit! I always get police officers in my section asking a bunch of questions," she said loudly. She shook her head as if the thought of serving a police officer disgusted her.

"Do you know her? I asked again.

She replied, "Yes, she comes in here all the time."

I asked, "What can you tell me about her?"

She rolled her eyes and said, "Look mister, I got a lot of work to do. I haven't made a lot of money today!"

I reached into my pocket and pulled out a one hundred dollar bill and handed it to her to entice into giving me information. Her eyes opened wider as she accepted the money; her attitude toward the subject warmed up. She appeared ready to spill her guts.

"Well, people say she was into some heavy shit! If you know what I mean," She said.

"No, I don't know what you mean, so why don't you tell me," I suggested.

She twirled her finger and said, "Drugs! Money! People say she was dealing drugs. I don't know if that's true or not, but I know she had a lot of money. Lotsss of moneyy!" she dramatized.

"Do you know any of the people she hung out with?" I asked.

She responded, "Cassandra hung out with her sisters and

all of the high rollers and ballers. None of them come in here during the day time, only at night."

"What do you mean by sisters," I asked.

"She was into that club stuff KAA or something," She said.

"KAA," I said. "You mean AKA?"

She smiled and said, "Yeah that's it. Sorry."

"Did she have any problems with anyone?" I asked.

She got excited and said, "I heard she got into a fight with a girl who works at Pure Passion!"

The waitress walked over to the swinging doors and escorted two white women to a table near mine. I had heard about the women, who worked at Pure Passion, a strip club in Whitehaven on Brooks Rd. The waitress came back over to the table. I asked her if she would show me some of the people Cassandra hung out with.

"Will I get some more money?" She asked with a smile on her face the size of Texas.

I sighed and said, "I'll see what I can do."

She grinned and said, "It's a date then. I'll see you tonight."

"What is your name?" I asked as I stood.

"Paige" I shook Paige's hand and she walked off.

I walked over to the black woman standing behind the cash register and paid for the coke. Then, I walked out of the club.

There was a message from Dr. Alice lying on my desk when I made it back to the office; it was quiet now. Monica and the rest of the department were out in the field. Dr. Alice was finished with the autopsy and her reports. She wanted to see me right away.

I walked over to Angie and told her, "Next time you get a message for me, please call me on my cell."

"Sorry!" she said with a big smile on her face.

I smiled at her on my way to the door. I thought about what Paige told me about Cassandra selling drugs. That would explain all the expensive things in their house. There was no way they could afford all those things on their salaries. Maybe someone came to rob them and killed James and his son in the process. If this was a simple robbery gone bad, Amos would be off the hook, I contemplated as I drove to the morgue to see

Dr. Alice.

The morgue is in the basement of Regional Medical Center off Madison Ave. It is always cold in the morgue which gives me the blues. The sight of Dr. Alice, the medics, and dead bodies always gave me a dreary and mute feeling. I hated going to the morgue and visiting the dead. Dr. Alice was sitting at her desk reading over some papers when I walked through the door. She smiled and told me to come inside.

Dr. Alice looks too beautiful to be a mortician. I am a fan of pretty faces, but don't get me wrong I am not a sucker for a pretty woman. Dr. Alice walked up to me and we stood face to face, and eye to eye. We starred at each other for a moment. We went out on a couple of dates about six months ago, but our jobs stood in the way of the relationship.

Finally, Dr. Alice broke the silence and said, "Are you thinking what I'm thinking?" She had a sexy look in her eyes.

It was an awkward moment for us both. We almost made love on top of her desk once. If you want to know the truth, I could make love to her right now, but not here at the morgue in the presence of the dead. The hairs on my arms stood straight up as I starred at her. She looked like she was possessed with a sensual spirit which was calling my name.

"Do you want to go for it?" she said teasingly with a sneaky looking smile on my face.

I shuffled my feet slowly like the Sand Man and said, "Yeah, let's do it."

"I don't believe you!" she said. I could feel her breath when she spoke.

"How about a date tomorrow night," I said.

"Chicken!" she replied.

She teased me by fanning her face with both of her hands. I thought about a lot of things I would like to be doing with Dr. Alice right about now.

I planned to show her I was not a chicken.

"Back to business, what do you have for me?" I asked.

"We found three different types of blood inside the house. Two of the blood types belonged to James and his son," she said.

"The other sample didn't match James or the kids. James had some fresh bruises on his face and I could get some D.N.A. which should point to the murderer involved in the struggle with James. Find a person that matches the D.N.A. sample and you got your man. That's not all I found out Jack. James isn't the little girl's biological father," Dr. Alice added.

She walked over to the counter and grabbed a plastic bag with some bullet slugs inside. She said James and his son were killed with a 45-caliber weapon and handed me the bag. I stood and grabbed her by the waist and pushed her up against the wall, and gave her one of those long hot passionate kisses like the ones you see in the movies.

Finally, I came up for air and said, "Tomorrow night at eight."

As I walked out the office, Dr. Alice was in a daze from the kiss. I surprised the hell out of her with that move. It was pay back for her calling me a chicken. She stood in the doorway and watched me until I got on the elevator. Even though it was not expected, she welcomed it. It has been a long time since I'd kissed a woman like that. After me and my ex-wife breakup, I never found another woman I liked until I met Monica. Then once my relationship with her ended I just quit dating all together.

I made it back to the office, and walked over to my desk and sat down. I was finding out more disturbing news about this case every time I turned around. I wasn't surprised at the news about the blood. I had a bad feeling in my gut and I just hoped it wasn't Cassandra's blood. It's possible that Cassandra was already dead by the time the killer went to her house. It may be just a matter of time before her body turned up. I put the plastic bag with the bullet slugs in the bottom drawer. They had to be taken to the evidence room.

I opened the Johnson case file again and stared at Cassandra's picture. "Where are you?" I whispered softly. Even though, I was afraid she was dead, I hoped for the best. I didn't know how I would explain her death to her parents after meeting them. I just couldn't fathom how a beautiful looking family like the Johnson's could have so much deception going on. On film, they looked like the perfect family sort of like the Cosbys.

I needed to talk with Amos but he was out of town preparing his brother's funeral arrangement in Jackson, Mississippi. I hated to bother a person during a time of mourning, but I was left with no choice. I was going to see him as soon as he got back in town. I was beginning to wonder increasingly if Amos was the killer, or if he was involved somehow. Maybe Amos was looking for the notebook or he could tell me what the numbers represented.

This case wasn't making any sense to me whatsoever which bothered me a lot. New suspicions surfaced when Alice told me James wasn't the father of Asa. Maybe Amos knew who the father was. I was going to turn up the heat on Amos as soon as he got back in town, and increase surveillance on him. If he was the killer, I was going to find some solid evidence so I could charge him with the murders. Amos had no idea he was a suspect. I planned to keep it that way, at least for now.

I called the chief to fill him in on what was going on with the case to see if he could get me a clearance to get down to the property room so I could check out one of my leads. I needed to talk with Yolanda Jenkins. The chief told me he would get back to me about getting a clearance to the property room. I thought about what Paige told me about Cassandra again. Where was all this money she was supposed to have? I wondered about the money for a second. If I could find the money trail, it would lead me to the killer.

Ron walked into the office wearing his old patrol uniform. I burst out laughing and said, "It's been a long time since you put that thing on. It looks a little tight on you," I blurted out laughing so hard I almost fell out of my chair.

"Yeah, Yeah, Yeah, laugh all you want!" Ron said with a smile on his face.

Angie walked over to Ron and joined in on the fun. "He looks so pretty," Angie said looking at Ron.

Her lips were poked out like she was going to give Ron a big kiss. I adjusted myself in my seat, and sat straight in my chair. Angie walked up to Ron with her arms extended like she was going to fly to Ron.

I wiped the tears off my face and said, "Okay Ron, I'm going to stop now, seriously. What do you know about the property room?"

Ron responded, "That place is off limits, but I've heard strange things about it. It's run by the sheriff's department." Ron walked over to his desk and grabbed his gym bag. Then, he came back over to my desk and said, "Why do you ask?"

"Nothing. I need to get down there and check out a lead," I replied.

"Well, all I can say is, be careful!" Ron said as he walked out the office.

Ron had about two hours to kill before he had to return to the church convention. I pondered again about all the money Cassandra was supposed to have. In the meantime, I decided to go back to the bank to have another talk with Samantha Morris. Maybe Cassandra and James had an account at the bank where Cassandra worked. The bank accounts could provide us with a lot of clues and answers about their house, cars, jewelry, and spending habits.

Ms. Morris was sitting at her desk talking on the phone when I walked up to her office. I waited at the door until she got off the phone. Within seconds of seeing me at her door, she hung the phone up, and asked me to come inside.

I stepped inside the office and Samantha said, "How can I help you Jack?" I smiled, because she was being cooperative which takes the edge of the investigation.

"I need to know if Cassandra or James had bank accounts here. Maybe in their children's name. If you need to see a warrant, I can leave and come back with one."

"There's no need for that. I know you are working on the case," Samantha said as she typed away on the computer.

She said "Yes, they both have a checking and savings account."

"How much money do they have?" I asked.

"Well, all together, it comes out to about …$4,000 with all four accounts," Samantha said.

I was expecting to hear A LOT more than $4,000. I sat

there with a perplexed look on my face.

"Is something wrong Jack," Samantha asked.

She could see the puzzled look on my face. "Can you tell me if they made any large deposits or withdrawals over the last six months or so?" I asked.

Samantha pecked away at the keyboard, then she looked at me and said, "Nope. No amount larger than two thousand dollars."

I shook my head in disbelief at the amount of the money that Samantha told me they had in their accounts. I thanked her and walked out of the office. I considered the new facts as I drove back to the office. If Cassandra had all this money, where was she keeping it? Maybe it was inside the house. I called Ron to see if he could get away for an hour. There is a good chance they hid the money in the house.

Ron was standing next to his red corvette dressed in blue jeans and a white t-shirt when I drove up to the house. He looked normal in regular clothing compared to him wearing that old patrol uniform. I got out of my car carrying two flashlights and a few latex gloves. I was determined to see if there was any evidence which corroborated what Paige said about Cassandra being a drug dealer with a big bank account. I walked up to Ron and handed him a flashlight and some gloves.

"We've got work to do," I said as we walked up to the house.

"What's going on?" Ron asked as we stepped inside the house.

"I think there could be some money and drugs hidden inside the house." I said.

"Where'd you get an idea like that?" Ron asked.

I responded, "A waitress at Alfred's told me Cassandra was dealing drugs. She said Cassandra had a lot of money."

"You think it's true?" he said.

"Don't know, but that would explain all the expensive things they have," I said.

It was cold inside the house. We split up and started searching the house. The search lasted about an hour; we didn't find anything. I was frustrated to be honest with you. Ron walked up to me and patted me on the back.

"Are you alright?" he inquired.

I was going nuts trying to figure this thing out. I reached down to pick up the flashlight. I assured Ron I was okay. We walked outside and stood on the porch. Ron had to leave so he could get to the church convention. None of my leads on the case turned up anything. The case was getting the best of me. It was dark out when I left the house. I headed home so I could shower and change clothes. I am going to Alfred's tonight. I want to look like I belong there, and hopefully, I'll find some solid leads in this case.

I left my apartment around 9:30 p.m. I decided to walk since Alfred's was just a couple of minutes away from my apartment. I was wearing dark brown slacks, a black button down silk shirt with a matching blazer, and some black loafers. The scenery inside the club had definitely changed. The music was very different when I stepped inside the door. The DJ was playing loud hip-hop music. There was a young-looking crowd inside the club and the place was packed.

There was merely enough room for standing. It was dark inside and the flashing disco lights hanging from the ceiling made it very difficult to see. I bumped into several people as I walked through the club. The smell of nicotine and liquor almost made me sick to my stomach. It has been a long time since I've been out to a club in an atmosphere like this. The club was mixed with blacks, whites, and other nationalities.

Everyone seemed to be having the time of their life. The crowd was jumping around to the music and chanting aloud to the music. I stood in the back corner of the club and checked out the crowd. I was looking for Paige to see if she had any new information for me, and I walked out on the patio to see if she was outside. She was nowhere to be found. Maybe she didn't come to work I thought as I walked back into the club and stood at the end of the bar. A white woman walked up to me to see if I wanted to dance.

"No thanks! I'm waiting for someone!" I yelled out.

"Jack, it's me Paige" she said, "the waitress from this morning!"

I couldn't believe the woman standing in front of me was the same girl I had talked with earlier. I didn't even recognize her. Paige was gorgeous. I admired the view of her body. She was wearing make-up now and her hair was curly. The red lipstick she was wearing made her look very sexy.

She was wearing a white blouse, and some black leather jeans that fit her body perfectly. Her 5" heels were covered in glitter. Paige and I danced for a while, then we walked over to one of the empty tables and sat down to talk. I asked Paige if she saw any of the people Cassandra used to hang out with.

"What?" she yelled back at me. She couldn't hear because the music was too loud.

I leaned forward to get up close and said, "Do you see any of the people Cassandra hung out with?"

"Yeah, they are all in the back of the club in the V.I.P section," Paige yelled as she lifted a Newport cigarette out of a pack.

She pointed to a table in the corner of the club. There were three men and two women sitting at the table. I tried not to stare at them, but I couldn't resist. The V.I.P section was packed as well. Paige told me it cost $1,000 per person to get back there. I asked Paige to come outside so we could talk.

The music was so loud it was impossible to hear. When I stood, I noticed Timothy Woods, the sergeant from the Penal Farm, James Johnson's best friend sitting at the table in the V.I.P. section. He was engaged in a heated conversation with another man. I wondered if the woman sitting at the table with Timothy Woods was Yolanda Jenkins.

I limped through the crowd trying to make it to the door. Paige and I made it across the room and walked outside. "Are you okay? You seem to be limping, "she asked with a concerned look on her face.

"I'm okay, I have a limp from an old football injury," I said.

My knee started bothering me from dancing. I just needed to walk it out. Beale St. was packed because the Memphis Grizzlies basketball game is tonight and the LA Lakers are also in town. I told Paige I needed her to get some information on the three men and two women that Cassandra used to hang out with. I wanted to know what kind of cars they drove and the tag numbers.

I needed pretty much any information she could get. I reached into my blazer and took out $200 and handed the cash to her along with my card. I told her to call me as soon as she got the info. She nodded as she puffed on the cigarette. I turned to leave and Paige said "You're not leaving already are you?" The night is young...let's party.

Paige was feeling it and she wanted to hang out with me. I would stay if the circumstances were different. I smiled at Paige and told her I had a long day, maybe tomorrow and walked off. She threw the cigarette out on the curb and went back inside the club. It was a beautiful night out, so I decided to go for a walk. It was a good day to exercise my knee; besides I needed to get my mind off the case for a while. I have been working on the case non-stop since day one.

The tall buildings downtown were bright. The reflections of light beaming from them lit up the streets and the sky was vivid with shades of dark blue. A homeless man was sitting at the bus stop eating some scraps off the ground. I gave him a few bucks as I walked by. The streets were still, except for a few cars headed down Third St.

A group of teenagers drove by hanging their heads out of the windows yelling loudly. There was a lot of activity going on at the back dock when I made it to C.J.C. I bent down and moved up close around the Clock Bonding Company.

I wanted to get a good look at things. It was dark on the dock and I didn't see anyone I recognized. There were people loading packages into the trunks of vehicles. None of the people getting in the cars were wearing C.J.C. or Sherriff's uniforms.

When the last car loaded up, a woman came out and started talking to a man standing on the dock when the car drove off. I wondered if she was Yolanda Jenkins. The man walked over to the wall and hit a button, and the garage door came down. Something weird is going on at the property room dock. I can feel it.

The dock was connected to the kitchen and the property room. Maybe the activity was nothing. Even though I already had enough on my plate to deal with, I had to make sure nothing illegal was going on. I just couldn't resist the temptation to investigate things.

I stepped inside my one bedroom apartment in the Old Exchange Building in downtown Memphis on Second Street, took my blazer off, threw it on the sofa, and sat down.

I turned on the television. An old repeat of the first 48 was on A&E. I stood and walked around the living room for a while. My knee was still bothering me. I walked over to the phone and checked the answering machine. There were no messages.

I walked over to the refrigerator, opened it, grabbed the chicken subway sandwich from the shelf, sat at my dinner table, nibbled on the sandwich, and went over the case aloud. I just couldn't get the Johnsons off my mind.

Two people were dead, one person was missing. Asa had lost her father and her only brother. There was a good chance Cassandra was already dead. There were no suspects, and no witnesses. We checked with the neighbors, but none of them saw or heard anything. Cassandra's BMW is missing and hasn't been located.

Cassandra may have been having an affair with an inmate, and Ron had a hunch she could be in a secret relationship with her brother-in-law. But I haven't found anything to support those accusations.

Amos and the victim had a big argument days before the murder, but no one knows what the argument was about.

A notebook was found on the baby, but no one knows what the numbers in the notebook signify. The notebook must be important or James wouldn't have gone to great lengths to hide it on his baby. Cassandra is supposed to be a drug dealer with a lot of money, but no money turns up at the bank or the house.

I sat on the sofa a long time. The fact that Asa was not James biological child was evidence Cassandra was unfaithful which presumably means her daughter's father is a suspect. I stood and turned the television off; then, I walked to my bedroom and shut the door behind me.

I drove to the office early Wednesday on Day 5, the morning of November 22nd. The skies were clear and the sun was shining. There was a good chance a cold front and rain were coming by the end of the day. I made several calls so I could setup more surveillance on Amos when he returned from Jackson. I had mixed feelings about Amos possibly being the killer, but I still thought he knew more than he told us.

It was a little after eight in the morning when Angie and Ron walked in the office. Ron spoke to me when he walked over to his desk. I subconsciously heard him, but I was deep in thought, staring at the blank computer screen, thinking about a theory I had developed about the case.

Ron walked over and touched me on the shoulder and said, "You were in another world."

I turned around in my chair to face him. We talked about the case for a minute. He wanted to know how things were going. I told him I wasn't getting anywhere with the case. He suggested things would get better; then, he walked over to Angie's desk, and they started talking to one another. The office became noisy as the other detectives shuffled their feet through the door. Angie brought coffee and doughnuts for everyone, but I didn't want any.

I had a hunch about something and needed to check it out. If Cassandra Johnson was sleeping with an inmate, maybe he had something to do with the murders. Maybe she got him out of jail, maybe he found out that Cassandra and James had a lot of money and set them up to get robbed. If Cassandra was charging money to change information around in the computer, maybe someone paid her to get them out of jail, and she didn't come through. So, they sent someone to kill her. It was important that I rule out every possible theory about the case. Even if it did sound farfetched, the theory sounds reasonable. I stood and left the office in a hurry.

I was on my way to the Court Clerk's office downstairs. The door was locked and the lights were off inside the office when I walked up. The clerks had already left the office to go to the courtroom. I headed back to the office to catch Ron. I wanted to ask a favor of him. Ron was still standing at Angie's desk running off at the mouth when I made it back to the office. Those two were spending a lot of time together lately. It doesn't appear they are worried about the strict fraternizing on the job policies around here. I walked over to my desk and sat down in my chair. I tried to wait on playboy Ron to finish talking with Angie but it didn't seem like he was going to stop.

Finally, I interrupted them and said, "Will you two blue birds knock it off for a second!"

Angie and Ron walked over to my desk and asked what was going on. "How would you like to be a baller?" I said to Ron.

"A baller! I'm already a baller you didn't know?" he claimed.

"Maybe in your dreams!" Angie said adding her two cents, to the conversation.

Angie walked back to her desk laughing at the remark Ron made.

"Seriously though, I might need you to go out to Club Alfred's and check some people out for me. See what they're in to."

"Just say the word," Ron replied.

He was still working security at the Church Convention, but he would find the time to help me anyway he could with the case. Ron walked over to Angie; she had a big smile on her face when he left. I walked over to Angie and asked her if she could get the names of the inmates Cassandra was accused of trying to get out of jail.

"Let me make some phone calls and see what I can do," Angie said picking up the phone.

Suddenly, a message came over the two-way intercom system for all available officers to report to Tri-State Bank, a few blocks away, on Main St. where a robbery was in process. I ran out of the office as fast as I could. Other detectives were right behind me. As I approached the scene, several patrol cars blocked the streets off. People standing in the hallway were taking pictures with their cellphones and watching the commotion. The uniformed patrol officers told the pedestrians to go back inside the building because this could turn out to be a dangerous situation.

I got out of my car and ran up to the uniformed officers who were bent down next to their patrol cars with their guns drawn. They looked like a couple of rookies. One of them was shaking badly; his eyes were protruded and he looked very nervous. I asked one of them if he knew how many robbers were inside.

"We don't know yet," the officer yelled.

Within seconds, the bank was surrounded with police officers and detectives. When I stood, I saw Ron's red corvette approaching the scene on the other side of the bank. Suddenly, the front door to the bank flew open and a burst of gunfire sped toward us. I hit the ground hard while the bullets penetrated the patrol cars. No one was hit, but a sharp pain rushed in my side. We couldn't return fire because we didn't know how many civilians were inside the bank. This was a bad situation.

I hopped to my feet; then, I ran over to the side of the bank with my gun out and looked around the wall to get a closer look at things. I noticed a black Ford F-150 truck parked in the row of cars in the front of the bank. I assumed the truck was the getaway vehicle. I tried to move closer to the front windows to look inside the bank, but it was difficult to see through the dark tinted windows.

Ron was on the other side of the bank leaning on a patrol car in shooting position. Everyone was ready. We had been here before. In fact, someone robbed this bank about two months ago. This was the only bank in the downtown area that has been robbed in recent years. The door opened again and everyone took cover. We didn't know what to expect from the robbers. I squeezed my Glock tight.

One of the robbers yelled, "Move those patrol cars now! Or I will kill one of the hostages."

The lead negotiator announced through the bull horn, "Move the patrol cars now." Several officers moved their cars immediately.

When the door closed, I ran back over to the patrol cars where the officers were. One of the uniformed officers had his eyes closed. He was bent down by the fire extinguisher near the street corner. It looked like he was saying a prayer. I bent down and ran over to the side of the green and white building across the street which was directly in front of the bank. My heart was beating fast, sweat was rolling down my forehead, and I was breathing hard.

Ron made his way over to me as I tried to catch my breath. He asked me if I was okay. I looked at him and nodded my head back and forth indicating I was fine. I was out of shape and all the running around made me kind of dizzy. I leaned up against the building to rest. There were about 40 police officers and patrol cars posted on every street corner in every direction on five city blocks. The robbers had no clear way out.

The last time this bank got robbed the crooks got away on foot. Not this time. Ron and I and the rest of the team were ready to protect and serve the citizens of Memphis. Captain Nelson of the robbery department, pleaded with the robbers to give themselves up over the loud speaker, but his request didn't seem to be working.

Finally, the front door to the bank flew open again. Three robbers with mask on their faces, armed with AK-47's came out of the bank with a white woman walking in front of them. One of the robbers had the woman by the neck. She looked terrified. The other two robbers were carrying three tan money bags.

The woman unsuccessfully tried to jerk away from the robber when she saw all the police officers. Captain Nelson came over the loud speaker and told us to stand down. At this stage, he wanted to ensure the safety of the hostage, who was in eminent danger. Everything came to a standstill as the robbers slowly moved to their truck. Suddenly, the red dye packs inside the money bags exploded, and a large thick cloud of red smoke and money flew in the air.

The force from the explosion knocked the robbers and the woman to the pavement. The robbers opened fire as they moved over to the parked cars in front of the bank. The woman eased over to the corner of the wall by the front door, and balled up into a fetus position. Shots rang out as the coast became clear to return fire at the robbers. It was a war zone out there. I heard the sound of glass shattering in the streets and bullets flying everywhere. One of the robbers stood and tried to run back inside the bank.

Ron got off two shots at the robber in a split second. The bullets took the life right out of his body as he fell dead to the ground. One of them was dead, and the other one was moving on the ground. We moved in closer with our arms stretched pointing our guns in the direction of the robbers; shortly afterward, the second robber died. The woman was covered with red-dye and surrounded by money, but she was fine. The medics rushed in, assisted the woman on her feet, put her on the stretcher, then she was transported to the hospital.

The spokesman for our department, Captain Nelson took over as television news trucks arrived on the scene. He always looked good for the cameras. I told Ron he was going to have to turn his gun over to the review board, so they could investigate the shooting to make sure it was justifiable. We all had to turn in our weapons after a shooting in accordance with departmental rules. Captain Nelson announced everybody who was needed in the investigation by the end of the week. I shook hands with Ron and the rest of the other officers. I said goodbye to the team, and headed back to the office.

I was happy none of the good guys were injured. However, I felt pity for the hostage who witnessed the murder. Death is one of the hardest events to witness. The sight of life leaving a body is harsh. A death scene hunts most people. There is nothing pleasant about seeing the human body's reaction to critical injury, or a dying man take his last breath.

4

Cassandra's BMW Discovered

The expression, *Live and let live*, popped into my head as I walked into the office. I thought those days were behind me now, but this was Memphis. Crime was pretty bad at times. I have shot and killed 10 men in my 22 years on the force. They were all bad guys, and the shootings were justified, but taking another life is nothing I am proud of.

I was still a little dizzy from all the running earlier. My body was completely still. I could feel the pulse in my arm. Angie walked over and kindly handed me a cold glass of water.

She asked me, "Are you okay?"

"I'm okay," I assured her.

My heart beat was normal again and I felt revived as I drank the water. Man, was it good. I really needed to be hydrated.

Angie handed me a yellow piece of paper with two names on it. One of the men on the list was serving time at the Penal Farm. I told Angie to call out to the Penal Farm and let them know I was on my way. I walked out of the office to use the restroom, then I headed out to the Penal Farm. I got on I-55 and took I-240 east. I was sitting in a small office at the Penal Farm waiting for Marcus Green to arrive. Marcus was one of the men Cassandra was accused of trying to get out of jail.

Two unarmed guards wearing green uniforms escorted Marcus into the office. He sat in a blue plastic chair facing me. I told the guards I needed to talk with Marcus alone. The guards didn't look too friendly. For a minute, I thought they weren't going to leave the two of us alone. Finally, after 20 seconds passed, the guards reluctantly walked out the office and stood outside the door. Marcus Green didn't look tough at all.

He was about 5'10 with a medium build, and he had a lot of

tattoos. He was wearing blue jeans and a blue button down shirt with yellow letters across the back that said S.C.P.F. Marcus was charged with possession of crack cocaine with the intent to distribute. We both stared at each other as if we wanted something from one another.

Finally, I asked him, "Do you know Cassandra Johnson?"

Marcus looked at me with a big smile on his face and said, "What if I do? Why does it matter to you?"

Marcus tried to look and sound like he was hard core or something. I wasn't fooled by his performance one bit. I wasn't afraid. I could take care of myself if it came down to it.

"I hear she tried to change some information in the computer to get you out of jail," I said. The smile he had on his face evaporated and his expression changed to anger.

He looked at me with tight eyes and said, "She was my bitch!"

Marcus began to make serious eye contact with me. I didn't believe what he said about Cassandra.

"Why would a woman like Cassandra get involved with a loser like you? I asked.

A smirk came on his face and he said, "What's the only two things in life you'll never see?" he asked.

I looked directly at him but I offered him no response.

"One of them is high and one is low," he said as he gripped his crotch.

"Are you trying to be funny? You think this is a game?" I said with a serious look on my face. "Cassandra is missing! Her family was murdered!"

"A ho' with heart!" he whispered." I tried to ignore the comment, but I couldn't.

"What do you mean by 'A ho with heart?'" I asked with a curious look on my face.

"Cassandra was just a wolf in sheep clothing. She wasn't cheap but she played The Price is Right. She was a high price piece of ass. She would spin the wheel as often as she liked. Oh! Let me guess. She got you fooled; don't she! She was into a lot of shit. She is just another pretty face. Some women toot a line of two, but Cassandra is about O's!" he declared.

"What are O's?" I inquired.

"Bursting one," he laughed.

I'm not sure he knows anything that can help me solve this case. If he knows something I don't think he is going to tell me, without something in return. I was tired of Marcus playing games with me. Either he was exaggerating or Cassandra was a sex addict.

I stood to leave and Marcus said mockingly, "I bet you looking all over the place for Cassandra, ain't you detective?" he stated.

I commented, "If you know where she..."

"Know what!" Marcus yelled out cutting me off. "What's in it for me?" he asked.

Sweat was rolling down the side of my face. Now the tables had turned. I knew he knew something.

"If your information turns something, I might be able to get you out of jail on a time cut."

His eyes looked like they were going to pop right out of his head. He swallowed and cleared his throat. I thought Marcus would probably do anything to get out of this hell hole, but he is smart.

Marcus stood and walked up close to me and said, "I need something in writing first."

Timothy Woods walked into the office and broke up the interview. He told me it was count time therefore Marcus had to go back to the cell block. The two guards standing outside the door came into the office and escorted Marcus back to his cell. I felt Marcus was going to tell me something about Cassandra before Timothy came through the door. Marcus had a strange look on his face, like he was afraid of Timothy.

I had never made a deal with a criminal before. If I didn't come up with something on this case soon, maybe that was about to change. I thought I could solve this case on my own, but I still wanted to know what Marcus knew.

It was a little past noon when I made it back to the office. It was quiet and peaceful inside when I walked in. Angie was sitting at her desk working on a stack of files. There were a couple of detectives standing at the window talking on their cellphones.

Ron walked into the office and went over to the desk and sat down. I walked over and asked him if he was okay. Ron had killed one of the robbers earlier at the bank.

Finally, Ron looked up at me and said, "I'm okay, I guess." He had a somber look on his face. I knew that look; killing someone, even a bad guy, is difficult to accept. It was his first time, but in this line of work, it might not be his last time taking someone's life.

We risk our own lives. This is not an easy job, but we choose it every time we walk down stairs through these doors to protect the citizens and visitors of Memphis.

I patted Ron on the shoulder and said, "If you want me to set you up with a counselor, let me know."

I walked over to my desk and sat down. Ron was on break from the church convention. I'm sure he was trying to get his mind off the shooting. Angie walked over to Ron and stood by his side and tried to comfort him. I sat at my desk and thought about Marcus calling Cassandra "A ho with heart!" I took the family picture out of the Johnson file and looked at Cassandra's brown eyes. Marcus' words: *A wolf in sheep's clothing* rung in my mind.

I put the picture back in the file, then I walked back over to Angie and Ron and said, "I went for a walk downtown last night, after I left Club Alfred's. When I got to the back of C.J.C., I saw a lot of cars parked at the back dock. A man was loading packages into the trunks."

"You think something strange is going on? I asked.

"I mean, it is a dock," Ron said implying that things are loaded at docks.

I answered, "I don't know yet, but you can bet your last dollar, I'm going to find out if something is going on."

"If you need my help, give me a call!" Ron said, and I walked back over to my desk.

Ron and Angie talked for a second, then Ron said goodbye and walked out of the office. I sat at my desk and looked at the reports and photographs Glenda left for me of the crime scene. Amos's truck came back negative for body fluids. The crime scene unit did find out Amos had a key to his brother's house on his key chain. I was surprised to hear that. I studied the photographs one by one. What's missing? I thought to myself as I stared at the pictures. The rain started coming down hard. I stood and walked over to the window and looked outside. The rain didn't look like it was going to last long.

Most detectives were returning from lunch. Cruz walked up to me and said, "Some chick called the office for you, but you were gone. She said she tried to call you on your cell, but you didn't answer."

"Did she leave a name?" I asked.

Cruz stated, "Yeah, she said her name was Paige." I thanked him as a got my cell phone out of my pocket.

After the bank robbery scene, I checked my phone and saw three missed calls from a number I didn't recognize and a text from Dr. Alice. I guess the missed call was from Paige. I called the number back but the voice message picked up after the first ring. I looked at the text message Dr. Alice sent. It was a remainder about our date tonight at the Peabody Hotel at eight.

I hit myself on the top of the head and said "Dammit!" Angie walked over to me and asked if I was okay, "I got a date tonight, but I got a lot of work to do. I really need to call it off."

"Is she special to you?" Angie asked.

"Yeah, very special!" I said with a smile on my face.

"Then go on the date Jack! You work enough as it is. Go out and have fun, have a good time!" she said.

I thought about what Angie said for a second. She's right a date would probably do me a lot of good.

"You're right Angie. I'm going out," I said.

Angie walked back over to her desk and got on the computer. I grabbed my car keys off my desk and walked out the office headed to Club Alfred's to follow-up with Paige.

The heavy raindrops pounded on my windshield as I drove south on Second St. headed to Beale St. I pulled up next to the curb in front of Alfred's, hopped out of the car, and ran inside the club. The lunch crowd was gone. There were a few people sitting at the bar drinking beer listening to soft music. The lights were dimmed and cigarette smoke moved through the air like little clouds. I walked up to Paige and tapped her on the shoulder; she jumped in her seat and turned around and said, "You startled me Jack!" She stood and told me to come outside to the patio so we could speak in private.

I noticed her hair was out of place and she was walking sluggishly as I followed her to the patio. When she reached a table, she sat on top of it, and propped her feet in the chair.

"The club was really busy today, but I managed to get some information for you," she said handing me a piece of paper.

"These people come to the club twice a week, and they definitely have money. One of the women works at Walmart in a mid-level position. I don't see how she can afford to pay VIP prices at the club working at Walmart. The other woman is a correctional guard out at the Penal Farm. All of them drive expensive cars too," Paige declared.

Paige took her shoes off and rubbed her foot. I studied over the list while I stood there. Paige wrote down a lot of information about the people Cassandra use to hang out with. I folded the piece of paper, placed it in my back pocket, thanked Paige, and handed her some more cash.

The rain stopped and the sun was shining bright. She escorted me back inside the club and I walked out the door. I was finally going to get a chance to talk with Yolanda Jenkins. I wanted to be able to identify the man and woman I saw standing on the back dock last night.

I was hoping Yolanda could tell me what was going on with Cassandra. It was quiet and empty in the basement when I stepped off the elevator. I glanced around, walked up to the stainless-steel door, and pressed the red button on the wall. A loud buzzer sounded, then the door popped open, and I stepped inside the room. There was a well-dressed attractive woman sitting at a desk inside an office talking away into the telephone.

There was another door with a black and white sign which stated: NO ONE BEYOND THIS POINT EXCEPT PROPERTY ROOM PERSONNEL.

Finally, the woman hung the receiver up, stood and walked over to me and said, "Can I help you sir?"

I introduced myself and told her I was investigating the disappearance of Cassandra Johnson. I asked her if she knew Cassandra. Her eyes shifted away from me, then they came back.

Finally, after ten seconds or so, the woman said, "I don't know anyone by that name." An obvious lie I thought. She looked very suspicious. She tried to clear her throat.

"Is Yolanda Jenkins here?" I inquired.

"I really need to speak with her," I added.

She replied, "She quit yesterday."

"What do you mean she quit yesterday," I said.

The woman reached into her coat pocket, took out a napkin, and wiped the sweat off her forehead. I assumed she was trying to cover something up, but she wasn't doing a very good job of it.

"Is your supervisor around? I asked.

"I'm afraid he's out-of-town on business," she said.

I smirked and asked, "When do you expect him to return?"

She responded, "He's due back in town next week."

I stood there for a second, thanked her for her time, and walked to the door. She smiled at me, walked into the office, and pressed the button on the wall. The door popped open, and I walked out of the room. I was disappointed that the interview led to a dead-end. My conversation with the woman confirmed to me something strange was going on in the property room. When Angie talked to the receptionist on the phone yesterday morning she told her Yolanda Jenkins didn't show up for work and now all a sudden she just up and quit.

I headed back to West Memphis to see if Yolanda Jenkins had come home. I didn't believe my eyes when I drove up to her house and saw yellow police tape surrounding it. I jumped out the car, walked up to the driveway, and stared at the scene. I was baffled the house I had just visited two days ago, was now a crime scene. The elderly neighbor I talked to the other day walked out of the house and stood in her driveway, waved at me and said, "Hi! It's the nice-looking policeman from

Memphis."

She was wearing a pink housecoat, matching house shoes, and a brown socks; a little white puppy was beside her. I walked over to the end of her driveway.

"What happened?" I asked.

The puppy tried to make a run for it, but I caught him before he could make it to the street. She covered her mouth with both of her hands and said, "They were murdered!"

I handed the puppy to her; then, she continued, "The police kicked the door in and found Yolanda and her son dead. I told them you had come by looking for Yolanda. I even gave one of them your card."

"Do you remember the name of the officer you gave my card to?" I asked.

"It was…" She looked up at the sky like as if his name was written in the clouds; then she said, "Reed! That's it, Reed!"

I thanked her, walked back to my car, and drove off. I was beginning to realize that the events in this case were connecting. One missing woman, two dead parents, two dead boys, and the missing woman and the deceased woman were friends and previously worked at C.J.C.

It just couldn't be a coincidence that family members at the homes of two old friends were murders in November. I returned to my office, went to my desk, and stared at the computer. Most of the detectives were gone and it was quiet in the office.

Angie walked over to my desk and asked, "Is everything alright?" She could tell by the look on my face something was bothering me.

I responded "It's Yolanda Jenkins!"

"Good you talked to her!" Angie said with a pleased look on her face.

I replied "No she's dead!"

"What!" Angie said surprised at the news.

I answered, "Yeah, the West Memphis police kicked in the door and found Yolanda and her son dead inside the house yesterday."

"Do you think it has something to do with Cassandra's

disappearance?" Angie asked.

I didn't know what to think about the case anymore. Things were becoming complicated.

Finally, I looked at Angie and said, "I don't know, but I'm going to find out what's going on. You can bank on it!"

I needed to contact the West Memphis Police Department to set up a meeting with Officer Reed. I need to collaborate with their department about these murders. I walked over to Angie and asked her to get the number.

"I'll get right on it Jack," She said picking up the phone.

I walked over to the window and looked outside. It was a dark beautiful evening. At 6:50 p.m. I looked at the clock on the wall. If the murders were connected that would mean, there was a killer on the loose.

I planned to notify Captain Dunn and the Chief, first thing in the morning. About five minutes later Angie called me over to her desk. The West Memphis Police Department was on the speaker phone.

"Hello, my name is Detective Jack Webster with the Memphis Homicide Department. Is Officer Reed in?" I asked.

The operator said, "One moment please." Some music played in the background.

"He's out in the field, would you like to leave a contact number? She asked.

I gave the secretary my information and thanked her. There was nothing more I could do in the office. I told Angie I would see her in the morning and walked out the door. I rushed home so I could take a shower and change clothes for my date with Dr. Alice.

I managed to make it to the Peabody Hotel a little after eight o'clock. Dr. Alice was standing at the front entrance when I drove by the hotel. Even though we went out on a date before, I'm getting butterflies.

I realize, in the past, I let my work get in the way of my relationships. Actually, I almost let work get in the way today. In fact, I told myself I wasn't going to mention anything about work, or any of the murder cases because tonight is going to be special, and we'll see what happens.

I was swept off my feet when I walked up to Dr. Alice wearing a blue, fitted dress that stopped an inch above her knees. She is as beautiful as ever. Her heels look very expensive and they make her as tall as me.

She had on a matching diamond earrings and necklace set. The smell of her fragrance took me to another world. I'm not sure I dressed right for the occasion after seeing her, but I am in the game - wearing dark, brown slacks with a white silk shirt and a matching brown blazer. A tie would have set my outfit off. I guess I'm too laid back these days. Next, time I will be on my 'A' game.

Dr. Alice and I walked inside the ballroom and the hostess escorted us to our reserved fancy table set up for two. There is nothing like a candle light dinner with a beautiful woman.

This table was near the window overlooking downtown Memphis. The lights were dimmed, soft love music played in the background, and it was nice and cozy. Everyone seemed to be having a good time. The environment was definitely a change of scenery for me.

We sat there a few minutes taking in everything and watching the couples dance. I called the waiter over to the table so we could order something to drink. We both ordered scotch. Something was different about our date this time. Things seemed magical as I sat there admiring Dr. Alice who looked like she just walked off the pages of a fairytale book.

I guess that is what's supposed to happen at the Peabody ballroom. "What's on your mind?" Dr. Alice asked with a pretty smile on her face.

I said with authority, "I almost forgot how beautiful you are."

"It's Alice tonight," she said.

"Okay Alice, you look stunning." I said.

She flipped her hair and said, "You're just saying that Jack. I bet you say that to all the women."

I replied "Nah', I don't have any women to say that too. I only have my eye on you and no one else."

Alice burst out laughing and said, "Stop it Jack!"

"I'm serious. Every second in life is important. I'm not into playing any games," I said. Alice tilted her head slightly; her smile faded from a bright light to lukewarm.

The waiter brought our drinks, sat them on the table, and took our order. It has been a long time since I felt this good inside. I was lonely after my divorce. I contemplated getting remarried someday. I am 43 years old and I am ready to use my experience to make the rest of my life better. I am not going to let anything stand in the way of love. At this moment, deep down inside, I know Alice is the woman for me. Even though something has been holding us back, I never stopped thinking about her. She makes me tick. She lifts my spirit.

"Would you like to dance?" I asked.

"Who told you I knew how to dance?" she stated.

"I just know! If you can't we'll just move our feet and avoid stepping on each other's toes," I stated; then I gave her a quick eye wink.

I stood, grabbed Alice by the hand, and escorted her out to the dance floor. I could see men admiring Alice out of the corner of my eyes. I didn't mind. It took an act of will power not to look at Alice. She looks incredible. I pulled her up to my body and held her tight in my arms as we moved around the dance floor. Our eyes met at the same time, and at that electric, moment we kissed each other lightly on the lips.

We floated across the dance floor. For a second, I felt light as if some magic ray had hit me. The music stopped and we were still in the middle of the floor dancing. Another song started playing, I held her hand as we walked back to our table, and sat down. I could stay in this moment forever – right here with Alice.

I finally let go of her hand and said, "I thought you couldn't dance."

"I never told you I couldn't dance Jack," Alice said with a smile on her face.

By then, the waiter arrived with our food. I had ordered Peabody Signature Filet Mignon which is a grilled filet with marinated Gulf Coast shrimp kabob & honey glaze. Alice had two oven-roasted Italian sausages in red wine with red seedless grapes served with braised red cabbage & fennel, with a red wine mustard sauce. Man, I was starving!

We sat there, ate, and talked for so long hours passed by. By 10:40 p.m. only a few couples remained in the room. I went over, paid the bill, then, we left. We drove back to my apartment. It was a full moon out tonight, so we decided to go for a walk down on the river front. We walked along the banks of the great Mississippi river holding hands and smooching. We stopped, watched the moonlight shine off the water cherishing the moments we were sharing together.

Alice looked at me with passion in her eyes and said, "I want to make love to you, Jack Webster." I was thinking the same thing if you want to know the truth. I knew Alice wasn't going anywhere tonight without making love. I kissed her again; then, we headed back to my apartment. I reached into my pocket to get the keys out to open the door, and dropped them on the floor. I was too anxious. Finally, I opened the door, and Alice pushed me inside and we attacked each other like there was no tomorrow.

It had been a long time since either one of us had made love. We were both ready. I picked her up in my arms and took her to my bedroom. I slowly undressed her as she stood before me. She reached out and touched my erect penis and said, "My god!"

I got undressed, then I turned on the stereo. Luther Vandross was playing. I walked over to the bed and licked Alice on the feet and made my way up her body softly rubbing her all over.

I was gentle with her. I went down and started performing oral sex on her. She started making sounds, then she said, "I want you inside me Jack." I got on top of her and felt myself slide in. Man, it felt good! We made love nice and slow. Everything was perfect and I thanked GOD for every moment.

Marcus Green beaten by guards at the Penal Farm

Back at the Penal Farm Marcus Green was fast asleep in his cell when the door popped open. Three guards ran in and one of them grabbed Marcus out of the bed and threw him to the floor.

"What the fuck was you doing talking to that police officer today nigger!" the guard said as they beat and stumped on him repeatedly.

"I didn't say nothing!" he yelled out as he tried to block some of the body blows with his arms.

"He just popped up, I don't know how he got my name," Marcus said in fear.

"Talk to him again and you a dead man!" the guard said.

One guard kicked Marcus in the face, stepped over him, and they walked out the cell. Marcus laid on the floor balled up in pain, moaning in need of some serious medical attention.

Detective Jack Webster

Alice and I laid in bed holding each other trying to catch our breath. I was emotionally happy and I wasn't going to let anything stand in the way of my relationship with her this time around. We had taken our friendship to another level by making love which was a deal maker in my view. We now belonged to each other. We were a pair, heading in a new direction.

"Where do we go from here, Jack?" she asked while looking at me with those big pretty blue eyes.

"I need you in my life, and I don't ever want this feeling to end." I said. I felt lucky to have a woman like her. I tried to express how gracious I was.

"I want to move in with you Jack," she said as she rubbed her fingers across my chest hairs. Her suggestion proved she is a humble woman because she owned a lavish Condominium in the suburbs.

"I would love for you to move in with me," I said. We laid there holding one another and finally went to sleep.

First thing November 23th Saturday morning, Day 6 of the investigation 7:00 am to be exact, I was on my way to the 11th floor of C.J.C. to see Captain Dunn.

When I laid my eyes on him, he was sitting in his chair with both of his feet propped up on his desk reading the morning paper. I slowly stuck my head in the door and Captain Dunn said, "Come in Jack."

I stepped inside the office and shut the door behind me. Captain Dunn was short with a beer belly, and a bald head. His face is pale and he can definitely use a tan.

I sat in the chair in front of Captain Dunn's cluttered desk in his cramped office which smelled like smoke. I thought the office was a fire hazard with all the files and paperwork scattered all over the place. I began to tell him about the notebook, the property room, and about finding out Yolanda Jenkins had been murdered. Captain Dunn never spoke while I went over the details of the case. I couldn't see how he could keep up with anything. A lot of old timers said Captain Dunn was once one of the best detectives the department ever had.

He took a cigarette and lit it while I was talking. I don't want my Dallas Cowboy football jersey and my blue jeans to smell like smoke all day. When I got through talking about the case, Captain Dunn told me to keep him informed. He told me to call if I ran into any problems, but he didn't offer me any advice. I walked out of the office to inhale some fresh air.

I walked into the office with a big smile on my face singing "Here and now" and humming. I spoke to Angie, walked over to my desk, and sat down.

Angie walked over and said, "I see your date last night must have been the bomb."

"What date?" Ron asked as he came in the office. "Who did you go out with Jack?" Ron asked with a curious look on his face.

Ron stood next to Angie and waited for an answer. "Come on man! Who is it? Who's the mystery woman?"

I finally gave into the questioning and said "Dr. Alice."

"I knew it! I knew there was something going on between y'all'," Ron said pointing his finger at me.

Ron grabbed a chair and said "Fill me in on the details." He had a big smile on his face.

Angie hit Ron on the shoulder and said, "Don't tell him anything."

"Hey that hurt!" Ron said to Angie rubbing his shoulder.

Ron was getting ready to head to the church convention at Bountiful Blessing Church of God in Christ on G. E. Paterson Drive in South Memphis.

"Speaking of dates, I see you two have been spending a lot of time together around the office lately," I said.

Ron smiled and Angie turned her nose up in the air and said, "I've got work to do. See ya'.'"

She walked back to her desk and started typing on the computer. Ron said goodbye and walked out of the office. Some detectives were getting ready to go out and serve a warrant on a guy they planned to question about a woman who was found dead in her car. I turned back around in my chair and started typing on my computer. I had to finish the report on the bank robbery and e-mail it to Captain Nelson. Then, I was going back out to the Penal Farm to interview Anton Norwood.

Homeless Male Billy Jackson

Billy Jackson was released from the Penal Farm about two weeks ago, and he is up to his old tricks again and already smoking crack like it ain't nobody's business. He looks and acts like a drug addict; he is un-kept, dark, and frail; he is one of the worse crackheads in the city. Most of his teeth were rotten from smoking crack for decades. He lives on the streets of downtown Memphis along with many other homeless people and junkies. Most of his family members disown him but every now and then, his mother sends his sister downtown to check on him and make sure he is okay. Sometimes she sends Billy money and food.

On occasion, when his brother wasn't at the house, his younger sister, Mary Ann, let Billy in the house to take baths, and put on some of his brother's clean clothes. His brother detested Billy because he had *sticky fingers.* Billy's mother and sister loved him and hated to see him out on the streets. Even though it hurt to see him back on the streets; his mother showed Billy tough love and banned him from the house. They had no choice; he couldn't be trusted. He lies like the devil and is quite cunning. Billy once convinced a tourist he was so desolate that he gave Billy the shoes off his feet. You know already, that Billy sold those shoes 15 minutes later.

Billy's mother could remember when he wasn't on drugs. He was a good son with a shot at life 25 years ago. Billy went off to college and started hanging out with the wrong crowd and got hooked on crack cocaine. Billy had been in and out of jail for 20 years. He had a record of petty crimes a mile long. Nothing too serious.

His record contained mainly auto burglary and drug possession charges. He broke into cars day and night to get cash or items which he could turn into cash or exchange for drugs. He used the porcelain off a spark-plug to break the car windows out. Billy would take the spark-plug, lay it on the ground, take a brick, and burst the porcelain into small pieces. One of those pieces could shatter a car window without making a sound when he threw it at the window.

Billy woke up about eight o'clock that morning. He was wearing a dirty brown shirt, blue jeans, and some old run down black tennis shoes. The skies were cloudy and it was about 58 degrees. Billy needed to get out to the Memphis International Airport before noon so he could break into some cars. There would be only one security guard watching the entire parking lot before noon which made it as easy as taking candy from a baby to get loot out of vehicles.

Billy walked around downtown panhandling money from everyone he saw. Finally, Billy got enough money to catch the city bus out to the Airport; he hopped off the bus the second it pulled up to the bus stop. When the bus drove off, Billy ran up to the fence, looked around to see if anyone was on the parking lot, then, he jumped over the fence.

He bent down and ran across the parking lot like a ninja, and stopped at the first row of parked cars. Two women came down the row and got into their car. His heart was beating fast and his face and hands were sweaty. Billy stood and peered inside the car looking for visible loot. Nothing was noticeable.

He searched several cars but came up empty handed. The sun beamed through the clouds. It was almost 12 noon. Billy was getting discouraged and he was about to leave, but he decided to check the black BMW parked at the end of the row. He walked up to the passenger side of the window of the BMW and looked inside. Billy couldn't believe his eyes. The keys were still in the ignition and there was a black purse sitting on the floor.

At first, he assumed it was a set up. Then, he walked away from the BMW looking around; then, he stopped, turned around, walked back to the car, and stood near the driver side door. He reached out to open the door, but he stopped. He looked around one more time. He hesitated for a second, then opened the door. The alarm didn't come on. He hoped in the car, drove off, wondering how lucky he was; then, he sped down Winchester Rd.

When he stopped at the red light, he reached down and grabbed the purse and went through it. His eyes bucked and he started to dance in the seat. There was $1,700 dollars inside the purse along with a smart phone, and a Glock 45 handgun.

Billy drove straight ahead, turned up the radio as loud as it could go, made a right on Elvis Presley Blvd, got on the highway right pass Brooks Rd. and headed downtown to Abel St. with a stack of cash to the crack house.

5

Billy Pawns Cassandra's BMW

At about 11:45 a.m., I was pulling into the parking lot at the Penal Farm looking for somewhere to park. I finally found a parking space after I drove around the lot the second time. I walked into the lobby to check my weapon in since there were no weapons allowed past this point. This was my third trip. The guards in the main building had gotten use to seeing me, so they buzzed me inside. I sat in the small break room waiting for Anton Norwood to come.

About 20 minutes had past and I was humming a song and patting my finger on the table. Finally, the door opened and Anton Norwood stepped into the room. I stood and introduced myself and we both sat down to talk. I asked Anton if he knew what Amos and James were arguing about the day before the party. Anton told me he had never met Cassandra before and that he didn't attend the party.

Anton told me he heard they were arguing about a stripper that worked at Pure Passion named Delicious. Apparently, James was having an affair too. I thanked Amos for his time and we walked out to the breakroom. I wasn't surprised to hear James was having an affair. Actually, nothing could surprise me about this couple. I headed to Pure Passion to talk with Delicious.

The parking lot was almost empty when I drove up to the strip club. There were about nine cars parked in the parking lot. I got out of the car and walked up to the door and stepped inside the club. A black woman with big boobs standing behind a glass window at the door asked me for the admission fee of $25. I took my badge out and flashed it at the woman and she told me to go inside. I took another peep at her boobs, then I smiled and walked into the club. The club was dead, I glanced around the large room.

There were about 20 men inside the huge club. The lights were dimmed, and the ceiling, and walls were covered with mirrors. The D.J. yelled into the microphone as the hip-hop music banged out of the black speakers. There were four half naked strippers on the stage dancing and sexing the poles. Several topless strippers walked around the club. The men were throwing money on the stage as the exotic dancers put on a show.

I sat down at one of the tables and watched the scene. Two men were sitting in the back of the club making strange sounds as the strippers gave them lap dances. A topless waitress walked up to me and asked me if I wanted a drink.

"No thanks. I'm looking for a woman that calls herself Delicious." I said.

"Are you a police officer?" the woman said.

"Do I look like one?" I asked.

The woman hesitated for a second and said, "Yeah."

I took out my badge and showed it to her. "I don't think she's here. Let me check for you," she said and walked off.

I sat at the table and enjoyed the show the strippers were putting on. They really knew how to use a pole. I watched them glide around the pole. One of the strippers walked up to me and asked me if I wanted a lap dance. I smiled at her and politely turned her down. It's no surprise I got an erection watching the naked sensual women walk around the club.

Finally, a woman appeared from behind the gold curtains; she walked up to me, and told me that Delicious wouldn't be back until tonight. I didn't think she was going to show her face anyway. In fact, I got the feeling Delicious wasn't going to be easy to find. I sat at the table for a minute and tried to calm myself down.

The strippers really had my hormones flowing as I sat at the table. I stood and walked out of the club. I headed back down Brooks Road and got on the highway and headed back to 201 Poplar. When I walked into the office, I asked Angie if

Officer Reed had called but she told me no one had called for me since I left.

Homeless Male Billy Jackson

Abel Street was in South Memphis about two blocks away from the church convention Ron was covering. Billy got off the highway on Lamar Avenue and headed toward E.H. Crump Blvd., then he made a right on Third St., and headed to Vance St. He sped down the street and pulled up next to the curb. He put the gun back inside the purse and hopped out of the car. He stopped in the middle of the street, did a little dance, and then he went inside the duplex apartments to smoke some crack cocaine.

Back at the crack house on Abel street. Billy was sitting on the old brown dirty sofa smoking crack with the purse lying on his side. No one had paid any attention to the purse because they were too busy getting high. Billy was spending money left and right. He thought he was king for a day and so did the other crackheads sitting around him feeding off his wealth like leeches.

One of the other black women walked up to Billy and whispered something in his ear. Billy smiled and stood. He was proud of himself for hitting a big lick that morning. Billy decided he was going to trade some money and drugs for sex. Two women escorted Billy to a bedroom in the back of the apartment and shut the door behind them. He forgot all about the purse lying on the sofa. Billy had a pocket full of money and all the crack he wanted. He didn't have to worry about anything. At that moment, he didn't have a care in this world.

One of the drug dealers walked into the apartment and glanced around the room to see who was inside. He wanted to know who was driving the black BMW parked out front. He saw the purse lying on the sofa and went over to see what was inside. He asked the crackheads if they knew who was driving the BMW parked outside. One of the women told him Billy was driving the car and the purse belonged to him.

The drug dealers name was Reco. He was dark, tall medium build, had long braids, and a lot of gold teeth in his mouth. Reco searched thought the purse and found the Glock 45, the iPhone, and a credit card that had Cassandra Johnson's name on it. He wondered if the credit card was any good because his girlfriend could hustle the card in the shopping malls. She could buy a lot of expensive clothes and jewelry to sell around the neighborhood. Billy came out of the room smiling from ear to ear. He was sweating like he was standing out in the hot sun.

Reco walked up to Billy and said, "Let me give you some crack for the iPhone, the Glock 45, and I want to rent the car for a few hours." He didn't say anything about the credit card he had found inside the purse. Billy thought about it for a second, then he said,

"What you gonna give me?" Reco reached into his pants pocket and took out a plastic bag of crack cocaine.

There was about 200 pieces inside the bag. Billy watched the bag like it was a naked woman dancing in front of him. Everyone on the room focused on the bag of crack Reco had. He gave Billy 30 pieces of crack for everything and asked him if the iPhone was an AT&T phone.

"Yeah it's an AT&T phone!" Billy said even though he didn't know what kind of phone it was.

Billy gave Reco the car keys to the BMW, and Reco walked out of the door. Billy sat on the sofa and continued to smoke with the rest of the crackheads. He had a pocket full of money and a hand full of crack. He wasn't worried about anything. As far as he was concerned, Reco could keep the car as long as he wanted.

201 Poplar St.

I was pacing in front of my desk thinking about the case. I remembered what my very first partner taught me about investigating cases. When a case isn't going your way, and your leads don't amount to anything, go away, and come back. In other words, start the investigation over. There was always

71

a good chance that you started the investigation wrong and missed something important. I sat down at my desk and went back over the case in my mind from the beginning.

I considered what I was missing, as I bounced the pencil off the top of the desk. Finally, it hit me to check out the last place Cassandra and James were seen alive which was B.B. King's club on Beale Street! I got out of my chair and walked out of the office and headed to the B.B. King's Club. Beale Street was about 10 city blocks from CJC. I drove to the Greyhound Bus station on Union Avenue and parked in the front of the station. It was a beautiful day outside so I decided to walk the rest of the way.

It was about two o'clock in the evening and there were a lot of people out today. I strutted down Third Street feeling good and looking at the nice-looking women as they walked by. I did a little window shopping when I got to the mall inside of Peabody Place. I saw some sporty shoes I liked sitting in the window. Beale Street was just up ahead and there was a crowd of people standing at the corner. Tourist come from all over the world to visit Beale Street and to hear the blues. The weather was great for this time of the year. It was just the first week of November and it was warm outside like it was June.

I made a right at the corner of Beale and Third Street. I could see the big black and white sign that was on top of the reddish brick building that said B.B King's Club. The club was located on the corner of Beale and Second Street. I could smell the fresh barbecue in the air when I walked up to the front door. There was a large sign standing outside by the door with today's special written in big black letters.

I stood at the door and watched the crowd of people walking on Beale Street taking pictures and having a good time. I opened the door and stepped inside the club and surveyed the scene. The B.B King's Club was much bigger than Alfred's as I compared the two clubs in my mind. I thought the clubs were definitely different from one another. The look was different and the crowd seemed to be a lot older looking.

The inside of the club was flushed out. There were pictures of movie stars and all kind of famous people on the walls. There was a large picture of B.B King hanging in the middle of the club. There were people all over the club laughing and eating. I saw a couple of women wearing shirts with B.B. King on them, standing at the end of the bar. I walked over to the bar and sat down. The bartender, a short blonde woman, with a sweet set of boobs was pouring Jack Daniels in some shot glasses. She told me she would be with me in a moment. The two women were standing at the end of the bar appeared to be on break. They were arguing about a tip that disappeared off a table.

The bartender walked up to me and said "How can I help you today?" the name on her shirt said Lindsey.

"I'm a homicide detective and I'm investigating the disappearance of Cassandra Johnson," I said as I showed her my badge.

"Don't know her," Lindsey said. "She was here last Sunday night for a big party the Penal Farm had."

"Oh yeah, now I remember. It's been all over the news," Lindsey said.

"Were you working the party that night?" I asked.

She responded, "Nope I was off. Thank God! But I think Diane was there." She turned her head and said "Hey Diane!" Lindsey yelled out to the two women at the end of the bar.

The music was playing loud. Lindsey yelled out again but Diane didn't pay her any attention. Lindsey told me the two women were best friends and that they argued all the time. Finally, Diane and the other woman walked down to Lindsey.

Diane looked at Lindsey and said, "What the hell do you want?"

"Didn't you work last Sunday night when the Penal Farm threw the big party?" Lindsey asked.

"Yeah, we both did. Why you ask?" Diane said.

Lindsey replied "This guy is a police officer and he's trying to find information about the woman that's been all over the news."

"What woman?" Diane asked.

Lindsey wailed "You know, the Cassandra Johnson lady!"

"Oh yeah! I remember her. She gave me a big tip," Diane said.

"You think everybody leaves a big tip," the other woman said to Diane.

The two-woman started debating again. Lindsey smiled at me and walked off. She had some more customers to tend to. I sat there and shook my head with a smile on my face while they argued.

"Ladies! Ladies! Please," I said admiring Diane.

Diane had a tan; she was short and petite with long black hair. The other woman was short and thick with a big butt, and she had short brunette hair. The name on her shirt was: Chrystal.

Diane stopped arguing with Chrystal and looked at me and said "I'm sorry about that, now what did you want to know?" with a smile on her face.

I asked Diane about the night of the party. I asked her if she could remember what king of mood Cassandra was in and if she remembered seeing anything strange that night.

"Well she seemed okay at first, but I don't think she was much into the party that much after talking to this guy," she said.

"What you mean he husband?" I asked.

She answered, "I don't think they were married. I mean, they didn't look the way a married couple looks. They were arguing in the back of the club by the back door. Cassandra tried to jerk away from him, but he didn't let go of her arm. She looked like she was about to cry. I thought he was going to hit her at first, but he didn't. They tried to play it off and act as if nothing was going on when we walked by."

Crystal was shaking her head in agreement with Diane. For once the two women finally agreed on something. "What did this guy do after the argument?" I asked.

"We didn't see him anymore after that." They responded.

"Do you think the two of you can recognize this guy again if you saw him?" I asked.

She said "I guess so, it was kinda' dark back there, but I guess we could." I thanked the ladies for their time, gave them a tip, and walked out the club.

With no traffic to fight, I pulled out on Union Avenue, made a U-turn and drove up to Third St., made a right and headed back to 201 Poplar. I walked in the office and went to my desk and sat down. Angie was talking on the phone and the other detectives were busy working on cases. I opened the middle drawer and got the list of names Paige had given me. I had decided it was time to check them out because nothing else seemed to be working. The first name on the list was Donnie Winters. Paige did some good job. Her list was detailed. In included the make and model of cars, and she even wrote down the tag numbers of the vehicles.

Donnie Winters drove a red Jaguar with a personalized tag that bore his first name. When Angie got off the phone, I asked her to call the DMV to get an address on Donnie Winter. Donnie used to hang out with Cassandra at Club Alfred's. Maybe he knew something that could help me with this case. I checked the criminal back ground database to see if he had been arrested but he did not have an arrest record. I was going to switch gears and focus the investigation on James. None of my leads on Cassandra turned up anything. I needed to find out who Cassandra was sleeping with. Amos Johnson was still in Jackson, Mississippi, but he was due back in town any day now.

I checked with the surveillance team watching him while he was in Jackson. Amos hadn't done anything to arouse their suspicion. I thought Amos would have tried to contact Cassandra by now, but he had not. I was afraid her body was going to turn up soon. I wondered were Cassandra was. Twenty minutes later, Angie walked up to me and handed me a piece of paper with Donnie's address written down. The address was just a block away from the Johnson's house. I jumped up and immediately walked out of the office. I knew the location. It was Donnie's car and it was known for drugs and all kind of criminal activity. I got on the highway at Alabama St. and headed south on I-55. When I drove up to the car wash; it looked like a ghost town outside.

I got out the car and surveyed the scene. There was a woman sitting inside the office smoking a cigarette and typing on the computer. I walked over to the large garage and looked inside, but the place was empty. I walked up to the glass door and waved at the woman to get her attention. The sign on the door said closed for one hour.

The woman looked at me and said, "We're closed, can't you read the fucking sign! I took my badge out and pressed it up against the window so she could see it. The woman sat there and blew cigarette smoke out of her mouth and nose. She looked at my badge like it meant nothing at all.

"If you don't open up, I'll call and have someone come out and kick the door in!" I yelled with an angry expression on my face.

I wasn't going to do that, but that line always seemed to work on people. Finally, the woman got up and stormed over to the door and unlocked it. When I stepped inside the office, the woman blew a cloud of cigarette smoke right in my face.

It was payback for making her open the door. I coughed and gagged as I stepped out of the office so I could get some fresh air. My eyes were watery and they were irritated. I felt sick from the carbon monoxide poisoning. I gained my composure after about two minutes, then I stepped back into the office.

The woman smiled at me and said, "How can I help you? As she walked over to the desk and sat down in the chair. I asked her if she knew where I could find Donnie Winters.

She replied "How should I know mister? I ain't no baby sitter!"

"Do you have a number I can contact him at? I asked.

"Nope," She said.

I came within inches of grabbing the woman and throwing her on the floor. She was just a teenage girl with a smartass attitude. She was wearing Gucci jeans, a Gucci shirt and some Jordans. She was very attractive but she had a nasty attitude. The woman took another cigarette out of the pack and before she could light it, I snatched the cigarette out of her mouth. I walked around the desk and grabbed her by the arms and slammed her face down on the desk.

I took my handcuffs out and slapped them on the woman and said, "You're under arrest!"

She began to weep and said, "What did I do? I ain't did nothing!"

I escorted her out to my car. I knew she was just a child, 20 years old maybe. I was going to teach her a lesson. I got in my car, dialed the two-way radio, and called in a fake call.

"This is Detective Jack Webster; can you send a patrol car out to Elvis Presley and South Parkway. I got a female, black, in custody that needs transporting. I'm charging her with assault on a police officer."

I laid the two way back on the seat and pulled out an arrest report and started filling it out. I knew from my days as a uniformed patrol office, that a woman would practically do just about anything to get out of going to jail.

She broke down fast and said, "What do you want to know?" I ignored the comment and acted like I didn't hear what she said. I kept on writing.

"Please Sir, I can't go to jail," she said. I was trying not to laugh at the woman but she sounded very funny when she spoke. I managed to keep a straight face. "Please I'll tell you what you want to know," she said.

Her voice sounded weaker and weaker each time she spoke. She pleaded with me but nothing was working. I gave in and picked up the two way and made another fake call. I told the dispatcher to disregard that last transmission on the female, black. I walked around to the back-passenger side door and let her out of the car. Some of the men that worked at the car wash were returning to work as I took the handcuffs off the woman.

I asked her where could I find Donnie, and I demanded a cell phone number on him. I told her if I found out she called Donnie and tried to warn him I was on my way, I was going to come back and take her ass to jail myself. I got back in the car and drove off. She told me that Donnie was probably at his pool hall on the corner of Fourth and Vance St. She told me to look for a red Jaguar.

Hustlers use Cassandra Wilson credit card at local Mall

Reco and his girlfriend, Tina, walked out of the Southland Mall on Shelby Drive carrying a lot of shopping bags. He reached into his pants pocket, took out the keys, and hit the trunk button on the alarm device. The trunk popped opened and they put the bags inside and closed it. Reco smiled at his girlfriend and gave her a peck on the lips. She looked like what the younger generation would call ghetto fabulous.

Tina had big boobs, a real big booty, and was just as tall as Reco. They hoped in the BMW and drove off headed to another store to use the credit card again. Credit card fraud was Tina and Reco's normal hustle. They knew through experience the credit card wasn't going to last long. Eventually, it was going to get cut off. It was just a matter of when.

Detective Jack Webster

I headed down Vance St. and drove pass the pool hall across the street from Foote Home projects looking for Donnie's red Jaguar. I needed to see if there was a crowd standing on the corner because this was a rough part of town. The Jaguar was parked in front just like the woman at the car wash said it would be. There was a black man standing in front of the door. I thought he was a look out man. There was a lot of activity going on inside the project.

I made a U-turn on Vance St. and headed back toward Fourth St. I drove up to the store across the street and parked at the end of the parking lot. I didn't want the man standing in front of the building to see me. He looked like a crackhead. They probably gave him some crack to stand outside and watch out for the police. I walked across the street and stood on the side of the pool hall facing Vance St. I took my Glock out and ran around the corner and told the man to put his hand up and get against the wall. I showed the man my badge and patted him down for weapons. He was clean.

I caught him off guard, and he was very nervous. I told him to knock on the door. He couldn't stop shaking to save his life. He walked up to the door and did a special knock.

I could hear some movement inside. The knock warned the guys the police were at the door. About two minutes later, the door opened and a large cloud of marijuana smoke came out of the door. I stepped inside with the guard man walking in front of me with my Glock out. I waved my badge in the air so everyone could see it.

"This is not a bust or anything like that. I just want to talk with Donnie," I said observing the discomforting expression of the guys sitting around the room.

There were about 10 guys sitting around, and an elderly man behind the counter. Anyone of them could have been Donnie Winters I thought as I surveyed the scene. The rap music banged out of the speaker over by the door. The inside was run down. Paint was peeling off the walls and there were pots sitting all over the floor which had caught water dripping from the ceiling.

One pool table sat in the center of the room; it was off balanced, and the green rag was worn. There were only two lights hanging down from the ceiling, and it was dark inside. No one responded when I asked about Donnie. I told the old man sitting behind the counter to turn the music off. I walked over to the wall and looked around the corner. No one was in the back. I walked around the room watching everyone. I asked the old man if he knew where Donnie was but the man shook his head signaling no.

I walked to the middle of the room and said, "Alright. Since no one in here can talk, how bout I just call in and have some of my buddies here in 10 seconds and haul all your asses to jail!"

I meant business. I reached into my pocket, got out my cellphone and started dialing numbers. "Ain't no need to do that? You want to speak to Donnie, here I am."

A tall stocky black man said as he walked out of the restroom from the back. Donnie was well dressed and he had a serious look on his face. I could tell he was the commander and chief, and these guys would do just about anything he told them to do.

Donnie walked up to me and said, "What's the deal?" I just want to talk to you about Cassandra Johnson."

Donnie looked at the rest of the guys and told them to leave the two of us alone. So, we could talk in private. Everyone stood and walked out the door at Donnie's request. I got a contact from all the marijuana smoke in the air. Donnie walked over to the counter and grabbed a glass with some liquor inside. He asked me if I wanted a glass but I turned him down. I put away my Glock and we both sat down at an old brown table to talk.

"What can you tell me about Cassandra Johnson? I asked.

Donnie sipped on the liquor then he said, "She was my nigga. We grew up together. She was one of 'the downiest' women I know." Donnie became very emotional when he spoke about Cassandra.

"You think she's dead?" I asked.

"Come on man! What the fuck you thank she's dead!" I got my guys out trying to find out who did this shit. Ain't nobody saying nothing!" I could tell he was from the streets by the way he talked.

I asked, "Do you know what she was involved in? Was she dealing drugs?"

He responded, "She was dealing with a nigga that ain't from round here. The nigga was big time!"

"Have you ever seen him before?" I asked.

"Nobody knows who this cat is. He didn't hang out at all, at least not with our crew. She told me she was going to get out of the game. She was going to stop for the sake of her kids. Shit fucked up round here. Everyone went through Cassandra to get to him," he said.

"Do you know why anybody would want to kill Cassandra?" I asked.

He replied, "Cassandra has a good heart. I don't know who would want to kill her."

"You think this was a simple robbery gone bad?" I inquired.

Donnie paused for a second then he looked at me and said, "You ain't listening man! Cassandra is one of us, nobody wanted to rob her. She fucked with everybody in the hood. She put a lot of niggas on their feet. If someone killed Cassandra, they killed a good woman."

"Do you know who Cassandra was sleeping with?" "I wish I could tell you, but I don't know."

I thought Donnie was telling the truth about Cassandra. I told Donnie Yolanda Jenkins had been murdered, and thanked him for his time and walked out of the door. I thought the interview went well as I drove back to the office. My cellphone started ringing as I drove down Fourth St.

I took my cellphone out of my pocket and said, "Hello," Angie was on the phone.

"Jack, you got a call from Detective Manson today. He said they got a hit on Cassandra's credit card. It was used at Southland Mall at Sammy's department store and at Footlocker," she said.

"Thanks a bunch Angie," I said and laid the cellphone on the passenger seat.

I turned the flashing blue lights on to stop traffic, then I made a U-turn on Union Avenue and headed toward the highway. I got on I-55 right off Union Avenue and headed to Whitehaven. The Southland Mall is located on the corner of Shelby Drive and Elvis Presley Boulevard. I got off I-55 at the Shelby Drive exit and drove straight across Milbranch Dr. and made a left turn at the light right into the parking lot.

I grabbed my cellphone off the seat and hopped out the car. When I walked in the door, I saw one of the mall security guards, and asked him to show me where Sammy's was located. He pointed to the end of the mall. Sammy's was located on the left side near Sears. I walked into Sammy's and asked a black woman if the manager of the store was in.

The woman yelled out behind the curtains and a young attractive black woman appeared from behind the curtains and said, "Can I help you?"

I showed the woman my badge and said, "I need to have a look at your surveillance monitors; a woman took me to the back of the store pass the rack of clothes into a small office with a computer sitting on top of a small brown desk. The office was neat and clean. She sat down in the chair and pecked away at the keyboard. I gave her a description of Cassandra while she typed on the computer.

She told me no one fitted that description came into the store today, but she did remember the woman who came into the store and used the credit card with Casandra's name on it. I watched the video but there was no sign of Cassandra. She pointed at the woman that used Cassandra's credit card. The video shows the woman leaving out of the store with several bags, walking up to a man who was waiting on the outside of the store.

The camera in Sammy's didn't pick up the man's upper body. Only his legs could be seen on the video. I thanked the woman and left out of the store and headed to the main office. I needed to look at the surveillance cameras to see if I could get a good look at the man's face. I headed down the crowded corridor to the main office.

When I walked into the office an elderly woman walked up to the counter and said, "Can I help you with something?"

I showed the woman my badge and told her I needed to look at the surveillance monitors to find a possible murder suspect. The woman nodded and called another woman.

A well-dressed unattractive woman walked out the back room and said, "What is it Bridgett."

She replied "This man is a homicide detective and he needs access to the surveillance monitors. There was a murder suspect in the mall today!" Bridgett looked excited.

"Come with me sir," the woman said as she escorted me to the back room. There were about 50 small monitors inside the dark room. She asked me which store the suspect was in today.

"Sammy's and Footlocker," I said. She pushed a few buttons and Sammy's appeared on all the monitors. I was going to get a good look at the man and woman because the screens were crystal clear.

I studied the monitors patiently. "That's them!" I said as I pointed to the man and woman standing outside of Sammy's.

They headed down the main corridor with several shopping bags in their hands. The man and woman walked up to the black bench in front of Footlocker. They sat the bags on the bench and the woman walks inside Footlocker. The man stood outside with the bags while the woman went inside the store. The man paced in front of the bench looking at his watch. He seemed more nervous the longer she took to come out of the store. Finally, the woman came out of the store with more bags and they walked off headed down the main corridor, and walked out of the mall.

The woman in the office hit another button and the parking lot appeared on the monitor watching them walk up to a black car, putting bags in the trunk. The man kissed the woman gently across her lips, then they get in the car and drive off. I jumped up in the air and smiled at the woman. I finally caught a break in the case. The woman gave me a copy of the video and I thanked her and walked out of the office. I took my cellphone out of my pocket, and called Angie as I headed to my car. I was so excited. We had Cassandra's BMW.

"Homicide department, how may I direct your call?" Angie asked.

"Angie. It's me Jack." I said, "I need you to call the dispatcher and have her put an APB on a black BMW. Suspects are one black male with long braids, gold teeth, and one black female, maybe driving around the Whitehaven area."

"Got it Jack," Angie said and hung the phone up.

The video monitor showed the BMW made a left on Shelby Drive and head toward Elvis Presley Boulevard; so, I headed the same way. I drove down Elvis Presley looking at every black vehicle I saw but the BMW was nowhere to be found. I drove around Whitehaven for several hours but came up empty handed. I thought they could be anywhere in the city by now. It was seven o'clock in the evening when I looked at my watch.

It had been a long day I thought as I headed back to 201 Poplar. The case was beginning to turn around as I sped down I-55 on my way to the office. Seeing Cassandra's BMW could only mean one thing. Cassandra was dead.

The Interrogation

Ron was sitting at his desk when I walked into the office. I sat down in my chair and laid the disc on top of the desk. For some reason, I was very tired. Ron walked over to my desk and asked if I was okay. He told me I didn't look too good.

I nodded at him and said, "I'm good."

I didn't tell Ron I was feeling light headed. I took the disk off the desk and popped it in my computer. I wanted to show it to Ron before he left to go to the Church Convention which would be over in about five days or so. The office was empty. It was Friday and most detectives leave early on Friday if they can. When Ron finished watching the disc, I asked him if he could meet me at Pure Passion at 11:00 p.m. He gave me a thumbs up, told me he would be there, and walked out.

I sat at my desk and watched the video repeatedly. I didn't like seeing Cassandra's car but I knew all along she was probably dead. I just didn't want to admit it. It was about 8:30 p.m. now and there was nothing more I could do at the office. I turned the computer off and headed to the apartment. When I opened the door to my apartment, the aroma of tuna casserole made its way to my nose. I thought I was in the wrong apartment for a second. I had forgot I gave Alice a key so she could move some of her things in.

Alice lived right outside of Memphis in Cordova. She was tired of the long drives and the lonely nights in her big house. Alice and I had fallen in love; the living arrangement worked out for the both of us. She was standing in the kitchen cooking dinner when I walked up behind her, grabbed her around the waist, and with great joy gave her a kiss on the neck.

"Something smells good baby," I said as I slowly made my way over to the sofa and sat down.

Alice walked over to me and said, "Hi baby, you look beat!"

I replied "I am beat, this case is kicking my butt!"

"Aww my baby had a long day," Alice said as she massaged my neck and shoulders.

My eyes rolled into the back of my head and I started moaning. Alice had the magic touch and it felt good. She asked me if we found Cassandra yet.

"No, not yet but I saw her car today on a surveillance video at Southland Mall." I said.

"Who was driving it?" she asked.

I replied, "I don't know yet. Might be the killers."

"They have to be mighty brave to be driving around town in a missing woman's car, you think?" she said.

I shook my head and said, "That's what bothers me, they look like a couple of kids."

Alice went back to the kitchen and fixed me a plate of tuna casserole. She poured us a glass of white wine and sat the food and wine in front of me on a stand in front of the sofa. I ate like a homeless man who hadn't eaten in a few days. Within minutes, I finished the casserole and asked Alice for another serving. She went back to the kitchen and fixed me another plate.

When she brought it to me she said, "You must really be hungry, or you like my cooking."

I was hungry but the tuna casserole was very good. Alice sat on the sofa next to me and waited for an answer to her question. I stuffed my mouth with casserole. Alice was not going to let me get off the hook without answering the question.

I picked up the glass of wine, then I looked at Alice and said, "It's the cooking baby. You go girl!"

Alice burst out laughing and hit me on my left arm. I continued to give Alice the details of the investigation while I ate. I told Alice about the notebook the nurse found on little Asa and about Donnie's claim that Cassandra was a drug dealer. She raised her eye brows as I filled her in. She asked me if I thought it was true. I didn't know what to believe anymore.

I looked at Alice and said, "I don't know."

It was almost time for me to leave so I could meet Ron at Pure Passion, but I didn't want to go. I wanted to stay with Alice. I thought she was going to be upset because I had to work tonight. This was our first night living together, but she wasn't mad at all; when I told her about my appointment with Ron, we went to the bedroom and laid in the bed together. I gently rubbed her smooth body all over and she closed her eyes. She was feeling good and told me not to stop. We laid in bed kissing and hugging each other.

Alice asked, "Why did you become a police?"

I glanced up at the ceiling; then, I looked at her and said, "Little Monica."

"Who is Monica?" Alice asked.

"Well, one day when I was a kid, I asked my father why the city only put speed bumps in black neighborhoods because I assumed they were some form of stereotype. I was eight years old when my father got a better job and we moved to a better neighborhood that didn't have speed bumps.

One day we were outside playing football. Monica was playing next to the curb and this car came out of nowhere speeding out of control and hit Monica. She was only 5 years old. She died on the scene and the car never stopped. I wondered if the speed bumps had been there, would Monica still be alive. The police never caught the driver."

I paused to cough then I continued. "My father told me speed bumps were put in place to send people a message in life. The message was slow down because you might be moving too fast. I told myself that day if I didn't make it playing football, I was going to be a cop." Alice was teary eyed when I looked at her. I wiped the corner of her eyes with my index finger. Alice got on top of me; we started kissing each other and made love.

Rico and Tina

Reco and Tina Dotson walked into the apartment on Abel St. about 10:30 p.m. Billy was sitting on the sofa smoking crack having a good time along with the rest of the users. The apartment was crowded and music was playing. Billy's eyes were wide open as if they were about to pop right out of his head. Reco had made so much money off the credit card that he walked up to Billy and gave him ten more pieces of crack cocaine. Billy still had a lot of crack left and the new pieces turned his new friends into loyal subjects.

Billy asked Reco if he would run up to the store on Third St. across from the Post Office and get him something to eat and Reco agreed. Billy told Reco he could keep the car as long as he gave him crack. Reco and Tina left out of the apartment and headed to the store. The church convention was just a block away from the store. There were three police officers standing outside drinking coffee when Reco and Tina pulled into the parking lot at the store.

Reco parked the BMW at the gas pump and walked in the store.

One of the officers noticed the BMW and said, "Check that out," as he pointed at the BMW.

"Holy shit! This might be our lucky day!" the short male officer said as he walked over to his patrol car.

He needed to check the flip computer to make sure Reco was the right suspect. He walked back over to the officers and confirmed the subject matched the profile of the individual on the radar. There was a lot of traffic coming in and out the store. The officers didn't want any innocent bystanders to get hurt. They didn't want the incident to turn into a dangerous situation. They called for backup.

The officers got in position to take Reco in custody when he came out of the store. Reco came out of the store carrying a couple of bags in his hands. When he stepped off the curb, the officers ran up to him pointing their Glocks at him.

"Get on the ground now!" the officers yelled. Reco dropped the bags and laid down on the ground face down.

Tina was sitting in the car smoking a blunt. She didn't even see what was going on. One of the officers ran over to the BMW opened the door, grabbed Tina, and pulled her out of the car. He put her on the ground and handcuffed her. Reco yelled out at the officers trying to find out what they had done wrong. About five more patrol cars arrived on the scene. The manager of the store came outside along with the customers to watch the action. A female officer told them to go back inside the store.

Reco kept yelling at the officers trying to find out why they were being arrested, but they did not respond. The officers walked over to the BMW and looked inside. There was a Glock 45 sitting between the console and driver seat. The officers searched Reco and found over $3,000 in cash on his person. When the officers assisted Reco off the ground, there was a bag of crack cocaine lying on the ground. He told the officers it wasn't his, but they weren't trying to hear it.

They put Reco and Tina into the back of one of the patrol cars. Tina was crying and shaking her head. They had no idea what kind of trouble they were in. Reco thought this was too much for credit card theft as the officers gathered around and stared at them. Reco then realized their troubles could be related to the car he rented from Billy. The officers transported Tina and Reco to 201 Poplar. The car was towed to the crime scene garage to be checked out for prints and evidence.

Detectives Jack Webster and Ron Stipanik

I sat in the parking lot at Pure Passion waiting for Ron to show up. I hoped the club wasn't going to be packed, but it was. The parking lot was filled to the max. I waited in my car about 10 minutes before I saw Ron's red corvette approaching. I got out of my car, walked out to the curb, and waved my hand in the air so he could see me. Ron pulled up next to the curb and hopped out of the car. We were both wearing bullet proof vests. I told Ron to be prepared for anything tonight, and he was ready.

There was a line of men waiting to get inside the club when Ron and I walked up. I took my badge out and flashed it at the men as we walked up to the front of the line. There were two muscular looking bouncers standing at the front entrance when we got to the door. Ron and I showed the bouncers our badges and they let us inside. I thought I was going to see the hot mama with the big boobs behind the booth, but a man was working the booth. The admission fee had changed to $50 now. I think the cover is kinda' steep to see a bunch of half-naked women dance around on a pole.

I imagined getting Alice to dance at home for me, maybe. The man behind the window hung the phone up and asked us for the admission fee. Ron and I laid our badges down on the counter at the same time. He shook his head at us and picked the phone back up and made a phone call. The man argued into the phone then he slammed the receiver on the counter.

He told me someone would be with us shortly. Finally, after 10 minutes passed, the phone started buzzing. He picked the phone up; thenm he hit a button on the wall, and the door popped open. Ron and I stepped inside the club.

A short man in a very expensive brown suit and dark shades was waiting for us on the other side of the door. The hip-hop music nearly blew my eardrums out. The man asked me what the nature of the visit was. I told him we needed to speak with a girl that goes by the name Delicious. He told us to follow him. It was standing room only inside the packed club. Ron was enjoying the show performed by eight strippers on the stage. He said, "This club is 'off the chain.'" There were about 40 half-naked strippers walking around on the floor mingling with the crowd.

There was a lot of marijuana smoke in the air. The smell of liquor and smoke made me sick to my stomach. I thought we were never going to make it across the room because we had to fight through clustered groups of happy men lusting over the women. I believe some of these men need therapy.

A man tried to grab one of the strippers dancing on stage, but the bouncers grabbed him and pushed him away. The crowd started getting wild. I looked back at Ron to make sure he was okay. He was into the show with a big smile on his face.

We were escorted through gold curtains to an office on the other side of the room. Once we entered, our escort closed the door and left. A man was sitting at the desk counting a lot of cash with two big frowning, Scarface looking, goons standing by his side. The light in the office was dim which cast a shadow over the desk. Therefore. Ron and I couldn't see the man's face.

Finally, the man stopped counting cash and said, "What can I do for you fine folks tonight?"

I responded, "I need to speak to one of the girl's that works here named, 'Delicious.'"

The man paused for a second then he said, "What business do you have with her... Is she in any kinda trouble? She's one of my best girls!"

Ron stood there and watched the two goons. He did not speak. I did all the talking. I told the man I needed to talk to Delicious about a man that was murdered.

I was beginning to get tired of all the bullshit and said, "We can do this the easy way, or the hard way. You're not going to like the hard way."

I had a feeling we were going to run into some trouble tonight. The office got quiet for a second.

He patted his fingers on the top of the desk and said, "If you ain't got no warrant, get the fuck out of my club!"

His goons walked toward us. Ron drew his weapon and said, "Take it easy big fellas!"

Ron and I backed our way out of the office. Ron still had his Glock pointed at two of them. He would shoot, if it came down to it. We walked out of the club and stood in the parking lot.

I headed to my car and Ron walked up behind me and said, "Where are you going!"

"Home," I said.

"You're just leaving! Just like that! Let's call for back up!" Ron was upset at the way things turned out.

"Call back up, for what Ron? What did they do wrong?" I asked.

"I don't know, hell, we'll make up something!" Ron yelled at me.

"I don't operate like that Ron! I go by the book! Now it's over! Go home and get some sleep!" I yelled back at Ron.

I was pissed off too, but I know how to let it go. Everything is going to work out. I hopped in my car and drove off. I headed toward Elvis Presley Blvd., and got on I-55 and headed north to downtown. When I made it back to the apartment, I took my clothes off and got in the shower. It had been a long day and I was tired.

I got out of the shower, put my boxers on, crawled into bed, and kissed Alice on the face. She did not move. I laid in bed and thought about the case for a minute staring at the ceiling. I didn't buy the information revealing Cassandra was selling drugs. I thought the man at Pure Passion was trying to cover up something. I had a bad feeling about it. Where was Delicious? I laid there and finally drifted off to sleep.

At eight o' clock that Saturday morning, I walked into the office with no idea the suspects driving Cassandra's car had been apprehended and were down stairs on a lower level inside the jail. Angie was straightening up around her desk listening to her iPod. She was really enjoying the music because she was dancing slowing passing the time away on her half day at work. I sat down at my desk and turned my computer on to finish the report on the bank robbery and e-mail it to Captain Nelson.

I'm not good at working computers. I would rather write the report by hand, like the good old days. After about two minutes passed, the computer was kicking my butt. I glanced around the room to see if anyone was free to help me with the report. I wasn't going to let false pride stand in the way any longer. The other detectives were busy working on their cases. Angie was still listening to her iPod and arranging the files on her desk.

Ron didn't understand why I wasn't upset about getting kicked out Pure Passion last night. I walked over to Ron and said, "You still thinking about last night?"

He frowned and said, "Yeah we got kicked out the club last night and I didn't like that shit man."

"I been kicked out of better places," I replied smiling.

"Well, it was hot in there," Ron said referring to the amount of heat the security guards had on them in the room.

"We didn't have a warrant. Nine times out of 10, she'll probably contact us or I'll have some patrol cars visit the parking lot and post up." I said.

He responded "Well, I think she's long gone by now anyway. She probably caught the bus out of town last night."

I walked back over to my desk and sat down. Ron was getting ready to head out to the church convention. They were having a mass service going on all day nonstop. Ron couldn't see how black people could stay in church so long, and neither did I. Ron told me his church service only lasted about an hour. He spoke to Angie on the way out. She put her iPod away. I continued pecking in the words for my report on the bank robbery.

Angie stood and walked over to me and said, "How did the interview turn out with the suspects?"

I looked at Angie with a puzzled looked on my face and said," What interview and what suspects are you talking about?"

"You don't know, do you?" she asked.

"Know what?" I asked with a curious look on my face.

"Uniformed patrol officers arrested several suspects last night who were in Cassandra's car."

I jumped up and gave Angie a big hug and said, "You got to be kidding me."

"Nope. I put the report on your desk this morning," she said.

"The murder weapon was in the car too, but the serial number had been filed off. They're down stairs on the lower level," she added.

Angie told me my daughter had called, too, saying she really needed to talk to me. That note was also in my message pile. I asked Angie to remind me to call my daughter back.

I had a big smile on my face. Hearing the news was like music to my ears. I grabbed the report off my desk, walked out the office, and headed over to the jail. I had to go down to lock up, and sign the suspects out before I could bring them up to homicide. There was no exception to this rule. I made it back to the office 20 minutes later. The suspects were in two different interview rooms waiting on me to conduct my interrogation.

I studied the reports; then, I went to the surveillance monitor room. I wanted to watch the suspects on the monitor to see what they were doing once they had been in the interview room for a while. Sometimes we get cues if a person is guilty by their body gestures. Guilty people are often defensive or avoid giving direct eye contact.

I asked Detective Davis to go around to the interview rooms and offer the suspects something to drink, and to see if they needed a smoke. Detective Davis was good at playing the role of good cop and I was going to play the bad cop.

I asked Angie to do a background check on the suspects for me. I wanted to get a feel for the suspects before I went to the interview rooms. I watched the monitors as Detective Davis offered the female suspect something to drink. She declined everything and started crying because she had been brought up to the homicide department. She did not like the idea one bit which was a sign of her innocence.

Detective Davis walked into the interview and headed to the room where the male suspect stood and started yelling out some demands. Detective Davis gave the man five cigarettes and a bottle of water, then he walked out the room. Fifteen minutes later, the male suspect stood, and paced the room. He walked over to the door and twisted the knob, but the door was locked. He walked back over to the table, grabbed another cigarette, and lit it with the lighter.

Angie brought the background checks back and handed them to me. I looked over the background checks to learn more about the suspects. The suspects were Tina Dotson a.k.a. Fabulous and Reco Parker a.k.a. Reco. Tina was on probation for identity theft which was her first felony. Reco had a record a mile long. He had been arrested on a murder charge before, but was released without being charged. I continued to watch the monitors after I got through going over the background checks.

Tina sat there with her head rested on the table. She did not move. Reco started yelling out loud again. He wanted to make a phone call, but it would be a while before they could use the phone. Tina tried desperately to stay awake, but she was falling asleep. I decided to interview Tina first since she was having problem trying to stay woke. I walked out the monitor room and headed to the interview room with the reports in my hand.

When I opened the door, Tina popped up looking wide awake. I pulled a chair from underneath the table and sat down. I laid the reports on the table in front of me and opened them. Tina was wide awake and alert. She was wearing a yellow jail uniform. Her hair was all over her head and her face was ashy. After spending a night in jail, she didn't look fabulous anymore.

I looked at her with one of my best angry looks and said, "My name is Detective Jack Webster with the homicide department and I'm investigating the murder of James and Marcello Johnson. I need to read your rights to you." Tina looked horrified when I mentioned the murders. I read Tina her rights and asked her if she wanted to give a statement.

Tina burst out and said," I ain't killed nobody!" before I could get through talking.

I told Tina she had to sign these papers before I could talk to her about the case. Tina shook her head signaling yes. I gave her the consent forms and a pen and she signed the papers and gave them back to me. I asked Tina several questions about the Johnson family, but she couldn't tell me anything about them. I asked Tina where she was last Sunday night around 10:00 p.m. She told me she went to a house party in North Memphis on Jackson Ave.

She called out names of some of the people at the party. She told me there were at least 50 people who could verify that she was at the party Sunday night. She didn't leave the party until 4:00 am the next morning. I asked her if Reco was at the party. She told me he was there, but he left before she did. She didn't know the exact time. I stood and walked out the room and shut the door behind me. I thought Tina was telling the truth, but I was going to check out her alibi.

I went back to the surveillance room to see what the other detectives thought about the interview. They were watching and listening while I interviewed Tina. The other detectives agreed with me they thought Tina was telling the truth. Tina told me Reco just showed up at her house the other day driving the BMW with the credit card. Reco told Tina he had rented the car from a crackhead on Abel St.

She said Reco rented cars from crackheads all the time. A

lot of people who smoke crack had nice cars and good jobs. When they run out of crack, they rent their cars out for more. I thought she was telling the truth about everything. I walked out of the surveillance room and headed down the hall to interview Reco.

At precisely 12 noon, I stood outside the interview room where the suspect was waiting assuming he was the real deal since he had a record a mile long. I had decided I wasn't going to go easy on him, like I was with Tina. I thought he might know more about the murders than Tina.

When I opened the door, and walked in the room Reco hopped out the chair and said pretentiously, "What's up with this bullshit. I ain't had no phone call. I got rights!"

I ignored the comment and told Reco to sit down in the chair. He stood there with an angry look on his face, like he wanted to try me or something. His jaws were puffed out like they were swollen.

I looked at Reco and said, "Sit your black ass down!"

I had a serious look on my face, and Reco got the message. Reco sat down in the chair with his lips poked out. I repeated the same procedure with Reco. It was important he understood his rights. I gave him a consent form and he signed the form as well. I opened the folder and studied it for a minute.

Then, I looked at Reco and asked him, "What do your friends call you on the streets?"

"My niggas call me Reco," he replied.

I asked, "Well Reco, do you know why you're sitting in this room?"

Reco scratched his head and said, "I ain't killed nobody if that's what you trying to say."

Reco's hands were shaking really bad. I looked down at the reports, then I looked at Reco and yelled, "We found your fingerprints all over the murder scene and you had the murder weapon in your possession! Can you explain that?"

Reco jumped up and said, "That's bullshit! Y'all trying to set me up! I ain't killed nobody! I bought that gun from a crack head name Billy!"

I stood and pointed my finger at Reco and said, "Sit yo' ass back down in that chair! Get up one more time and I'll…"

Sweat started running down his forehead. He sat down and wiped the sweat off his head with his arm. "Two people are dead and one is missing and guess what? You and Tina are driving around town in the missing woman's car, using her fucking credit card!"

Reco looked perplexed, and his hands were shaking again. He was very nervous. I had Reco right where I wanted him.

Billy the Morning after Reco's Arrest

Back at the apartments on Abel St., Billy was lying on an old sofa in the front room with a woman he had been getting it on with all night. Billy stood and stretched his arms and legs; then, he walked to the back, glanced around the apartment when he stepped out of the bedroom wondering if Reco had come back to the apartment last night while he was sleep. Billy walked over to the bedroom and opened the door. There were several people inside asleep but Reco was not in the room.

Billy shut the door and headed outside to see if the BMW was parked out front, but the car was gone. The last time Billy saw Reco was when he asked him to go to the store and get something to eat. Billy walked over to the front yard. He asked around to see if anyone had seen Reco but no one had seen him since the night before. Billy hadn't eaten in two days and was hungry so he decided to walk to the store on Vance St. and Fourth St. to get something to eat.

Billy reached into his pants pocket to see how much money he had left. He had about twelve hundred dollars left and six pieces of crack. Billy thought he was doing good to have that much money left after a whole day of freaking with women and smoking crack. As a matter of fact, for the first time in his life, Billy felt like he knew what it is was like to be a playboy.

Detective Jack Webster

At about 1:15 p.m. in the afternoon, I walked out the interview room. Reco told me the same thing Tina said claiming he had rented the car from a crack head named Billy in exchange for crack. Reco told me he didn't know where Billy got the gun or the car. I tried to catch Reco up by telling him that his finger prints were found on the murder scene. I even told Reco we had a witness that could place him at the scene the night of the murders, but Reco didn't buy any of it.

I thought Reco was telling the truth. He wasn't the killer. I told one of the uniformed patrol officers to escort Tina and Reco back down to lock up. I could hold them in jail for ten days under a murder investigation. But, I could charge them with auto theft and identity theft. Reco was facing crack cocaine and possession of a fire arm charges too.

Reco told me Billy was homeless and lived in downtown Memphis in a cat-hole, but he always came to Abel St. to smoke crack at the apartment. Every detective and police officer in the city of Memphis knew about Abel St. It was two blocks south of Beale St. at the end of Vance and Third St. I called Captain Dunn and updated him on the investigation and told him about Tina Dotson and Reco Parker.

I told Captain Dunn I needed a search warrant so we could bust the apartment on Abel St. to find Billy. He told me he was going to call the judge on duty and get the warrant. I sat at my desk waiting for Captain Dunn to call me back. I told Angie to call the Narcotics Department to see if Detective Robert Jones was in because I needed him to tag along with the team. He knew the area like the back of his hand. Detective Jones and I were partners at one time when we were uniformed patrolmen.

Ron walked in the office and spoke to everyone. He glanced around the room and noticed we were pulling out bullet proof vests. He knew we were gearing up for something. Ron walked up to me and asked what was going on. I told Ron about the interview with Reco Parker and Tina Dotson, and finding Cassandra's BMW. I told him we were waiting on Captain Dunn to call back, so I could go and pick up a search warrant from the Judge's chambers.

Ron was on his break from the church convention and decided to go with the team to serve the search warrant. Abel St. is two blocks away from Bountiful Blessing Church of God in Christ. It has been a long time since I had to serve a search warrant, but I am ready.

Detective Jones was dark, tall, and stocky. When we were partners, he was thin and lanky. We hugged when we saw each other, talked for a brief minute then, I introduced Detective Jones to the rest of the team. He wore a bullet proof vest over a black jumpsuit, and had on black combat boots. He had busted apartment units in the complex several times and knew the place very well. He briefed the team about the apartments on Abel St. so everyone would know what to expect.

Billy Jackson

Billy walked to the store on the corner of Fourth St. and Vance St. eating a double cheese burger and drinking a coke. It was 55° outside and the skies were clear. Billy ate the burger nonstop like it was going to be his last opportunity on earth to eat.

A short framed, attractive woman with small boobs walked up to Billy and asked, "What's up with you?" He was still eating the burger and did not respond.

"I wish I had some meat to eat, I'm hungry too!" she said to Billy with a smile on her face. Billy almost chocked on the burger.

He coughed, spit on the ground, and looked at the woman and smiled. Her invitation took him by surprise, and he licked his lips and told her to wait until he bought some more crack cocaine.

Billy stood at the corner of Fourth St. and Vance St. waiting for the light to change. Then, he ran across the street to see if anyone was at the pool hall, but it was closed. He walked across the street to Foote Homes Project and stepped inside the fence. Billy stopped on the side of one of the apartment complexes and glanced around to see if anybody was looking. The coast was clear so he reached into this pants pocket and took his money out. He counted out $100. Billy did not want to get robbed by one of the gang members or drug dealers; so, he hid the rest of the money in his sock.

Billy stepped around the apartment complex and headed down the walkway pass groups of people standing around listening to loud music banging out the windows. Several people sat on their porch smoking cigarettes and marijuana. Children were running around playing and having a good time. Billy got nervous as he got closer to several guys huddled in a circle shooting dice. An argument broke out between two of them about some money. When Billy walked up a man with a gun sticking out his black shorts told Billy to stand over to the side of the apartment.

He walked up to Billy and said, "What you trying to get?"

"I got a hundred," Billy said nervously.

The man walked to the front of the apartment and peered around to make sure the police were not in sight. He walked over to the window and knocked two times.

A black woman with gold teeth came to the window and said, "What's up?"

"I need a hundred-dollar pack," the man said in a low tone of voice.

The woman disappeared from the window. About 20 seconds later she appeared at the window and handed the man a plastic bag containing 12 pieces of crack cocaine. He handed the crack to Billy, who looked at the bag quickly to make sure it was real.

"It's real nigger, we don't play games round here!" the man retorted looking at Billy.

Billy gave the man the money and walked off. Billy's friend, Terriann, was sitting on the curb wearing a black shirt, some tight blue jeans, and sporting a pair of brand new white Air Forces Ones when Billy walked out the projects. She lived in an abandon house behind the store on Fourth St. She turned tricks with men to support her habit. Billy walked up to Terriann and said, "Come on!" Terriann stood and escorted Billy to the abandoned house behind the store on Fourth St.

201 Poplar St.

Back at the office, I sat at my desk waiting patiently with

the rest of the team for Captain Dunn's call. A search warrant had to be signed by a judge for the search to be legal. It was 1:55 p.m. when I looked at the clock on the wall. Angie had left for the evening. Finally, the phone rang and I ran over to Angie's desk and noticed the first ring. It was Captain Dunn, he told me the search warrant was at the court clerk's office downstairs. I hung the phone up and told the team, and I would meet them in the garage. Ron and the rest of them, and I walked out the office together.

The team consisted of 12 detectives and six uniformed patrol officers who would follow behind in three patrol cars. We were going to use two black Suburbans with dark tented windows that the narcotic squad always used. Ron went in the closet and got the ram, a device made from steel used to knock down doors.

About 10 minutes later, we hopped in the suburban and pulled out of the garage to Poplar Ave. headed west across Third St., made a left turn on Second, and headed South. Detective Jones had to wear a mask over his face to keep his identity concealed from people on Abel St. because he was an undercover agent who made a lot of drug transactions in Memphis for the Narcotics department. It was important that no one on Abel St. saw his face.

I informed the team in a short briefing that Reco couldn't remember what Billy was wearing. But, I recalled that Billy was a dark skinned, short, skinny man with badly, rotten teeth. Reco said Billy would probably be in the second apartment downstairs in the living room.

We made a left turn on Vance St. and drove up to the traffic light. Abel was the first street on the right, just across Third St. Detective Jones told the driver to hit the gas hard once we turned on Abel St. He said there would probably be a look out man standing in the street watching for police officers. The light turned green and we headed across Third St. When we made the right turn on Abel St. the driver punched the gas pedal like he was driving in the Indy 500.

When we drove up to the apartments, Detectives Jones jumped out the suburban before it came to a complete stop.

Within seconds, he had the man sitting under the tree on the ground pointing his Glock at the man's head, and was coercing him to ease the shotgun from underneath his legs.

A woman walked out of the apartment upstairs when she saw the team creeping up, and yelled from the top of her lungs, "Heads up." Detective Jones handcuffed the man, while several team members ran inside pursuing her.

Ron and Detective Jackson ran up to the second apartment and hit the door with the ram and yelled, "Memphis Police Department!" gun shots rang out toward Ron and Detective Jackson as the door flew off the hinges.

Ron was hit and fell to the ground hard. Detective Jackson hit the ground too, but he was okay. The rest of the team opened fire. My feet pounded the ground as I ran over to Ron to see if he was okay. The bullet proof vest did its job. Ron was okay, but the bullet had knocked the wind out of him. The whole scene was out of control. I helped Ron to his feet and we ran into the apartment to help the team get occupants of the apartment unit under control.

Within minutes the team had everything under control, and everyone in the apartment lying face down on the floor. One person was dead and three people had been shot. At this point the severity of the injuries is unknown. I called them in, and emergency vehicles were headed our way.

Food wrappers, empty beer bottles, and debris was scatted across the apartment; human blood and fluids stained the floor, and gave off an odor. The floor was covered with broken glass, and walls contained many bullet holes. I walked around searching for Billy. In seconds the apartment was crawling with medics and uniformed patrol officers. The medics rushed the people who had been shot to the Regional Medical Center. The detectives and uniformed patrol officers turned the place upside down, but Billy was nowhere to be found.

We found several grams of crack cocaine and marijuana in the back bedroom where a black male had been killed. Everyone with a crack pipe in their possession were charged with drug paraphernalia and transported to 201 Poplar. Dr. Alice walked into the apartment, stepped over the body lying on the kitchen floor, and went to the back room where the man had been killed. She spoke to me as she walked by. I nodded at her, walked outside, and stood in the front yard surveying the scene.

Detective Jackson walked up to me and said, "He's not here Jack. We turned the place inside out. One of the women said Billy went to the store to get something to eat and never came back."

Billy Jackson

During the apartment raid, Billy was lying in the bed butt naked at the abandoned house of Fourth St getting high and having sex with Terriann. He had no idea what was going on Abel St. Billy asked Terriann to light a candle so he could find a piece of crack he dropped on the bed. She lit another candle; then, he asked Terriann to give him oral sex while he smoked the crack and she happily agreed.

Someone knocked at the front door while she was giving him head. Billy told her not to stop. The person at the door knocked even harder and longer. Billy yelled out and told them to go away, but the knocks continued. When Terriann finished pleasuring Billy, she put on a pair of shorts, a shirt, and ran to the front room to see who had been knocking at the door. Terriann came back to the room with a woman walking behind her.

Terriann introduced Billy to the woman with long blonde hair as Dirty White Girl. Dirty White Girl was wearing a white a long thick sweater, a t-shirt, and some black jeans. People around the neighborhood called her by that name because she was known for playing tricks on men she dated for drugs and money. She was low down and would do anything to get high. She couldn't be trusted.

Terriann sat on the bed next to Billy, and Dirty White Girl found a spot on the floor. Billy gave Terriann another piece of crack and they sat there and continued to get high. Dirty White Girl fired up one of her rocks, smoked it, then she looked at Terriann and said, "Y'all know the narcotics just busted Abel St."

Billy hopped out the bed and said "When did this happen? I was just around there a few minutes ago!"

"They around there right now!" Dirty White Girl said as she put another piece of crack on her crack pipe.

Billy got dressed and told Terriann he would be right back. He reached into his pocket, took out $50 and handed it to Terriann. Billy put his shoes on and walked out the house to go see what was going on. He walked through the trail in the bushes to avoid narcotics. Billy thought if the narcotics had busted Abel St., they would probably hit another spot in the neighborhood. When Billy got to the middle of the trail, there was a crowd of people gathered around watching the scene. He watched with the rest of the crowd. There were several patrol cars and emergency vehicles parked in front of the apartments. A Channel 3 news truck was on the scene as well.

Billy glanced around to see if he knew anyone in the crowd, but he did not. A man wearing a brown jacket and green pants came out the apartments on Abel St. and walked up the trail headed toward the crowd. When he walked up to the crowd standing in the trail, a man with a thick mustache and a long beard asked him what was going on at the apartments. He announced that the police were looking for a black man named, 'Billy.'

Billy overheard the conversation. His heart started beating fast and, he wondered why the police were looking for him as if it was impossible for them to connect him to the BMW. The man in the brown jacket and green pants continued telling to the crowd what happened at the apartments. After hearing about the raid, Billy's became nervous. Then, he eased off from the crowd without anyone noticing him.

7

Retaliation Death Order

Captain Dunn drove up to the apartments, hopped out the car, slammed the door, and went inside the apartment to review the scene. I was standing in the front yard talking with several uniformed patrol officers when Captain walked by. I gave them a good description of Billy, told them to drive up to the corner of Fourth and Vance St. to see if they could spot Billy.

Captain Dunn stormed out the apartment and walked up to me and said, "What the fuck happened Jack?" this was supposed to be a simple search for a goddamn crackhead! Now I got one man dead and three clinging on to their life!"

Bystanders heard captain Dunn's voice. His face turned red when he yelled at me. I tried my best to explain what happened to Captain Dunn, but he was too upset to hear what I had to say. The other detectives stayed clear of the fireworks. When Captain Dunn got through chewing me out, he told me I was going to answer for what happened at the apartments today.

Captain Dunn walked back to his car and drove off. Detective Jackson walked up to me and asked if I wanted to canvas the neighborhood to see if we could find Billy. He had to be around the neighborhood somewhere. Detective Jackson rounded up the team and we got back in the Suburbans and drove off.

Billy Dodges the Police

Billy hid in the bushes behind the store on Vance St., scared and very nervous waiting for the commotion to settle. His hands were shaking. He could see the patrol cars and the black Suburbans as they drove by. He thought they were looking for him in the neighborhood now. Billy was confused and wanted to get high.

Billy walked out to the end of the store, looked around the corner, and watched the intersection of Fourth and Vance St. for about three minutes. No patrol cars or Suburbans had pass by in a while. He planned to run over to the projects to buy some more crack to smoke, and then go downtown where he would be safe.

A local prostitute standing across the street made eye contact with him. She nodded at Billy. He spoke to her as he ran by. When he made it inside the fence, he walked over to the apartment complex and leaned up against the side of the building. His heart was jumping out his chest. He wanted a piece of crack so bad he could taste it.

Billy reached into his sock and pulled out $200 worth of wrinkled and foul smelling bills, headed down the walkway, and made a connection with the drug dealer. He took the long way downtown, and headed down Danny Thomas Blvd.

Detectives on Billy's Trail

About 5:00 p.m. in the evening, a few minutes after the bust, there was no sign of Billy anywhere. We had been around the entire neighborhood dozens of times. I thought it was going to be hard to locate Billy. He lived in the underground world with the rest of the junkies and homeless people. I called off the search and told the team to head back to the office.

Ron got a uniformed patrol officer to drop him off at Bountiful Blessing Church nearby. It was a narrow escape for Ron today. The man who shot Ron was shooting a desert eagle. If Ron hadn't been wearing the bullet proof vest, he would be dead.

The team and I walked into the office and sat down at our desk. It was a disappointing day because we didn't find Billy. But, I had a plan. I knew two places downtown Billy might go: The Union Mission on Poplar Ave. and the Salvation Army on Danny Thomas Blvd.

I've been in the department longer than anyone else, and being the oldest detective in homicide adds up to experience, but in this line of work learning never ends. Every member of the team is important because everyone brings something different to the table.

I told the team, "You guys did a good job today."

"Thank you," several detectives said in unison.

Angie walked in. She had left her son's iPod and came back to get it. Angie walked up to me and asked me if I was okay. I told her I was fine, and shared with her about the events on Abel St. today.

When I told her Ron had been shot, she covered her mouth with one hand and said "Oh my God!" her eyes were full of fear. I told her the bullet didn't penetrate his protective vest.

Angie sighed and said "Thank God!"

She reminded me to call my daughter, and walked out the office in a hurry because her son was waiting for in her in the car. I had forgot all about the phone call from my daughter. I made a few calls to see if the downtown uniformed patrol officers could keep checking Fourth and Vance St. for Billy. I was going to head to the Union Mission and Salvation Army after I called my daughter.

I had to find Billy because I needed to know where he got Cassandra's BMW from.

I reached in my pocket and took out my cell phone to call my daughter. The rapes of the teenage girls popped in my head as I dialed her number. It had been a long time since I talked to her. We laughed and a great father and his daughter conversation on the phone for about 20 minutes. She needed some money to buy some new Jordans for the big game against Hamilton High next Friday.

I told her I would bring the money by the house in the morning. I was looking forward to seeing her. I wondered if Alice was still at the apartments on Abel St. I plan to ask her if she wants to go out tonight to grab a bite to eat. I have not eaten any solid food today. I am hungry! I texted Alice to see if she wanted to go out. It was 6:30 p.m., and I am headed to the Union Mission to see if I could find Billy.

Billy Arrived in the Cat hole

Billy avoided the police, made it to the cat hole downtown, sat down on the brown cardboard box on the ground, reached into his shirt pocket, pulled out the plastic bag, took his crack pipe out, reached inside the bag, selected the biggest piece, put it on the pipe, lit it, inhaled slowly, and blew the smoke out.

Within seconds, faster than morphine gets in the veins, he was high as a kite; the pupils of his eyes enlarged like ping pong balls. He forgot about Abel St., the police officers, everything. For a few minutes, he was in his element without a care in the world.

Union Mission

I pulled up to the Union Mission on Poplar Ave., parked on the side of the building, got out my car, walked up to the door, and stepped inside. A short man wearing a winter hat with a large stomach was behind the desk checking a black male into the mission. The building smelled like old socks and shoes. I walked up to the attendant and showed him my badge.

"I am looking for a homeless man name Billy" I informed the attendant who was wearing a name tag which said, "Tom."

"I don't have a last name on Billy, but he is slim, his hair is matted, and he has really bad teeth," I added.

"Let me check with someone. I will be right back," he told me. Then, he walked away from the desk to see if any of his co-workers knew anyone that fit Billy's description.

I stared at the men coming in the door to eat dinner, surveying their faces as they walked by. I could see more men approaching the mission through the glass doors outside.

Finally, Tom came back to the desk and said, "I'm sorry, but I'm afraid nobody knows anyone by that name or by that description."

Tom checked the files on his desk to see if anyone had been to the mission whose first name was Billy in the past six months. Tom said he would keep an eye out for Billy, and told me to check at the Cavalry Street Men's Mission on Third St. I gave him one of my card, asked him if I could take a look around, he nodded his head up and down, and buzzed me in.

I walked over to the television area to have a look at the men who were watching a college football game. None of them came close to looking like Billy. I walked outside to the smoking area, went to the dining area, but none of these guys looked like Billy. I walked back to the front desk, thanked Tom, and walked out the door. There are only three homeless missions in the area. I headed to the second mission downtown - The Salvation Army which was a block away from C.J.C.

Reco and Tina Taken to the County Farm

Reco and Tina were processed and booked into the system at the jail. She was transported to Jail East near the Penal Farm which housed females. Reco was assigned to A-pod on the 5th floor. The 5th and 6th floors were called the penthouse because the pods were laid back. All the hardcore inmates were housed on the fourth floor.

When Reco made it up to the floor, a skinny black man wearing a light green deputy jailer's uniform told him to get up against the wall. He laid his property on the floor and stood against the wall. The deputy jailer searched Reco on the floor and stood against the wall, and searched Reco's property to make sure he didn't have any contraband like cigarettes, marijuana, or lighters. The jail frowned heavily on things of that nature. Then, Reco, who had an angry look on his face was escorted to his assigned housing unit.

He blamed Billy for his arrest because Billy had rented him a car belonging to a missing woman. When the rusty steel bars opened, Reco walked inside the pod. Deputy Smith called him up to the desk and she assigned him to a bunk. Reco thought she was a very beautiful woman with short black hair, light skin, a small waist, and curvy hips.

Deputy Smith looked at Reco and smiled then she said "You look like you are mad at the world!"

Reco shook his head and said "You don't know the half of it!"

"Things can't be that bad," she said trying to get Reco to

smile.

Reco mumbled something under his breath then he walked over to his bunk and dropped his property on the floor. Reco finally got a chance to use the phone. He walked over to one of the blue telephones hanging on the wall.

Searching for Billy

I was standing in the lobby at the Salvation Army on Danny Thomas Blvd. across the street from C.J.C. waiting for a woman by the name of Mrs. Dent over the homeless program to come speak with me. If this wasn't his spot, there was only one more mission left in Memphis for homeless men. I was surprised Billy had never been to Union Mission because a lot of homeless men seek shelter there. I searched the premises and looked at every man at Union Mission.

Billy was not there. I was beginning to think Reco was lying about Billy because he was nowhere to be found. I knew from experience a lot of homeless men stay at the mission at some point or another. Winter was just around the corner and it was getting ready to get cold. I hoped Billy would show up sooner rather than later.

A woman with short blonde hair and a small, petite body came out to the lobby and introduced herself as Mrs. Dent; she was over all the programs at the Salvation Army. I told her I was a homicide detective, showed her my badge, and explained I was looking for a homeless man named, "Billy."

When I gave her his description Mrs. Dent smiled and said, "That would-be Billy Jackson. He's been in and out of the program for years now. He always leaves once he gains his health back."

I smiled at Mrs. Dent, then I let out a sigh. I asked her if she had a recent picture of Billy and an address to his next of kin. She told me to wait and disappeared through the glass doors. About three minutes later, she came back, and gave me the information I needed. I was so relieved, she helped me solve a big piece of the puzzle. I thanked her and left.

Billy Parties on Beale St.

Billy left the cat hole where he was getting high, and headed on Beale St. to party. Many homeless people and junkies go down on Beale Street on the weekends to hustle tourists or to have a good time.

The homeless and junkies panhandle as long as the police officers can't see them bothering anyone. Billy wasn't going on Beale St. to panhandle. He had plenty of money. He was going to drink and have a good time like the rest of the people.

Reco hooked up with Crips on the County Farm

"Find Billy and make him pay," Reco said to his crew on the phone. Then, he got off the phone, walked over to his bunk, and sat down. Reco looked around the pod which housed up to 120 men, and surveyed the scene. One television hang from the wall, and six blue telephones lined on the wall near the door. There were two stainless steel walk in showers, four sinks, and five toilets in the rest room.

An inmate walked up to Reco and said "You banging?" He wanted to know what gang Reco represented.

Reco stood and said, "What's up cuzz!" he waved his hands in the air in the form of the letter C.

Reco was a member of the Crips. He and the other man did a special hand shake and introduced themselves.

"My name is Dré," he replied cheerfully.

Dre was 5'9 and he had a real nasty scar across his nose; the word 'Crip' was tattooed on his neck. Dré escorted Reco around the pod and introduced him to the rest of the Crips in the unit.

"You got anything to smoke?" Reco asked Dré.

Dré replied, "I got a plug in the jail, but I got to do something first."

"I got to get someone to go to Walmart and get me a reload," Dre added.

Reco didn't know what Dré was talking about, so he explained the business to Reco. When Dré finished talking

Reco walked back over to the phones and made another call.

Reco hung the phone up and walked over to Dré and sat down on his bunk. Reco told Dré his sister was on her way to Walmart. She told him to call her back in 20 minutes. Dré told Reco once he got the reload everything would be good. Dré asked Reco how much he told his sister to get. Reco told her to get $100. Dré smiled at Reco and they did the handshake again.

Detective Jack Webster

At 8:30 p.m. I sped down I-55 on my way to Whitehaven. Billy's mother lived at 877 Raines Rd. across the street from my old high school. Alice texted me back while I was in route and told me she would be ready to go out at 9:45 p.m.

I didn't call ahead of time because there was a good chance Billy was there. If I had called, she would probably warn Billy; then, he would leave. I got off the highway at the Brooks Rd. exit, and drove down Elvis Presley Blvd.

I switched lanes and came within inches of hitting a red van. The driver really let me have it with the horn. When I pulled up to the front of the house, the lights were on inside the house, and there were three cars parked in the driveway. I pulled up next to the curb opposite of Hillcrest High School, walked across the street, walked up to the door, and rang the doorbell.

A nice looking young woman opened the door and asked, "Can I help you?" I introduced myself and showed her my badge. She seemed really surprised the law was at her door. I believe she thought I was there to tell them something bad happened to Billy. She ran off screaming out for her mother before I could explain the nature of my visit. A young man and a younger woman returned to the door with an elderly woman, who invited me in the house.

Immediately I said, "I am not the bearer of bad news," as I stepped inside the house.

The women sighed and looked at each other and said, "Thank God!"

I told the elderly woman I needed to find Billy right away

to discuss a car Billy recently came in contact with. The young man who came to the front door with the women walked back down the hall, and disappeared into one of the rooms. He appeared unconcerned. They informed me they hadn't seen Billy, and they took my card and offered to call when they saw him again.

I made it home about 9:30 p.m. Alice was sitting on the sofa watching ER when I came through the door; she was dressed and ready to go. I spoke and gave her a kiss; then, I went to the bedroom to take a quick shower and change clothes. I remembered how good the barbecue smelled at B.B. King Blues Club, so I decided to take Alice on Beale St. She had never been there. I got dressed, we walked out the door, and walked since it was a beautiful night, and Beale St. was only a 10-minute walk from my apartment.

Alice was wearing a gray Nike jogging suit and some white Airmax. I had on blue jeans, and a black button down shirt. We both wore jackets because it was a little windy out. I liked walking because it always took my mind off things. Now that Alice was back in my life, I had somebody I could talk to. There was a lot of traffic on Third St., and 100s of people headed to Beale St.

The street was packed at Beale and Third. There were people everywhere on both sides of the walkway and in the middle of the street celebrating. The Memphis Grizzlies had beaten LeBron James and the Miami Heat earlier. Memphis won 15 games in a row. The crowd was so loud, I could barely hear myself think. Some people shuffled up and down Beale Street holding oversized plastic glasses of various mixed drinks, especially Walk Me Downs, an alcoholic mixed drink, containing Blue curacao, Gin, White rum, White tequila, Vodka, 7-up, and Sour Mix, listening to the sounds of live blues music.

Every club was lit up with bright lights, and people were standing in long lines waiting to get inside. We stood and waited for the traffic light to change, and noticed cops were out in full force. Two little black boys flipped their way down the middle of Beale St. and the crowd went wild. As we walked further, we saw the police arresting an angry group of intoxicated white guys who had gotten kicked out of a club. The light changed and Alice and I headed to B.B. King's club. I could smell the aroma of barbecue as we walked up to the front door.

When we stepped inside, a live band was entertaining the crowd, and I saw the waitresses Diane and Crystal; they were very busy. A few people were dancing as we passed by. The hostess escorted us to a table in the middle of the club next to the window facing Beale St. Alice rocked slightly enjoying the music.

Diane walked over to the table and said "I thought that was you standing at the door, but Crystal thought you were someone else." I introduced Diane to Alice.

Diane smiled and said, "Have you caught the guy that killed Cassandra yet?"

"Not yet, but I'm working on it," I said.

Crystal walked up to the table and Diane said, "I told you it was Jack. I'm always right!" They started arguing again and I told Alice, Diane and Crystal were best friends, who debate about everything. Alice smiled and shook her head as they walked off.

"Now to you! You haven't said two words all night. Is something wrong?" I asked.

"Actually, I'm taking everything in," she said and smiled shyly, "I've never been out like this before."

"How do you mean?" I asked.

"Well. This is very different for me. I'm used to formal dates. This is why I love you Jack Webster. You bring out the wild side of me."

She added, "I've never been on historic Beale Street before. Walking down here was adventurous."

I was pleased Alice was having a good time. The waitress came and we ordered the B.B. King Rib Tip special which included 50 rib-tips, baked beans, dinner rolls, and coleslaw or potato salad. Alice ordered a glass of white wine. I just couldn't stop staring at her. She is simply beautiful. Her smile is charming. She is perfect for me.

We sat there, ate, talked, and enjoyed each other's company. After dinner, Alice and I hung out. I didn't have any cash on hand, so I walked across the street to use the ATM machine. I wanted to buy Alice her first <u>Walk Me Down</u>.

Suddenly, Billy staggered out a club with a beer in his hands wearing a black jacket, a brown shirt, and gray pants. He walked up to Alice and asked her what her name was.

He could hardly stand up straight. Alice frowned when he opened his mouth. She quickly walked down to the crowd of people standing by the curve side bar listening to the live band. Then, Billy walked off and disappeared into the crowd.

I walked back over to Alice and stood in line to get the <u>Walk Me Downs</u>. I took $400 out my saving account because I had to give my daughter $250 in the morning. I brought the drinks which were in a tall plastic glass, and we headed down Beale Street. We walked around with the rest of the crowd enjoying the Beale Street atmosphere. From the looks of things, I'd say Alice was enjoying her <u>Walk Me Down</u>.

We waltzed up and down street holding hands and having good time. We both needed a break from our jobs. I didn't feel like a homicide detective and I liked the feeling. I was on top of the world when I was with Alice. I stopped and gave her a long kiss standing in the middle of the street. Her lips were so soft. She is a great kisser. I could get use to having her around for life. When Alice and I came up for air, a crowd applauded; we both smiled and bowed slightly.

I can't think of anything else I'd rather be doing right now. At some point of time, I imagined me and Alice getting married and living a happy life together. Alice looked at her watch and it was almost 1:30 a.m. She had to do her weekly reports in the morning, so we headed home. In our line of work, a day off is rare. We are always on call. We made it back to the dark apartment at 1:42 a.m.

The <u>Walk Me Downs</u> did its job on Alice. She was really feeling good, dancing and laughing as I escorted her to the bedroom. When I let go of her hand, she fell straight in the bed like a ton of bricks. She called me to the bed, I climbed into the bed, she got on top of me, and we kissed for a longtime, slid our clothes off, and got under the covers.

Alice looked at me with those pretty blue eyes and said, "I love you jack Webster."

I borrowed the lyrics of an old R&B song and replied, "My life would be nothing without you." We were lost in the moment, and we laid there and fell asleep in each other's arms.

Reco's Second Day at the County Farm

Reco and Dré woke up at 7:30 Monday morning. They were sitting at one of the tables over by the bars waiting for one of the deputy jailers to drop off Reco's package. Most of the inmates were still asleep.

The deputy running the pod was busy talking on the telephone at the desk. Reco's sister had went to Walmart the previous night and brought the reload. All they had to do now was sit back and wait on the cigarettes and the marijuana. Reco couldn't wait. He needed a smoke bad to calm his nerves. Reco and Dré sat at the table waiting for the deputy jailer to bring Reco's package.

Dré asked Reco, "What you in for?"

Reco told Dré, "Man I rented a BMW from a crackhead named Billy. Turns out the car belongs to a missing lady. And check this. Her family was murdered last week."

"Some of the gang is out in the free world looking for Billy, but, so far, no one ain't' seen that punk!" Reco retorted.

"Man that's fucked up!" Dré stated.

An argument broke out between two inmates over a card game. Some of the inmates gathered around and cheered them on. The pod got loud but nothing happened. The deputy jailer called both inmates up to the desk to resolve the problem, and gained control of the situation without calling for back-up. Everything went back to normal.

Five minutes later, a short woman with short braids in her hair wearing a uniform walked up to the bars, nodded at Dré, dropped a small brown bag inside the black garbage can, and walked off. Reco watched out for Dré as he slowly made his way up to the bars, reached inside the garbage can, got the bag out, and tucked it under his shirt.

Dré walked over to Reco, handed him the package, walked to Dre's bunk, and sat down. Reco looked in the bag, then he smiled at Dre, and they walked off. Dre walked over to the bunk, grabbed the white spray bottle of bleach sitting on the floor next to his bed, and walked over to the restroom area where Reco anxiously awaited his return.

Dré reached under the bench and grabbed a sponge under the tub and got down on his knees in front of the toilet. Dré told Reco to watch out for the deputy.

If an inmate got caught with any kind of tobacco products, he or she would automatically be written up and sent to lock down pending disciplinary actions. On the other hand, if caught with marijuana he or she would be taken back down to intake and recharged with possession of marijuana.

Dré took the sponge, drained the water out the toilet, sat on the bench so they could blow the smoke from the marijuana and cigarettes in the toilet. The draft from the toilet was strong enough to suck the smoke down the pipe.

Then, they sprayed bleach in the air to kill any excess smell of the marijuana or cigarettes, and got high just like they were in the free world. Most deputy jailers had no idea what was going on, but some of them knew and walked the other way.

Reco walked out the restroom with cigarettes and marijuana left, and a big smile on his face. He got in his bunk, laid down, and watched the scene.

Billy Monday Morning

Billy woke up Monday morning to sunlight beaming down on his face with a bad hangover. He got so drunk Sunday night that he slept on the side of the Greyhound bus station on Union Ave. in downtown Memphis. Billy stood to his feet, dusted them off, and walked into the crowded and very noisy bus station to use the restrooms.

He walked out of the restroom to the canteen shop and stood in a long line waiting to buy a cup of coffee. People stared at Billy like he was a green man from outer space. Billy looked up at the clock hanging on the wall which read: 9:30 a.m. He walked over to Squirrel Park to get something to eat. Then planned to head back over to Terriann's house.

Squirrel Park is downtown on Second St. next to the Exchange Building where Jack lived. A lot of churches and different organizations go to Squirrel Park to feed the homeless on the weekends. The park adopted its name because the park is a key habitat for squirrels. Billy headed to Second St., made a right turn at the corner of Monroe and headed down Second St. The sound of gospel music flowed out of large speakers. Everyone was having a good time praising the Lord.

Billy ate so much food he didn't want to move. Then, he sat on a brown beach with two more homeless men watching the squirrels run up and down the trees.

John, an elderly man with short blonde hair, a snow-white beard, walked up to the bench and said, "Would you guys mind if I prayed for you?"

All the men consented to prayer. Billy and the other men stood and joined hands with John.

John said, "Father God, bless each of us. Give us guidance, wisdom, peace, and love in our hearts and souls."

Billy said, "Amen." Billy shook John's hand and walked off headed back to Fourth and Vance St.

Detective Jack Webster

I woke up to the sound of an alarm clock going off a little pass 7:00 a.m. Alice was already gone. It was a beautiful Monday morning. The sun was out and there wasn't a cloud in the sky. I wondered how long this good weather was going to last. After all, it was November. I headed to the bathroom to take care of my personal hygiene so I could go and see my daughter.

I drove across town and pulled in the driveway at my ex-wife's house at 10:00 a.m. I had to run to the office first. I got there later than I expected, got out the car, and walked up to the front door to ring the doorbell, but there was a note

117

attached to the door.

I grabbed the note off the door and read it:

Dear Dad, Coach Mack called a surprise practice this morning. He wants the team to be ready for the big game against Hamilton Friday. We can beat the whole team today if we played, but you know how coaches are. He wants to make sure the team is ready. Sorry, I couldn't be here when you came by, but I'll spend the weekend at your place soon. I promise! You can leave the money under the flower pot by the door.

I love you always.

P.S. Love Stephanie.

I left the money under the flower pot, got back on the highway at Shelby Drive, and headed N. on I-55. I turned the radio on and a Luther Vandross tune was playing. I was disappointed I didn't see my daughter. It's been a long time since Stephanie and I spent some time together. I am definitely looking forward to the game Friday night. I was going to make sure she kept her promise.

I headed to Calvary Rescue Mission to see if anyone knew Billy Jackson. I need to make contact with him ASAP. I got off the highway at the Lamar Ave. exit, headed toward E.H. Crump Blvd., pulled in the parking lot, parked at on Third St., got out the car, looked around, walked up to the door, and rang the doorbell.

Gang members on Billy's Trail

Billy headed back to Fourth and Vance St., walked down Second St., made a left turn on Union Ave., walked toward the Greyhound Bus station, and made a right turn on Fourth St. Billy shuffled pass the large crowd of people which included tourists, and others carrying backpacks in the Historic Beale St. area. Women were showing off their legs, and the young men were flexing their muscles.

Billy was just a few blocks from Terriann's house; he hurried along. He was ready to get high. He had an after taste of crack in his mouth. When Billy walked up, there was a small crowd standing in front of the pool hall on Fourth St., but no one seemed to notice him right off. He tapped a young black girl on the shoulder and asked her what happened. She told Billy two guys got into an argument inside the pool hall over a dice game, and a fight broke out between them.

Billy turned and headed to the store to buy a new pipe. When he came out of the door, Dirty White Girl was coming toward the store. Billy spoke to her as he turned the corner to go to Terriann's house. Dirty White Girl ran to the front of the store and peered around the side of the building watching Billy.

Billy walked up to the abandoned house and called out for Terriann to open the door. Dirty White Girl turned around and headed back across the street to Foote Home Projects to let Reco's gang brothers know Billy was back in the neighborhood.

Gang Murder

It was 6:00 p.m., almost dark, when I walked into C.J.C. and headed to the elevators. The building was quiet, peaceful, and almost empty on the weekends. There were no lawyers, no clerks, bailiffs running around, and no people to fight for a spot on the elevators. The custodians and housekeeping workers were visible.

No one knew Billy Jackson at the Cavalry Street Men's Mission on Third St. I drove around the neighborhood for a long time, but Billy was nowhere to be found. His mother and sister told me he always hung out downtown on the corner from Foote Hood Apartments, but no one had seen him.

I starting thinking maybe Billy was the master of disguise as a ghost. Billy's mother told me she would give me a call when she heard from him. I believed her. She seemed like an honest woman.

I was going to walk around the downtown area to see if I could find Billy. But first, I wanted to check the database to see what his criminal background check revealed. I sat down at my desk and pecked away at the computer. Billy's had a record a mile long. He had been in and out of jail since the early 90s. For the next hour, I studied over the Johnson file and Billy's background check. I tried to print the information out of the computer but nothing came out of the printer. I tried again, but got nothing. I looked over at Angie's desk out of desperation hoping she was here, but the seat was empty.

Detective Bell was talking away into her cellphone sitting at her desk. The other detectives were going over case files. I thought about calling out to Detective Bell but I would pay the cost. She was another one who complained a lot. She was worse than Monica. You name it, she complained about it.

Detective Bell was one of those people who thought there was a conspiracy against her. She was a damn good detective. Out of the seven female detectives in homicide, she was the best one. I stood and walked over to her desk. When she looked up and saw me standing there, she told the person on the phone she would call them back.

She hung the phone up and said with a smile on her face, "Now what do I owe the pleasure of this visit?"

"I was wondering if you would show me how to print a criminal background check out." I said.

"So, the Great Jack Webster needs my help!" She couldn't resist taking a cheap shot at me. I stood there and let Detective Bell have her fun.

She stood and said, "Let me see what I can do."

We walked over to my desk, then she typed in the information, and the printer came to life, and two seconds later the background check came out the printer. Detective Bell handed me the printout and walked to her desk and picked up her cellphone. I thanked her, but was surprised because she didn't complain. That was a first.

Billy had been arrested 37 times mainly for petty crimes, but several arrests was for auto burglary. There was nothing on his record that suggested he could kill anyone. But you never know what people are capable of in this day and age - 2013. Unlikely suspects have committed horrific crimes.

Reco calls off the Hit

Reco laid on his bunk coming off the effects of the marijuana high. His eyes were red, but he was feeling normal again. The bunk bed next to Reco belonged to a trustee, who worked inside the jail cleaning the hall. He sat on his bed and introduced himself to Reco.

"Hey what's up? My name is Peter," he stated.

Since he was an elderly man, all the inmates called him pops. If an inmate was over 40, the younger inmates called them old school, but elderly inmates are generally called, "Pop."

"Ain't' much going on. I'm Reco," he replied.

"What you in for?" Peter asked.

Reco told Peter the same story he told Dré about Billy and the car. He told Peter some of his Crip brothers were going to take care of Billy for him.

"Do you think that's a wise thing to do?" Peter asked in a tone of voice which came across as sarcasm.

Well, let me run this by you, "If your Crip brothers kill Billy, then you are going to get stuck with the murder charges. You were the last one the police caught in the car!" Peter said. "You get what I'm saying."

It dawned on Reco that he was going to need Billy to clear his name. Reco sat there and thought about what Peter said for a minute. Then, Reco hopped out of bed suddenly and went over to the phone to call his brothers to call off the hit.

Terriann and Dirty White Girl Party on Beale Street

Terriann had been out on an overnight date with one of her regulars, who was a big-time spender. She got out of his rented black Hummer on the corner of Fourth and Vance St., and walked into the store to get some change. The corner was dead. When Terriann came out of the store, Dirty White Girl was standing on the corner trying to catch a date.

Terriann walked up to Dirty White girl and asked, "What's up Bitch! Trying to make that money?"

"A bitch trying to get paid, but it's slow tonight," Dirty White girl replied. "Look like you can throw me something," she added.

"Come on with me. I got you. You can retire tonight," Terriann stated.

Terriann made $300 and told Dirty White Girl she was going to get both of them high.

"Go down to the house and wait on the porch. I'll be right back," Terriann said.

Terriann walked over to the pool hall to buy some crack, but the guy she was looking for wasn't inside.

She came out of the pool hall and went across the street to

the Foote Homes Projects to buy some dope. It was dark outside and Terriann didn't like going over to the projects at night because it was dangerous at times.

When she turned the corner, there weren't many people standing out. An argument broke out between a man and woman in one of the apartments as she walked down the walkway. The big green garbage dumpster was over flowing with trash and gave off a loud stink.

When Terriann got to the end of the walkway, the lookout man told her to stand up against the side of the apartment complex. The police were bad at night. The drug dealers tried to keep the walkway clear of traffic.

The lookout man asked Terriann, "What you need?"

She told him, "A 50 pack."

He came back and handed Terriann seven pieces of crack wrapped in aluminum foil. Terriann handed him the money and disappeared into the night.

Too Late for Billy

Reco was in a heated discussion on the telephone. It was too late. They had already taken care of the business with Billy. There was nothing he could do about it now. Reco yelled into the phone and slammed the receiver against the wall. Everyone stared at Reco as he walked over to his bunk with a sad look on his face.

Peter knew it was too late. Reco was so upset he discussed the event with Peter, a complete stranger. Reco told Peter he had talked with one of his Crip brothers and had been informed that they had already caught Billy and took care of him.

Peter shook his head and asked, "What you going to do now?

"You gonna' have to come up with something," Peter added. Reco sat there for a second with his head down.

Then, he looked at Peter with a worried look on his face and said, "I don't know." Reco laid down on his bunk looking like a sick puppy.

The night was young and beautiful. Terriann and Dirty

White Girl sat in the house and got high; then, they decided to go on Beale Street to party. Terriann lit another candle for more light, she changed clothes, and fixed herself up. Terriann went to another room inside the dark and empty house and came back dragging a black garbage bag containing clothes. She told Dirty White Girl to go through the bag so she could find something to wear.

When Terriann got dressed, grabbed the candle, she went to the bathroom and looked in the mirror at herself. When she walked into the hall, she told Dirty White Girl to stop moving around. Terriann thought she heard a strange moaning and scratching sound against the house.

She walked back to the bedroom and said, "Do you hear that?"

"Girl you just high and paranoid!" Dirty White Girl said.

"You probably right," Terriann said as she reached inside her shirt pocket and got her money. Dirty White Girl blew the candle out on the floor inside the bedroom and they left.

Detective Jack Webster

I made it back to the apartment at 10:20 p.m. Alice had fallen asleep on the sofa. I kissed Alice on the face.

She woke up, smiled up at me and said, "There you are baby."

I went to the bathroom to wash up. I had worked up an appetite. I came out of the bathroom and walked over to the kitchen and rubbed up against Alice's body. She was in the kitchen warming up some scallop potatoes, lamb chops, steamed vegetables, and a slice of apple pie. I sat down at the dinner table and ate my food while I discussed the case with Alice. I told her I still hadn't found Billy, but I was able to get a last name and an address on him last night.

I even told Alice I had spoken to Billy's mother and sister the previous night, and they agreed to contact me the moment they heard from him. Alice thought I was really getting somewhere with the case now, but I felt the investigation was still going slow.

I looked at Alice and said, "Enough about me, how did your day go today?"

Alice told me there was a three-car pile-up on I-240 earlier. Two teenagers were thrown 50 feet from the car. They were pronounced dead on the scene.

"Teenage drinking and driving is at an all-time high these days," Alice said.

I finished eating my food and went back over to the kitchen and fixed another serving. I brought the apple pie to the table with me. Alice really liked the fact that I loved her cooking.

She went over to the fridge, opened it, and grabbed a bottle of white wine. She asked me if I wanted to join her but I didn't want any wine. She poured herself a glass, walked back to the sofa, and sat down. When I started talking again, Alice had shut her eyes, but she quickly opened them again. She had a long day at work and she was very tired. Alice was trying very hard to stay awake but the wine sealed the deal. I crammed a piece of apple pie into my mouth, washed it down with some water, and took Alice to the bedroom. I took her clothes off and put her in the bed. She was knocked out. I took off my clothes, hopped in the bed beside her which was a great feeling.

Billy's body identified

Terriann woke up at 7:00 am the next morning to the sound of police sirens and a loud pounding at the front door.

She got off the mattress, and yelled, "Who is that knocking on that damn door like that?"

When she opened the door, she was greeted by cool air, and three police officers standing on the porch. One of the uniformed officers grabbed Terriann by the arm and snatched her outside. When she stepped off the porch, she saw yellow police tape surrounding the house. She stood still with a puzzled expression.

"What's going on," she asked.

"Come this way with me," one officer demanded in a nasty tone of voice.

There were about nine patrol cars in front of the house along with two emergency vehicles. A large crowd had gathered at the corner of Fourth and Vance St. There was blood all over the steps. The last person she could remember being with was Dirty White Girl. Terriann left her downtown on Beale St. with two black guys. The uniformed patrol officers took Terriann to one of the patrol cars and put her on the back seat to take her downtown to get some information from her.

A group of police were huddled around a body on the side of the house covered up with a black sheet. People stood on their porches, and in their yards watching the scene. Detectives Cruz and Jackson heard the call on the scanner, and arrived on the scene, got out of a White Dodge Charger with dark tinted windows, walked up to the uniformed patrol officers standing in the street, and asked them who discovered the body.

One of the officers told Detective Cruz some kids on their way to school spotted the body lying on the side of the house, ran home, told their parents, and one of the parents called 911.

A police officer said, "The woman in custody lives in the abandoned house where the body was discovered."

A second officer said, "We are taking her downtown to question her."

Detective Jackson walked over to the rear of the patrol car were Terriann was sitting, opened the back door, and asked her, "Can you come with me to see if you can tell us the name of the unidentified man on the side of this house?"

Terriann said, "Yes," and she got out of the police car and starting walking nervously behind Detective Jackson. When they reached the side of the house near the room where Terriann slept, Jackson stopped, and looked gently at her; then, one of the police officers bent down, and removed the black sheet.

Terriann's eyes bucked wide open, she covered her mouth, and suddenly cried out shaking her head violently – NO BILLY NO!

.... **To Be Continued** ....

Read .... *Death by Association* Vol 2 *Deception*

NOTE

[1]Shelby County, Tennessee "History"
https://www.shelbycountytn.gov/index.aspx.

Death by Association **Volume 2** *Deception*

By Anthony Ellis

Blog: meredithetc.com

facebook **Meredith** *Etc*

Meredith*etc*

Author Page http://meredithetc.com/death-by-association/

Death by Association **Volume 2** *Deception*

Meredith Etc ▪ 1052 Maria Court
Jackson, Mississippi 39204-5151

Keywords: murder mystery, fiction, Memphis, prison contraband, prison guards

A Two Volume Novel
First Printing
Trade Paperback Edition printed by CreateSpace
Hardback edition printed by Nook Press
Published by Meredith Etc
Black & White on White paper
Vol 1 & Vol 2 - 288 pages

Available on the World Wide Web as an eBook
Printed and bound in the United States of America

Visit Anthony Ellis' author page online.
http://meredithetc.com/death-by-association/

Book Summary

Death by Association **Vol. 1** *Retaliation*

Abstract
4 parents, 3 sons, 1 homeless man murdered, 1 wounded: all victims of association

    Death by Association is a two-volume murder mystery by Anthony Ellis. In **Volume 1** *Retaliation* the story begins with the Memphis Homicide Department searching for clues concerning a missing woman, a double parent-child homicide, and ends with the department searching for a serial killer.

    In **Volume 2** *Deception* detectives attempt to solve the mystery to prevent the fourth parent-child double murder but the culprit has infiltrated the Homicide Department and is two steps ahead.

    Detective Jack Webster and the homicide team search ferociously for evidence… buried beneath a pile of deception.

Summary of the Johnson Homicide Case

On the morning of November 18, 2013 at 5 a.m., Detention Officer Amos Johnson discovered his brother, James Johnson's, corpse with his infant daughter, Asa, laying on his chest. Amos's son Marcella was mortally wounded in his bed. James' wife, Cassandra Johnson and her black BMW were missing.

Sources lead Chief Detective Jack Webster to a multi-million-dollar illegal prison contraband operation, and on a relentless murder path involving a parent – son double murder pattern. *Death by Association* **Volume 1** *Retaliation* ends with the gang murder of a petty criminal who pawned Cassandra's BMW for drugs.

Death by Association **Volume 2** *Deception* climaxes when Jack Webster tries to stop the next double murder, and discovered the killer is two steps ahead.

Apartment of Detective Jack Webster

Tuesday, November 26, 2013

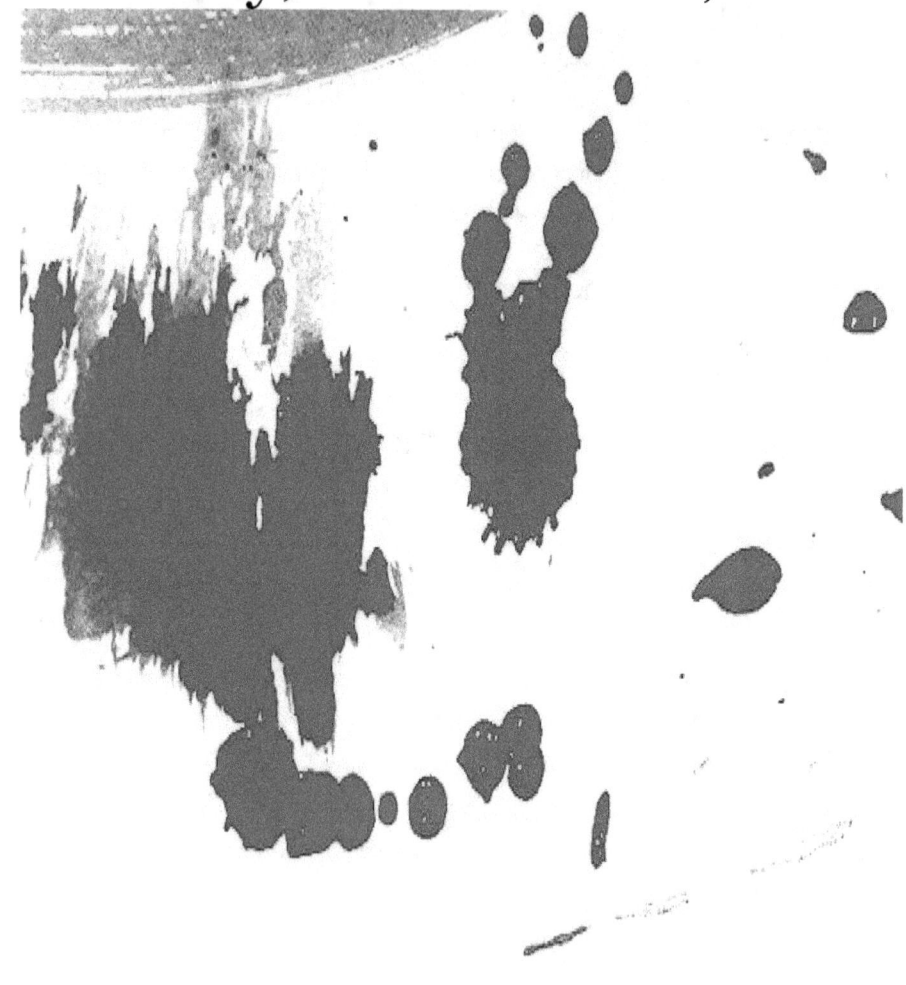

1

Tiffany & George Roseland

I was in the kitchen fixing breakfast for Alice; she was still asleep in bed. She didn't have to go to work until noon, unless she received a call about a body.

I took breakfast to the bedroom on a tray, shook Alice lightly, and said, "Breakfast in bed!"

Alice rolled over, stretched her arms and said, "You shouldn't have Jack. What's the special treatment?"

I bent down to kiss her, but she turned her head. She told me she had a bad case of the morning breath and waved for me to get back. I settled for a peck on the side of her face.

"I just wanted to do something special for you today - just because." I said.

Alice got up and went to the bathroom to take care of her personal hygiene. I turned the television on but the sunlight beaming through the curtains obstructed the view. I am going in late this morning. So, I walked over to the window, shut the curtain, and hopped in bed. Alice came out the bathroom and got back into bed too.

Then, she inspected her breakfast: two eggs sunny side up, two pancakes, two pieces of toast with butter, three pieces of bacon, and milk. Alice took the fork, closed her eyes, and tasted the eggs and pancakes. Her eyes popped opened and she looked at me shaking her head. I was pleased the food passed her inspection.

The expression on her face indicated she was enjoying the food as she was eating, I looked at her and said, "What do you think?"

She nodded at me and said, "It's really good, Jack!"

I asked her what she wanted to do tonight, and what she wanted to do for Thanksgiving Thursday.

"I'll go out later and buy some desserts, cranberry sauce, and other items from Kroger, and I'll made some cornbread dressing tomorrow tonight," she said.

"A quiet holiday dinner sounds good to me," I stated.

"Next year, I'll be better prepared and we'll put together a feast and have guest over," she added.

"We can spend Christmas at my place if you like," she suggested.

"Sounds like a deal," I replied.

It was a beautiful morning outside and I was planning to have a wonderful Tuesday morning with my new love, and the worse unexpected thing that could have ever happen this morning, happened. Both of our cellphones started ringing at the same time.

I picked up my phone and said, "Hello!"

Detective Jackson said, "Jack. I'm over here on Fourth, right before you get to Vance St. We got a body Jack! You need to look at this body Jack. It's Billy, Jack, the guy you been looking for."

"Dammit, please tell me it isn't so!" I yelled into the phone.

"I'm afraid so Jack," he said.

"I'm on my way," I said and threw the cordless phone on the bed and looked at Alice. I could not believe it. Not Billy. I was frozen in silence. My plans to have a wonderful day had just went down the drain, and maybe the case too.

Alice tapped me on the shoulder and said "What is it Jack?"

"They found the guy I have been looking for, dead on Fourth St." Alice had gotten the call from the morgue about the same body.

She smiled at me and said," Everything will be okay!"

She got out of the bed and started getting dressed. Fourth St. was just three minutes away from the apartment. When she finished getting dressed, we left the apartment at the same time and headed to Fourth St. to view the murder scene.

`   Alice and I arrived on the murder scene in two separate cars within seconds of each other.

I got out the car and walked up to Cruz and said, "Are you sure it's Billy?"

He replied, "The woman made a positive ID Jack."

"Where's the body?" Cruz took me over to the side of the house.

The uniformed officers took the black sheet off the body. "Jesus Christ Cruz! Look at what they did to him!"

In all my years working on the force, I never saw anything like this. Billy was severely beaten, and he had been sodomized. His guts were hanging out of his rectum. Insects surrounded his body. Jackson ran out to the curb and regurgitated.

The officer covered the body and I walked away shaking my head. I wasn't prepared for that this morning. Dr. Alice walked up to the body with a mask covering her mouth and nose. She was wearing special gloves used to examine bodies. Terriann was still sitting on the back seat of the patrol car crying. A large crowd gathered on the side of the store on Vance St., emergency vehicles and patrol cars blocked traffic off on Fourth St. and Vance St., and drivers honked their horns because they had to detour to get to their houses.

Dr. Alice recognized Billy immediately as the person who walked up to her Saturday night on Beale Street. I walked over to Cruz and asked him if there were any witnesses to the murder, and he said, "No." I was upset because I had just told his mother he was alive and now this. Cruz offered to notify the family but I told him I had just talked with his mother and sister for an hour two nights ago. It would be best if I notified them.

It is never an easy job to tell someone their love one was murdered, but this time, it was something I had to do. I walked around and surveyed the scene. The street reminded me of a scene out of *The Twilight Zone*. There was broken glass in the street, empty beer cans and paper all over the place.

There were several abandoned houses on the street. Some houses looked like a strong wind could blow them down. The termites were feeding off the old ply-wood that covered the windows. A pack of wild dogs were lurking nearby. I asked the uniformed patrol officers to search the Woods behind the house for evidence. Cruz said Terriann lived in the abandoned house, but she wasn't around yesterday. She told Cruz one of her friends who goes by the name, Dirty White Girl was in the neighborhood yesterday and she might know who did this.

I walked over to Jackson and stood in the middle of the street wondering what Billy, a man who used drugs and broke into cars to get high, could have done to enrage someone like this. His mother told me he used to be a good son before he got hooked on crack. Like many people, Billy had some bad breaks in life. I walked back over to the body and stared at Billy. While, Dr. Alice and the medics examined the body, I felt obligated to find out who committed this horrible crime.

I couldn't get Billy's mother off my mind. I could still see her face. She told me her only wish was to see Billy straighten his life up before she died. Billy told his mother he was going to stop using 100 of times and she believed him, but he never kicked the habit. I thought about my own daughter when Billy's mother was talking the other night. Addiction could happen to anyone's child. I've struggled with alcohol. I walked down to the corner of Vance St. to see what Jackson had come up with. He was talking with some of the people standing in the crowd getting aggravated because no one would give him any information about the murder.

"That's how it is in black neighborhoods. People don't want to be considered snitches and give information to police, but if a crime involves their loved one they will disclose information," Jackson said.

He is right. I asked a few questions too, but no one I talked with knew anything either. From the look on Jackson's face, he was just as upset as I was, if not more. He wanted some information on the murder as quickly as possible. Someone knew something but they probably couldn't talk to us with a large crowd watching or they could end up like Billy. We handed cards out to people who would take them. Jackson and I headed back toward the murder scene and went door to door asking questions.

I didn't think we were going to get any information out of the crowd. I had forgot all about finding out where Billy had gotten Cassandra's BMW from; at that moment, I was concerned with finding out who did this to Billy.

Near the crime scene, one of the uniformed patrol officers was standing near a bloody tire iron lying in the grass which had to be what the assailants used on Billy. One of the Crime Scene Unit Officers bagged it up and tagged it as evidence. It was a little past 3:00 p.m. when I glanced at my watch.

There was nothing more I could do on the murder scene. I headed out to Whitehaven to see Billy's mother. I wanted to inform her of her lost immediately. Billy's case was assigned to Cruz and Jackson. I was going to help them with the investigation anyway I could. I didn't really know what I was going to say to Billy's mother. Delivering her this news wasn't going to be an easy task. I drove to Union Ave. and got on I-55 and headed south to Whitehaven.

When I pulled up in front of the house, there was only one car in the driveway, so I pulled in, parked, got out the car, walked up to the door, and rang the doorbell. A short dark woman was standing in the yard next door arguing on the phone. She paused her conversation to tell me her neighbors had gone to a church.

I asked the woman what time they normally returned home and she said," Real late, nighttime."

I thanked her, and headed back to my car. I could hear the loud cheering coming from the football field on the other side of the school. I drove over to the field, parked and hopped out of the car so I could watch the boy's football practice at my old high school. This was the field where it all started for me, where I learned to love the game of football under the leadership of Coach Randy Walls. He was hard on me, but he kept me on the right track. I am eternally grateful for his tough love. We won three State Championships in a row.

My mother and father died in a train wreck when I was 10 years old. My aunt Mary raised me, but Coach Walls was like a father to me when I was a teenager. According to ESPN, I was the top receiver in the nation coming out of high school. I received several offers from all the big-time schools, but I accepted a full scholarship to play for USC. I was projected to get drafted to the NFL, but I got hurt in a game my senior year in college. I went airborne to catch a pass in the end zone in a game against UCLA. When I planted my left leg on the ground, the safety hit my knee and tore my ACL. That was the hit that ended my dreams of becoming an NFL football player. I lost my love for the game after I got injured.

When I came back home from school, I decided I was going to fight crime. I completed training at the Memphis Police Academy and became a cop. That was 22 years ago. And now I am standing on the side of the field thinking about the good old days with other onlookers watching the team practice.

I appreciate Coach Walls for being a role model and an inspiration in my life when I was a kid. Back then, Coach Walls made us practice until we got every play down packed. Seems nothing has changed, as I watched Coach Walls yell at the receivers for running the wrong passing routes.

When practice was over, I walked out to the field clapping my hands as I got closer to the team. Coach was talking to the boys and didn't recognize me at first. When I got close, he took the green cap off his head, and wiped the sweat off his forehead with his arm and asked, "Jack, is that you?"

"The one and only!" I said with a big smile on face.

"Hot dog, Cat-Eyes Webster! Man, how have you been?" Coach Wells said; we hugged and embraced one another.

"Man, it's good to see you!" Coach said as he shook my hand.

Coach introduced me to the team and bragged about me when I was a receiver. I still held the record for the most touchdown catches - 95. His bragging gave me a great feeling. At first, he couldn't believe his eyes. I couldn't either. He told the team practice was over and they sprinted up to the locker room like a herd of cattle. It's been a long time since the two of us saw each other. During my college years, I always went to the school when I came back home in the summer.

Coach and I sat down in the small office and talked. He still had a picture of me signing the letter of intent to attend USC hanging on the wall. I took the picture of me in 1987 off the wall, removed the dust off the top of the frame with my hand, and smiled.

Man! That was a good year for me. When I looked up at

the clock hanging over Coach's desk, it was 8:45 p.m.

"Coach, I have to be leaving because I have a stop to make," I said. We stood, shook hands, and embraced again.

Coach smiled at me and said, "Cat-Eyed Webster! It's really good to see you again. Drop by anytime. I looked around the office one more time, sighed, then I walked out the door.

I drove back over to Billy's mother's house but no one was at home. I headed to Elvis Presley Blvd, made a right, and headed to Brooks Rd. where I once lived. I really enjoyed talking with Coach. Our conversation took my mind off things.

"Cat eyes," I hadn't heard anyone call me that since high school. I have cat eyes. When the sun shines directly in my face, my eyes change colors.

As I got on I-55, and headed north to downtown, a song by the O'Jays was playing. I called Alice and told her I was going to stop by Subway and get something for us to eat.

She said, "Subway sounds like a good idea because I am beat down."

"Get me a 6" chicken sub and a chef salad," she stated.

Examining Billy's body wore her out. I made it home about 15 minutes later. I almost dropped the soft drinks when I opened the door to the apartment. I was trying my best to juggle the bags. Alice got off the sofa and helped me with the food. She was wearing one of my long white shirts and pink panties and pink socks.

I gave her a peck on the lips, then I went to the bathroom to wash up. When I came back to the kitchen I told Alice to go back over to the sofa to relax. I was going to serve dinner. I grabbed some napkins, dried my hands off, and poured Alice a glass of red wine. She usually sipped on a glass of wine to mellow out at night.

I brought everything over to the living room and sat it down on the coffee table. Alice was watching *CSI Miami* when I sat down. It was a very good show, but I was never at home to watch television these days. My job keeps me busy most of the time. We started eating and Alice was looking at me with a funny look on her face. She smiled at me, I smiled at her, and we continued to eat. I got into the television, and I could see

Alice staring at me out of the corner of my eye.

I looked at Alice and asked, "Is something wrong?"

Alice looked at me and said, "Well, I got something to tell you baby! But you got to promise me you're not going to be alarmed by the news!"

"Okay, I promise," I was curious. I wanted to know what she had to tell me. She sounded so serious. I was all ears at this point.

Alice looked at me with those big pretty blue eyes and said, "Do you remember the other night when we came out of B.B. King's Club, and you walked across the street to the ATM machine?"

"Yeah, I remember," I said.

"Well, Billy Jackson walked right up to me and asked me what my name was." I was surprised, and I jumped up off the sofa and said, "You're kidding?"

"No, I didn't know you were looking for him. You never told me."

"Dammit!" I said as I hit myself. I never would have imagined Billy on Beale St.

Billy was right there in the palm of my hands, and I didn't even see him.

"It's sad, he was right there in our presence, and now he is gone," Alice noted.

"Yes, he could have told us a lot about Cassandra and how he ended up with her car," I added. I sat back down and finished eating my food.

Alice looked at me and said, "I'm sorry he had to die such a horrific death too."

I was a little disappointed, we tried, but it just wasn't meant for me to catch Billy. When we got through eating, I turned the television off and we headed to the bedroom.

On the morning of Wednesday, November 27, 2013, I made it to the office about 9:30 a.m. I wasn't feeling well. I had just told a mother that her dreams of seeing her son turn his life around wasn't going to ever happen because her son was gone. It was one of the worst things, I had to do all month. I sat at my desk and stared at my daughter's picture sitting on top of the counter screen. I promised Billy's mother I would find out who was responsible for his murder. He didn't deserve being tortured to death.

Angie walked over to my desk, and asked me, "You okay?"

I told her about Billy's mother. She seemed very empathetic. Then, she told me Officer Reed had called and left his cell phone number for me. She laid the number on my desk, and walked away. I tried not to be so hard on myself, but I could still hear her voice in my head.

At the Police Academy, we are taught to never let a case get personal, to keep our feelings out of it, but that isn't always so easy to do. Billy's murder motivated me to get to the bottom of things. I called Officer Reed, and he told me to meet him at Yolanda Jenkins's house at noon. I got a call last night from the surveillance team which was watching Amos. They informed me he made it back to town about 7:00 p.m. last night.

I stood and walked out of the office. I was on my way to the garage to see Bella in the Crime Scene Unit. I needed her to take a picture of Amos when he came to pick up his truck. I will have Angie call him when I get back to the office. I had a plan. I am going to ask Amos about the argument he had with James when he comes to the office to sign the release forms for his truck.

Bella and another woman were going over Cassandra's BMW for prints when I walked into the garage. I stood nearby and waited. Finally, she looked up and saw me standing by the desk.

She walked over to me and inquired, "What's up Jack?"

I nodded my head. Then, I asked her, "How's it going with the car?"

She replied, "Well, we found a lot of prints inside the car and on the truck. There were dry blood stains in the trunk."

I didn't like the sound of that. I was silent. I felt a charge go through my body, like electricity, when she told me about the blood. I explained my plans to Bella and she agreed to take Amos's picture when he came to get his truck. I was going to show the picture to Diane and Crystal to see if they could recognize him. I needed to know if Amos was the man

Cassandra argued with that night at the party.

West Memphis, Arkansas – Home of Yolanda Jenkins

I was back in West Memphis, Arkansas on a cool and sunny day outside of Yolanda Jenkin's house waiting for Officer Reed. I got out of the car, stood in the driveway, hoping the elderly woman next door was going to come outside, and give me an update on the latest talk going on around the neighborhood about the murders. I was curious about Officer Reed's assessment of the case.

Finally, a blue police sedan pulled up to the house, a tall white man got out the car, walked up to me, and we introduced ourselves. Officer Reed was wearing a dark blue police uniform and some dark shades. He started telling me what he thought about the murders as we walked up to the house. I know you're not supposed to judge a book by the cover, but I personally doubted his abilities; he looked - 23 maybe. He probably got the job because his father and uncles were on the force. Officer Reed told me there were no witnesses to the murders.

We walked around and surveyed the ransacked house, but it was not as bad as the Johnson's house. He assumed the killer came in through an unlocked window in the den. He was confident in his observation, but I respectfully disagreed with his findings. There were large shoe tracks coming from the back door to the backyard. The killer cut the phone line to disable the alarm system.

"The killer must have picked the lock," I said to Officer Reed who was standing right up on my heels as I checked the door knob to the house.

Officer Reed scratched his head and said, "I didn't notice that the last time I was here. FBI guys who were here asking questions about Yolanda Jenkins didn't mention the loose locks."

I was startled and asked sharply, "FBI was here?"

"Yep, they looked around and asked a whole bunch of questions," he confirmed.

The two FBI agents who were at the Johnson's house ran

across my mind. I was curious about their involvement. I had thought about them since that day. There had to be a connection to the murders. There was no doubt in my mind about it.

"I appreciate your time Officer Reed," I said as we walked back to our cars.

"You're quite welcome, and I appreciate your input," he replied.

I was almost positive the murders were linked and something was going on. I was pretty sure we hadn't heard the last of this killer. Ron was sitting at his desk when I made it back to the office.

He appeared to be okay after being knocked down the other day. I asked Angie to call Amos so he could come to the office and sign the release forms for his truck. The office was loud as usual. I sat at my desk and studied over the case file for the next 30 minutes or so. I looked through the pictures of the Johnson's house. The phone line wasn't cut, but I noticed the same shoe pattern at Yolanda Jenkins house. I stared at Yolanda's picture. I couldn't help but wonder why someone wanted to kill her and her son.

Something heavy is going on here. I can't pin point it, but I'm going to find out one. Ron left the office to go to the Church convention. Amos walked in the office at 4:50 p.m. Angie pointed Amos over to my desk, and he walked over and sat down beside me. I acted as if I were searching for something in my desk drawer to allow me enough time to observe Amos's demeanor.

He looked like he hadn't been to sleep in days. He didn't look so good. He had bags under his eyes. I asked him if everything was okay. He said his father had a stroke after the funeral, and he'd been helping take care of his father, and the family had been through a lot. I hated to probe him for information, but I had no choice in the matter.

I popped the question about the argument he had with James. Amos looked down at the floor; then, he looked at me and said, "You're going to find out anyway, so I might as well tell you now. I had an affair with Cassandra.

That was the last thing I was expecting to hear. Ron had gotten that part right. Amos dropped the bomb shell right in my lap. He said James was spending a lot of time at Pure Passion and the argument was about James spending too much time at Pure Passion with a stripper named Delicious, and I was encouraging him to focus on his marriage. I wondered why Amos was concerned about how much time James was spending with a stripper.

He said, "James forgave me, and we were working on our relationship."

I actually believed him. I asked him, "Can you take a DNA test to clear your name?"

He said, "Yes, I will." Then, Amos signed the papers and walked out the office.

I didn't ask him about the notebook. He was in bad shape, so I just let it go for now. I called Bella to let her know Amos was on his way to pick up his truck. I took out the list of names Paige gave me and decided to go see Tiffany Roseland. She hung out at Alfred's with Cassandra. I was hoping she would be able to tell me something solid.

I put Yolanda's picture back inside the Johnson's case file, walked out of the office, got on the highway at Alabama St., headed south on I-55., got off at the Shelby Dr. exit, headed to Elvis Presley Blvd., and made a left turn at the light. The parking lot was full when I drove up. In fact, there was never a time the parking lot at Walmart isn't full. I parked by the door, got out the car, and walked inside. The store was packed with shoppers.

Based on the selections in the baskets, some people were picking up things for Thanksgiving. I walked over to the Customer Service Department to see if I could find out where Tiffany Roseland worked. The Customer Service lines were just as long as the lines at the cash registers. I took my badge out and flashed it to jump ahead of the crowd. As I made my way to the front of the line, I couldn't believe so many people could fit into one store. It was very loud. I finally made it to the counter and asked an employee wearing a uniform for the manager. She paused for a second; then, she got on the microphone and summoned a supervisor.

I stood back and watched the shoppers as they waited. Two of the customers got into an argument with another woman for butting in line. They resolved the problem without incident. About 20 minutes later, a short woman with long black hair, and large boobs walked up to the counter. The cashier looked at me and pointed her in my direction. The name on her blue Walmart shirt was, "Betty."

She walked up to me and shook my hand and said, "How may I help you?" I flashed my badge and completed her sentence with, "Jack, please call me Jack."

I continued, "I need to speak with Tiffany Roseland."

"She hasn't been to work in three days. No one's seen or heard from her," she said in a concerned tone of voice.

"Do you have an address on her," I asked.

"Sure thing, I'll be right back," she said and disappeared into the store.

Five minutes later, Betty returned and handed me a white piece of paper with Tiffany's address on it. I thanked better. Tiffany lived on Neely Dr. off Raines Rd. I knew the location, and proceeded to my car to head to Tiffany's house. I pulled out of the parking lot, drove down Elvis Presley Blvd, made a left turn on Raines Rd and headed west. It was almost dusk dark outside when I drove up to the huge English Style house. There was a blue Hummer and a cream-colored Mercedes SUV parked in the driveway. I pulled in next to the Hummer and got out the car with my flashlight.

The lights were off inside the house when I walked up. As I got closer to the door, I noticed it was open. I could smell a rancid odor coming from inside the house. I took out my gun, called for backup, and went inside. It was dark and quiet. I could hear my feet going forward. A fresh odor got stronger as I headed up the stairs. My intuition told me to go back outside and wait for back up, but I kept moving until I ran across two dead bodies: a black woman and a little boy. Then, I immediately turned around and walked hurriedly out of the house to get some fresh air.

Now things are getting crazy; two women and their sons

were killed perhaps days or hours apart. Their deaths were eight or nine days after James and his son were murdered.

Within minutes, the house was crawling with medics and uniformed patrol officers. I walked to the backyard and glanced around. The phone line had been cut just like at Yolanda's house. Detective Bell and Monica arrived on the scene and went inside the house. I walked into the house and checked with one of the officers. It had been confirmed. The victim's Tiffany Roseland, and her son George Roseland had been shot in the head and chest and were both dead.

There was a pattern to the murders, but I hadn't figured it out yet. First, there was James Johnson and his son murdered, and Cassandra Johnson was missing. Then, Yolanda Jenkins and her son; and now Tiffany Roseland and her son; one male, two women, and three boys' dead. All three boys were murdered with one of their parents. These murders are linked. We may have a serial killer on our hands with this unusual killing pattern.

I walked to my car and headed home. Detective Bell and Monica were going to take charge of the case. I wasn't up to hearing all the loud talking and complaining, not tonight anyway. I turned on the radio as I headed home and thought about the case. Something was going on, and it wasn't over. I was sure of it.

I felt the urgency to figure things out - fast. More lives hung in the balance. It was 9:55 p.m. when I walked in the door, just in time to watch the 10:00 p.m. evening news. There was a note lying on the sofa for me: your plate is in the oven. Alice had fried chicken, cooked macaroni and cheese, spinach, and homemade biscuits. I wondered how she became a doctor and learned how to cook so well.

I went to the kitchen, got my plate, went to the sofa, and sat down to watch the news. The news didn't mention anything about the murders. We didn't want reports discussing any murder patterns. Those details don't need to be revealed to the public, at least not for now.

When I finished eating, I laid back on the sofa and watched the Tonight Show. I planned to wait on Alice to come home. I flipped through the channels trying to find something to watch. There was nothing interesting on television. I stood and walked to the bedroom, laid in bed, and thought about the case. Something was definitely going on. Things were probably going to get worse before they got better.

2

Forest Hills Cemetery

Juan Mendoza, a proud Mexican, worked hard six days a week to send money home to Mexico to help support the rest of his family; he dreamed of the day when he had made enough money to bring the rest of his family from a life stricken with poverty in Mexico. Juan worked during the day, and went to school at night.

He enrolled at S. W. Community College on Union Ave., so he could get his GED. On his lunch breaks, he studied over his school work, and listened to Rosetta's Stone's English language tapes to help him become more fluent in the English. He had been working in the U.S. for two years.

Juan made a name for himself in the landscaping business, and landed several contracts including the Forest Hills Cemetery on Elvis Presley Blvd. and Person St. in South Memphis.

Juan and his crew arrived at Forest Hills about 7:00 a.m. Wednesday morning, November 27, 2013. He drove a black GMC truck into the parking lot, they got out, started the Zero Turn lawn mower, drove them off the trailer, and went to work.

Juan always started at the back and moved his way upward, while listening to his black Sony Walkman headphone set. Not long into his work routine, he came upon on a small patch of grass that had been dug up from the ground. He had never seen the small hill before; so, he paused for a second. Then, he continued moving through the hilly lawn.

When he got ready to pull off, he noticed something sticking out of the ground out of the corner of his eye. He got off the zero, turned, and walked up the hill to see what it was. He jerked when a human foot came in full view from a shallow grave which obviously had been put there by a local undertaker; he fell to the ground, grabbed the rosary from his neck, and started praying. Juan jumped to his feet, ran to the office as fast as he could to notify the manager.

Detective Jack Webster

Several detectives were gathered around in a huddle having a conversation when I arrived at the office at 8:00 a.m. There was a big write-up about the game in the morning paper. From what I could hear, it sounded as if they were talking about the big basketball game Friday night.

Cruz and several detectives walked over to my desk and Cruz said, "Jack, isn't this your daughter?" as he handed me the morning newspaper. There was an article in the sports section about Stephanie with a big picture of her standing next to her Coach. I didn't know what was going on until I read the subheading. It was a proud moment for me seeing my daughter in the newspaper. It brought back old memories when I was in high school and my football scores made the paper every week, but the sports writer really gave Stephanie her props.

"I got fifty bucks on Hamilton," Cruz said.

The bets started coming from left to right. Before I knew it, I put $400 on Stephanie's team.

I was waiting for Detective Bell and Monica to arrive. I wanted to know what they had on Tiffany Roseland's case. There was no doubt in my mind there was a connection, but how and why was a $64,000-dollar question. I wasn't going to tell them I thought the cases were connected. Not yet anyway. There was more going on with the case than it seemed. Three parents and three boys were murdered. Then, Billy was killed. As I sat at my desk going over the case, a call came over the two-way. There was a body found at Forest Hill Cemetery. The Crime Scene Unit and K-9 were already on the way.

I decided to head out to the cemetery to have a look. I got on the highway at Alabama St., took I-55 S., got off at the Parkway exit, headed to Elvis Presley Blvd., made a right turn, and headed to Person St. As I drove up to the cemetery, I saw the K-9 unit searching around the wooded area with the cadaver dogs. There were several Crime Scene Unit officers digging up what appeared to be a grave site.

A Hispanic uniformed patrol officer was getting some information from Mexican workers. The manager and several employees were gathered around watching the scene.

I turned to walk away and one of the Crime Scene Unit officers shouted, "We got a body!"

I walked over and looked in the hole. There was a decomposed body inside. The manager of Forest Hills was shocked and she covered her mouth with both of her hands. There wasn't supposed to be a body back there. Plus, it was not buried properly. The computer file didn't list a body in the rear of the seminary either.

I called the murder in, and the cemetery became a crime scene. A Hispanic uniformed patrol officer revealed to us what the Mexican workers told him.

"Juan Mendoza told me he was cutting the lawn and saw a foot out of the corner of his eye," the officer stated.

We didn't need the Mexicans for anything at the moment, so they were free to go. Two television news trucks pulled into the parking lot. They must have heard the call go out on the police scanner. I told the uniformed patrol officers to keep the news reporter at bay. I didn't need them on the scene, not there, not now.

When the Crime Scene unit officers got the body out of the hole, I walked over to have another look. Judging from the looks of things, I presume the body is a female. There was a blue party gown on the body and a ring on the right hand. When I looked up, Dr. Alice and her team had arrived on the scene.

"I missed you last night and this morning," I whispered to her as she walked up.

She smiled and I read her lips, "love you."

We began to search the area to make sure there was no more evidence lying around. I walked back over to the body and observed Alice and the team. Alice told me the body had probably been there at least 10 days. There is so much evil in the world. I wondered what the world was coming to.

One of the medics reached into one of the pockets, pulled out something, and yelled, "Detectives, I got an I.D. on the body."

I put my gloves on and he handed me the I.D. I wiped the I.D. off and looked at the name. It was disturbing news. It was exactly what I was afraid of all along, Cassandra Johnson.

Suddenly, I felt a surge go through my body. I was beginning to feel certain disturbing things about this case. I sighed aloud and walked away and stood off from everybody, not sure what to do next. I need to find out more about Cassandra. What could she have done for somebody to do this to her. Uncovering her body took quite a while. Dr. Alice and her team rapped things up with the body around 9:00 p.m.

An officer walked over to me and asked if I was okay. I shook my head and said "Yes," but it was a lie. I was hoping to find Cassandra alive. Once again, I dreaded being charged with the task of informing the next of kin – Cassandra's parents. I worked all day and forgot to eat again. I asked Alice if there was anything in particular she wanted to eat tonight.

She said, "I have a taste for some barbeque."

"I'll see later at the apartment," I told her.

Then, I blew her a kiss, and walked off. When I got near my car a black female reporter asked me to identify the body.

I threw my hand up and said, "No comments," got in my car, and drove off. I headed to A&R Barbeque. It was just a block or two from Forest Hills Cemetery.

It was 10:15 p.m. when I made it to the apartment. Alice was sitting on the sofa watching *The First 48 Hours* when I walked through the door. I laid the food on the table and went to the bathroom. I was really hungry. I had worked up an appetite. When I came out of the bathroom, Alice had already fixed our plates, and poured two glasses of white wine. She walked up to me and gave me a big hug and a long kiss.

"I missed you baby," she said with a big smile on her face as our lips departed.

We kissed again, then, she looked at me and said, "You thinking what I'm thinking?"

"I sure am," I said with a smile on my face.

Actually, I wasn't thinking about making love, but I didn't want to disappoint her. We sat down, ate juicy baby-back ribs, coleslaw, potato salad, and dinner rolls. I even stopped at subway and got Alice one of those chef salad's she liked so much. We sat there and ate and talked about the case. I reminded Alice my daughter was going to be spend the weekend with us. She was excited and looking forward to meeting Stephanie.

"The DNA I found underneath James fingernails didn't match Amos's DNA," she said. I wasn't surprised to hear the news about the DNA. I didn't believe Amos was capable of killing his own brother, after seeing him at the office. The guilt and remorse about the affair with Cassandra was enough for him to deal with. Alice let me know she would have a partial autopsy report on Cassandra by noon tomorrow.

Alice finished eating, went to the bedroom, gave me a sexy look, and told me she would be waiting. I sat there for a couple of minutes with a lot on my mind, stood, looked around the room, and decided I would go see Cassandra's parents first thing in the morning. Alice and I had a pleasant night.

The next morning when Cassandra's mother opened the door she greeted me, "Happy Thanksgiving Jack."

"Happy Thanksgiving to you too," I replied.

"You poor man, you have to work on holidays," she stated in a serious tone of voice.

"Well it's complicated, in my line of work, we take turns working holidays. The next ones if on me," I responded.

"Well good, have a seat," she added.

It's amazing because Cassandra's parents took the news of her death better than anyone I'd ever seen. Their inner strength reminded me of an old saying my Aunt Mary used to say, *God's greatest gift to us, is death!* As a child, her words were confusing, but through, Cassandra I see another side of death living in Asa.

I made it to work at 9:00 a.m. Thursday morning. Angela had placed a large banner on the wall which read, "Happy Thanksgiving" in large bold letters. Ron was sitting at his desk waiting for my arrival. The church convention was finally over, but he had to start his in-service training (seminars for new detectives) in the morning; it was going to last another week.

"I hope you brought chicken and dressing, turkey legs, and mac and cheese with you," Ron said laughing lightly.

"Man, I didn't smell anything like that when I left home. We've been working nonstop. When I was growing up we could smell food cooking the day before Thanksgiving. I used to lick cake bowls, and pinch food out of pans," I recalled.

"My oldest sisters cook like that, but I don't get to lick the bowls. My nephews do that," he laughed.

I know Ron is eager to get back to work on the case. In the middle of Ron's laughter, Captain Dunn stepped into the office and walked over to my desk. I'm guessing he heard about the suspects who were apprehended in Cassandra's car. He thought I was going to charge them with the murders. We were still nowhere on the case. I didn't have any evidence leading to a solid suspect, and I had been working around the clock on the case. I gave Captain Dunn a long briefing about the details of the murders over the course of an hour or so.

Even though I had a lot of information on the case, I felt I didn't know enough.

"The mayor is breathing down the Chief's neck and he wants someone charged, and he wants them charged soon!" he said sternly. Then, he stood up abruptly and walked out of the office which was his way of making a statement.

Ron walked over to my desk and said, "What was that all about?"

"The chief wants this case solved. The mayor is asking a lot of questions," I said to Ron.

Angie walked over to my desk and handed me the pictures of Amos, Bella left for me. I grabbed my car keys, and Ron and I walked out of the office at 11:00 a.m. I wanted to go see Diane and Crystal before the lunch crowd.

When we arrived, there were about 10 people inside the club, and Diane and Crystal were standing at the bar. We walked up to the bar and I introduced Ron to Diane and Crystal. Diane smiled at Ron and said, "He's handsome. Are you married or dating anyone?"

Ron smiled at Diane and said, "Nope, but I'm looking for a good woman."

I shook my head and said, "Let's get back to business." I handed Diane the pictures and asked her if a picture of Amos look like the guy arguing with Cassandra at the back of the club the night of the party. Diane studied the pictures for a few seconds then she handed them to Crystal.

Crystal gave me the pictures and said, "He was here that night, but he's not the guy." Diane agreed with her.

"Are you sure?" I asked. They both nodded and said Amos wasn't the guy.

Ron wrote his number on Diane's hand and we walked out of the club. I got a text from Alice as we headed back to 201 Poplar St. There was an ASAP behind the text. I dropped Ron off at C.J.C., and headed north on Poplar Ave. to the morgue. I sped pass the traffic, made a right on Dunlap St. and headed to the hospital. Alice was sitting in her office with the door open when I stepped off the elevator. She stood and walked around the desk and met me in the doorway.

"You really put it on me last night," she said pleasantly.

As we stood in the office and kissed, I was proud of myself. She walked back to her desk and sat down.

Her expression changed. "What is it?" I asked.

Alice looked at me with a sad look on her face and said, "I'm afraid I got some bad news Jack. The killer buried her alive, and she was about three months pregnant."

I stood there at a loss for words. Amos told me Cassandra was pregnant, but I wasn't expecting to hear she had been buried alive. I was shocked about the news. She caught me off guard. I told Alice I would see her tonight and walked out of the office.

It was 2:30 p.m. when I made it back to C.J.C. I had worked through lunch and was kind of hungry. I walked over to the canteen to get something to eat. I had a bad feeling about the case now. Whoever killed Cassandra had to have a personal vendetta against her. That's the kind of thing you do to somebody when it's personal. The killer was trying to send a message. Everything about the case was changing.

I thought it was going to turn out to be a relationship gone badly. I was wrong. I was sure of it now. Now, I had to figure out who had it in for Cassandra. I ordered a couple slices of pizza, a large fry, and a diet coke. Angie was sitting at her desk eating a baked potato when I walked into the office. When I sat down to eat I noticed a white envelop on my computer.

I looked inside. Enclosed was $50, and a note from Ron, "Here is your money for my bet payoff."

I had forgotten all about the bet we made about Amos and Cassandra. Actually, Ron was right about one thing. Amos and Cassandra did have an affair with each other, but Amos was not the murderer. I finished eating and got back to work. Most of the detectives were gone and it was quiet in the office. I went over Cassandra's personal history again. Nothing seemed to click inside my head.

Cruz and Jackson walked into the office. I called Cruz over to my desk and asked him if they had any suspects on the Billy Jackson case.

"Not yet, but we're working on it. We could use some help to track down the white girl." Cruz said.

"It'll try to get Ron to help out," I said and Cruz went to his desk.

I stood and walked over to Monica's desk to see what they had come up with on Tiffany Roseland. Monica said they had come up with very little.

The killer came through the back door; the phone line had been cut, both victims were shot twice, and the house was ransacked. The neighbors hadn't heard a thing. Monica opened the file and I looked at the picture. I had seen Tiffany Roseland before. I couldn't pin point it, but I had seen her somewhere. I thought it was time for us to head to the classroom to use the blackboard.

Detectives Bell, Monica, Jackson, Cruz, and I headed to the classroom to see what we could come up with on the murders.

"This will only take a few minutes," I assured them.

"Good," Monica said, "Unlike some people, we have holiday plans."

Reco Parker & Tina Dotson charged with Capital Murder

Down on the first floor of C.J.C., Captain Dunn, District Attorney Jerry Gibson, and the three uniformed patrol officers who had apprehended Reco Parker and Tina Dotson were inside the media room getting ready to hold a press conference announcing that Reco Parker and Tina Dotson were being charged with the murders. The mayor had received a lot of bad publicity. With an election coming up next year, a conviction on this case, would look good on his behalf. District Attorney Jerry Gibson was planning to run for Sheriff of Shelby County.

The state was charging them with Capital murder. Since there were three crimes involved. Burying a pregnant woman alive is grounds for Capital Murder. The state was going to seek the death penalty. Captain Dunn didn't want to go through with the press conference because Jack told him Reco Parker and Tina Dotson didn't commit the murders. But, Captain Dunn was left with no choice in the matter. He had to stand with the mayor.

I want to solve this case more than ever now because politics is making a lie out of justice. We put the Johnson family at the top of the black board. Cassandra's name was written at the very top of the board. In the middle, everybody wanted to know why I thought she was the whole key to solving all the murders. The way in which Cassandra was killed was different from all the other murders. The killer shot everyone else with a hand gun except for Cassandra. He took the time to bury her alive.

The big question is why did the killer make Cassandra suffer?

If we can find out the answer to this question, we will find the killer. The killer sent a message that Cassandra's murder was personal. We looked at the connection between the women. Each woman had a son, and they were all 27 years old. Cassandra and Yolanda grew up together and they both worked at C.J.C. previously. We didn't have anything on Tiffany Roseland.

Since Cassandra and Yolanda both worked in the property room at one point or another, we were going to set up surveillance outside of the property room to see what we can come up with. I told Detective Bell and Monica about the activity I saw on the back dock the other night, and they volunteered to set up a stake out. I asked Cruz to check the database to see if anything came up on Tiffany.

The only thing we know about the killer is that he is tall, and wears a unique kind of shoe. I didn't tell them I think there are two killers, not just yet, I had to be sure. I didn't want to confuse anybody, and in any investigation, everyone's observations are important. I have a feeling about it; there is a dark secret to these murders.

It was about 3:30 p.m. when we walked out of the classroom. The rest of the detectives left for the evening. I went to my desk to make a phone call. I called my good friend Melvin Bush over at the Bureau. I needed him to check the background on the three women to see what he could come up with. We need leads fast. Time is moving way too fast.

Neither of the three women have any local arrest, but I wanted to see if there is anything on the federal level. Melvin told me he would see what he could find out and get back to me. I reached in the middle drawer and got the notebook and the Johnson file to work on the case at home this weekend if I get the chance.

My daughter is coming over Friday; so, I'm not going to be able to go to the office. Spending time with her is important. She is growing up fast. I stood and walked out of the office. When I made it home, Alice was in the kitchen. She made some groceries the previous day.

I am looking forward to me and Alice's first Thanksgiving together and spending the weekend with the two most important people in my life – my two greatest reasons on earth for being thankful.

Alice purchased fruit, snacks, and various juices for this weekend. I walked over to the kitchen and attacked the back of her neck with my mouth.

She giggled and turned around facing me with a big smile

on her face and said, "Hi baby!"

"What's for dinner, baby? I'm starving," I asked.

"I had some Thanksgiving dishes catered from Kroger's," she replied.

I went to the bathroom to wash up, and went to the kitchen to fix my plate: baked hen, cornbread dressing, potato salad, jellied cranberries, wheat rolls, sweet potato pie, and German Chocolate cake. When Alice finished putting the food up, she poured two glasses of white wine, and came to the table and sat down. We talked about everything from music to government issues; she was in a good mood.

Maybe Alice wants a child of her own someday. I had never given the thought any consideration until now. She would make a good mother. A child would probably make her life complete. I could see a little Jack Webster running around, too. We went over to the living room and sat on the sofa after I finished eating. The 10:00 p.m. news came on. The top story was about the rapist who was currently terrorizing the Whitehaven area. Two more girls had been raped. The media called him the "Come with me rapist."

The name was given to him because the girls who had been raped said the rapist told them repeatedly, "Come with me."

I was going to ride around the neighborhood to investigate, but I hadn't found the time. When the news continued, the next story shocked the hell out of me. I couldn't believe my eyes. I closed my eyes for three seconds, then I opened them again to make sure I wasn't seeing things. It couldn't be so.

It was a press conference at the jail. Alice looked at me and said, "Congratulation! Reco and Tina were charged with the murders." I looked at the television, but I couldn't believe what I was seeing.

"I didn't know anything about it," I finally said to Alice.

I was dumbfounded about the press conference. The longer I sat there, the angrier I became. I had just told Captain Dunn Reco and Tina weren't the killers. Alice could tell I was upset. She looked at me and asked if I was okay, but I didn't respond. I was disgusted at the mockery of justice they were making. I sat there on the sofa, mortified. I couldn't even look at Alice.

She knew I was the lead detective on the case. I had no idea about the press conference. Alice grabbed the remote and changed the channel. She took my hand and softly rubbed it with her smooth hands. Then she stood and went to the bedroom. Alice decided she was going to work early in the morning, so she could get off for the big game tomorrow night. I sat on the sofa in silence. I grabbed the tall glass of wine and took a long deliberate drink and stared at the television.

I know politics is behind the whole thing. The press conference was a political stunt to make the mayor and the district attorney look like they had solved the murders and had the city's crime under control. I am not going to standby quietly and let two innocent people get convicted for a murder they didn't commit.

Friday morning, I woke up early and made it to the office at 7:30 a.m. Alice left the apartment before I got out of bed. I dressed in some blue jeans, an old USC football jersey, and my red and white Airmax, and headed to the office; it was empty and quiet when I arrived.

There were two more people on the list of names to investigate. I was going to meet with them today. Angie walked in the office at 8 a.m. wearing a blue dress that fitted her body so perfect, I nearly forgot what my name was. I imagine she is going to make some guy the luckiest man on earth one day. Most of the detectives were coming through the door. Detective Monica gave me a strange look. I'm not sure what that look is about, but I guess I will find out.

The pressure was on, at least for me, to solve this case and not let two people go down for a crime they didn't commit. I stood and walked over to Detectives Bell and Monica and told them we needed to get the ball rolling on the murder cases. I told Cruz and Jackson the same thing. I didn't hesitate to ask them to work late, if we had too. Detective Bell and Monica didn't mind the overtime. Cruz and Jackson were going to the big game tonight, but they agreed to get right back to work when the game was over.

Time wasn't on our side anymore. Eleven days ago, this

time, this case started with the death of James and his son. I walked over to my desk, grabbed my car keys, and walked out of the office on my way to the Penal Farm to see Lieutenant Renee Peterson. I got on the highway and took I-55 to I-240, and headed east to Sycamore View, got off at the Summer Ave. exit and sped pass traffic.

As I drove up to the parking lot, I could see several guards standing outside talking and smoking cigarettes. I got out of my car, walked inside the lobby, asked the white female guard for Lieutenant Peterson, and handed my Glock to her. She pointed to the Lieutenant standing outside with the rest of the guards. I walked outside, stood by the door, and looked directly at her.

She threw her cigarette on the ground, stepped on it, and walked up to me and said, "Detective Jack Webster. What took you so long? I been expecting you."

I was surprised at the way she introduced herself. She was very attractive, and a very sexy walk. Certain women give off that "come follow me" vibe that drives a man wild. She was one of them. I couldn't help but notice how young she is. She is young to be a lieutenant at a correctional facility. Go figure!

"So, you used to hang out with Cassandra Johnson?" I asked. She took her green cap off her head, threw her hair to the back, then she put the cap back on again. I couldn't help but wonder where I had seen her before. Maybe it was from one of my previous visits out here to the Penal Farm.

"I knew James and Cassandra very well. We used to hang out together," she said as we walked through the lobby and headed into the Penal Farm.

"Did they have any kind of problems with anybody?" I asked as we headed down the sidewalk.

She was on her way to check the buildings she was assigned too. There was a lot of activity going on. About 10 guards ran pass us in a hurry. Inmates were on yard call and we passed several who were on their work details.

There was a backup call in one of the buildings. The voices of the call over the two-way could be heard through the speakers on her side. An inmate had been stabbed. After being distracted for a few minutes, we continued our conversation.

"James had quite a few enemies on the job. Nobody really liked him. He thought he was better than everybody, and he acted that way," she said.

"That's why no one attended his funeral," she declared.

That was a good question. I was so busy focusing on Amos. I didn't realize that no one from the Penal Farm attended the funeral service. When Renee and I walked out of the building, she lit her cigarette. We stood in front of the building and talked.

"What about Timothy Woods, James Johnson's best friend. Didn't he attend the funeral?" I asked.

Renee burst out laughing and said, "Best friend! That's the understatement of the year!"

I stated, "I thought they were best friends. So, how would you describe the relationship?"

"One word: acrimonious!" she proclaimed.

"Cassandra had an affair with Timothy about a year ago."

"He didn't mention anything to me about it," I noted.

"Why would he, you're a homicide detective investigating the murder of a guy he grew up with! I hate to say it but Cassandra was a dominatrix; she loved to have sex," she added.

"James was a nice man, but he patronized Cassandra. She was my friend, but it is what it is!"

"I heard when she was 18 years old, she dated three men in the same circle: the captain of the football team, the school counselor, and the assistant principal," she said in a low tone of voice, "she demanded privacy and respect."

Then, she added, "Men call Cassandra a player because she takes charge of her men."

Cassandra appeared to be a complicated character. After her third cigarette, we ventured back onto the sidewalk and headed toward the lobby.

"Are you sure you don't know anything she may have done to someone to make someone want to kill her?" I asked again.

Her eyes shifted away from me when I asked her the question. Finally, she looked at me and said, "I told you all I know detective."

"What time did you leave the party?" I asked.

"I have a little girl and a boy. I left around midnight," she noted.

I thanked her for her time, and walked off. I got the feeling she knows a lot more than she said. I also believe she wants Cassandra's killer found. But to be on the safe side, I am going to get an unmarked car to follow her around. We must follow every lead. Everyone is suspect in a murder case and especially in this case because we might have a serial killer or two killers on our hand.

Suddenly, I wondered if Renee and her son were next.

3

The Green Dots

If you see what a person is like on the inside the first time you met them, you probably should avoid them the next time you see them.

Anthony Ellis

I got in my car and headed back to the office. I wondered if James knew who Cassandra was before he married her. Who knows, maybe he felt he could help her or change her. I couldn't help but wonder about Cassandra's sex life. This case may not be about a jealous man. There is more to it than that, and there is no doubt in my mind Renee knew more than she told me.

The office was loud and noisy as usual when I walked through the door. There was an elderly black couple sitting on the side of Angie's desk when I walked by. Angie was busy talking on the phone.

When she hung the phone up, she walked over to my desk and told me, "Tina Dotson's grandparents have been waiting here to see you for several hours."

"Okay, give me a second," I told Angie.

Tina must have called them after she was charged with the murders. I walked over and introduced myself. The elderly woman didn't look too friendly.

She stood and said, "I'm Emma Dotson. My grandchild told me to ask for you Mr. Webster. Now, I know she's not a saint, but she didn't kill nobody! She didn't kill those people y'all say she killed. Now you find out who did, and let my baby go!"

She had a worried look on her face. "Don't you worry Mrs. Dotson, I'm going to get to the bottom of things. I promise you that Tina will be okay."

"Thank you, Mr. Webster," she said and they walked out the office.

"You are welcome ma'am," I said touching her shoulder lightly.

I walked back to my desk, sat down, and couldn't help but think about what Renee told me about Cassandra. I wonder if any of the guys Cassandra was sleeping with had anything to do with the murder. I glanced at my watch at 1:40 p.m. I am meeting Alice back at the apartment so we can go to the game together which starts at 5:30 p.m. I am looking forward to seeing my daughter play.

I haven't seen Ron in a couple of days, but I am sure the in-service training is going well. Ron said he was going to help Cruz and Jackson locate Dirty White Girl in his spare time. I wonder how the search is coming along. Alvin Myers, who worked for Waste Management was the last name on the list. Maybe he can give me something to go on. I have enough time to head out to Waste Management, then head home, and get ready for the big game.

I walked out of the office. Angie ran out of the office and yelled my name just before the elevator doors closed.

"There is a call for you on line one," she said fast. I stepped off the elevator, walked back into the office, and grabbed the phone and said, "Hello."

Bella from the Crime Scene Unit was on the phone. She said with enthusiasm, "Jack, I got some good news for you. The cell phone we found in Billy Jackson's pocket belonged to Cassandra Johnson. If it's not damaged, we may be on to something."

"That's great, keep my posted, thanks for the call," I said and hung the phone up. I jumped in the air like I had just won the lottery. Finally, some good news. Things are starting to look up. Detective Monica walked up and asked what was all the noise about?

"Billy had Cassandra's cell phone in his pocket. We may be able to find out who she talked to the day she was murdered," I said.

I was so happy I could kiss Monica. Well, maybe not that

happy. I walked out of the office and headed back to the elevators. At first, they thought the phone if Billy's pocket didn't work because it was dead.

In most murder cases, the victim talks with the perpetrator the day of the murder. Usually, the victim knows the killer. There was no doubt in my mind Cassandra knew her killer. There wasn't much activity going on at the land field when I drove up. The smell was unbearable. It smelled like someone had just dumped some sour food on top of my head. The smell was just that bad. When I walked into the nasty office, the smell wasn't much better.

A white man with a toothpick sticking out of his mouth was sitting at a desk behind a counter in a chair yelling on the telephone. He slammed the receiver down, looked at me and said, "Now what the hell do you want?"

He was very loud and rude. I took my badge out, showed it to him, and asked for Alvin Myers. His whole demeanor changed when he saw my badge.

"He's out on his route. What's he done now?" He asked shaking his head.

"That guy is always into something. He's a damn good driver, just can't seem to keep his nose clean," he said.

"He's been in trouble before?" I asked.

"Has he!" I've given him chance after chance. He just got out of jail about four months ago. He's my best driver. One of these days I'm going to fire him for good!" he added.

"What's he done now?" he inquired of me.

"He's not in trouble. I just need to talk to him about a woman he used to hang out with," I noted. "Do you have a picture of him I can see?" I asked.

He started to peck on the old modeled computer. "We don't have a printer but this is what he looks like," he told me turning the computer screen around so I could see the picture.

"When do you expect him to return?" I asked.

"He drives the Westwood and Orange Mound Route. He never makes it back before 7:00 p.m. at night." I didn't have time to wait around for him. I was in a hurry. I thanked the old gaffer and walked out the door at almost 4:30 p.m.

It was Friday, rush hour traffic. I headed home to get ready to go to the game. I got on the highway, took I-55 to midtown, and got off at the Union Ave. exit. The traffic was thick on every street. I hit the siren and pulled out of the lane and sped across the red light. I had to get home in time to take a shower, put on some clean clothes, and I didn't want to be late. Alice was already dressed and waiting when I walked through the door. I gave her a peck on the lips and trotted to the bathroom.

I put on some jeans, a L.A. Laker's Jersey and my Airmax. I wore the L.A Laker's Jersey because my daughter's school colors were black and gold. She was very excited about attending the game. Alice wore some black jeans, a yellow button down shirt, and some white Nikes. As we drove in front of Hamilton High School there were several uniformed patrol officers directing traffic.

There were cars everywhere. I pulled up, showed the officer my badge, he moved the barricade for me, and I drove into the parking lot and parked. It was 5:10 p.m. when Alice and I walked into the loud and crowded gymnasium. There was white and blue on the right side and black and gold on the left side. The fans are out tonight. It's amazing this many people can fit inside a high school gym.

There was a lot of police at the game. A fight broke out in the middle of the floor with the students at the last two games. I saw my ex-wife Amber and her husband Roosevelt sitting up toward the middle, behind the team. Alice and I walked over to the stands because coach always reserved those spots for the parents. When we sat down, I introduced Alice to Amber and Roosevelt. Amber appeared surprised.

From time to time she looked at Alice and observed her. The fact that Alice was younger than me and beautiful as hell, played a big part in the way Amber was looking. I enjoyed every moment of it. The crowd went wild as the two teams ran out of the locker rooms into the gym.

Stephanie glanced up the stands to see if we were here. We all stood and pointed at her at the same time. I showed Alice who she was. Her number was 24. She is 16, and already 6'1. It seems like she is getting taller and taller every time I see her.

The starting lineup went out to the center of the court for the tip off. Stephanie looked at us one more time, and I pointed at her, and gave her a thumbs up. Hamilton won the tip off and went down the court and scored two points easily, and their fans became louder and louder as the game went on.

I glanced around the gym to see if I could spot Cruz or Jackson, and some of the other detectives in the crowd, but there were too many people inside the gym for me to single them out. They were here watching and hoping for a win, just like I was. Channel 13 News was covering the game. I saw one of the sports reporters who used to interview me when I was in school. Man! Is he old now, but he is hard at it. Alice is into the game rooting everyone on. My life style is different from hers, but she has been enjoying herself.

Every time my daughter made a basket, Alice cheered aloud. Amber observed Alice out of the corner of her eyes. I got a kick out of Amber's curiosity. The game was close. Hamilton was up by 11 at halftime. Whitehaven trailed the whole time, except for the time when they tied the game up at 45. Hamilton maintained a scoring lead. Stephanie had scored 26 points by halftime.

I asked if anybody wanted anything to eat from the concession stand. I was hungry. Nobody wanted anything to eat. Alice told me to bring her a coke back. We were going to take Stephanie out to eat if they lost. The winners were going to T.G.I. Friday's. Alice didn't want to spoil her appetite. There were several people standing in line when I walked up. Cruz and Jackson walked up behind me and Cruz tapped me on the shoulder. He was smiling when I turned around.

Those two were always together. They remind me of Will Smith and Martin Lawrence on the movie *Bad Boys*. Except Cruz is Hispanic and Jackson is white. I shook their hands and said, "What's going on guys?"

I could see the dollar signs in their eyes. "You want to pay up now or later?" Cruz asked.

"The game isn't over yet. We got two more quarters to play," I reminded them.

"I'm telling you Jack. Whitehaven is too weak for

Hamilton. Your daughter needs some help!"

"We'll see," I said.

I ordered two cokes, a chili dog with extra cheese, headed back to the stands, and sat down just as the third quarter started. One of the Hamilton defenders stole the ball away from a Whitehaven point guard. She went down the court like a rocket and scored two points like it was nothing. The Whitehaven cheerleaders kept on cheering trying to get the fans involved in the game. Hamilton was killing us under the basket. The Coach called a time out. The game went back and forth. The teams traded baskets.

Stephanie jumped in front of a pass and stole the ball, went down, and did a NBA layup that got the Whitehaven fans back into the game. I couldn't' believe it, myself. I didn't know she had it in her. The Whitehaven fans came to life. All you could hear was go Whitehaven Tigers. With 20 seconds to play and the game tied at 69, Hamilton took the ball out. They passed the ball around and tried to run the time out. When the clock reached ten seconds, the guard for Hamilton drove the lane and passed the ball underneath the basket to the center. She went up with the ball and scored two points.

The referee called a foul on the play. I couldn't believe it - nobody could. The boos really started to come at the referee for his bad call. The Coach was furious. Up by two points, the Hamilton Center went to the line to shoot one free throw. Everybody in the gym was silent. The Whitehaven fans were praying she missed. The referee handed the center the ball. She bounced the ball a couple of times, looked at the basket, and shot the ball. It seemed like the slowest shot I had ever seen.

The ball hit the rim and one of the Whitehaven players got the rebound and called a time out with four seconds left on the game clock. It would come down to a final shot. We were down by two points. The referee handed the ball to the girl. Suddenly nervous and paranoid, I couldn't watch. I wanted to close my eyes, but I had to watch. Alice had her fingers crossed. Amber and Roosevelt were praying.

The Whitehaven girls got in a straight line. Stephanie pushed off the line, ran to the far-left corner of the court, the center threw the ball to Stephanie. She bounced the ball one time and let it fly.

The Hamilton defender jumped into the air and tried to block the ball, but she missed. I stood to my feet. Hundreds of fans stood to their feet. I thought the ball was never going to come down. The ball hit the rim of the basket, bounced up slightly, and went in. It was a three pointer. The game was over. We had won. The Whitehaven fans went wild. My daughter was still standing in the corner starring up the court at the rim.

The rest of the team ran to the corner and jumped on her. I couldn't believe it. It was so exciting. We hopped around in the stands like bunny rabbits. All I could think about was Cruz and Jackson. I would pay anything to see their faces right now. The uniformed officers took over to make sure nothing jumped off. They quickly got everybody moving out of the gym.

Alice, Amber, Roosevelt and myself walked down to the court and waited for the celebration to end. The team was celebrating their victory.

Amber walked up to me and said, "She's beautiful. I've seen her somewhere before."

"You probably saw her on the news. She's the chief Medical examiner for Shelby County," I said with great pride.

Stephanie and the rest of the team finally got off the floor. Stephanie ran over to me and jumped into my arms. Man, she's heavy. She said she was going to ride with the team to T.G.I. Friday's for the victory dinner.

All the team parents were invited to come. Alice liked the idea of going to T.G.I. Friday's. The news reporter interviewed the Coach and the team. My baby could play just like she told me she could. As we stood there and watched the interview, I was appreciative the team had just made me $400 richer. The team went to the locker rooms to change into their clothes. Alice and I headed to the car. Amber and Roosevelt left for T.G.I Friday's. I was trying to wait for the traffic to die down.

The patrol officers did a great job keeping the traffic moving. I got in front of the team bus and escorted them to T.G.I Friday's. I turned on my blue lights and sirens. I headed north on Bellevue St. toward midtown and made a left turn on Union Ave. T.G.I Friday's was in downtown Memphis on the corner of Union Ave. and Third St. We parked behind the Greyhound Bus Station.

Stephanie got off the bus carrying her black and gold gym bag. I grabbed it and sat it on the floor board under the back seat when she walked up. The three of us headed inside T.G.I Friday's. The place was packed on the inside when we stepped through the door. T.G.I Friday's always host a dinner celebration for the winning high school team on Friday night. Alice congratulated Stephanie.

Amber stood and waved her hand in the air so we could see her. We walked over to the table and sat down. I noticed most of the parents who were married were dressed alike. Which seemed quaint in this day and age. Amber and Roosevelt were even dressed alike. We all talked and laughed about the game. It felt kind of awkward at first, being with Amber and Stephanie. It was the first time we had been together at the same table since the divorce two years ago. Man, it seems like a long time. I got over it.

Being at the table reminded me of the times when we were a happy family. I was happy to be with my family. Alice and Stephanie were hitting it off pretty well. They were talking like the two of them had known each other for years. Finally, the waitress came and we placed our orders. We decided not to drink any liquor around the kids. I ordered the 25-inch quarter house steak and potatoes. Alice order the ribeye steak, cooked medium.

Amber and Roosevelt ordered the steak dinner also. Stephanie ordered the baby-back rib special. When the food arrived at the table, we ate, talked, and had a really nice time together. The Coach stood and got everybody's attention. He called Stephanie up to the middle of the restaurant. She stood and walked up to the Coach.

"Tonight, the game ball goes to Stephanie Webster," he said and handed her a small black and gold basketball.

Everybody in the restaurant started clapping and stood to their feet. "Speech, speech!" the crowd demanded.

Tears rolled down Stephanie's eyes as she held the ball. She called the rest of the team to the middle of the floor and said "This game ball is for the team."

Alice and Amber got teary eyed. Okay, a tear or two ran down my face as well. I was proud of my daughter for calling the whole team up with her. Amber and Alice took pictures with their cellphones, and so did many of the parents.

We sat and had such a good time it was 11:30 p.m. when I looked at the clock on the wall.

The coach stopped by our table and said, "Good dam' tiger" on his way out of the door.

We stood and said our goodbyes and left. Amber winked at me on her way out which was her way of approving of Alice. When we made it back to the apartment, Stephanie and Alice sat on the sofa and continued talking. I went to the back to get some bed linen for Stephanie. She was going to sleep on the sofa. Stephanie and Alice made plans to go shopping.

Alice was going to take her to the morgue and show her around. Stephanie was impressed that Alice was a doctor, and a Chief Medical Examiner. Their Saturday activities will give me a little time to work on the case. I went back to the bedroom, and left the two ladies alone, so they could chitchat.

I woke up around 6:00 am in the morning. Alice was in the bathroom getting ready for her day with Stephanie. I hopped out of bed, and stretched my legs. I didn't get much sleep last night. I had a bad dream. The case was on my mind. When I walked into the living room to check on Stephanie, she was going through the Johnson case file.

From the looks of it, I'd say she had been up all night. The television was on BET, and her iPad and phone were lying next to her.

"What's up champ," I said kissing her on the forehead.

"Good morning dad. I was just looking at the case file on the Johnson family. Have you caught the killer yet? She asked.

"You know that is private information in that file," I noted.

"Yah' daddy, I know," she replied as if I had asked her something she already knew.

"Nope, but I been working on the case day and night

trying to catch the creep," I said looking for something to eat in the refrigerator.

"It's sad that somebody would kill these people over some Green Dots," she said as she flipped through the notebook.

I nearly bumped my head on the refrigerator. I walked over to the sofa and said, "What did you say? You mean to tell me you know what those numbers are inside the notebook?" I asked.

I had a curious look on my face. "Yeah'. They're Green Dots reload dad, money!" she said. I sat on the sofa next to her so she could explain.

"Green Dots, is the name of a prepaid debit card through participating stores, but most people get them at Walmart," she stated. Then, she reached into her purse and took a green credit card out, then she continued.

"You take one of these numbers out of the notebook, call the 1-800 number on the back of the card. Give the person the 14-digit number and the money transfers to the credit card in seconds. Mom got me one about a year ago. She wanted to teach me how to be responsible with money. Everybody knows about Green Dots, except for detectives. From the looks of it, the Johnson's were rich!" she said.

She handed me the notebook. I sat on the sofa in complete silence. Stephanie stood and went to the bathroom to get ready to leave with Alice. I couldn't believe it. I had asked about 100 people what the numbers were and nobody had a clue. My 16-year-old daughter comes over and solves the 16-digit number issue in one night. Kids!

I sat there on the sofa speechless. Stephanie had no idea, but she may have given us something we didn't have on the case. A motive. She had just helped me solve a big part of the case.

Alice came out of the bedroom, put her arms around my neck, gave me a big kiss and said, "Good morning baby. What are you going to do while we're gone?" she asked.

She was in a good mood this morning. I told her I was just going to sit around the apartment and work on the case. She offered to fix me some breakfast, but I told her it was okay.

When Stephanie came back, I reached into my pocket and took $300 out and handed her the cash. She grabbed the money and said, "Thanks Dad!"

"Now you two go have some fun," I said. Stephanie and Alice left. I went to the bedroom to get dressed. I was going back to Walmart to see how much money was in the notebook.

I was back at Walmart fighting through the crowd of shoppers. The lines were as long in the morning as they were at night. I walked right up to the front customer service line, caught a few stares from the customers who had been waiting in long lines, but I ignored them. I was on official police business. I asked an unattractive female worker for the manager palming my badge in my hand. She told the customer standing in line to wait a second, got on the microphone, and her voice echoed over the loud speaker.

A man with a "Grant" name tag, wearing a light brown tie, a white button down shirt, and some brown Duck Head slacks came from behind the customer service counter. The clerk told him I was a policeman.

He walked up to me with a warm smile and hand thrust forward and said "How may I help you detective?"

"Jack, please call me Jack," I insisted.

We shook hands and I told him that seven people had been murdered so far and our investigation pointed to Green Dots. He escorted me to a very spacious room in the back of the customer service department with several women sitting at large expensive desks typing on computers and talking on phones. Fax machines, copiers, and shredders were scattered throughout the room.

Grant introduced me to a very nice and cordial employee, named Royce. I pulled up a chair and sat down beside her desk while Grant explained the purpose of my visit. I handed the woman the notebook and she went to work. Grant offered me a cup of fresh coffee and I accepted.

"If you need anything, anything at all, just let Royce know," he said and walked out of the room. Royce flipped through the pages and pecked away at the computer.

I sat there so long, I didn't even notice how much time had

passed. I played free cell and solitaire on my phone and went inside the store and bought some soap and some car wax to break the monotony. Royce worked on the notebook, nonstop, for five hours. There was a text from Alice on my phone when I took it out of my pocket. Stephanie and Alice were cooking dinner and wanted to know how much longer I was going to be. I didn't know it was going to take this long. I texted her back and told her I was at Walmart on official police business and hopefully wouldn't be much longer.

My butt was numb from sitting so long. I stood and stomped on the floor. My leg had fallen to sleep. The feeling finally came back to my leg. I didn't see how Royce could sit there and type on a computer that long; maybe she is a robot or something. I walked out of the room and went to the restroom.

It was 5:45 p.m. when I looked at the clock on the wall. I had spent the whole day at Walmart. Stephanie was going to be mad at me. I tried not to think about it though. I was going to make it up to her. I knew just the thing, money. I went to the ATM machine and took $100 out. Money can't buy love, but it buys things a teenager wants. I went back to the room and sat in the chair. Finally, after 40 minutes passed, she stopped typing.

She was finished, finally. Royce stood and walked over to the printer and got the printout.

She walked up to me with a smile on her face and said, "Here you are Mr. Webster," handing me the notebook and the printout.

She had some really nice legs. I stood and glanced at the printout, then I looked at Royce and said, "There must be some mistake!"

"No Mr. Webster, the numbers are correct," she said with a smile on her face. She sat back down in her chair and went to work on another issue.

My heart started pounding fast and sweat started rolling off my face. Wrinkles formed on my forehead. I tried to conceal my emotions but it was unbelievable.

"It couldn't be," I mumbled aloud. There was $2.5 million worth of Green Dots written inside of the notebook. I thanked

Royce for her time and walked out of the room. I still couldn't believe it. I was holding $2.5 million dollars in my hand. This money is connected to one man. I can't imagine how much other officers are making off smuggling contraband into the prison.

I got in my car and headed home. A lot of negative thoughts ran through my mind. I could do a lot of things with $2.5 million dollars. I turned the radio on to clear my mind. I tried not to think about the complications of the case, but I couldn't elude the present. Now, I had a motive, but there was still something else going on with this case, I didn't understand. Why kill the kids? They didn't have anything to do with the money. That bothered me.

I could smell a roast cooking when I walked in the door. Stephane and Alice were standing at the stove when I came in so busy cooking and talking they didn't even hear me. I walked up behind them and scared the living hell out of them. Their eyes were enlarged like snowballs and they both jumped and hit me at the same time. I started laughing at the two of them.

"That's not funny," Alice said and gave me a mean look.

I just couldn't resist. Alice took Stephanie to the beauty salon earlier. They had the same hair style, and got their nails done too. Women!

"What do you think Dad?" Stephanie asked as I surveyed her hair.

"It's beautiful baby. It makes you look like a woman." I said, then, I gave Alice a kiss and went to the bathroom.

My knee was bothering me again. I was still a little stiff from sitting so long in Walmart.

Alice was setting the table when I came out of the bathroom and sat down. I was starving. I hadn't eaten all day. Stephanie was tending to the food. Alice told me Stephanie did most of the cooking. I didn't know my daughter could cook. They brought a roast with gravy, potatoes, carrots, and rice to the table. Alice baked a chocolate cake and some homemade bread. The steam from the food gave off a good smell. Plus, it looked good.

We paused to bless the food, each other; then, we ate. Well,

Stephanie and Alice watched me as I took my first bite. I said another prayer without the two of them knowing, then I tasted the food.

I nodded and said, "Not bad, not bad at all, actually, it's delicious!" I wasn't just saying that because she was my daughter. I was impressed with her cooking abilities. She was becoming a young woman right before my eyes.

"Did you find out how much money was in the notebook?" Stephanie asked.

"You figured out what the numbers were?" Alice inquired.

"I didn't. Detective Stephanie here told me what the numbers were. Yep, she told me this morning." Stephanie had a big smile on her face.

"Is there anything that you can't do?" I said to Stephanie.

"When I figure out what that is, I'll be sure to let you know," she retorted.

"Go Ms. Thang!" I said. Stephanie and Alice burst out laughing at my comment.

"Well, how much was it?" Alice asked. They both had a curious look on their faces.

"You're not going to believe me if I tell you."

"Try me," Alice said. They both stopped eating and stared into my direction.

"$2.5 million." Their mouth popped wide open and they stared at me, like they had been frozen solid.

"You're kidding me!" Alice finally said.

"Nope, I wish I were," I admitted.

"What are you going to do with the money?" Stephanie asked.

"Can we keep it?"

"No! We can't keep it!" I said.

"When all this is over I'm going to give some of the money to Cassandra's parents for their grandbaby. I am going to suggest they set up a trust fund."

"Where do you suppose, they got all of that money?" Alice asked.

"That's a million-dollar question," I said.

"What type of work did they do?" Stephanie asked.

"James was a guard out at the Penal Farm and Cassandra was a bank teller."

"Maybe she stole the money from a bank," Stephanie proposed.

I finished my first plate of food. Then I said, "I don't think she stole it from a bank without anybody noticing the money missing."

"How else would you explain the money?" Alice said. I didn't have an answer to that question, but I intended to find out.

"At least you have a motive now," Alice said.

"Tell me about it," I countered.

We sat there and ate and talked for a long time. Stephanie and I decided to do the dishes. Alice went to the back to take a bath, and get ready for bed. She had to go in early the next morning.

"So, what do you think about Alice?" I finally asked as we loaded the dishes into the dishwasher.

"She's Gucci! I really like her," Stephanie said.

"What's Gucci?" I asked. She looked at me and shook her head.

"Dad! You don't know what Gucci means?" she replied as if I was a dinosaur.

"Nope. That's why dads aren't allowed at the malls," I said playing the dumb dad role. I don't know a lot of things, but I know that Gucci is a high-end designer.

"It means she's cool. She's down," Stephanie said.

"Oh," I said as I shook my head.

I told Stephanie I wanted her to help me pick out a ring for Alice. I was going to ask her to marry me. I told her to keep it a secret for now. We went over to the living room and sat on the sofa. I asked her about her boyfriend. I had never met him before. She told me it was nothing serious. I popped the question. The question every father wants to know when it comes to their teenage daughter. I asked her if she was having sex yet.

"I thought about it, and we almost did but I didn't. I wasn't ready. He wanted me to," she admitted.

I was relieved she wasn't having sex yet. I know that day is coming, but I told her that abstinence was the key. I told her to call me if she ever needed to talk about anything. She already knew that. I just wanted to make sure she knew I would be there for her. We talked about the importance of protection. I didn't want to be a grandfather, not at 43. We sat and talked for a long time. I was proud of my daughter. I reached into my shirt pocket and took $100 out and gave it to her. She gave me a big hug. I stood and said good night, then I went to the bedroom.

She has a good head on her shoulders. She is going to be a fine young woman one day, and hopefully on a career path without children.

4

Clues and Old Dues

I ordered surveillance outside of C.J.C. at the back dock, December 1-3, 2013. Nothing out of the ordinary happened the first night. I checked with the unmarked unit watching Renee's house, but nothing was happening there either. I think the killer is going to strike Renee and her son which is consistent with a pattern.

I went down to the crime scene lab and waited for Bella. She is going to ride out to the Penal Farm with me and post up. I don't think Cassandra's murder has anything to do with the Green Dots. There is something else going on. I can feel it. My plan is to take a picture of Timothy Woods, Donnie Winters, and Alvin Myers, and show the pictures to Crystal and Diane to see if they recognize one of them as the man Cassandra was arguing with at the party. Cassandra did have an affair with Timothy, and God knows who else. Jealousy could be the motive.

Bella came out carrying one of those state-of-the-art, high tech camera's and said, "Ready to go."

We hopped into a white unmarked suburban truck with tinted windows and drove off. The temperature was in the low 50s, the air was cool, but it was nice out. I got on the Hwy. at Alabama St., took I-55 to I-240, and headed east to Summer Ave. I turned on the radio. A Jay-Z tune was playing. Bella didn't talk much on the way to the Penal Farm, but she was bobbing her head enjoying the music.

I asked her about the camera. She told me it was a Sony TXJ2700 which was the latest model on the market. I almost choked when she told me what it cost: $5,000. I was amazed at the camera's features. Pictures could be taken from 50 yards away. It had night vision, and could take pictures under water.

The only thing the camera couldn't do was take a picture through walls. She said they were still working on that technology. I got off the Hwy. at the Summer Ave. exit and headed to the Penal Farm.

There wasn't much traffic to fight like earlier. I drove into the parking lot about 1:40 p.m., circled around the lot to see if I could spot Timothy Woods black Cadillac Escalade, and bingo, there it was. I pulled around back and parked as close to the K-building lobby as possible in the parking space facing the entrance. The guards change shifts at 2:00 p.m.

Several guards were walking briskly through the parking lot trying to make it to work on time. It was quiet inside the truck as we waited patiently for Timothy to come out. At 2:10 p.m. the guards came rushing out of the lobby like a herd of wild animals. I guess I would run out of there too, if I had been locked up for eight hours with 100s of disrespectful criminals.

The guards were so busy trying to get to their cars no one noticed us. We sat there and watched the door. Finally, about 40 minutes later, Timothy came out and stood at the door conversing with an attractive, female guard with a caramel face.

"That's him!" I said to Bella. Bella took several shots of Timothy at different angles.

When she was satisfied with her work, she came back to the front seat and said, "Let's go."

I pulled out of the parking lot and headed back to the office. She told me she would have the pictures ready in the morning by 8:00 a.m. I asked her about the sim-card just before she got out of the truck.

"The technician is still working on it, but I will call you as soon as she gets through."

She said goodbye and got out of the truck. I took the suburban back to the garage and headed to the office. Ron was sitting at the desk when I walked in.

"What's going on buddy?" I said to Ron as I stood at my desk.

Ron stood, walked over, and shook my hand. "I'm good. I'm just ready for this training to end."

This was my first time seeing him in about a week. "How is the search coming with the girl?" he asked.

"We can't seem to locate her anywhere. It's like she just up and disappeared off the face of the earth," I replied.

"What's been going on with you? How is the case coming along?" Ron asked.

"I still don't have a suspect yet, but I found out what the numbers in the notebook are."

"What are they?" he inquired excitedly.

"You are not going to believe me, if I tell you," I said.

"Try me," Ron said.

"How does $2.5 million sound?"

Ron's eyes bucked wide open and he said, "C'mon man. You kidding me."

"I wish I were," I said smiling.

"Dammit, that's a lot of money. Where the hell did they get $2.5 million from?"

"I don't know, but I going to find out," I added.

"That's a hell of a lot of money. Anybody could have killed them for that much money" Ron contended.

"Tell me about it. Speaking of money," I hinted to Ron about our bet.

"Yeah, yeah, yeah! I know," Ron said reaching into his coat pocket and pulled out $50. He betted on the game last week. Ron gave me the cash and said goodbye. He walked over to Angie's desk and waited for her to get off the phone. I got back to work on the case. Most of the detectives were out in the field.

I sat at my desk wondering where James and Cassandra got all that money. I didn't have a clue, but I knew someone probably knew. Cruz and Jackson walked through the door. I stood and threw my right arm in the air like I was shooting a basketball and smiled at them. They were impressed my daughter made the winning shot. Actually, I couldn't have been prouder.

I sat back down and studied the case for the next hour trying desperately to put two and two together, but nothing was clicking. I didn't want to admit it, but the case was going south, cold! What was I missing? I kept asking myself as I sat at my desk. There was something, but I couldn't see it. It was about time for me to pay Marcus Green another visit. I was convinced he knew something. I just had to figure out how to get him to talk. I wasn't going to be able to get him out on time cut, not now.

The District Attorney was sure Reco and Tina had committed the murders. There was no use talking with the Chief now that the mayor was involved. The case was out of his hands for now. I was alone on this one, all alone. I hadn't heard from Melvin Bush yet. He was away on a big assignment, but he has never let me down in the past.

I stood and walked over to Angie, who was working late and asked her to call the Penal Farm in the morning and set up an interview with Marcus.

"I'll take care of it Jack," Angie said.

When I leave the office, I plan to stop by and see how Detective Bell and Monica were coming along with the stake out.

By 8:00 p.m., there was nothing left for me to do at the office. I stood to my feet, but my mind was racing. I was going to go see Marcus tomorrow, and I hoped he would tell me what I needed to know.

Then, I walked out of the office on my way to go see Detective Bell and Monica. I parked behind the red Mazda truck, got out of the car, walked up to Detective Monica's black Toyota Four Runner, and tapped on the window. She unlocked the door, and I hopped inside. They were in the middle of their rap session about life again.

"What's going on ladies?" I asked but they kept talking.

I am not sure what I got myself into, coming out here to see these two ladies. I watched the traffic as the cars drove by. There was a box of pizza sitting on the back seat along with a cooler of bottled water, and a big bag of barbeque chips.

I thought they had picked the perfect spot. A car drove up and we all ducked low in the seats, but it was nothing. The car made a U-turn and headed the other way.

"What's up, Jack?" Monica finally inquired.

"What's been going on?" I asked.

"Nothing really to tell. We hadn't seen anything suspicious at all. Nothing. The only movement we've seen at all is the garbage trucks, the food service trucks, and supply trucks.

"Are you sure you saw something suspicious that night at the back dock?" Detective Bell asked me.

"I don't know what was going on, but I saw what I saw," I assured her.

"Besides growing up together, this is the only place Cassandra and Yolanda were connected too. That's why I got the feeling something strange is going on," I added.

"Give it a few nights, and if nothing comes up, then we'll call it quits," I insisted.

They continued their conversation about how unfair life was treating them. All the bitching and complaining was so annoying.

"Time out please!" I shouted getting their attention.

There was complete silence. I decided to change the conversation.

"Let me share an old story my Aunt Mary used to tell me. When I complained about life all the time," I said and they both turned slightly giving me their attention.

> It might help the two of you out. One day a flock of birds flew south for the winter because the weather was getting cold. As they were flying, they ran into another bird headed in the same direction they had just came from. They stopped in midair and told the bird about the cold weather he was about to fly into. They asked him if he wanted to fly south with them.

I paused to cough, then I continued.

> The bird thought about it for a second, and decided to keep going north.

> They said their goodbyes and flew their separate ways. Well, the weather got so cold that the bird froze solid as he was flying. He fell to the earth, landed in a cow pasture,

and assumed he was going to die. About five minutes later, a cow came by and saw the bird lying helpless on the ground. The old cow felt sorry for the bird and shitted on top of the bird and walked off.

The bird knew he was going to die now because he was frozen solid underneath a pile of shit. Life was over. About five minutes later the bird noticed something. It was warm under the pile of shit. The bird thawed completely out and he was ready to go. But the bird still had one little problem. He was still underneath a pile of shit and had to get out.

My cell phone rang and I cut it off, then I continued.

Instead of the bird digging himself out of the shit, he started whistling real loud. In other words, the bird started bitching and complaining about being underneath the shit. A cat happened to be playing in the cow pasture that day and heard the bird. The cat searched for the bird, and dug through the shit. When the cat got to the bird, the bird looked at the cat and smiled then he thanked the cat. He thanked the cat for getting him out of the shit. The cat smiled at the bird then he ate that shitty ass bird.

Now the story has three morals.

I reached into the cooler to get a water for Monica, then I continued.

The first moral has something to do with the cow shitting on top of the bird. Everybody that shits on you in life, is not necessarily your enemy. The cow shit thawed the bird out when he was freezing to death. The second moral has something to do with the cat getting the bird out of the shit; everybody that gets you out of shit in life, ain't your friend. The cat got the bird out of the shit, but ate him.

And the last moral has something to do with the bird being under a pile of shit in life. If you're not willing to dig yourself out of the shit, keep your mouth shut. If the bird wouldn't have been bitching out loud the cat never would have found him. If being a detective isn't working for the two of y'all, maybe it's time to quit. We get tired of hearing all the bitching and complaining at work every day. I love both of y'all, and y'all are two damn good detectives, but maybe it's time for something else. The women had serious looks on their faces when I got through talking. I said goodbye to them and got out of the car and headed to the apartment. Women!

Some people don't know when they're blessed. I hoped they got something out of the story. Maybe it's time they sat down and took a long hard look at their lives.

There is a full moon tonight, and it is cool out; there isn't a cloud in the sky. Alice was sitting on the sofa watching ER on television with a glass of white wine in her hand when I walked through the door. I walked over and sat down beside her. I gave her a long, hot kiss.

"You want me to fix you something to eat?" she asked with a smile on her face.

She was wearing a long white t-shirt, nothing else. I didn't feel much like eating tonight. I wasn't hungry. I had a lot on my mind.

"No, I'm okay," I finally said to Alice.

"What's wrong baby, it's the case again, isn't it?" she said in a soft tone of voice.

"Yep, I'm not getting anywhere. I'm no closer to finding the killer than I was from day one." I said disappointed.

Alice grabbed my hand and rubbed it gently. A heavy, tense silence followed for the next minute or so.

"I don't like it, but I'm afraid the case needs new information soon. Dammit!" I said as I hit the sofa with my hand. I startled Alice.

"It's going to be okay baby. Find me some DNA, and you will get this guy," Alice said as she put her arms around me and laid her head in my chest. The case was not going well, but my personal life was *on the money.*

Monday morning, I thought about the case in silence.

James and his son were found dead 14 days ago. Six people are dead: two children, 4 adults, and two of the three adults were parents. Two children were killed with their parents. By 8:45 a.m., I was sitting at Bella's desk in the Crime Scene lab waiting for her to finish developing Timothy's pictures, so I can take them to the BB King's Club to see if Diane and Crystal could identify Timothy as the man arguing with Cassandra that night at the party.

I had a feeling Timothy withheld information from me. Bella came out of a small dark room with five, 8 x 10" full color, photographs of Timothy. I thanked her and immediately headed to BB King's Club and showed the pictures to Diane and Chrystal. Diane sat at the bar and rubbed her temple.

She looked at Crystal and said, "That's not him, but he was at the party too. The guy was much taller than him." Crystal nodded.

"I'm sorry Jack, but he's not the guy," Crystal stated.

I put the pictures back inside the envelope and stood there a few seconds. I patted the pictures in my hand as I looked off into space. I was certain they were going to tell me Timothy was the guy. I thanked the ladies and walked out of the club disappointed. I needed another lead fast.

I was beginning to become discouraged with each uneventful, passing moment. When I got to the office, I asked Angie if she called the Penal Farm, and sat up the visit.

"He's at the Med in the Prison Ward. Marcus Green was attacked. He was in critical condition, but is stable now," Angie said.

I was surprised at the news. I wondered what happened as I went to my desk and sat down. I had to make a few calls to the jail. I needed to check on something. I was curious about the garbage pickup schedule. I called over to FBI Headquarters to see if Melvin was in. The receptionist told me he was still out on assignment. I hung the phone up. I really needed to talk with Melvin. I stood and walked out of the office. Then, I headed to the Med to see Marcus.

By noon, I was standing at the nurse's station inside the Prison Ward on the fourth floor. I signed in and checked my weapon in at the counter with one of the hospital guards. One of the nurses told me Marcus had been in the Ward about a week. He had already been through a couple of minor surgeries. The hospital guard unlocked the door to the room and I stepped inside. Marcus was lying in the bed facing the wall. He had no idea I was in the room. The room was empty except for a black chair, the small hospital bed he was in, and a restroom.

The window facing a reddish brick wall had rusty steel bars. At the prison ward, inmates are locked away in these small hospital rooms until it's time to go to another part of the hospital or back to jail. If you've never served any time before, you wouldn't believe how incongruous the conditions are. Boredom doesn't even begin to describe what it's like. A convict I once interviewed on death row told me how it was to star at the same slabs of concrete 24/7 and repeat the same daily routine: rise, stand, stop, walk, eat, okay...

When the guard locked the door behind me, I walked up to the door, and looked at the chart hanging on the door. Marcus had four broken ribs, his left lung had been punctured, his right jaw bone had been broken, and he had massive swelling to the head. He had just returned from a nearby hospital. Marcus was hurt bad, but he would live.

Finally, he rolled over and stared straight at me. I looked into his green eyes and wondered if he was going to tell me anything about the case. The top of his head was wrapped in white bandages. There was a silver jaw brace attached to the right side of his face. His left eye was barely open, based on his facial expression, I guessed he was glad to see me.

I sat in the empty chair beside the bed and asked Marcus if he could talk. He shook his head signaling he could. He sat up in the bed as best as he could. He was in pain.

"What are you doing here Detective Webster?" he asked. His voice was very low, like a whisper.

He uttered something, but I couldn't understand. His breathing came in harsh rasps, and his eyes constricted when he tried to speak.

I asked Marcus several questions about James and Cassandra. Marcus didn't hesitate to answer any of my questions. I could tell he was in serious pain, and it was hard for him to speak, but I needed to know more than he told me that day at the Penal Farm.

That tough boy I saw the first time we met was gone. His whole attitude was different. After the rough start, Marcus began to sound much better. His voice got stronger as we talked. An attractive black female nurse entered the room while we were talking. She had to check his vital signs and give him some pain medications. She smiled at me on her way out of the room.

I sat there and listened to everything Marcus told me about James and Cassandra. A lot of it was shocking, but I wasn't surprised. I asked him about the Green Dots I found inside the notebook. I couldn't believe what he told me after that. I sat in the chair in disbelief because his story about the Green Dots sounded very paradoxical.

I was beginning to think the pain medicine the nurse had given him was taking over. He asked if I was going to be able to get him out on probation. I told him I was still working on it. He started smiling and became happy. He looked drunk from the medicine. There was nothing more he could say. I sensed he was telling the truth. I told him, "Take care." I stood and walked up to the door and knocked. The guard opened the door and I walked out of the room and headed back to 201 Poplar St.

At 3:30 p.m., I called Bella and told her I was on my way to pick her up. I sped down Poplar St. headed to C.J.C., parked my car on the north side of the jail, and went inside the garage to get the keys to the white suburban. I still had some reservations about the story Marcus told me about James and the Green Dots. He said James made all that money selling cigarettes and marijuana to inmates inside the Penal Farm.

It seemed impossible to come up with $2.5 million off prisoners. Marcus told me James and Anton had a big falling out over the business one night. When the three of them were inside the Intake Department, James found out Anton and Cassandra were sleeping together. But, Anton told me he'd never met Cassandra.

Bella was standing outside ready to go when I drove up.

She hopped in the truck and I drove off. I made a right turn at Danny Thomas Blvd. and headed south toward Union Ave. I made a left turn on Union, sped pass traffic, and made a right on Bellevue Park directly across the street from Donnie's car wash. It was time to get a picture of Donnie Winters so I could show it to Diane and Crystal. I didn't think he was involved but I had to dot every 'i.'

Most witnesses lie or tell half-truths. This whole case was very complicated and with $2.5 million in the mix, the suspect list was growing. There were several cars parked on the lot at Donnie's when we pulled in. I didn't see his red Jag, but I knew he had several cars. I turned the radio on and it was time for Bella and me to play the waiting game again. Bella was wearing a black MPD, Crime Scene Unit shirt with some khaki pants, white ankle socks and black Nike Airmax. Her Glock was on her left side. I took a couple of peeks at her nice brown legs.

A Lil Wayne tune *How to Love* played on the radio. I never mind listening to rap music for others when we are on a stake out. I used to sample the music my daughter listened to when she was younger to make sure it was appropriate. Bella was into the song. She was probably 25, fresh out of college.

"How long have you been on the force?" I finally asked, when the song went off.

"A little over two years now," she said.

"What about you Jack?" "Twenty-two long, hard years," I said as I shook my head.

"How do you like it so far?" I asked. "It's exciting and turning out to be all that and more. I love the excitement and the adventure," she replied.

I predict Bella is going to be a good cop. We sat there waiting patiently. Several cars pulled into the parking lot and parked. Suddenly, the park came alive. Several young black boys raced over to the court to play basketball. Young couples walked around holding hands. The elderly women shuffled around the track trying to stay in shape. There was a crowd of people standing by a car smoking marijuana listening to music.

I ignored the smoking. We were on an important mission.

The sun was starting to fade quickly. When I glanced at my radio clock it was about 5:45 p.m. Still there was no sign of Donnie so far. I wondered if I should have gone to the pool hall first to check and see if he was there; finally, after 30 seconds passed, Donnie's red Jag pulled into the parking lot at the car wash. He got out and leaned against the driver's door.

He was talking and laughing into his cell phone. I told Bella he was our man. Bella quickly got out the truck and in position to take the pictures. She pressed a button on the camera and a flashing red light appeared. The lens came out about six inches, and Bella let the camera rip. I saw the bright lights and flashes from inside of the truck. Several people walking on the tracks stared in our direction. When she got through she came back to the front of the truck and I pulled off. We headed back to 201 Poplar St. It was dark outside when I drove up to the Crime Scene lab. I thanked Bella and shook her hand before she got out of the truck. Then, I drove around to the garage to check the Suburban back in.

I liked Bella professionally. We talked for a long time today. It was 6:15 p.m. when I made it back to the office. Ron was sitting at his desk typing on the computer. Angie was busy organizing a bunch of files sitting on the cart. I asked her if anyone had called and left any messages for me. She said no one had called.

"The in-service training is over, and I can get back to work!" Ron finally spoke.

"That's great because we could really use your help on these cases," I said.

"Angie told me you went to the Med to see Marcus Green. Why is he in the hospital?" Ron asked.

"Somebody jumped on him. Beat him half to death." You think it has something to do with your first visit?" Ron asked.

"I don't know. We didn't talk about it much," I replied.

"Did he tell you who jumped him?" Ron inquired.

"He said, "He didn't see his attackers, but I think he's afraid to tell. He told me how James made all that money, but you're not going to believe it. I still don't believe it myself!" I said.

Ron walked over and sat in the brown chair on the side of

my desk. "I'm all ears," he said as he sipped on the coffee.

"Marcus told me James and Anton were smuggling cigarettes, rolling tobacco, and marijuana to inmates into the Penal Farm."

"You were right. I don't believe it." Ron said.

"You mean to tell me James made $2.5 million selling cigarettes to inmates!" Ron said laughing at me.

"Get the fuck out of here. You don't really believe that do you?" Ron asked, "I know better. You're serious about this, aren't you?" He continued.

According to Marcus, one cigarette cost $10. There is 20 cigarettes in a pack which went for as much as $400. He said the rolling tobacco went for as much as $600 because it was more tobacco in the pack. One street size blunt, or a $5 bag of marijuana cost as much as a $150."

"Damn! How could they afford to pay for it?" Ron asked as he shook his head at the thought of it.

"He said most of the inmates tell their families a good lie, so they will get Green Dots. Most drug dealers have access to money," I stated.

I paused to check my text message, then I continued. "He told me he distributed the contraband to the inmates for James after he checked the Green Dots to make sure they're legit. James told Marcus, Cassandra was going to get him out of jail, but it never happened. He claimed selling contraband is big business inside the Penal Farm because inmates are willing to pay any price for contraband," I noted.

Ron stood and went to get some more coffee and came back then I continued.

Marcus told me several officers brought stuff in, but not like James. He was the man out there. He also said Anton was a big gambler and lost everything at the Casino in Tunica about two months ago. Anton told Marcus he was going to get even with James. Now, here is the killing part about all of this. Anton was sleeping with Cassandra.

"Damn! She was fucking everybody." Ron said.

"Marcus gave me the names of a couple of inmates Cassandra was doing. "A ho' with heart," I mumbled under my breath.

"What did you just say?" Ron asked with a curious look on his face. "A ho' with heart." Marcus used the phrase when he talked about Cassandra. He said that's the only two things in life the average person will never see: "A ho' with heart." He thinks there is nothing a woman won't do for a man if she's in love or down with him. In his view, heart is strength.

Ron smiled and said," I don't know about all that. Cassandra didn't look like the type of woman who was sleeping around. She was drop dead gorgeous. I just don't get it."

I couldn't help but think about what Marcus said about Anton and Cassandra. Anton told me he had never met Cassandra before.

Anton seemed like an honest man. I believed him for the most part. However, no one I had interviewed told me the absolute truth. No one can be trusted. It is a continuing refrain in the case that nobody is telling the truth. Ron and Angie left and I was the only one in the office, as usual. It was 8:50 when I gazed up at the clock on the wall. I turned my computer off, and walked out of the office to go see how the stake out was coming along.

5

A Ho' with Heart

"A ho' with heart," lingered in my mind as I headed to my car. There is little moral standing in the world James and Cassandra lived in. I have respect for women, even Cassandra. But you have to wonder about their contractual marriage. They lacked morality and had great understanding. On the other hand, in my first marriage we had morality, but no understanding. Aunt Mary always said, "Balance is the key."

I thank God, my world is going well. My life took a 90 degree turn overnight. I've changed; change begins with self. I enjoy one aspect of my personal life. I have a healthy relationship with my daughter's mother and step-father. I have a wonderful woman, and she and my daughter are bonding together. My daughter respects my woman. My ex-wife respects Alice, too.

My daughter called and asked when I was going to get the ring and ask Alice the big question. I told her I was going to do it soon. I was so happy my daughter is a part of my new life. She is looking forward to helping me pick out the ring. She is really excited. She has learned to balance her life and her love.

I parked behind Detective Monica, and got out of my car. She unlocked the door as I walked up "Hi Jack!" They both said at the same time as I got into the truck.

"What's going on ladies," I said. Detectives Bell and Monica were in a good mood.

They smiled at me. I wasn't expecting the warm welcome. There was a different look on their faces. I thought they were going to be a little upset with me, but I was wrong.

"I want to thank you for telling us that story last night Jack. We really got something out of it. We didn't know we were such a big distraction around the office. I would like to apologize for any trouble I may have caused," she stated.

"It's nothing like that," I said to them.

"You two are the best female detectives I know. I know my life is in good hands whenever I partner with you or Bell. I know y'all got my back when I'm out in the field. That's more important to me than anything," I said to both of them.

I patted both on the shoulder. They smiled and said thanks. We sat and watched the back dock on Washington Ave as the traffic moved up and down the street. Within three minutes, a garbage truck pulled up to the back dock and a black man jumped out. I was about to get out of Detective Monica's truck when it hit me.

"That's it!" I yelled as I got back into the truck.

"What are you talking about?" Detective Bell asked.

"The garbage truck pick up is on Monday, Wednesday, Friday, and Sunday. Today is Monday. Follow that truck," I said to Detective Monica.

"You sure about this Jack. You want to follow a garbage truck?" Monica asked as she pulled out and drove down the street to catch up with the truck.

The garbage truck headed down Washington Ave., made a right on Danny Thomas Blvd., and headed south toward Union Ave. Detective Monica followed close behind. The truck made a left turn on Vance St. and drove up to Foote Home Projects.

Detective Monica pulled up to the curb and killed the lights. There were five cars parked on a side street with several men standing outside. The driver hopped out the truck and walked up to the huddle of black men. It was dark outside but we managed to see what was going on. The man ran back to the truck, climbed on the step, pulled a large black bag out, took the bag over to the men, and they divided the contents.

One of the men reached into his car and took a dark colored gym bag out and gave it to the truck driver. He looked through the bag, then he zipped it back up and walked back over to the truck. He hopped inside the truck and drove off. It was clear to us he wasn't picking up trash.

We followed the truck down Vance St. Then he made a right turn on Bellevue, and headed toward Lamar St. Detective

Bell and I took out our Glocks and got ready to take him at the light. When the truck came to a complete stop at the red light, Monica drove around to the front of the truck, and turned the flashing blue lights on as she stopped inches from the truck. We hopped out running pointing our Glocks straight ahead.

"Get out of the truck with your hands on top of your head!" Detective Bell yelled out. We had the driver covered. The door flew open and the man hopped out the truck shaking.

"Turn around and face the truck," I said as I pushed him up against the truck. I put my gun away and patted him down for weapons. Monica had her Glock pointed right at his head. Detective Bell climbed up in the truck to search the bags.

I told the man to turn around and face us. Monica shined the flashlight in his face, when he turned around. I looked at the man's face, I couldn't believe my eyes. It was Alvin Myers, one of the guys that used to hang with Cassandra and Yolanda at Club Alfred's.

"We got cocaine and money!" Detective Bell shouted out of the truck. I couldn't believe how my instinct lead me to follow that truck.

Detective Bell threw the bags out of the truck. They were filled with bagged up cocaine. Monica placed her handcuffs on Alvin and we gave each other a high five.

"Good work detectives," I said to them.

Monica escorted Alvin over to her truck. He was very nervous and quiet. I called for a transport cruiser. Suddenly, out of nowhere two black suburbans with tinted windows pulled up to the scene. Several FBI agents got out and walked up. A tall white agent wearing a black suit asked who was in charge. I had seen him before at Cassandra's house the day after the murders talking with Captain Dunn and the Chief.

"I'm in charge," I said to the agent. He walked up to me and introduced himself. We stepped over to one of the black Suburbans and talked for a while. His voice was heavy and his eyes wandered when we spoke. Several cars slowed down as they passed to see what was going on. Agent Benson told me Alvin's investigation was part of a FBI sting. He explained some of the details and he showed me the paperwork.

He told me he would come to the office and explain everything. I had no choice but to let him go. I walked over to Detectives Bell and Monica and said, "Let him go."

"You just letting him go like that?" Monica asked.

"Are you going to take the cuffs off or do you want me to do it for you," Agent Benson said.

"Back off!" I yelled. I didn't like it either, but I had no choice. The powers that be, were in control.

The ladies were as upset as I was. Detective Bell reluctantly walked over to Alvin and took the handcuffs off him. The rest of the agents grabbed the bags with the money and cocaine and put them back into the truck. "I hope you haven't messed things up," a short white agent said. Agent Benson escorted Alvin to the truck; he got in and drove off.

As the agents walked toward their car, I retorted looking directly at them, "That's how you look at, but we are investigating multiple murders."

I walked over to the ladies and tried to comfort them. It was hard, but I managed to put a smile on their faces. I threw my arms around their shoulders and squeezed them tight.

"Come one ladies, let's go home," I said with as much enthusiasm as I could muster up.

Monica said, "That's fucked up." We got back in the truck and headed back to 201 Poplar St.

No cop or detective likes it when the FBI shows up at a scene and takes over. I told Detectives Bell and Monica what Agent Benson told me about the FBI sting in the property room. The news took us by surprise.

"This shit isn't right. It's not supposed to happen!" Detective Bell complained loudly.

"They didn't say it, but I believe Alvin Myers is an FBI informant," I stated.

I felt her pain in a way. She was right; something weird was going on in the property room. There was too much suspicion going on that day when I spoke to the receptionist.

It was almost 12:00 a.m. when I made it to the apartment. Alice was lying in bed reading a book with the television on when I opened the door to the room. She was startled when I walked in, and she jerked.

"You scared me!" she said as I walked up to the bed and gave her a kiss. I was tired. I took my clothes off and got in bed.

"Stephanie and her team won against Westwood High School. I told her you were very busy working on the case, and would be at her next game," Alice said.

I like that Alice went to the game and established an independent relationship with Stephanie. That was a good thing. I told Stephanie I was going to make it to a lot more of her games. I was going to do better. Fighting crime can be demanding sometimes, but I am learning to find balance.

"I almost forgot," I said as I rolled and looked at Alice. "Do you remember if James Johnson smoked?" I asked.

"His lungs were perfect. James was in excellent physical condition. Why you ask?" she said.

"I saw a lot of cigarettes and rolling tobacco inside the garage that day. There were a hundred packs or more." Marcus was telling the truth about James selling contraband.

I still couldn't believe he earned $2.5 million selling cigarettes and marijuana inside of a correctional center. The Penal Farm has about 5,000 inmates. Maybe he did. Alice moved over close to me and I kissed her softly on the face. Her skin was soft, smooth, and warm. I liked the way she smelled - like wild roses. We laid in bed cuddling and it was lights out.

Back at the office Tuesday morning, I sat at my desk going over the case files. The dark secret about the murders still twirled around in my head. I kept asking myself what was missing. Something about the case was staring me in the face. Maybe I was trying too hard. Soon, the office became loud and busy as usual. A couple of detectives engaged in debate about something petty.

Detectives Bell and Monica walked in the office carrying boxes. They walked over to their desk and started putting their things inside. The other detectives gathered around quickly to see what was going on.

I stood and walked over to the crowd and said, "What's going on?"

Linda shook her head and said, "They resigned!"

"What!" I said out loud as I moved through the crowd to get to Detectives Bell and Monica.

"What's going on?" I asked.

"We thought about the parable you told us the other night and we decided it was time to try something different Jack," she said smiling.

My eyes became watery. "Y'all don't have to leave us Monica. Are you sure about this? We need y'all," I said. I was stunned. Nobody wanted them to leave.

"It's best for us," Detective Bell finally spoke up.

We were like a big happy family. Detective Bell and Monica had been on the force for 11 years. They were like sisters to me, even if they did complain all the time. They were my friends, all our friends. We all had love for them.

"Y'all just gon' leave us like this without letting us throw a going away party," I protested.

"We'll get together and have a special party, agreed?" I gave Monica a long hug then, I hugged Detective Bell.

Everybody participated in a group hug. When they finished packing, we grabbed the boxes and walked them to the door. They both stopped, turned around, and glanced around the room one more time.

"I'm really going to miss this place," Detective Bell said as she wiped tears away with the back of her hands. We said our goodbyes and hugged one more time and they left. It was a sad occasion, losing two of my best detectives. Monica turned and nodded at me. I sighed as they headed to the elevators.

Ron stepped off the elevators and walked up to me and said, "What's going on?" Cruz, Jackson, John, Stevie and several more detectives got on the elevator with them.

"Detective Bell and Monica just quit," I finally told Ron. I stood there watching the elevator.

"You alright?" Ron asked.

I punched the wall lightly. "You okay?" Ron asked again. He put his hand on my shoulder. I couldn't help but wonder if I was too hard on them the other night. I was beginning to question my judgement. Had I influenced two of our finest detectives to quit when we needed them the most?

"Dammit," I said. "There was nothing I could do about it now.

"I'm okay," I said to Ron as we stepped into the office.

I filled Ron in on my conversation with the ladies during the stakeout. We just lost two of the best female detectives this police force has had.

There was complete silence in the office. Everybody looked like they had lost their sisters. I sat at my desk and thought about the good times we shared together. I remembered when Detective Bell first walked through the door. Her first name is Peggy Sue. She had everybody starlit the first day she came. Detective Bell hated her first name and told us to call her Bell or Detective Bell.

I remembered about four years ago, Cruz messed around and called her Peggy Sue. She lit into Cruz like *a bat out of hell*. She could hit like a man. He never called her by her first name again, nobody did. We laughed at Cruz a long time about taking that 'lick.' They both are good strong women. I am going to miss them dearly. I wish them the best.

The office came back to life. It was still a little quiet, for the most part. "How is it going with the search?" I asked Ron who was pecking away on the computer.

"We still haven't located her," he replied.

"It can't be that hard to find a white girl in a black neighborhood now, can it?" I asked.

"That's just it Jack. She vanished," he concluded.

"That's why I think she knows who killed Billy," I said.

"You don't think the killers found out we are looking for her and did something to her, do you?" Ron asked.

"I hope not. We got enough going on as it is."

Captain Dunn, Agent Benson and a FBI agent walked through the door and came to my desk. I had been waiting on Agent Benson to show up. Captain Dunn didn't look too happy.

"What's going on Captain," I said as I stood.

"I believe you know Agent Benson," Captain Dunn said.

"We met last night, unfortunately,' I said.

"I'm afraid you need to hear what he has to say Jack,"

Captain Dunn said with a serious look on his face. The office was quiet.

Several senior detectives gathered around to hear what Agent Benson was about to say.

About two years ago, a detective pulled over a car speeding on I-55. The driver was on his way to Atlanta, Georgia. When the detective walked up to the car, the man was nervous. The detective searched the car and found over 50 kilograms of cocaine in the trunk. He questioned the man and found out some disturbing news. The man said they was transporting the cocaine to Atlanta for Danny Herbal, the property room supervisor. The detective contacted our office and we have been watching the property room for two years now.

"Excuse me, but what does this have to do with me," I said cutting agent Benson off. "I was about to get to that. It has a lot to do with you, Detective Webster. The detective that started this investigation was Curtis Nickels, your old partner."

"Everything seemed to stop around me when he said my old partner's name. My heart felt like it was about to stop. I started trembling. I couldn't believe it.

Ron tapped me on the shoulder. Then asked me, "Are you okay?" I was in a daze. Finally, I came back to earth.

Everybody was staring at me. "We believe Danny Herbal is responsible for the death of Curtis Nickels, Jack. We think he found out Curtis was investigating him, and he shot him right outside the back dock at night, and we didn't have surveillance set up."

"You almost messed things up last night," the other agent said. "Stay out of our way Detective Webster,' he said and looked at me.

Before I knew it, I had grabbed the agent by the shirt and pushed him against the wall.

"You look here. I don't give a fuck about the FBI, he was my partner and best friend." His face turned red. Captain Dunn started yelling at me. I jerked away from everybody and walked away.

"Stay out of this Jack, and that's an order," Captain Dun yelled. Then, captain escorted the agents out of the office.

Ron asked me if I was okay, but I didn't respond. I was angry. Suddenly, flashes of Curtis popped in my head. I could never forget the cold-blooded murder of a friend. I could remember every little detail about it. Nothing had diminished from my memory about his murder. It all came back to me, like it happened yesterday. I felt an urge to go and get drunk. I wanted to get away, just say to hell with everything, but I couldn't. I had to deal with this without the bottle. I couldn't and wouldn't go back to drinking. It nearly killed me the last time.

I finally looked at Ron and said, "I'm okay."

"Are you sure?" he asked.

"I'm fine, really!" I said.

Ron was concerned like the other detectives who were standing around me. Several men patted me on the shoulder and went back to work. Most of them don't know what it is like to lose a partner. It is an experience I hoped they never have to go through.

I looked around the room; then, I walked out of the office to go see Bella so she could take pictures of Donnie to show Diane and Crystal. Suddenly, I had I feeling everything was going to be fine. My therapist once told me: bad situations always seem to work themselves out, if we stay in the solution. She was right. I needed to stay out of the way and let the powers that be handle the situation.

The FBI was going to get their man, they always do, right! Agent Benson said the operation was almost over. He told me Cassandra and Yolanda's death didn't have anything to do with Danny Herbal. He was sure of it. They had to make sure Jacqueline Owens, the undersheriff, wasn't involved in the murder. She was running the drug operation. Can you imagine her selling the same drugs law enforcement takes off the street right out of the property room back on the streets to someone else? Agent Benson said the sheriff of Shelby County didn't know anything about it. He was clean.

I headed to Beale Street. It was packed and very loud in the

B.B. King's Club when I stepped in the door. Crystal was standing at the bar talking to Lindsey.

I walked over and said, 'What's going on ladies?"

"Hi, Jack," they both shouted.

"Big crowd today," I commented.

"Yep, B.B. King is coming to the club tonight," Crystal informed me.

"Oh! I bet that's going to be fun," I said smiling.

"Tell me about it," Crystal added.

"I got some more pictures for y'all to look at," I said.

"Where's Diane?" I asked.

"She's in the powder room; she'll be right back," Crystal noted.

I took the pictures out of the envelope and showed them to Crystal. She took the pictures and glanced at them quickly and said, 'That's not the guy. I've never seen him before, he's handsome. I wonder if he's dating anyone."

I wondered how she remembered every man that came in the club. I was beginning to think too much time had passed, and they weren't going to be able to recognize the guy.

Diane walked up to me and spoke. I handed her the pictures and she looked at them. She handed them back and said the same thing. Donnie Winters wasn't at the party. She asked me to tell Ron hello. I said, "I'll give Ron the message," said goodbye, walked out of the club, and headed back to the office.

I finally found out who was responsible for the murder of my last partner, and I believe it was meant for me to learn the truth even though the truth brought back painful memories. When I walked in the office everyone stared at me. I stopped in the middle of the room and said, "I'm fine. It's over. Back to work!" Most of them remembered what I went through two years ago, when Curtis first got killed. I went to my desk and sat down. Angie walked into the office and sat down at her desk. She wasn't being her old self lately. She had been acting strange.

I called Ron over to my desk and asked him if he noticed a change in her. "She's going through a tough time right now;

her son is in the hospital."

"What's wrong with him?' I asked.

"Poor little guy has the flu. She told me not to mention it to anybody, so don't say anything about it," Ron said.

"What's his name and what hospital is he in?" I asked.

"Brian Richardson and he's at Methodist University Hospital," Ron stated.

"Oh, yeah, Diane told me to tell you hello," I mentioned.

"We been talking on the phone. I'm thinking about asking her out. She's hot!" he contended.

"You two would make a nice couple," I said to Ron.

He said goodbye and walked out the office. I made a few calls to get some information on Anton. I was going to get an unmarked car to follow him around to see what he was up to. I didn't have a suspect and I was going to have to move on to another case soon. I took out the Johnson file and looked over my notes one more time.

I wondered if Renee Peterson knew why her friend was dead as I looked at her picture. I still couldn't remember where I had seen her before. I sat there and went over all the evidence repeatedly. The first thing that came to mind was James and Marcello. What stood out the most was the fact they had been murdered slovenly.

The other murders seemed organized, like a professional hit. A hit man would know exactly where to shoot a person in the head with a powerful hand gun. Without blowing their brains all over the place. That's why I believed there is more than one killer involved in these cases. Secondly, the phone lines to the houses had been cut. I knew the same person who killed Yolanda Jenkins and Tiffany Roseland had been to Cassandra's house.

The same shoe print was at all three houses. If the killer buried Cassandra, why did he go to the house? The only answer I could come up with was the little boy. He went to the house to finish the job off. When he got to the house James and the boy were already dead. That's it, the boy was already dead when the killer got to the house. He knew the killer. Whoever killed the women and children had a deep hatred for them.

The physical evidence in the cases ruled out the possibility of robbery. Nothing of value had been taken from the houses. I had been thinking about the pattern to the murders. I was aware of particular facts, but I hadn't figured it out yet. That was probably the reason Renee Peterson and her son was still alive. They were being watched around the clock. I knew it was there, but I was missing it. There was another clue staring me in the face.

Why kill the little boys?

Was it part of the plan?

If I could find out the "answers" to the puzzle I could solve the case.

When I stood and turned around to leave, Agent Benson was standing in the doorway. He was alone this time. The office was quiet; everybody was gone. He walked over to my desk and said, "I apologize for Agent LaFraud, he was way out of line."

He continued,

> I know how it is to lose a partner. I lost my partner of eight years about six years ago in New York. He was gunned down right in front of me. He fell in my arms. It took years to finally get over it. We didn't catch the killer until last year. I just wanted you to know you're welcome to tag along when we go after this guy.

I shook his hand and we talked for a long time. I told him about Marcus Green and the guards at the Penal Farm. He said he would get on it right away. After we finished talking, we exchanged numbers, and walked out of the door at the same time.

Alice was in the kitchen cooking when I walked through the door. The smell of fresh baked cornbread, chicken, and black eyed peas penetrated the house, like music to my nose. She didn't hear me come in, because the television was loud. I went to the bathroom to wash up. It had been a long day. When I made it back to the living room, Alice was setting the table. "I didn't hear you come in baby. Why didn't you say anything?" she asked.

"I didn't want to disturb you," I said as I walked up to her and gave her a kiss. Then, I held her tight in my arms.

Her breast and stomach pressed against me, felt good. I held her for a long time. I didn't want to let her go.

"Is everything alright?" she asked when I let her go.

"I love you baby," I said. I was okay. I hadn't realized it earlier, but it seemed like a big burden had been lifted.

I guess the news about Curtis was something I really needed to hear. I couldn't explain it, but I felt good. It was a different kind of feeling, an inner peace. It was the higher power of God dwelling in me. Alice brought the food over to the table and sat down. I blessed the food, and we started eating.

"How was your day?" I asked.

"My day was wonderful. Nobody got killed today, can you believe that," she said, "Nobody got killed in Memphis today! That was some good news baby."

"How was your day?" she asked.

I was in the middle of stuffing my mouth with some fried chicken and cornbread and couldn't speak at first.

"My day was really good. I got some great news today," I said pausing, "I found out who killed Curtis Nickels."

"Really, now that's some good news," she said.

Alice knew Curtis well. They worked on a few cases before. It was an honor to be able to tell her his murder will be vindicated. I have looked forward to this day for a longtime.

I was glad Agent Benson came by to include me in on the case. I would just about do anything to help apprehend Danny Herbal. Alice had finished eating and excused herself from the table. I sat at the table and enjoyed the moment.

Early Wednesday morning, I was back at the crime lab waiting for Bella to arrive to the Penal Farm to get a picture of Anton. Anton told me he wasn't at the party, but he also said he never met Cassandra before. I was hoping Crystal and Diane would be able to identify Anton as the person who was arguing with Cassandra at the party. The identity of the person arguing with Cassandra would change the whole perspective of the case.

I had a feeling about Anton. According to Marcus, Anton was involved with Cassandra. I wasn't sure, but I had a good theory on one part of the Johnson case. The surveillance team followed Anton all night. He spent most of the night at the Horseshoe casino in Tunica, Mississippi losing at the Black Jack table. According to the team, he lost around $7K.

He was pretty upset about it. He almost got kicked out of the casino. Bella walked in the door just before 8:30 a.m. She spoke and said she would be ready to go in about three minutes. I nodded as she walked by. There was still no word back on Cassandra's sim-card. I was really hoping to hear something soon. I wanted to know who Cassandra had been in contact with the day she was killed.

Bella came out all set to go. I stood up, and we walked out the lab. Bella and I chitchatted about a lot of things. I was beginning to get to know her a little more with each passing day. She told me a joke she heard Kevin Hart say the night before at his comedy show. He was in town at the FedEx Forum. I laughed for a long time. The joke was funny, I needed the laugh. It had been a longtime since I enjoyed a laugh like that.

There was a lot of traffic at the Penal Farm when we drove up. I didn't know if we were going to be able to get a picture of Anton. We drove around all the check points to make sure our cover was secure. I wasn't going to be able to follow him around all day. He would get suspicious if he noticed us following him. I couldn't let that happen. I pulled into the parking lot on the left side of the Penal Farm where all the vehicles entered and exited.

Bella and I sat in the truck and surveyed the scene. There was a lot of traffic: 18 wheelers, vans, police cruisers, and several county vehicles coming in and out of the gate. I didn't know if we were going to be able to take the pictures. I didn't even know if Anton was the person who was arguing with Cassandra to be honest with you. I was going on a hunch, a deep sense down in my gut. I just had a feeling James knew his attacker, and let him inside the house.

We put a lot of man power on these cases. This was the most difficult case I ever worked on. I've never been so troubled in my 22 years on the force by a case. The Johnson Family investigation really had me *running like a chicken with its head cut off.* The worse part about it is not being any closer to finding out who the killer was. Bella was listening to music as always. I leaned back in the seat and watched the scene. Finally, after 45 minutes a white van with a Shelby County Penal Farm written on the side pulled up to the guard shack.

Anton hopped out of the van with his back facing us, and gave a guard a piece of paper. Bella couldn't take the picture but I noticed something. Anton had a white Styrofoam cup in his hand and he spit inside the cup. He chews tobacco. I sat up in the seat and bright light popped in my head. I remembered Alice told me the other night to bring her some DNA to test, and I would get my man, if it matched. Anton got in the van and pulled inside the Penal Farm.

Bella looked at me with an inquisitive expression on her face. She could tell something was going on inside my head. I explained everything to her. I still wanted her to get a picture, but the DNA would be a whole lot better. I switched seats with Bella so she could drive. We were going to follow him to see where he was going, when he came out, if the opportunity presented itself, I was going to get the cup out of the van. Bella and I posted up and waited. The 50 ft. gate opened and Anton drove out, stopped at the corner, made a left turn, and headed toward the front of the Penal Farm.

Bella followed far behind being careful not to get up close. Anton pulled into the main parking lot of the Penal Farm at 11:45 am, and slowly drove down the lanes checking the parked vehicles. According to news reports, there have been a rash of auto burglaries at the Penal Farm in the last few months. Inmates were getting released and coming back up to the parking lot and breaking into the guards' vehicles. Anton pulled out of the parking lot and headed to the Adult Offender Center which housed low security inmates. We stopped at the pond, pulled over to the side of the road, and waited for Anton to return. Traffic was thick and several cars drove by.

Mark H. Luttrell Correctional Center (MLRC), and a federal penitentiary are also on the Penal Farm. We saw women on yard call across the pond at MLRC which is one of two female prisons in Tennessee. Anton came back up the road, headed straight past us in a hurry. I feared he was going to see me, but he didn't even look our way. He headed back toward the Penal Farm. Bella followed cautiously behind him.

He went back to the main parking lot, pulled up to the lobby, and blew the horn. A black female guard came out of the lobby, and handed him a piece of paper along with what appeared to be cash. He pulled out of the parking lot, headed toward Summer Ave, stopped at Tiger Mart, got out of the van, and went inside. Bella pulled in the lot and parked three spaces down from the van.

I could see Anton inside the store. I can't take a chance on trying to grab the cup here. There was a chance he would see me. Anton walked to the counter with soft drinks in his hands. He paid for the drinks, came out, hopped in the van, and pulled up to the street. When the traffic stopped, Anton zoomed across the street, pulled into Burger King's parking lot, parked on the side of the building, got out the van, and went inside. Now is the time.

Bella pulled into the parking lot, parked on the passenger side of the van, hopped out of the truck, and headed toward the door. She peeped out the window and threw one arm up in the air signaling the coast was clear. I got out of the truck, surveyed the scene, nobody was in the parking lot, so, I walked up to the passenger side door, grabbed the handle, opened the door, grabbed the nastiest looking cup, and shut the door; then, I got back in the truck. Bella came out of Burger King with a cup in her hand.

Anton was walking close behind. I eased down on the floor. Anton was trying to hit on her; she is beautiful. Bella cut the conversation off, but Anton was very persistent, forcing Bella to maintain a distance from the truck. My heart pounded hard as I waited low on the floor of the truck. About two minutes later, Anton gave up, got in the van, and drove off.

"Good job!" I said to Bella as she got in the truck.

She laughed at me. "He is clingy. Good job to yourself. Let's get out of here."

I struggled to get up off the floor back into my seat. Bella pulled out of the parking lot, and we headed back to 201 Poplar St.

Bella told me, "We'll know something on the sim-card by tomorrow afternoon."

"Good to know," I replied, and I thanked her for her time and drove off.

That was some good work she did today. I didn't even have to coach her or anything. She is smart, and has a lot of common sense.

I checked the truck back in, headed to my car, and drove to the morgue to see Alice. It was very cold and I could feel my body trembling. Alice and some of her co-workers stepped off the elevator engaged in a conversation. She didn't even see me standing in her office.

A short woman pointed at me and said, "A handsome man is in your office," she smiled at me when they walked up.

Alice looked at me with those big pretty blue eyes and said, "He's already taken!"

The women smiled as they walked off. Alice and I walked into the office, and she shut the door behind us. I carefully placed the cup on the counter. She threw her arms around me and she smacked me on the lips.

"What brings you to my 'neck of the woods'," she asked.

"I got some good news. Well, I hope it turns out to be some good news," I said.

I handed her the cup. "I got some DNA of a suspect for you to test. Do you think you can use it?" I inquired.

"What is it?" she asked. "It's chewing tobacco mixed with spit and saliva.

"I should be able to get a good match from this," she confirmed.

"How long do you think it's going to take?" I asked.

"It shouldn't take too long baby. A few days or so," she conferred.

I gave Alice another kiss on the lips, told her I would see her tonight, and we walked out the door. I hope the case is finally turning around. It is another beautiful day. It hasn't rained in two weeks. The sun is shining, but the wind hollers when you're in a shaded area.

Cruz, Jackson, a white man, and Kimberly were standing by my desk when I walked in the office. I was curious and wanted to know what was going on. Angie was standing nearby. I walked up to the crowd and said, "What's going on?"

"Good you're back" Cruz said.

"I got some good news buddy. This guy does security out at the airport." Cruz paused to check his phone, then he continued, "He saw the press conference the other night on the news, and remembered seeing Cassandra's BMW parked in the lot for days. He retrieved the video footage. Take a look at what he came up with."

Cruz pressed a button on my computer and a video appeared on the screen. Two black men pulled up in Cassandra's BMW, parked, got out of the car, and hopped into a dark colored van. We couldn't make out the tag number but it didn't look like Tennessee plates. We jumped around and gave each other high fives. I shook the airport security guard's hand and thanked him. We needed to get some information from him. I turned around to ask Angie to get his information, but she was gone. Ron walked through the door, I asked him if he saw Angie, and he told me she had just left to go to the hospital.

I asked Kimberly to get the information from the guy. I let out a big sigh, then I sat down. This is some good news. Things were starting to turn around. Cruz put an APB out on a dark colored GMC van without a state license plate on it.

The office was quiet and different when I glanced around because Detectives Bell and Monica were no longer in our department. The office had an empty feel. The kind of feeling like something big is missing. I couldn't believe I was actually admitting it. I missed all the noise. It's true, *the grass is not always greener in another pasture.* I walked out of the office, headed to the store to pick up some items so I could cook for my baby tonight.

Murder in the alley off Front Street

Later that night, a black Mercedes pulled into the alley off Front Street in downtown Memphis. A woman with brown skin, wearing a long black wig, a long brown leather coat, dark shades got out of the car, looked around, and walked around to make sure nobody was around; then, she walked back to her car, and got inside, killed the lights, and waited.

About six minutes later, a blue GMC van pulled halfway into the alley and stopped. She blinked the park lights twice. The van slowly pulled into the alley and the dark colored man wearing a green camouflage outfit and black boots got out of the van, looked around, then he walked up to the driver's door. The window slowly came down and the sound of gun fire erupted as she shot him six times in the chest. The man fell to the ground hard, and died on the street. She rolled her window up, drove to Front Street, and disappeared into the night.

6

Hitting the Hit man

I made it to the apartment at 9:30 p.m. with steak, potatoes, and chef salads from Subway to surprise Alice with dinner when she comes in from work. I was in good spirits, and feeling good about the case. I know my way around the kitchen too. I could do a little something. I put a bottle of Besieger wine on ice, opened one of the drawers, grabbed my old white apron, and went to work. I turned the television to ESPN to see what was going on in the world of sports.

Geneva Burks

Geneva Burks, an 88-year-old elderly dark skinned woman who was born and raised in the Orange Mound Section of town, is a retired Memphis School teacher and one of the three oldest members of New Hope Baptist Church. She is highly respected in the community. She volunteers at the local Red Cross five days a week, and would practically give a person the shirt off her back. Her husband, Tom Burks of 60 years lost his battle with prostate cancer, and died four years ago. The couple had three adult children: two boys and one girl. Her daughter is a Memphis school teacher.

Ms. Burks lost two of her sons to the streets; her son Jerry is living on the cutting edge of the streets. In his world, he is 'on the come up' making a name for himself. He engages in a lot of risky, criminal activities to build his notorious reputation. Roy was the opposite of Jerry. He engaged mainly in petty criminal activities to support his drug addiction. After he reached manhood, his occupation switched from furniture salesman to beggar. Because Roy feared Jerry, Roy was usually persuaded to get into all manner of crimes. Despite their shortcomings, Ms. Burks loved her sons dearly.

She was sitting on the sofa at home watching the 10:00 p.m. news when a special report aired showing Cassandra's BMW and a dark colored GMC van at the airport. When she saw the news report, she couldn't believe her eyes. A terrible feeling of shame came over her body. She stood to her feet crying, while looking at her two sons, Jerry and Roy Burks in a deceased woman's BMW.

She cried out in a thunderous voice, "Lord have mercy," when she heard a voice say, "If you have any information to help solve this crime, please call Crime Stoppers…"

Detective Jack Webster

Alice walked in the door at 10:15 p.m., into the living room, and I picked her up in my arms like she was a little girl and hugged her tight.

I sat her down and said, "I love you baby."

"I see you're in a good mood, and something smells really good. I didn't know you could cook like this," she said.

"I wanted to surprise you tonight, now go get washed up so we can eat baby," I said smiling.

While Alice went to the back and washed her hands, I went to the kitchen and started fixing our plates. She came back to the kitchen and meticulously sat in a chair at the table.

"It really looks good!" She said when I sat her plate in front of her.

I baked two ribeye steaks, and two baked potatoes which I stuffed with sour cream and butter. I placed the salads in a small bowl, poured wine in two wine glasses, and placed the silverware on the table.

"I'm so happy you're in a really good mood, tonight. How is the case going?" she inquired.

"I never felt better about the case and you," I admitted.

"What's going on?" She asked as we ate our food.

"We got a big lead on the case. One of the security guards at the Airport brought a video tape to the office tonight of Cassandra's BMW entering and exiting the parking lot," I said.

"Two black guys got out of the car and hopped into a dark colored van," I added.

"That's great baby. See, I told you things would turn around. Can you see the men on the video?" She asked.

"It wasn't that clear but with a $1,000 reward from Crime Stoppers, someone will call in with some information. They always do. The news aired the video tonight," I stated.

I got my food, sat at the table, and talked for a long time. I added, "Plus, I'll glad Rico and his girlfriend can now get off the hook. They were falsely charged with murder last week."

"That's right baby; justice must prevail," Alice replied.

Alice finished eating and went to bed. She was tired. She has never come home this late before. I went to the living room and watched a little television. The special news report about the BMW came on again. I studied the video carefully. I believe the two men are in their late 30s or early 40s. I feel confident our department is going to catch these guys and give the Johnson family some peace.

The office was quiet when I made it to work Thursday morning. A week ago, I told Mrs. Ellison's we found Cassandra's body, and promised we would get justice for their family. Ron called and said he finally got the call from SWAT, and was leaving for his sniper training. I was happy for Ron but this was a bad time to lose another detective. We were already shorthanded after losing Detectives Bell and Monica, and now Ron. I sat at my desk and made a few calls to check on the surveillance team. So far, everything was normal.

Renee Peterson and her family were okay and Anton wasn't doing anything suspicious. He spent most of his time at the casino when he wasn't at work. I talked to Agent Benson last night. He told me the operation was just about over, and it was just a matter of time before they made some arrests connected to the property room. I was ready and waiting. Angie arrived at the office before 9:00 am, came in, and went straight to her desk.

I walked over to her desk to see how she was doing. She didn't look well at all. I could tell she wasn't up for a conversation. I told her to let me know if she needed anything.

She nodded at me. I walked back over to my desk and went over the case mentally. I still had to figure out why the boys were killed.

Jackson walked through the door, I called him over to my desk, and he looked kind of funny without Cruz. In fact, I don't believe I've ever seen the two of them apart. I asked him, "Has the dark GMC van been spotted yet?"

He said, "There are no hits on the van, but several calls about the two men in Cassandra's BMW came in."

We were standing at my desk talking when Cruz walked through the door escorting Ms. Burks, a nice looking elderly black woman to my desk and pulled a chair out which she sat in. After clutching her purse in her lap, she looked directly at me with a somber look on her face, and said, "This is one of the hardest things I ever had to do in life."

"Ma'am' I do understand," I told Ms. Burks.

Cruz pulled us over to the side, and told us what was going on. Ms. Burks saw the video about Cassandra's BMW last night on the news. The two men in the BMW were her two sons. She was here to turn them in. We spoke with her for a couple of hours.

She continued, "As a parent, I can't live with myself knowing my boys could be involved in something like this and be silent," she paused, "so here I am."

"Yes ma'am.'" Cruz remarked.

I understood her pain too; we all did. Everyone in our department deals with all kinds of people. Some people harbor their children who break the law, others help from a distance, some abandon their troubled children, and unfortunately some children become dangerous to themselves and their families.

When the interview was over, I thanked Ms. Burks and Detective Linda escorted her out of the office. It takes a special mother to turn in her own children. She gave us their full names and description, and a lot of pertinent information about their characters and tendencies.

She said solemnly, "I can't believe Roy did this."

I told Cruz to get the crew together. About 20 minutes later, I was standing in the classroom going over the details about the situation at hand to 10 detectives. It was time to hit the streets, and find Jerry and Roy Burks. Ms. Burks told us Roy had a drug problem and would probably be on the corner of Lamar Ave. and Airways St. sitting on a blue milk crate begging for money. We walked out of the classroom and headed to the garage to load into unmarked Suburbans.

Roy Burks woke up about 10:30 a.m. on the outside of the men's restroom behind the Exxon Tiger Mart on Lamar Ave. After his feet hit the ground, he sat on a blue milk crate, took his pipe out of his coat pocket, and attempted to hit it one more time, but nothing was there. He grabbed a broken hanger, stuck it inside the pipe, pushed the screen to the other end of the pipe, then, he put it away. He lit the pipe with the lighter, closed his eyes, and blew the hot air out of his mouth. He was disgusted at his morning luck and walked to the corner so he could panhandle and collect money.

We pulled out of the garage, headed north toward Danny Thomas Blvd., made a right at the light, made a left turn on Union Ave. and headed to Bellevue Drive. There wasn't much traffic out, so we made it to Lamar Ave. and our destination: Airways St. in five minute.

It must have been hard for Ms. Burks to give up her sons. There are still a lot of good, hardworking, honest people in the world. I would have done the same thing. Right is right, and wrong is wrong.

Ms. Burk told us Roy was tall, 6'2, skinny, and bald like his father. I could see Roy sitting on the curb with a brown card board sign in his hand begging people for money just like his mother said. Airways St. and Lamar St. is one of the busiest intersections in Memphis. I told the driver to drive pass Roy and head east on Lamar Ave.

We were going to circle around and take Roy from behind. We made a U-turn at Burger King and headed toward Tiger Mart, stopped at the red light, and the Suburbans got in position. Then, Roy came out of the store, walked over to the parking lot, lit a cigarette, and headed toward us.

We all pulled out our guns at the same time and demanded loudly, "Get on the ground."

We rushed in from all directions and surrounded Roy. He spit the cigarette out his mouth, and laid down on the ground face down. John slapped the handcuffs on him, we assisted him up off the ground, and he shook his head, and remained silent. His clothes were apparently dirty, and he had a really bad odor.

Detective Ashley read Roy his rights. Cruz called for a patrol cruiser to transport Roy to 201 Poplar St. To me he was just another person with a drug problem, but there is no excuse for breaking the law. I knew he wasn't the killer. But, I am willing to bet he knows important details about the kidnapping and murder of Cassandra Johnson.

Several cars pulled into the lot to see what was going on. People watched the scene from the inside of the station. I imagine most of the customers know Roy, have given him a few bucks from time to time, and are wondering why he was being arrested.

About 10 minutes later, a patrol cruiser pulled up. Two white female uniformed patrol officers got out of the cruiser, and walked up to the scene. I asked one of the officers to transport Roy down to 201 Poplar St. and take him to lock up. However, he needed a shower; the fresh jail clothes would help.

Roy had a pipe, two lighters, and $4.06 in change on his person when he was searched for weapons. We got in the Suburbans and followed behind the cruiser. I prayed Roy could give us something to help us catch the killer.

I listened to the rest of the detectives discuss the case as we headed back to the office. Each detective had their own theory. This case had everybody way off balance. I don't normally admit it, but so am I.

Back at the office, there was a message from Bella lying on my desk. The tech was finished with the sim-card and they wanted to see me right away. John went to the jail to sign Roy out and bring him to the office so we could interview him right away. Cruz and Jackson could start the interview with Roy.

I excused myself and walked out of the office to the Crime Scene lab. When I made it to the lab, Bella and a female crime scene unit officer were sitting in the computer room. They were going over the sim-card when I walked up to the door and knocked. I could hear their conversation from the hall.

"Come in Jack," Bella said as she introduced her partner Claudia, a computer Wiz to me.

"We got some really good news for you Jack," Bella said as Claudia pecked away on the keyboard.

"It took me some time, but I was able to transfer everything off the sim-card over to a disc. Take a look at what I found," Bella said.

About 30 text messages appeared on the screen with the initials A. N., Anton Norwood. "Looks like he was stalking the poor woman," Claudia said.

"Tell me about it," I replied.

Most of the texts were about money; then he asked her if she wanted to get together several times. She turned him down and told him she didn't want to see him again. She even told him she was trying to work on her marriage. Anton texted her back and asked to borrow $6,000, but she told him, "No."

His last text message to Cassandra said, "You still belong to me bitch."

Her reply was, "Your colors are showing. Take 15 deep breathes!"

I asked Claudia if she could give me a printout of the text messages. She hit a button and the pages shot through the paper feeder. I thanked both of them and walked out of the office. I was beginning to believe my theory about one part of the Johnson case. James knew his attacker and let him inside the house. There was no doubt in my mind now Anton killed James and his son. However, I was going to need proof.

I needed a match on the DNA Alice found underneath James Johnson's fingernails. Without a DNA match, we only had circumstantial evidence against Anton. When I made it back to the office, there was a woman with blonde hair sitting at the receptionist desk. I walked over to John and asked him what was going on.

"She's the new receptionist, her name is Cynthia. Angie quit."

I was dumbfounded and asked, "Did! she say why?"

"Nope', she said they didn't say why and she didn't ask." I

wondered if her son was alright as we stood at my desk.

"He spilled his guts Jack. I ain't' never seen anything like it. He told us everything he knew. It seemed like the more food we brought him, the more he talked."

"What did he say," I asked.

"Dude was hungry," he added.

According to Roy, one night his brother, Jerry, pulled up on the corner driving Cassandra's BMW; his friend Tony was on the passenger's side. Jerry told him to get inside the car. Roy said he didn't want to get in because he knew the car was stolen. Anyway, he got in and Jerry drove to Forest Hill Cemetery and a dark male was waiting for them in a blue van.

When they got out of the car, the man handed them some shovels and they started digging. When they got through digging the hole, the man opened the door to the van and a woman was lying inside asleep. Roy tried to run, but they caught him and brought him back. They made him help put the woman in the hole and bury her. His brother threatened to kill him if he talked. John's eyed tightened and he shook his head when Roy finished talking.

"Did he say who the guy in the van was?" I asked.

He said he never saw him before until that night, but he said the man had an accent and was from out of town. The guy paid Jerry $10K, and Jerry gave Roy $500 after they took the car to the airport. He told the investigators where his brother and Tony were.

"I checked their background. These two are the 'real deal' Jack. Armed robbery, drug charges, attempted murder you name it," Cruz proclaimed.

Cruz and Jackson came out of the interview room with Roy walking in front of them. They escorted him back down to lockup. I walked over to my desk, called Captain Dunn, and asked him for two arrest warrants. He reminded me about the last warrant we served on Abel St. Things didn't go as planned on that 'go round.' I told Captain Dunn things would go a lot smoother this time! I hung the phone up and got the team together.

It was time to hit the streets again and go on another man

hunt. Two dozen of the department's finest police officers and detectives wearing protective vest with the letters MPD in big white letters on the front and back were standing in the garage when I stepped off the elevator with the arrest warrants. The team was heavily armed with assault weapons because Jerry Burk and Tony Carter were considered armed and dangerous. I preferred my Glock 40. I never leave home without it.

Cruz and John had already briefed the team, and we got into the Suburbans and pulled out of the garage. Roy said Jerry and Tony ran a dope house out of the Pepper Tree Apartments on Graceland Dr. Everybody knew the location. The Apartment is just down the street from Hillcrest High School.

Once upon a time, the Pepper Tree Apartments was a privately owned luxury apartments. The owner sold them to the City of Memphis years ago. The whole place *went down to the dumps* and became a haven for criminals. We got on the highway at Alabama St., and took I-55 to Whitehaven St. Roy gave us a good description of Jerry and Tony, and we had their mug shots from their last arrest. Jerry was 6'2, had long gold braids, and all of his teeth were gold at the bottom. Tony was 5'7, he stuttered really badly, and wore a long red Mohawk.

The traffic was light when we got on the highway; we made it to Whitehaven St. in about seven minutes, got off the highway at Brooks Rd., and headed down Elvis Presley Blvd. to Raines Rd. We looked like a governmental convoy with all the Suburbans and patrol cruisers following one another. Jerry lived in the first townhouse at 1521 Graceland Dr. on the corner. The sun was fading around 5:45 p.m. when I glanced at my watch.

We made a left turn on Raines Rd., headed down to Milbranch St. and pulled into the Mapco Mart on the corner. I told the rest of the team to stand by while we headed to the apartments to check things out. We drove back up Raines Rd., made a left on Graceland Dr., and slowly moved down the street. Several people were standing out smoking marijuana, drinking, and listening to music.

There were a lot of little kids running around playing. I noticed a lot of people going and coming from Jerry's apartment. The apartments were an adaptation for criminal activity but they seemed even more foreboding at night. We headed back to the Mapco Mart to get the rest of the team. The team was standing in the parking lot when we pulled up. I got out of the truck and suggested it would be best to take them from the side of the apartments.

We were going to surround the apartment and move in with force without them knowing what hit them. We loaded up, headed up Raines Rd. and pulled into Hillcrest Community Apartments and came out at the alley.

A couple sitting in a blue Ford F-150 parked in the alley was engaged in a heated discussion. John walked up to their truck, tapped on the window, and when the male rolled it down, John asked them politely to leave. He was very upset but he obliged and drove off.

Two uniformed patrol officers carried the ram as we surrounded the Apartment and got in position. We stood at the doors cocked and loaded. As soon as I got ready to give the signal to hit the door with the ram, the door flew open and we came face to face with Tony Carter in the door way with a gun sticking out of his pocket. His eyes bucked wide open when he saw all the guns pointed in his face.

I think he started to reach for his piece, but his hand stopped in mid-air. He froze. Two detectives grabbed him by the collar of the shirt, slung him to the ground hard, and removed his weapon. The music banged out of the stereo as we stepped inside the apartment.

There were three half naked black women lying on the living room floor high as a kite, watching rap videos on BET. We took them into custody and two policemen escorted the women outside. The whole house smelled like marijuana. We split up and searched the apartment. I headed upstairs with Cruz, Jackson, and Kimberly Wells.

The team found several guns, 10 kilos of cocaine, and $70K in cash. There were four small children in one of the bedrooms asleep. Jerry and Tony are operating a sizable drug operation. I was relieved we got Jerry and Tony, and took them into custody without anyone getting injured.

Neither one of them said anything. They didn't even ask why they were being arrested. That was a first. Usually people want to know why they are being arrested. I could tell by the look on their faces I was dealing with some heavy weights. I got the feeling we were going to have a difficult time with these two. The next time I gazed at my watch it was 9:35 p.m. The time flew by so fast.

We let the women and children go free. The apartment was a Section 8 Housing unit and they were not on the lease. I allowed the women to gather their things. I felt sorry for the kids, and gave the women some of the cash we confiscated.

Cruz said, "You follow the book about everything, but break it for something so small."

"Putting those kids in the system won't be better than the life they have with their mother. It's not about being poor," I retorted.

I told two of the uniformed patrol officers to escort the women and children to a motel of their choice.

There was a large crowd watching the scene from afar. We locked the door to the apartment and headed back to 201 Poplar St. It was late when we got back to the office. I told John and Linda to take Jerry and Tony down to lock up and book them for murder. I decided to interview them first thing in the morning.

I got out of the suburban and took my vest off. I shook hands with the rest of the team, and told them, "We did a good job today."

I said goodbye, and headed to the car. Cruz and Jackson could handle the paperwork. I was tired and my knee started bothering me again. It was such a long day I forgot to eat lunch again. I wondered if Alice had cooked anything as I drove to the apartment.

I was so hungry *I could eat a horse.* When I opened the door to the apartment, I couldn't smell anything, nothing. The apartment was dark and empty, like nobody had been here for a long time. I laid my keys and cellphone on the kitchen table and went to the bathroom. Alice was working late again.

I drove to McDonald's on Union Ave. since it stayed open

24 hours. When I came back to the living room, my cell was blowing up. I walked over to the table and looked at the number. It was Deidra, a detective who worked the downtown area.

I pressed the talk button and said hello, "Jack, this is Deidra. We got a body downtown off Front St. in an alley."

"Can't you take care of it?" I asked.

"Yeah," she added, "but I think you should know about this one Jack. It's got your name written all over it."

"Why do you say that?" I asked.

"It's the guy in the blue GMC van from the airport video," she stated.

"Dammit! I'm on my way," I said and walked out the apartment.

I could have walked to the crime scene but I drove. As I pulled in the alley, I could see Alice, her crew, and several uniformed patrol officers standing next to Deidra and Andrea, her partner.

I got out of the car and walked up to the scene and asked Andrea, "What's the deal here?"

"Not much to tell Jack. Looks like someone shot him multiple times in the chest area. No witnesses," she noted.

Alice said, "Judging from the looks of the body he has been dead for at least a day."

She added, "His name is Obie Solieu; he's from Dakota, and looks Indian. We found a Glock 45 and Red Roof Inn hotel key in his pocket."

I walked over while Alice was on her knees examining the corpse. I asked one of the medics to take off one of his black boots, so I could look at the bottom of it. The boot was made in Lebanon. I turned the boot over, and it looked like the shoe print I saw at all three houses. I have never seen a pair of boots like these before. They were special made.

There were a few drops of dry blood in the cracks of the shoe. I got the hotel key and told two of the uniformed officers to tag and bag the boots, and follow me The Red Roof Inn was a few blocks away on Pauline Dr. and Union Ave. The hotel was quiet and still when we pulled into the parking lot. A short woman with gold hair was standing outside the office door smoking a cigarette.

I got out of the car, walked up, and asked her, "Can you point me in the direction of the manager."

"Look no further, you found me," she said as she blew smoke out of her nose.

I introduced myself and explained why we were there. She escorted us to the room so we could open the door. As we approached the room, I could see the light from the lamp shinning inside the room. We took our guns out and told the manager to stand back.

One of the uniformed patrol officers opened the door and yelled, "Memphis Police Department" as we rushed inside. The room was clear. I could tell the man was organized when I opened the drawers. There were four green camouflage outfits neatly folded along with some white boxers. The room was well kept. There were several bottles of water inside a small brown refrigerator.

One of the uniformed patrol officers found a green duffel bag underneath the bed containing a black briefcase along with an AR 15 machine gun with a silencer. I opened the briefcase and there were several handguns, silencers, bullet clips, about $2K in cash, and the names and addresses of all the victims and their sons.

There was a circle around Renee Peterson and her son. He was a hit man for hire. There were dots on a sheet of paper showing a weather mapping of Memphis. There was a check beside November the 3rd, 6th, 15th and December 8th on the map. I glanced over the map, but I couldn't make any sense of the map. We put everything back inside the green duffel bag and left.

I told the manager to make sure nobody entered the room. The crime scene unit had to dust for prints. I told the uniformed patrol officers to take the bag to the evidence room and tag it into property. I took the maps and headed to the car. By then, it was 2:20 a.m. when I looked at the clock on the radio.

I called the surveillance team watching Renee and her

family, and told them to abort the mission. I headed back to the apartment to get some sleep. Alice was still at work when I made it back to the apartment. I was tired and worn out. I went straight to the bedroom and shut the door behind me. I had a long day ahead and I needed to get some rest before I interviewed Jerry and Tony.

7

Killer Strikes Butterworth Dr.

Thursday night I had a bad dream about the case, woke up out of my sleep, and got out of bed. Alice was asleep. I went to the living room and sat on the sofa. I couldn't get the case off my mind. There were several questions bothering me. Who killed the hit man and why? Nothing made sense to me. I am confused and very apprehensive.

I have a scary feeling the killings aren't over. It hit me that the person who hired the hit man is still out there and will kill again. I stood and went to the kitchen so I could fix some breakfast. About 20 minutes passed before Alice appeared in the kitchen. She walked up behind me and leaned against my body.

"Something smells really good baby. Sorry I've been working late these past couple of days. We've had a lot of work lately," she said.

I turned around and kissed Alice. She was wearing one of my long white t-shirts and some pink house shoes.

"You don't have to apologize baby. I know how demanding your job is," I replied.

I had already boiled some water for her coffee. She always started her day with a fresh cup of coffee. I poured her a cup and she went over to the sofa and turned the television on. I was just about finished cooking: cheesy grits, scrambled eggs, ham, and buttered toast.

I reached in the fridge got the orange juice and brought everything to the table. Alice stood and came to the kitchen table and sat down to eat.

"Was the guy in the alley the man you was looking for?" she asked.

"He was the killer, but I believe somebody hired him to kill the women and their sons since he came up dead," I noted.

"Do you have any idea who?" Alice asked.

"Nope, there maybe someone else on the loose," I said.

"You don't think it was Anton Norwood, do you?" she inquired.

"I don't think Anton hired the hit man, but I do believe Anton killed James and his son. I'm waiting for the DNA results," I added.

"I should have the results back real soon baby. Maybe tomorrow," Alice stated.

I was glad to hear her news. I smiled at her, and we continued our conversation. I was just ready for all of this to be over. This is absolutely a complicated case. I can't imagine the end, nobody can. I stood and went to the bathroom to shower. I was eager to get to the interrogation room.

The Koreans have an old sayings: *quitting while you're a head, is really not quitting.* The thought popped in my head when I thought about Jerry and Tony taking $10K to bury a woman alive. Some people just don't know when enough is enough. It is sad how violence was blooming at an all-time high in the city.

I arrived at the busy office Friday morning at 9:30 a.m. I had called a head of time and asked John to go down to lock up and sign Jerry and Tony out. I walked over to my desk and sat the maps the hit man had in his hotel room in my chair. I solved one piece of the puzzle. I knew that the 3rd, 6th, and the 15th, were the days he murdered the other victims. I'm not sure what December 8th represents, but it could be the day he was planning to kill Renee and her son. We put surveillance on her house December 1st. Five days later, Renee and her son are fine.

John walked over to my desk and said, "They are all yours."

I asked him, "What kind of body gestures have they been making while they were sitting in the interview room."

He told me, "Both of them are calm and cool, real respectful as if nothing has happened."

John thought Tony was probably the weakest link between the two, so we decided to start with him. I grabbed the case files, we headed down the hall, and went to the interview room. I opened the door, we stepped inside, and I introduced John and myself to Tony as we took our seats. He couldn't look us straight in the eye. He stared at the table. I opened the file and studied it for a second. John stared at Tony with a mean expression on his face. John normally played good cop, but we reversed our roles.

"How is it going this morning Mr. Carter?" I finally asked.

"Do you know why you're here today?" I added.

Tony did not speak. John stood up, and slapped the table and said, "Answer the fucking question! Do you know why you're here?"

Tony swallowed and he looked at me and said, "No I don't" in a low tone of voice. He was very nervous.

"Oh, you want to play dumb with us this morning. Do you remember the woman that you helped bury? John said forcefully.

How much did Jerry pay you for your part in it? Did he give you $500 like he gave his brother?" John asked.

For some reason, I didn't think John was acting. He was really upset. Tony's eyes and lips started moving as if he was about to tell us something.

Finally, he stuttered, "I want to speak with a lawyer." It took Tony forever to get those words out.

"You goddamn right, you gonna' need to talk with a lawyer. You're facing the death penalty!" John shouted.

There was nothing more we could say to him after he asked for a lawyer. He had the right to have one present.

"Are you sure you don't want to give us a statement? I implored. We can help you now. Once we walk out that door, it's over" I said.

He sat there and looked down at the floor. John and I walked out of the room. We headed down the hallway to interview Jerry Burks. Suddenly, Detective Linda rushed down the hallway saying my name.

We turned and walked toward her and she stopped to catch her breath

"What is it Linda?" I asked.

"It's Renee Peterson Jack. She's been shot and her son was kidnapped!"

"When did it happen?" I asked.

"Her house" I said. "Dammit!" I yelled as I threw the files on the floor. Linda picked the files up and John and I hurried to the elevator. I told Linda to make sure Jerry Burks and Tony Carter got back to lock up before we got to the elevator.

I got on the highway at Alabama St., took I-55 to Whitehaven St., heading to Renee Peterson's house on Butterworth Dr. across from Havenview Middle School in Whitehaven, and turned the sirens on and sped pass the traffic. I believe my driving scared the - shit - out of John. His arm was hanging tight on the arm rest as if he was gripping for dear life. My adrenaline escalated because I had just called off the surveillance leaving two people vulnerable.

I got off the highway at Shelby Dr., headed toward Milbranch St., pulled up to the red light, and made a left. Cars slowed down as I made the turn. Butterworth was just up ahead to the right. As I drove up in front of the house, I saw the medics rushing Renee to the emergency vehicle on a stretcher.

I pulled up to the curb and we got out the car. I ran over to the ambulance to check things out. I asked the short black female EMS worker if Renee was going to live. She said she wasn't sure if she was going to make it. She closed the doors, and they drove off in a hurry with a police escort. There were several patrol officers on the scene.

Detectives Paul Wells and Rayford Coleman were assigned to the case. John walked over to assist the patrol officers standing in the street trying to keep the large crowd at bay. I walked over and stood beside Paul while he asked an eye witness some questions.

She said, "I saw a new model black Mercedes pull up in the driveway, and a black woman wearing a long brown coat and dark shades walked up to the door."

She continued, "She opened fire at Renee while she was coming out the house. Then, the woman grabbed Renee's son, got into the car, and drove off fast.

She added, "I ran inside and called 911 immediately."

I walked over to the house and surveyed the scene. There was a large puddle of blood in the doorway and three bullet casings lying on the ground. Coleman came out the house carrying the little girl. She was okay; she hadn't been touched. Coleman took the little girl over to one of the patrol cruisers and put her on the black seat. She looked scared and apparently, her mother's blood was on her green dress.

Coleman walked up to me and said, "I don't understand it. Why take the boy and leave the girl, Jack?"

He continued, "This woman is mighty bold to do this in broad daylight."

"She didn't care about witnesses," Coleman said.

"Whoever she is, an evil force drives her," I stated.

"Did anyone put an Amber Alert out on the boy?" I asked.

"It went out about 20 minutes ago," Coleman said.

The crime scene unit and the television news truck pulled up. Bella and several crime scene officers got out of the truck and headed toward the scene. I asked Paul if the woman got a tag number off the Mercedes as he walked up. He said the neighbor was scared and ran into the house when she heard the first shot. She didn't come back outside until we got here. I'm anxious to catch this woman.

I felt responsible for all of this because I called off the surveillance last night.

"Goddammit!" I shouted as John walked up to me. He knew what was wrong with me.

"This isn't your fault Jack. You didn't know! Nobody knew this was going to happen. Nobody Jack!" John said.

I knew John didn't blame me, but I believe we would have gotten our killer if surveillance had not been aborted.

John patted me on the shoulder. I stood there and glanced around the scene one more time wondering how different the course of events would have been had the surveillance team watched the house a few more days.

John and I headed to the car. There was complete silence in the car on the way back to the office. John handed me a picture of Renee's son which didn't help matters any. He was about five years old. He looked happy and healthy. He and his little sister stood side by side as they posed for the photo. I was back at my desk trying to figure out what to do next. I tried not to be upset, but I felt like I have made a terrible mistake.

I opened the middle drawer and put the picture inside. I couldn't get the little boy off my mind. I could still see his face, his innocent smile so pure and warm. I made a few calls to see if the black Mercedes had been located yet.

"Are you okay?" John asked as he walked up to my desk.

"You didn't know Jack. You couldn't have stopped it from happening," he assured me. I worked a case years ago, and just last month they found the female body inside a trash bag in a land field. We still haven't solved her case.

"I'm okay, but I have to find the little boy before it is too late," I said.

"We're human, nobody's perfect. Detectives have to think ahead!" John proclaimed.

Detectives Paul Wells and Rayford Coleman walked into the office and Paul told me Renee made it through the first round of surgery.

Paul said, "She was shot in the neck and stomach with a 38 special. The doctors said she had about a 50/50 chance of survival."

"Great," John said cheerfully.

The thought of Renee having a chance to live gave me some solace. I decided I was going to the hospital to see her, and stood and walked out the office. Inside the Methodist University Hospital, I was standing at the nurse's station talking to a female nurse. I tried to get as much information as I could about Renee's condition.

The nurse told me very little; then, she said, "Be patient the surgery nurse will give an update soon."

"Thank you," I told her, and headed down the hall to Renee's Surgical Unit.

"I'm Detective Jack Webster, can I see Renee Peterson?"

"Let me get her nurse," the attendant said and she walked through two double doors.

The nurse returned and said, "Hello sir," pausing several

seconds and continued, "Renee Peterson had a cardiac arrest earlier, lost a lot of blood, is in a coma, and is not breathing on her own."

"May I see her?" I inquired.

"Briefly," she replied. Follow me.

I walked up to the side of the bed rail and stared at her. Her eyes were open, but she was nonresponsive. "Who did this to you?" I whispered, as I looked at her. I couldn't help but wonder if she knew the woman who shot her. I gently grabbed her right hand and said, "If you know who did this to you, squeeze my hand?" she did not respond. I laid her hand on the bed and listened to the breathing machine pump oxygen into her body.

I have to fix this. I am going to find this woman, and I am going to get her son back. I slowly turned and walked out of the room.

I stood at the elevator with negative thoughts running through my mind about the case. When the doors opened Melvin Bush, walked off the elevator.

"Jack, how is it going?" he said as he shook my hand.

"Fancy meeting you here," he said.

"Man, am I glad to see you. I been calling and calling you man!" I said.

"I was in Houston, Texas on a man hunt. I just flew back in town today. My son is about to have his first child. His wife is in labor right now. I'm going to be a grandfather," Melvin said with a smile on his face the size of China.

"Congratulations man," I said as we shook hands again.

He gave me a cigar. "I was wondering if you found out anything on those four women I told you about?" I asked.

"I sent that information to you before I left for Texas. I even called and talked with the receptionist. I faxed it to her. She told me she got it while I was on the phone with her."

"You mean Angie?" I asked.

"Yes, that's her name." he confirmed.

"I never got your fax. Her son was sick and she probably forgot to give it to me. Do you remember what the information was?" I inquired.

"I found out they were involved in an accident in Jackson, Mississippi. Cassandra had been charged with vehicular homicide, but the case vanished off the records," he said.

"Did it say why?" I asked.

"Nope' that was all in the information I could find," he added.

I congratulated Melvin again, he walked off. I got on the elevator, and headed back to the office.

It was quiet inside the office, and most of the detectives were gone. I opened the case file and studied if for the next 40 minutes. I put the four women's pictures side by side and stared at them. I know I've seen them together somewhere before. A secret is beneath this picture. My cellphone started ringing and I reached into my pants pocket and took it out. It was Alice. I pressed the talk button and said hello.

"Jack I got the DNA back. It is a positive match!" She said sounding very excited.

"Don't forget Stephanie's game tonight at the school," she said.

"I wouldn't miss it for the world." I said goodbye and hung the phone up.

That was music to my ears. I called John over to my desk and told him to round up the team. Then, I called the surveillance team to see where Anton was. He was at the Horseshoe Casino in Tunica, Mississippi. I told them to keep an eye on him and stay put until we got there. I called Captain Dunn to inform him about the news on the DNA match. He said he was going to call the Sheriff and let him know the situation.

Tunica was out of our jurisdiction; so, we needed the Tunica Sheriff's department's involvement. We have worked with the Sheriff on other arrests. Finally, after nearly three weeks, we were in the process of making an arrest on the case. John and the rest of the team came over to my desk, and I filled everyone in on the details. It was about to go down at the Horseshoe Casino. We checked our weapons, put on our protection vest, and headed to the garage.

8

Horseshoe Casino

Without incident, at 12:45 p.m., eight of the finest detectives in our unit loaded into black Suburbans headed to the Horseshoe Casino in the Casino district in Mississippi. We drove west on Poplar St., made a left turn on Second St., and headed south. Then, we made a left turn on Calhoun St., turned right on Third St., which turns into US Hwy. 49 which was thick with traffic. The skies were gray, but the sun was creeping through the clouds.

I was right about Anton all along, and I despised the prick for murdering Marcello Johnson. The memory of his brain matter on the wall was still fresh in my mind. Life without the possibility of parole isn't going to be enough punishment for Anton. It took us about 12 minutes to reach Horseshoe Casino. There were 40 or so vehicles in the huge parking lot. The surveillance team was parked at the front door waiting for us to arrive.

We got out of the trucks and gathered around the side of the casino. I had to make sure everyone approached the situation with extreme caution. We couldn't take a chance on anybody getting hurt or killed. We headed inside to assist the local sheriff to take Anton Norwood into custody; there were more people than we were expecting to see.

The sound of slot machines and small Jack Pot bells banged around the room. It was very loud and noisy inside. A live rock band was performing on stage in the bar. Everybody seemed to be having a good time. Casino managers, pit bosses, and employees were shuffling their feet around the place; a commotion started at the Black Jack tables. I got the feeling it was Anton. Sure enough, he was arguing with three Casino managers. We could hear the conversation as we got closer. I told the team to spread out and surround the Black Jack table. When the short white female manager turned around, Anton looked me straight in the eyes. It seemed liked everything stopped at that moment. I could hear my heart pounding.

He appeared frightened, and he reached into his pants and pulled out a gun. Suddenly, Anton grabbed the manager by the neck and put a choke hold on her. She started gagging and her face turned red.

"Stay back! or she's a dead woman!" He screamed jerking the woman under his tight grip pointing his gun at her head.

I threw my hand in the air and signaled for the team to stop. People started running for their lives when they saw what was going on. The casino was in chaos; the managers and security quickly attempted to gain control of the room. The local boys did a good job of getting the people to safety.

"We got you surrounded Anton. Why don't you give yourself up?" I pleaded with him. We all had our Glocks aimed at him. I thought he was going to hurt the small woman.

"Let the woman go," I declared. Anton glanced around looking for a way out. By then, casino security was in on the action.

I said calmly, "It would behoove you to give yourself up! We've got the whole place surrounded Anton."

"I'm not going to jail detective. I didn't mean to kill James and his son. It was an accident," Anton yelled.

"I know Anton. I know all about it. Let me help you. Look at what you're doing. We can fix this, but you have to give yourself up," I said trying to console him.

Sweat rolled down his forehead. The woman was trying to put up a struggle, but Anton held her tight. He slowly moved toward the front of the Casino. He had the upper hand and there was nothing we could do. He had the gun pressed up against the woman's neck with the hammer cocked back.

He eased out the front door, and surveyed the scene. I could hear police sirens wailing from afar.

"If you try anything, I'll blow her away. I ain't' got nothing," he pleaded. No one wanted anyone to get hurt because we knew he was a desperate, crazed and vulnerable man.

I told the team, "Stand down." Casino security was advised to pursue him with extreme caution.

Anton demanded a car or he would do something crazy. There were several people standing out in the parking lot. His demands were quickly met. Detective John ran to one of the Suburbans and pulled it up to Anton. He got out of the truck and backed away. About nine Tunica Sheriff's cruisers arrived on the scene. Anton quickly moved to the truck and sped off fast. John and I jumped to our feet and ran to the other truck and took off.

We had to leave the rest of the team behind. Anton sped down the narrow Rd. leading to I-55. The Tunica Sheriff's department followed suit. I fired several shots at the tires but missed. I stuck half of my body out the Window so I could get a good shot off. We were going over 80 mph. I tried to focus, but the strong wind attacked my face. I had to make this shot. John fired two more shots trying to disable the car before it got on I-55. I was wishing Ron was here. He could make this shot with both eyes closed. John aimed, and pulled the trigger. The left tire blow out. The Suburban sped out of control, Anton drove into the guard railing, bounced off the railing, flipped over on the driver's side, and came to a complete stop about 20 feet away.

Anton crawled out of the truck and staggered over to the medium. We pulled up. He was hurt pretty bad. His face was covered with blood, and a piece of glass was sticking out his side. Mississippi Sheriffs, John, and I aimed our weapons, and advanced slowly toward Anton. He still had the gun in his hand, but it was apparent that he was weak and losing strength with each step.

"Give yourself up, Anton. You need some medical attention," I shouted.

He pulled the glass out of his side and tried to steady himself. The Tunica Sheriff's Department blocked traffic off with the patrol cruisers.

"Drop the gun, Anton. Let us help you!" I shouted again to deaf ears.

I could tell by the look in his eyes, this wasn't going to have a happy ending. Four Sheriff's moved in on the scene with their weapons drawn at Anton.

"I'm not going to jail, Jack. No way!" he shouted. Anton smiled at me, then he took off running toward the guard rail. He hopped over to the other side of I-55., dropped the gun on the ground, and looked back at me as I ran toward him. I knew what he was about to do. Anton ran out into the path of an 18-wheeler truck. I turned my head, I couldn't watch, I heard the loud thump, brakes screeches, and then, it was over.

Chills went through my body. The truck came to a complete stop about 500 ft. down the road. A loud hiss came from the truck, and a cloud of black smoke came out of the chrome pipes. I had seen a lot of terrible deaths in my life, but nothing had prepared me for this. Anton's blood and human body parts were scattered on the highway. The Sheriff's ordered more cruisers on the highway to block the view from drivers.

His head had been severed from his body and his brains were spread out. As we got closer to the truck, the driver was pacing in front of the truck. He looked hysterical. Anton Norwood's death was an extremely, bloody scene.

"I didn't see him! He came out of nowhere! Oh, my God!" The man yelled sobbing.

He threw both hands on top of his head. "It was an accident. He came out of nowhere!" The man repeated.

The front of the truck was covered with blood. John freaked out when he saw what was left of Anton.

"Where is the rest of his body?" John asked. No one could answer that question. I could hear sirens as the Tunica emergency vehicles arrived on the scene. Anton never made it across the Mississippi State line, so Mississippi officials had to handle the incident.

"Stay with me John," I finally said trying to help him keep it together. Tunica sheriffs were consoling the truck driver.

He shook his head and walked back to the truck.

"I don't understand it, why did he do it?" A male Sheriff asked.

"I guess he couldn't live with himself for what he had done to James and his son or maybe he preferred death to jail." I said.

I walked over to the Captain and Lieutenant and introduced myself. I explained the situation to them. It was about 5:20 p.m. when I glanced at my watch. My daughter's game started at 6 p.m.

I gave the sheriff a business card and asked him, "Please call our office and someone in Homicide will fill you in. I must leave now."

He said, "I will. Take care and be safe."

I walked to the truck and got inside. We pulled out onto I-55 and headed back to Tennessee.

It was a tight squeeze inside of the truck, but we all managed. John had already called for a tow truck to come and get the Suburban Anton was driving.

"Are you okay?" I asked John.

I don't know who looked worse, John or the truck driver. It was hard. My memory of James and his son will forever be with me.

We made it back to 201 Poplar St. about 5:45 p.m. We said our goodbyes. I got out of the truck, and went to my car. I didn't want to be late for my daughter's game at Whitehaven High School. I hopped in the car, turned on the sirens, and headed to Alabama St., got on I-55, and rushed pass traffic. Cars moved over to the other lane as I drove by.

We aren't supposed to use the sirens unless it's official police business, but I bend the rules occasionally. I got off the highway at the Shelby Dr. exit. Once I drove on Elvis Presley Blvd, I turned the Sirens off, and made it to school five minutes later. The parking lot was packed. I had never seen so many cars at a girl's high school basketball game before. Whitehaven was hosting Carver High School. Both teams were unbeaten, 7 and 0. It is going to be a good game from what I had heard on the radio.

I pulled up to the uniformed patrol officers who were standing at the barricades, and hit the blue lights. They moved the barricades aside, I pulled into the parking lot, hopped out of the car, and ran up to the door. I flashed my badge at the ticket window, and they let me inside the gym. Carver High School colors are orange and white. But, black and gold was everywhere because this is a home game.

The team was in a huddle when I walked over to the Whitehaven High School side. Alice stood and waved her hands in the air so I could see her. She was sitting next to Amber and Roosevelt. I stood by the team so Stephanie could see me when they came out of the huddle.

"Knock em' dead tiger!" I shouted at her. She looked at me with a big smile. I made my way through the cluttered bleachers and took my rightful seat next to Alice. I greeted everyone. I hadn't seen Amber and Roosevelt since the Hamilton game.

Alice had on a Whitehaven High School shirt and so did Amber and Roosevelt. I asked Alice where she got the shirt from. She said Stephanie gave it to her, and my shirt was at home. Those two were developing a relationship with each other. Whitehaven was up by two points at halftime. Both teams headed to the locker rooms.

The Carver High School cheerleaders walked out on the floor to do their dance routine. Everyone cheered ecstatically. I could barely hear myself think. The girls got into a special formation and did several routines. When they got ready to end the routine, four of the girls did some flips and landed facing the Whitehaven fan base. In front of the formation, the crowd went wild. When four cheerleaders bent down, a bright light went off inside my head as I remembered the picture Mrs. Ellison showed me of Cassandra at Whitehaven High School some years back. I jumped to my feet.

"Are you okay?" Alice asked.

"I got to go. I will explain later!" I kissed Alice and left out of the gym in a hurry. I remembered seeing four women (Cassandra and three cheerleaders) together in the living room on a picture.

I headed to Cassandra's parents' house. I hated to drop by unannounced, but I had to follow this hunch. All four girls went to high school together. I knew I had seen them somewhere before. As I drove up to the house, I saw Mrs. Ellison standing in the kitchen through the window. I pulled into the driveway, and got out of the car. The headlights shined through the window from my car.

Mrs. Ellison opened the door and said," What took you so long dear."

"It's me Mrs. Ellison, its Jack," I said.

"Oh my, I'm sorry. I was expecting my husband," she said as she smiled.

"That's alright Mrs. Ellison." She invited me inside and shut the door behind me. She was cooking dinner.

"I'm sorry to come over unannounced but I need to see something," I said.

I explained the nature of my visit and she escorted me to the living room to have a look at the pictures. Little Asa stumbled into the room with a doll in her hand. She was trying her best to walk and talk. I asked Mrs. Ellison how she was doing, she told me Asa cries a lot at night and she wonders around as if she's looking for something.

Mrs. Ellison said, "I believe Asa knows her mother, father, and brother are missing."

I responded, "Poor baby," and told Mrs. Ellison, "The man who murdered James and your grandson confessed earlier today. His name was Anton Norwood. He used to work with James. He took his own life earlier," I added.

She stated, "I'm going to pray for his lost soul."

"I'll call James' mother and tell them the news," she declared.

James' mother lives in Jackson, Mississippi. I told her the hit man hired Jerry and Roy Burks to bury Cassandra. She told me she had forgiven him for what he did to her child. I believed her.

She added, "They were going to answer to God one day."

I asked her several questions about the four girls. She told me they all grew up together and went off to Jackson, Mississippi after high School to attend Jackson State University.

I asked her, "Do you recall them being involved in a car

accident in college?"

"No, I don't know anything about them being involved in a car accident," she noted. We talked about the details of the case for a long time. I thanked her for her time and stood to leave.

Mrs. Ellison grabbed my hand and said, "Please find out who is behind my daughter's death. She didn't deserve to die like this."

Mr. Ellison walked in as I was leaving and said, "Take care son, and thank you for all of your hard work.

Mrs. Ellison looked so serene. I told her, "I promise Mrs. Ellison. I'm going to find out who did this if it's the last thing I do." She smiled at me, then I walked out the door.

I never made a promise like that before, especially to the parents or love ones of a victim. But I was going to do everything in my power to find the murderer. I now believe the woman who attempted to kill Renee and kidnapped her son is connected to the other murders. I turned the radio off so I could think.

I heard a buzzing sound coming from the console. I opened it when I stopped at the red light. It was my phone. I had forgotten I put it on vibrate at the game. I had several text messages from Alice and Amber. When I opened my mailbox, it was disturbing news. Stephanie had been injured. She was in the emergency room at the Methodist University Hospital. I turned the siren on, made a U-turn, and headed toward the highway.

I came close to running into a white Lexus. I sped down I-55 breaking just about every traffic rule in the book. I got off the highway on Union Ave., made a right on Pauline Dr., then a left on Madison Ave., and pulled up in front of the Methodist University Hospital. I got out of the car, and rushed inside to the Nurse's station.

An elderly nurse pointed me down the long hall. Stephanie was in room 101A. As I got closer to the room, I could hear a lot of cheering coming from inside. I opened the door, stepped inside the room, and people were celebrating. Amber, Alice, Roosevelt and most of her team mates surrounded her bed. They were so loud they didn't even know I was in the room. I walked up to the bed and Stephanie was smiling like she had just won a million bucks.

"What happened?" I asked as I made my way to the bed.

"She sprang her left ankle," Alice said.

I let out a big sigh of relief and said, "Thank God! It's not serious."

I rubbed the top of her head and said, "You okay champ?"

"We won the game daddy. Wow!" She said with a lot of excitement.

Winning a game against a rival school was important. My daughter was a tough cookie. Everyone was signing their names on her bandage. I grabbed the pen and signed my name too. About 10 minutes later, a female nurse walked into the room with a pair of crutches in her hand along with some papers.

"She's ready to go. Here's the discharge papers.

I need for one of the parents to sign," the Nurse said. Amber signed since she is the custodial parent.

The nurse gave the release instructions and said, "Make sure she stays off her leg as much as possible and keep that ankle elevated. Here's a prescription for pain."

"Does this mean I can miss school?" Stephanie asked.

"Nope!" We shouted. Amber gave her the crutches, and I helped her out of bed.

We walked out the room. I told Alice I would see her back at the apartment. I kissed Stephanie on top of the forehead, and told her to call me soon. She nodded and walked off.

I headed in the opposite direction to see Renee Peterson again. I needed to check to see how her vital signs were.

"How is she doing?" I whispered to the nurse I had spoken with two days previously.

The nurse smiled at me and said, "She came out of the comma this morning. She's a fighter, but she is weak. She's hanging in there."

I noticed the breathing machine was gone, and Renee was breathing on her own. "You really care about this woman. In all my years working at Methodist University Hospital, I've never seen a detective so concerned about a victim. Keep up the good work detective," She smiled at me and walked out the door.

Renee was heavily medicated and asleep. I stood over her bed and said softly, "I'm going to find out who did this to you Renee, and we're going to find your son."

I gently placed my hand on top of her hand and looked at her deeply; then, I walked out of the room. I called the Amtrak Station to see when the next train left for Jackson, Mississippi. The ride will give me the opportunity to think clearly because I need to find some new clues about the killer.

First thing Saturday morning, December 7, 2013, I was standing in a long line waiting to board the 4:15 a.m. Express Train to Jackson.

I had my black gym bag and Alice had packed me a few sandwiches and a couple slices a cake. I had been working so hard on the cases I was neglecting my body of food which was not good. Being a homicide detective in a big city can be demanding at times. We must learn to balance our lives or the job will take over.

We boarded the train and the attendants escorted everyone to their seats. I turned on the head light, then I took the case file out of my bag. There were still a lot of unanswered questions about this case bothering me like: Who killed the hit man and why? I studied the map he made trying to come up with a reason why he killed the victims on those days. I knew the answer was staring me right in the face. Suddenly, a female train attendant came down the aisle asking if anyone wanted some coffee or breakfast.

I ate two of the sandwiches Alice made for me while I stood in the long boarding line. There were two black women sitting two seats up from me. I couldn't help but watch the married man stare at the woman's legs. His wife was sitting by his side asleep. She did have some nice legs though. The little girl across from me woke up and stared at me as I studied the case file.

"Hi mister, what is your name?" she asked.

"My name is Jack, what is your name?" I inquired.

"I'm not supposed to tell strangers my name, but I guess

it's okay since you're a police," she determined.

"How do you know I'm a police office?" I asked.

"I can see your gun sticking out of your shirt," she said as she pointed to my waist.

"My name is Delphine but my friends call me Keke," she stated.

"That's a pretty name. Where are you going?" I probed.

"We're moving to Jackson, Mississippi. My father found a better job. That's my mother and father sitting in front of you asleep," she said pointing.

My cellphones started vibrating inside my pocket. I reached into my pocket and took it out. Ron was calling.

I told the little girl, "It is nice meeting you." Then, I answered the phone. Ron and I talked for a long time. He was back in town. I told him Angie quit. He was gone out of town when she left. He told me he was going to check on Angie and her son to make sure everything was okay.

He said, "I got a date with Diane tonight."

"Good for you both," I told him.

Then I told him to say hello to Angie for me and give her my blessings. We hung up and I continued studying the case file.

At 11:50 a.m., a male train attendant came by and announced we would arrive in Jackson in about 10 minutes. I put the case file back into my bag, and zipped it up. I gave Keke the cake and said goodbye! When the train came to a complete stop, the train attendant made the announcement to passengers to exit the train for Jackson, Mississippi. I got off the train and walked down the concrete stairs to the ground floor.

The place was packed. There were several people standing in the long ticket lines. The whole room smelled like fresh popcorn and butter. I walked outside to get away from the loud noise. There were a lot of cars parked on Mill St. Captain Dunn told me a JPD officer would be waiting for me. I spotted a patrol cruiser, and walked over to it.

"Are you Detective Jack Webster from Memphis?" A woman's voice said from behind me. I turned around as she walked up.

"Yes, I am," I said. She was very young and slim.

We shook hands and got into the cruiser. She had the figure of a model. She was wearing a dark blue patrol uniform with a protective vest underneath, and she introduced herself as we drove off.

"My name is Teresa Reed," she said.

"Please call me Jack," I said. "Would you like to check into your hotel room first?" She asked.

"Not right now, I said.

"So, what would you like to do first Detective Webster?" she inquired.

"I was hoping you could take me to the Hinds County Court House," I said.

"No problem." She crossed Capitol St., and made a left on Pascagoula St. The court house was just up ahead. There were several law enforcement patrol cruisers parked on both sides of the busy Street. Teresa told me Police Headquarters and the Sheriff's Department were located side by side. There were several people headed to the Court House as we drove up and parked.

"Is there anyone in particular you need to see?" she asked.

"I need to see someone in the District Attorney's office because I am trying to find out what happened in a vehicular homicide case involving four female Jackson State University students," I replied.

We went through the metal detectors and signed in. We rode two elevators to get to the top floor where the District Attorney's office is located. A very well dressed woman greeted us.

She said, "Good morning, how may I help you?" She was very polite.

I introduced myself and showed her my badge. I explained the nature of my visit and told her about the murder cases I was working on in Memphis.

I told her I needed some information about four female Jackson State University students who were involved in a hit and run case about eight or nine years ago.

"Do you have their names?" She asked. I gave the woman

their names and she wrote them down. I told her that Cassandra's last name would have been Ellison at the time of the accident. The woman invited us to take a seat, and walked into a nearby office area. She called one of her co-workers, a white woman walked over to her desk, and whispered something into the woman's ear. They both walked over to another office and went inside.

They shut the door behind them. "I wonder what that was all about." Teresa said.

"I don't know, but it didn't look good." Teresa and I sat down in the cushioned chairs and waited patiently for their return. About 20 minutes later, the door opened. A white man in a brown suit came out of the office with the women. One of the women pointed him in my direction.

Teresa and I stood and he invited us to go into a meeting room with him. He handed the names back to me and said, "I'm afraid we can't help you sir. That case was sealed."

"What do you mean, the case was sealed! People are dead, and a little boy has been kidnapped!" I declared in a deep voice.

The office got quiet and everyone stared at me.

"I'm sorry Detective but there's nothing I can do," he said assuredly.

"I don't make the rules. You'll have to speak with the Judge who heard the case, but they are all gone for today," he concluded.

I glanced around at everyone and stood there for a second. I couldn't understand why he couldn't give me the information I needed. "A little boy's life was at stake!"

"Come on Jack, let's get out of here. There has to be another way," Teresa concluded.

I turned and we walked out of the office. I was disappointed. I assumed getting information to solve this murder from Jackson was going to be easy. Teresa made a few calls once we got outside. She hung the phone up and told me she had a plan. We got into the car and drove off.

Teresa called one of her friends who worked at the Jackson Municipal Court Clerk's office.

"What's the plan?" I asked as we headed down Pascagoula

St.

"If they attended Jackson State, then we should start there," she replied.

That sounded like a good idea. I didn't have anything to lose. I didn't know what to think anymore. I didn't even know if I was going to find out anything helpful on this trip. There comes a time in every murder investigation where a wild goose chase is all you have. I just hoped the trip will give me a new lead! We made it to Jackson State, home of the Sonic Boom of the South, in 10 minutes. She parked on the side of the music department, and we got out of the car.

I listened to music coming out of the building. Some of the band members were rehearsing. There weren't many students out as we walked down the concrete tile plaza.

It brought back a lot of memories of the times when I was at USC. Man, those were some of the best years of my life. Several young ladies dressed in pink and green with words Alpha Kappa Alpha painted in big pink and green letters were standing under a tree.

Teresa and I decided to start with them. Maybe one of them could tell us something about Cassandra and her three friends. Since they were in the sorority too. We walked up to the tree and introduced ourselves. I asked them several questions about the accident. I gave them the names of all four women, but none of them recognized the names. These women said this was only their second year at the university.

Cassandra and her friends were here about nine years ago. They were too young to know anything about the accident. One of the ladies told us to check with the campus police, and the student affairs building. We thanked her and walked off. It was 12:40 p.m. when I glanced at my watch. I was beginning to become anxious.

Teresa and I decided to split up. She headed toward the campus police department. She knew some of the guys on the force. I walked across the plaza and headed toward the old reddish brick building and went inside. There was a very attractive, well dressed woman sitting at the receptionist desk. Her perfume smelled very good.

I took my badge out and showed it to her as I introduced myself. I explained the nature of my visit, and asked her some questions about the accident. She told me she had only been working at the school five years. But she told me I was in luck. One of the deans was here; she picked up the phone, and made a call. An elderly woman came down the hall and escorted me to an office at the end of the narrow hallway. She shut the door behind us, and I sat in the brown chair in front of a large desk.

She sat down and said, "How can I help Mr. Webster?" I explained the situation to her and asked if she remembered anything about the four women in the accident. She remembered the accident, and filled me in on the long narrative about the accident. She even remembered the names of three of the women. She told me they were drunk, and Cassandra made the other girls keep quiet about the accident.

She didn't know the name of the five-year-old boy who died in the accident, nor did she know his mother's name. She told me the mother spent a lot of time after the incident at Whitfield, the state asylum in Rankin County. The sorority kicked the women out of the organization, and they were expelled from the university. I bet Cassandra's parents didn't know she had gotten expelled. Mrs. Ellison never mentioned it.

She said the case was sealed because Cassandra's Alpha Kappa Alpha sorority's council placed her in a first-time offender program and requested the court seal the case after Cassandra completed her brief probation. I thanked her for her time and left. Teresa was sitting in the lobby when I came down the hall.

"Did you find out anything?" she asked as she walked up to me.

"Yes, the dean gave me a lot of details about the incident. I need to get out to Whitfield Hospital," I said.

"She asked. "What's out there?"

She didn't remember the woman's name, but she told me the woman was committed to Whitfield for a while after the death of her son. We got in the car and drove off. I was about to find out the name of the woman whose son was killed by Cassandra which hopefully would lead us to the killer.

Teresa got on I-20 and headed toward Pearl, Mississippi. I thought I was a fast driver. Teresa was driving like a woman on fire. There was a lot of traffic on the highway. We made it to the hospital in about 15 minutes. Teresa and I got out of the car and walked into the hospital. A receptionist, who looked like she was about to leave, was standing at the desk.

Teresa and I walked up and I introduced ourselves to the woman; we displayed our badges, explained the nature of our visit, and asked her if she remembered anything about an accident where a five-year-old boy was killed in a car accident by a JSU student.

"You're talking about Jeanette, Jeanette Gilbert," the woman said.

"You remember her?" I asked.

"Of course, I remember her. She was in and out of here for a long time after her son was killed.

She committed suicide about two years ago." The woman sat down and pecked away entering data on the keyboard.

"Yes, she jumped into the Ross Barnett Reservoir. They never found her body; some people claimed nobody could have survived that jump, and some say she could have," the woman noted.

"Do you have a picture of the woman?" I asked.

"I don't have access to patient's files. You'll have to speak with a doctor," she declared

I was afraid she was going to say that. "Is there a doctor here now?" I asked.

"As a matter of fact, Dr. Olivia Sergeant just walked out of the door. If you hurry, you might catch her!" she said hurriedly.

"Thanks!" I shouted as Teresa and I headed for the door.

When we got outside, there was a woman getting into her car in the middle of the parking lot. Teresa took off like she was running a relay race in the Olympics. I tried to keep up with her, but I couldn't. Teresa stopped behind the car as the woman backed out. Then I heard the brakes. Dr. Sergeant was startled when she saw Teresa in her rearview mirror.

She got out of the car and said, "Are you okay?"

I made it to the car, and asked Teresa if she was okay. She

nodded her head back and forth. "I was out of breath," Teresa told Dr. Sergeant.

"Are you Dr. Sergeant?" I asked.

"Yes, and I'm in a hurry." She turned and headed back to her car.

"I need to talk to you about a former patient of yours. Jeanette Gilbert!" Teresa blurted out.

Dr. Sergeant came to a complete stop, slowly turned around and stared at me as if she had just seen a ghost. I told her about the murders in Memphis, and asked if I could look at Jeanette's picture. She immediately turned off her car ignition, gathered her purse, and told us to follow her. She escorted us inside to her office. The inside of the hospital reminded me of a scene out of a Steven King's novel. The building is as old as dirt.

Teresa and I stepped inside the office; she shut the door behind us, walked over to her desk, and sat down.

"I haven't heard that name in a long time. Jeanette Gilbert committed suicide."

"I heard her body was never found," I noted.

"In all my years as a psychiatrist, I've never treated a person with so much rage and hatred in their heart. She had built up a lot of resentment toward her former friends in the car when her son was killed. She was like a ticking bomb waiting to explode. I saw an evil presence inside her eyes once. I was afraid of her," she professed.

"Did she ever talk about revenge?" I asked.

"She never said anything directly, but two years ago, after she escaped, one of the orderlies found a diary she had been hiding. She wrote in the diary that she was going to kill the four women and their sons on each boy's fifth birthday.

"My heart stopped when Dr. Sergeant told me that."

"That's it!" I shouted out loud.

"Dammit! What's wrong Jack?" Teresa said.

"The dates the hit man wrote down were the fifth birthdays of the little boys. It was their birthdates!" I said happily.

It was right there in my face and I didn't see it. It was

staring me in the face the whole time.

"Do you have a photo of Jeanette Gilbert?" I asked. The clock was ticking. Teddy Peterson's birthday is tomorrow, December 8th.

Dr. Sergeant stood and walked over to the closet and unlocked the door. There were several file cabinets inside the large closet. She came out the room with a thick brown file and placed it on top of her desk. I walked up to the desk to get a good look at the picture. When she opened the file, pointed to the picture, I backed away from the desk, and bumped into the wall. I felt like I was having a heart attack. My heart started pounding. I couldn't believe my eyes. It couldn't be so. This wasn't happening. This was just a bad dream. No! It was a nightmare.

When I came out of the trance, Teresa and Dr. Sergeant were staring at me.

"Are you okay?" Teresa asked.

"Yes, I'm good," I said.

I thanked Dr. Sergeant and ran out the office. Teresa was right beside me. Jeanette Gilbert is Angie!

Angie quit the force and attempted to kill Renee the following day. She was one step ahead of us and she intentionally didn't give me that fax from the FBI. That evil witch deceived us all.

I told Teresa I had to get back to Memphis. A little boy's life was at stake.

9

Jeanette Gilbert

According to local legend, Voodoo Village is a small wooded area located in Memphis at the bottom of the Westwood Community at the end of Raines Rd. Local people have been telling a story for years about two people who saw evil spirits in Voodoo Village. According to one legend, two teens once had car trouble down there and they have been missing ever since. She looked out of the side window and thought she saw something in the woods. Then, the boy climbed to the front seat and turned the head lights on. There were several people walking slowly toward the car, like zombies in the Michael Jackson Thriller video.

The male teen tried to start the car, but it wouldn't crank. Then, they dived out of the car and took off running up Raines Rd. The next morning, the local police searched the woods, but there was no signs of life. The car was still parked at the end of the road where the teenagers left it.

There is only one abandoned house at the end of Raines Rd. No one has lived in it for years. Over the years, local residents swear they saw people in the woods gathered around fires dressed in ceremonial robes like devil worshipers. All who made it out of the area alive said they had car trouble when they tried to leave. Nobody goes to the end of Raines Rd. anymore after dark.

But, Ron was on his way to Voodoo Village to see Angie, who we now know is Jeanette Gilbert, a former cheerleader, and a childhood friend of Cassandra. Ron called Diana, told her he would meet her at the club around 9:00 p.m. after he checked on a friend to make sure her son was okay.

Surprisingly, Theresa is very resourceful. At 7.35 p.m. I was on a JPD helicopter headed back to Memphis with

Detective Charles Waters, who was picking up classified items at 201 Poplar St. I discussed the case with him during or flight, and he left me with one thought: desperate people take desperate measures. Angie had every one fooled. She acted so professional. Charles is right, Angie is desperate now. No one would have guessed in a million years she was behind the murders she helped us investigate. She was part of the homicide family, part of the bond we shared with one another. We thought she was one of us.

I feel betrayed, angry, and hatred toward her all at the same time. Nothing compared to what she did. I was speechless. I had an awful pain in my heart, a deepened hurt. I considered Angie a member of our family. She was a vicious killer and a wolf dressed in sheep's clothing.

Ron pulled up at the 19th century English style house at the end of Raines Rd., got out of his car, and studied the surroundings. He couldn't believe Angie lived in an old run down house. The grass was dead and most of the windows were cracked. The wind had blown a lot of the shingles off the roof, and several wooden planks on the right section of the porch were missing.

Ron walked up on the porch, knocked on the door, and waited for about three minutes; then, he knocked on the door again. No one came the door. He was beginning to think he was at the wrong house. Angie had given him the address a long time ago when they were planning to go on a date, but they never connected. He reached into his coat pocket and took his cellphone out.

He looked at the address: 27444 Raines Rd. He backed up and looked at the address on the house. This was the right address. He walked up to the door and twisted the door knob. The door came open and he yelled out for Angie. His voice echoed through the house. He stepped inside and glanced around the dark house.

He moved closer to the stairs and yelled out Angie's name again. A figure appeared at the top of the stairs. It was dark, and he could barely see.

"Is that you Angie? It's me Ron. Jack told me that you quit.

I just came by to check on you."

"You shouldn't have come here," Angie said. She slowly started coming down the stairs. "I hate you came Ron," she continued.

The pilot told me we would be landing in Memphis in about four minutes. Suddenly, I reached into my pants pocket and took my cellphone out to call Ron to warn him Angie was seeking revenge against four of her former sorority sisters. The phone rang several times.

Finally, Ron said hello. "Ron its Jack! I found out who the killer is!"

I shouted into the phone. The helicopter was very loud.

"What, I can barely hear you!" Ron yelled.

"Ron! Angie's the killer!" I said as clearly as possible.

"Angie!" He said in disbelief.

"Ron! Ron! Are you there?" He shouted. Then, I heard a disturbing sound: gun shots!

"Ron! Can you hear me?" Suddenly, the phone went dead.

The helicopter landed on top of the roof at C.J.C. I jumped out of the helicopter, bent down, and ran inside the office. I told the female patrol officer to get the dispatcher on the phone. I needed an address on Angie Richardson. The dispatcher told her there was no one by that name on the registrar. I told her to try Jeanette Gilbert. I paced around the room waiting for an answer.

She came back and said there wasn't a Jeanette Gilbert in the department. "C'mon! Think Jack" I mumbled. Time was running out.

"Where are you Ron?" I said.

I started pacing again and it hit me, Ron has a corvette which has an OnStar system. I gave her Ron's tag number and information and asked the dispatcher to get OnStar on the line.

I ran out the office headed to the elevators. Two patrol officers were standing next to their cruiser engaged in a conversation. I ran up to them, flashed them my badge, hopped inside the cruiser, and took off. I called the dispatcher, and she told me Ron's Corvette was on Raines Rd. pass Westwood St. I headed toward Alabama St., and zipped on the highway.

I turned the siren on and sped down I-55 headed to Whitehaven. It has been a long time since I've been behind the wheel of a patrol cruiser. I got on the radio and called for back-up. I got off on Brooks Rd. and headed down Elvis Presley Blvd. weaving in and out of traffic.

I made a right on Raines Rd. and headed toward Westwood near my destination. Strangely enough, it was dark outside and the wind was howling, as I got out of the car and looked around. I took my Glock out, and loaded a full clip. I bent down and ran up to the house. I checked the door knob but, it was locked.

I counted in my mind: one, two, and three, hit the door as hard as I could with my shoulder, and the door flew open. I peeped inside, then I stepped in the house which was dark and very cold. I could barely see. I had a real hard time trying to focus. I slowly moved through the house calling out for Ron. I stepped into something sticky. I bent down to see what it was.

When I took my cellphone out and pressed the button so the light could shine there was blood on my hands. My heart beat accelerated as I headed toward the stairway praying I had not just passed Ron's blood. The light on my phone slowly started to disappear. After taking three or four steps, my phone went dead. The stairs squeaked, but I continued with caution.

"Angie! If you are listening to me, please give yourself up! I don't want to hurt you. I know all about your son Angie," I shouted as I got to the top of the stairs.

"I know how you feel. I'm sorry but there is another way out. Think of Brian! He wouldn't want you to do this," I pleaded.

The house was quiet, except for the sound of the wind hitting the shutters.

"What have you done to Ron and where's the little boy!" I yelled out assuming she caught Ron off guard because his car was out front.

There was a dim light coming from the room at the end of the hall. The fear of the unknown started to set it as I got closer to the door. A sixth sense kicked in, I could feel Angie's presence. I knew she was watching and waiting to ambush me.

I wondered what kind of trap I was walking into.

My heart was pumping fast. I stood at the door almost afraid to go inside. I stepped to the side, opened the door, slowly looked inside, and discovered the little boy gagged and tied to the bed. His big white eyes glowed through the light peering in the window. I did a quick sweep around the room and looked inside the closet. The room was clear.

I ran up to the bed and untied the boy, then I took the gag out of his mouth.

"Are you Teddy Peterson?" I said. He was shaking pretty bad. He shook his head signaling yes. I told him I was a policeman and I was going to get him home. He did not speak, but I could tell he understood me.

"Let's get you to safety," I said and grabbed his hand.

With my Glock in my right hand, we quickly walked out of the room, and headed toward the stairs. Suddenly, a dark shadow appeared over us and I felt a cold sharp blade in my back. Then something bashed me in the back of my head. I tumbled down the stairs hard, and dropped my Glock. All I could think about was saving the little boy.

I could feel the strength leave my body. I was paralyzed. Blood rushed out of my head and back side. When my eyes finally focused, Angie stood over me with a shiny object in both hands held over her head. It was at that moment everything in my life flashed through my mind: Stephanie, Alice, Amber and my friends. I could feel my heart beating heavily.

I looked Angie straight in her eyes, and saw the dark evil presence Dr. Sergeant warned me about. Her arms started coming toward my heart. I closed my eyes and let my higher power's will be done.

I started to understand something clearly at last; there was nothing I could do to stop her. Suddenly, I heard a powerful, thunderous sound. I knew the sound. If you've ever heard a Smith & Wesson 44 revolver and a Glock 45 sound off at the same time, that's the sound I heard. If you've never heard this sound, then, you don't know what power sounds like. When I opened my eyes, Angie was laid back dead on the stairs. The force from the bullets took her up a few stairs.

When I looked up, Bell and Monica were standing over me.

"How did you know?" I asked.

"We heard you come over the police scanner!" Monica said.

"Thank you!" I said as I stared at them. Little Teddy came down the stairs.

"Ron! We need to find Ron, he's inside the house!" I said. I could hear the sirens wailing as the cavalry pulled up to the house.

Suddenly it was lit up outside the house, and the place was crawling with police officers and detectives. I stared at Angie's body lying on the stairs. It all seemed unreal. The uniformed patrol officers found Ron in the basement. He was still alive, but in need of immediate medical attention. He had been shot twice, and had lost a lot of blood. The EMS workers came in, got Ron, worked on him in the back of the ambulance and rushed him to the hospital.

A joyous feeling came over me when I thought about Bell and Monica, whom I had worked with for years, saving my life. The medics put me on a stretcher, and wheeled me out to the ambulance.

"I never liked that broad! It was something about her. I caught her going through your desk one day," Monica declared. "I kept one eye on her after she made that move," she added.

Cruz, Jackson, John, and Davis arrived on the scene as I was being put inside the ambulance. They rushed over and wished me well.

I proudly said, "I'm fine. Detectives Bell and Monica saved my life!"

"We are not detectives anymore Jack. You haven't seen our commercial on television yet?" Bell said.

"We're private investigators now," Monica said.

They handed all of us a card. I was happy to take one. As a matter a fact, I took several. I planned to refer them to other people. They were the best at conducting investigations.

Alice and her team drove up and she ran over to the ambulance.

"Are you okay baby!" she said. Her eyes were consumed with fear. She heard an officer was down.

"I'm okay," I said extending by hand toward her.

"I love you Alice," I said softly.

"I love you too," she said.

"I'll see you at the hospital." The medics closed the door and pulled off. I was so happy to know Teddy Peterson was safe, and his mother's chances of surviving were improving with each passing day. Their family was going to have a happy ending.

The men in our department were shocked to learn Angie was behind the senseless, and horrific killings. In a way, I kind of felt sorry for her, losing her son. I had never seen so much evil in a person's eyes before. I was devastated about everything. But, most of all, I was glad it was finally over. Angie was truly a mad woman with two personalities. She killed innocent children seeking revenge against Cassandra. The other ladies were passengers in the car. The ladies died because they associated with Cassandra.

10

The Pink Teddy Bear

For the next three days, I was cooped in a small hospital room at Methodist University Hospital for observation. The computerized axial tomography machine known for short as a CAT scan revealed I had a minor concussion. Angie really did a number on my back. I am still bruised from falling down the stairs too, but I feel a hell of a lot better than I did Saturday.

I am lucky, no, blessed to be alive. I can't thank Bell and Monica enough for saving my life. Ron is just fine. He is at Methodist Hospital on Union Ave. He is getting released today. One good thing came out of this. We saved a little boy's life, and had a mad woman put away in HELL where she belonged.

I got a chance to spend a lot of time with my daughter and Alice since I have been confined to a hospital bed. They have bonded very well. There are so many flowers and get well cards in my room you would think I am in a greenhouse. Someone even sent me a pink teddy bear. I'd say Cruz and company are behind the teddy bear. Can you imagine someone sending a tough guy like me a pink teddy bear?

I laugh every time I look at the thing. I even had the chance to see Renee Peterson. She is doing a lot better. Her mother brought her children to the hospital over the weekend. We talked for a long time. She told me she never suspected Jeanette Gilbert was behind the murders because the Jackson Police Department told them she committed suicide two years ago.

She was very sorry for what happened to Brian Richardson. I thought about the little girl, who was killed by a hit and run driver when I was a kid. No child or parent should have to go through an ordeal like that, nobody should. This is one case for the record books. This is the first time I was ever injured on the job. I will never forget Angie (Jeannette). She gave me a new outlook on life. It's too short!

I plan to live the rest of my days on earth to the fullest. You never know when it's going to end. I was lying in bed watching ESPN when the phone started ringing. It was John informing me Agent Benson and company were going after Danny Herbal today. When I hung up the phone up, I removed the blood pressure cup off my arms. Then, I got out of bed.

My heart was still pounding from hearing the news. The hairs on my arm stood straight up. I told John to get my gun and come pick me up. I was still a little weak, but I could manage. One of the female nurses came in the room to see what was going on. The alarm went off at the nurse's station.

"What you doing Mr. Webster?" she asked.

I looked at her and said, "I got to go!"

"But you can't leave, you're still sick!" she pleaded.

"I don't have a choice!" I said and politely walked out of the room.

John was waiting for me at the front of the hospital when I got off the elevator. I got in the car and John drove off.

He handed me my Glock. John told me we were meeting Agent Benson and the team on the corner of Raines St. and Elvis Presley Blvd. Danny Herbal had a mansion in Twinkle Town, a subdivision in Whitehaven off Winchester Rd. As we drove up to the busy parking lot, I saw several FBI agents standing in a huddle.

Agent Benson was going over the details of the raid. Unaware I had been hospitalized, he nodded at me when he looked up. "Glad you could make it," he said.

"I wouldn't miss it for the world." Agent Benson introduced us to the rest of the team and told them we were going to tag along. One of the agents handed John two protective vest with the letters FBI across the back in big white letters.

Agent Benson informed us another team was about to hit the property room at 201 Poplar St. as we speak. He said there were about 15 men inside the house, and they were heavily armed and so were we. There were three dozen FBI agents in all, and two more watching the mansion. We outnumbered them 2 to 1.

We got inside the vehicles and headed out. It is about to go down. The agents said there were two look out men walking around the yard with AK 47 machine guns. The plan was to sneak up on them without getting into a gun fight. John asked me if I was okay. My adrenaline had kicked in and I was good to go. Agent Benson explained to the team that John and I we were just observers for the record. They understood what he meant.

There were several luxury cars and trucks parked in the driveway. Three dozen FBI agents surrounded the mansion. We were in luck. The lookout men were inside the small house smoking marijuana with a woman. We snuck up on the men and the woman and took them into custody with no problem.

We got in position and waited for the signal. Agent Benson came over the loud speaker and shouted FBI raid. Then all hell broke loose. Shots rang out toward us. One of the agents went down hard. We took cover and opened fire at the house. There was a man on the roof. One of the agents shot him, and he fall off the roof on the ground to his death.

It was like a war zone. Bullets were flying everywhere. There was a black man asleep inside a green hummer. He opened fire and shot another agent. We opened fire at the hummer as he tried to drive off. He crashed into the side of the house, jumped out shooting, and was quickly shot down.

I looked at John to make sure he was alright. They had us at bay. Finally, one of the agents got the grenade launcher and fired a grenade inside the house. A small explosion went off. The agents moved closer to the house, went inside as the gun fire came to a halt. There was blood and dead bodies all over the place.

One of the men ran out the back door. John and another agent took off behind him. The house was severely damaged. Smoke and dust polluted the air. I glanced around the room looking for Danny Herbal. "Look out!" one of the agents yelled as he opened fire toward me. I hit the floor fast. One of the men had a gun pointed right at me. The agent killed him.

Agent Benson and two more agents headed upstairs. I continued to search around for Danny Herbal. There was a lot of debris scattered everywhere. I headed to the back of the house and heard gunfire upstairs.

We discovered a man and a woman dead on the floor next to an agent. The other agents tried to give their comrade CPR but he was gone. I knew he was gone. I've seen death 100s of time. I heard a loud thump down the hall. I eased down the hallway with my Glock out. When I got to the last room at the end of the hall Danny Herbal was standing over an agent with a gun to his head. Agent Benson was moving helpless on the floor. He had been wounded.

"Drop the gun Danny its over!" I yelled. He looked at me baring his teeth together.

"Detective Jack...Jack Webster. What a surprise to see you here," he said calmly.

"Drop the fucking gun and get on your knees. Last chance!" I shouted. My eyes narrowed out of anger.

Danny could tell I meant business. He threw the gun over by the bed and smiled at me.

"I was going to kill this agent, just like I killed old Curtis Nickels," he said jeeringly.

Danny moved away from the agent, looking me straight in my eyes. I felt the rage in my heart and I wanted to kill him, right then and there.

"Curtis begged for his life Jack. He begged like a little bitch!" Danny said tauntingly. My fingers started twitching.

"What's the matter Jack? Oh, I forgot, you're a bitch just like Curtis Nickels. He couldn't keep his nose out of my business," He said angrily.

"Get on your knees!" I shouted. Several agents rushed into the room and took Danny Herbal into custody. The medics came in and tended to the wounded.

Agent Benson looked like he was going to make it. He had been shot in the arm. The bullet went straight though. I left out the room and headed outside. There were reporters and news television trucks everywhere. The whole scene was a mess. Several more FBI sedans pulled up too.

The medics were taking care of the wounded and wheeling the dead out in black body bags. John and another agent got out of one of the sedans.

"Did you catch the guy?" I asked.

"Nope, he got away. Damn! It looks like a war zone out here!" John said.

Three agents escorted Danny Herbal out the house.

"Were you selling drugs out of the property room?" a white anchor woman asked.

"They ain't got nothing on me. My lawyer will get me out. The charges are going to be dropped! The justice system will be on my side. I'm clean," Danny yelled out.

The agents put him in the back seat of the sedan. "Now that was an indefensible statement if I ever heard one," I said to Ron.

Agent Benson walked up to me with his right arm wrapped in a splint and said, "It was a good bust. We found over 100 kilograms of cocaine inside the house. But there was no money inside the safe. Just some more books full of 14 digit numbers." John and I looked at each other, then we looked at Agent Benson and laughed.

"What's so funny?" he asked.

"Green Dots!" John said. Agent Benson had a curious look on his face. I explained what Green Dots were to Agent Benson. They are like having your very own Swiss Cayman Island off shore account right in the palms of your own hands. It's the new way to hide money from the government. I asked Agent Benson to clear his schedule for the next few days. I told him to take the notebooks up to Walmart on Elvis Presley and ask for Grant.

"One more thing Jack. You could have killed Danny Herbal back there and nobody would have known. Why didn't you do it?" he asked.

I took my badge out, smiled at Agent Benson, and held it in the palm of my hand. I shook his hand, then I looked at John and said, "Let's go home John, let's go home." John and I walked to the car and we drove off.

On the drive back to the office, John turned the radio off, turned toward me and asked, "Why didn't you kill him Jack?"

I smiled and said, "I could have killed Danny Herbal. I wanted to bad but killing him would make me no better than Angie or Anton. We speak for the victim's. There isn't a day that goes by I don't see the victims inside my mind. If I had killed him, I would have changed shoes with him, and he would be a victim and I would be a criminal.

William Shakespeare once said: *To thine own self be true.* John nodded at me. He understood where I was coming from.

It was about 9:00 p.m. when I walked into the apartment. Alice was sitting on the sofa watching the television. She got up, walked over to me, and gave me a hug. She had a worried look on her face.

"Are you alright. One of the nurses told me you left the hospital before you were discharged. I've been worried sick about you!" she said.

We kissed and hugged for a long time. I assured Alice I was just fine.

I asked her if there were any leftovers in the fridge. "You know I don't believe in leftovers baby. I'll fix you something."

"Sounds good to me" I had worked up an appetite.

"Call me when it's ready. I'm going to take a long warm bath," I said.

"You want me to join you?" she asked. She gave me that look and smiled sheepishly.

"You can if you want to!" I said.

"I'll give you a day or two. You need the rest baby," she proposed.

I returned to the office, Friday, December 13, 2013. I received a warm welcome back from all the detectives. There was a newspaper on top of my desk when I sat down. The FBI operation about the property room was on the front page. They arrested 27 property room workers. Jacqueline Owens, the undersheriff, was found dead inside her house. She took her own life with her service pistol.

There was a big picture of Agent Benson and Danny Herbal on the front page. Ron walked into the office carrying a bag in his hand. He was now an official member of the SWAT team. I shook his hand and congratulated him. He looked over at the receptionist desk and stared for a brief minute. The devastation Angie left behind was still fresh.

We were still discussing how she was maneuvering in the department. It was going to take some time, but *time heals wounds*. Bell and Monica walked into the office and handed me a notebook with Green Dots inside.

"We found it on Angie that night," Monica said.

"You think she did all of this for money?" Ron asked.

"It's usually about the money Ron, but Angie was seeking revenge, and probably ran into the money," I said.

I had been so busy working on the cases I didn't even know it was missing. I gave Bell and Monica a big hug and thanked them for saving my life.

"Anytime," they both said at the same time.

"Drop by to see us sometimes, private investigators."

Bell and Monica left. Ron had finished clearing out his desk, and walked up to me. We gave each other a man hug.

We shook hands and said our goodbyes. He looked around the office one more time, then he walked out. I stared at the receptionist desk where a woman I thought of as a friend once sat. Cruz came through the door and walked over to my desk.

"I got some good news Jack. We just had a meeting with the County Farm phone company supplier. We have the recorded inmate conversations in our possession. We found out who killed Billy Jackson," he said soberly.

"I was happily surprised by the information, and I stood to my feet."

"Who did it?" I asked. "It was Reco Parker. "He ordered a hit on Billy for renting him Cassandra's BMW. I got him on tape," he added.

"The gang task force is out on the streets right now as we speak. We'll have someone in custody tonight," Cruz noted.

I gave Cruz a high five for that good news. I was going to stop by Billy's mom house and share the information with her. Cruz said Jackson was at the County Farm in the process of getting Reco Parker released, and going to bring him to the office. I called the chief and told him the news about Anton, Angie, and Reco. The chief told me he was going to call the mayor and the district attorney right away.

I would give anything to see their faces when the news was revealed to them. Jackson walked into the office with Reco Parker. Cruz walked over to my desk and said, "Go ahead Jack, do the honors."

"I wanted to be the first to tell you we found Cassandra's killer, and we know you and Tina are innocent. We're going to drop the charges today."

"Reco jumped in the air and started celebrating."

"Wait a minute, I'm not through. We are charging you with the murder of Billy Jackson. We got you on tape. We know about your Crip brothers too," I stated.

His face turned stone. "Get this piece of shit out of my face. Book him!" I sat at my desk and closed out the cases. I needed to type a report but it could wait.

Detective John came over to my desk and told me the West Memphis police department called. They found a white woman dead in the woods behind the Pilot Flying J. She had been stabbed several times. Her name was Tammy Phillips aka Dirty White Girl. Apparently, a trick she tried to rob, killed her. She was last seen at the truck stop with a truck driver. Store video footage showed her in the store alone at the counter buying a Miller's Light. She was in the morgue in West Memphis, Arkansas for several days before her prints came back with an identity.

John said Terriann moved out of the abandoned house, and checked herself into drug rehab. She was getting her life together.

Cruz and Jackson walked over to my desk and Jackson said, "Look at what just walked in. Damn!"

I turned to see what they were looking at. A young sexy black woman was talking to the receptionist.

She was one of the sexiest women I had even seen years. Even with a bun in the oven, she was hot and beautiful. Cynthia, the new receptionist, pointed her in my direction. She had smooth legs, and she looked like she had just walked off the cover of a magazine. She was wearing a mini skirt and shoes with 6" heels. When she walked toward me, I knew she had to be: Delicious, the stripper, from Pure Passion.

I can definitely see why they called her Delicious. She walked over to my desk and said, "Are you Jack Webster?" John, Cruz, and Jackson were standing close by like puppies.

I smiled and said, "I'm Jack. Can I help you?"

"My name is Delicious. One of the girls at the club told me you were looking for me."

"Excuse me guys, can she have some privacy," I said in a serious tone of voice.

Somebody got to have some sense in our department! They reluctantly walked away. I pulled out a chair, offered her a seat, and we talked. We had a long conversation. When we got through, I gave her my card, and told her to call me in the morning. She was pregnant with James baby. She told me James got her an apartment, and took her out of the club life.

He paid her tuition for nursing school the week before his death. She told me she quit stripping after his death and honored his wishes, but with no money coming in, things were getting rough. I told her not to worry because James heirs would be taken care of. She doesn't know, but I am planning to give some of the Green Dots to Delicious for her child and some to the Ellison's for little Asa. It is the right thing to do. Plus, James and Cassandra's estate would be divided and placed in Trusts for his two children.

Agent Benson called and told me Marcus Green was working with the FBI to bring down the officers who were bringing the contraband into the Penal Farm. The warden was on board with the undercover operation. Marcus was getting a second chance to turn his life around. Roy Burks was in protective custody inside the jail. His brother Jerry Burks put a hit on his life for giving us a statement about Cassandra's murder. I was finished and just about ready to close the Johnson Family murder case.

On this 13th day of December, 12 days before Christmas, there was one more thing I need to do before this day ends. I have put it off long enough.

I went to the hospital. Alice was inside one of the large auditoriums giving a lecture to interns. It was dark inside when I stepped in the large packed room. Alice was standing on stage facing an overhead screen hanging from the ceiling.

When she got through with the lecture, she asked if anyone had any questions about today's lesson.

"Yeah! I got a question!" I shouted.

"Will you marry me?" I asked.

It got real quiet in the room. You could hear a pen drop. She turned the lights on and everyone was staring at me.

I stood and said it again loudly, "Will you marry me?"

Alice stood on the stage like she was in a trance. I walked fast toward the stage. All the student's eyes followed me every step of the way. Alice was very surprised and emotional. She covered her mouth with both hands.

I grabbed her hands and said, "Will you marry me, Dr. Alice?"

Alice was still shocked and surprised. A few tears rolled down her face. We stared in each other's eyes.

Finally, Alice said, "Yes! Yes! I will marry you Jack Webster!" the interns cheered us on as we stood there and kissed.

The lights went off and the spotlight beamed on us.

"I love you Alice," I finally said.

"I love you too Jack!" we kissed again.

Yeah, life is good. I get a second chance at love. I'm gonna' love this woman like my life depends on it, stay away from the booze, and admire all the beautiful women keeping in mind: *Ain't no woman like the one I got.*

THE END.

ABOUT THE AUTHOR

Anthony Ellis is a native of Jackson, Mississippi, and a longtime resident of Memphis, Tennessee. He is the author of *He Got that Package*, a fiction story which includes auto-biographical accounts about his prison stay in a Tennessee Correctional Facility. *Death by Association*, Vol I *Retaliation* Vol II *Deception*, a two-volume novel, is his second work. He previously attended Jackson State University (Jackson, MS), and was a member of the Sonic Boom.

Buy Other Meredith Etc Book Titles
www.meredithetc.com

Make Comments on Anthony Ellis's Author Page
http://meredithetc.com/death-by-association/